OYSTER BLUES

MICHAEL McCLELLAND

POCKET STAR BOOKS
New York   London   Toronto   Sydney

This book is a work of fiction. Names, characters, places and incidents are products of the author's imagination or are used fictitiously. Any resemblance to actual events or locales or persons, living or dead, is entirely coincidental.

 A Pocket Star Book published by
POCKET BOOKS, a division of Simon & Schuster, Inc.
1230 Avenue of the Americas, New York, NY 10020

Copyright © 2001 by Michael McClelland

Published by arrangement with ibooks, inc.

ISBN: 0-7434-7731-6

First Pocket Books printing February 2004

10 9 8 7 6 5 4 3 2

POCKET STAR BOOKS and colophon are registered trademarks of Simon & Schuster, Inc.

Cover design by Rod Hernandez

Manufactured in the United States of America

For information regarding special discounts for bulk purchases, please contact Simon & Schuster Special Sales at 1-800-456-6798 or business@simonandschuster.com this novel is for my fathers

Ellis McClelland

and

Henry Swofford

OYSTER BLUES

1

The rum alone would not have been enough to make Harry shoot them like he did. Nor would the heat, the sex, or the simple revolting arrogance of it all. But when Happy Harry Harper woke up that sticky September morning, hung over, hot and irritable, to see two thumb-sized palmetto bugs fucking on the wall opposite his bed, something inside him just snapped.

Harry reached under the wadded-up blue jeans he was using as a pillow and pulled out his .38 automatic. He thumbed off the safety and, without taking time to ruin his shot by aiming, pointed and fired. The gun spit fire and thunder, ripping a silver-dollar–sized hole in the weathered gray wood of his rented room.

Bug bits and wood splinters exploded out into the steamy Dominican sunshine. Harry grabbed his throbbing head, cursed himself for mixing gunfire and hangovers, and collapsed backwards onto his rickety cot. The cot spun dizzily underneath him, and for a moment Harry thought he might throw up. He took a moment to double-damn his luck and his judgment, then put the gun back under his pillow and went back to sleep.

Let's face it. Harry was just not a morning person.

The loud gunshot from the upstairs room scattered the chickens she was feeding in the courtyard outside, and Juanita Peron breathed a quiet curse at her *yanqui* guest. Normally, she let her *yanqui* tenants stay about a month before calling her cousin Jorgé to run them across the island to the American embassy in Santo Domingo. That gave them plenty of time to drink too many bottles of rum on tab, eat lots of the curried chicken and pork Juanita made especially mild for their *yanqui* tastes, and get drunk enough to smash several of the expensive-looking pottery vases her sister Eliza made five-at-a-time in her tourist booth at the portside market in Puerto Plata. Jorgé would take the humiliated *yanqui* to the angry embassy staff, who would advance him cash against whatever U.S. credit he could produce. Then Jorgé would give the embassy men their gri-gri, take out his own 15 percent, and return the rest to Juanita.

This particular *yanqui*, though—this Harry Hopper—he was crazier than most. He didn't go with the whores at La Bonita, or chase Juanita herself, and he wouldn't buy the cheap green ganja Jorgé's second son Paulo sold other *yanquis* by the fistful. He didn't try to take money from the card players in La Bonita's downstairs bar, no matter how hard they tried to make themselves look like stupid islanders. He did drink—he drank perhaps more than any other *yanqui* she had ever had, Juanita thought, chasing rum shots with Red Stripe beers and then more shots—but he drank by himself. Sometimes he went for long walks on the beach down the hill from Juanita's, stumbling along beside the water turned gray and smoky by the gold miners who had come and raped the hillside and fouled the water before admitting there was no gold in Cielo Bay and then leaving. On quiet nights, she could hear him shooting coconuts with that big pistol of his, and laughing and shooting again. She never was sure if he was laughing when he hit them, or laughing because he missed. But he laughed a lot.

Mostly, though, this *yanqui* read books. He would sit for hours under the tangled grape arbor behind Juanita's chicken shed with a book in one hand and a rum glass in the other, or stretched out on the cool concrete of the mine's abandoned loading dock, reading. His books were paperbacks, all old and torn. Juanita couldn't read the English titles—could not have read them, in fact, even if they had been in Spanish—but the day she went through the *yanqui*'s gym-bag luggage while he slept out in the arbor she recognized a certain sameness to the covers. They all seemed to have pretty girls looking frightened, or bodies lying face-down and bloody, or both. And almost always, there was a gun somewhere on the cover. Often it was leaking smoke.

The *yanquis* who ended up at Juanita's end-of-the-line boarding house were usually very angry men—angry at a woman, angry at the world, angry at themselves—

3

and Juanita knew how to deal with that. Sometimes, they were sad, usually because of a woman, and Juanita knew how to deal with that too. But despite the drinking, and the shooting, in a strange way it seemed like this particular *yanqui*, this Harry Hopper, was almost content. And Juanita had no idea at all how to deal with that.

It made her very nervous, and anxious to get this particular tenant out of her home as quickly as possible. But Harry Hopper didn't seem to be in any hurry to leave, and he actually had cash of his own, even if it was only Dominican Republic pesos and not the American dollars that were worth far more in both buying power and prestige. He didn't mind when she demanded rent prices twice that paid by the islanders who lived in the much nicer rooms downstairs, and didn't even complain when she asked to be paid in advance. He ate the hottest jerky chicken she could serve up without so much as asking for extra water, and somehow seemed to sidestep all the pottery knickknacks she kept shifting around the house, no matter how well concealed they were, or how drunk he was. He didn't even seem to mind that she kept mispronouncing his name, which she knew damn well was Harper, with an *r*.

Juanita wouldn't deny that Hopper was a fine tenant, and certainly he was good for her pocketbook. Still, he made her nervous. And now, with two other *yanquis* in town—nearly unprecedented, at least since the mine closed—she could easily replace, even double, the income lost if he were to move on.

Those other two *yanquis*, of course, were just as

4

crazy as most Americans who ended up in Cielo Bay. They stayed on their little sailboat up by Tomato Creek day after day, never coming into town. They even tried to cover the boat with branches so no one could see it—as if no one would notice a thirty-foot-long brush pile with an aluminum mast!—rather than simply admit they had been blown into Cielo Bay during last week's storm and couldn't sail well enough to get back out. There were a dozen fishermen in town alone who could get those fools out in minutes, but they held off, knowing the true value of a *yanqui* and respecting the ability of Juanita and Peres (who owned La Bonita, the only bar still open in Cielo Bay) to milk those *yanquis* dry. The fishermen knew that anyone who ran off the Americans early would suffer Juanita's anger; they knew too that anyone who helped her along would get a little gri-gri.

Juanita tossed the last bit of cornmeal to her still-skittish chickens, glanced again toward the upstairs room and shook her head in disgust. Crazy *yanquis*! Sometimes she believed God had given them all the money to make up for not giving them brains.

Juanita picked up the plastic bucket she used to carry the chicken feed, still marked Blue Bay Gold in fading black stencil, and walked around the corner of her house to the small barn behind it. She noted with satisfaction the fresh hole darkening the side of the upstairs bedroom. She could fix it for next to nothing, Juanita knew, with some scrap wood and a bit of plaster. But the *yanqui* would not know that. At dinner tonight she would tearfully explain the difficulties of obtaining a carpenter this far from the city, she decided, and see if Hopper would once again reach so calmly into his bottomless wallet.

Juanita rounded the corner to the barn door and then stopped dead still. She raised one hand to her mouth, turned backwards so she could bite her knuckles in shock. The grain bucket dropped from her nerveless fingers and hit the bare earth floor with a hollow *plonk!* that seemed to echo on forever.

Campeón lay on the ground before her, his neck twisted sideways, blood pooling around his mangled head. He lay framed by the light spilling through the open door like Jesus in the paintings at the church in Plata. Majestic, still, silent. Juanita let out a single despairing moan, then rushed forward and dropped to her knees before Campeón.

Tearfully, she slipped her small hands under Campeón's still-warm corpse and lifted. He rose easily, lightly, as if there were no weight left in his empty body. His head swung loosely at the end of his neck, and several drops of bright red blood dripped from his open beak to spatter in the dust at Juanita's knees.

Juanita closed her eyes and sniffed loudly. Mighty Campeón, her prize gamecock, the king of her courtyard and pride of her heart, was dead.

True, the bird had been old, and half-blind and unfit even for stud, and Juanita knew that her neighbors thought her foolish to keep him around. But she still remembered when the gangly rooster had been the undisputed master of the fighting pit, wild, furious, unbeatable and untameable. She remembered watching breathlessly as Campeón destroyed opponent after opponent, shredding them even after they were down and still, unconcerned with the shouts and curses of the men surrounding him there in the makeshift arena in the hills above Cielo Bay.

There was something historic and noble about the bird, about the way he fought on and on regardless of the odds against him or how many wanted him to fall. He captured her imagination and then he captured her heart, strutting in the firelight beside the pit, clawing at the body of a downed opponent without a single mark on him. Once, making love with her man Hector after a night at the cockfights, Juanita had called out "Campeón!" at the moment of pleasure. Hector jumped up and cursed her, enraged and humiliated, sweaty, angry, his shiny-wet brown penis already limp. He had gone to Puerto Plata and thrown a three-day drunk. Even though she came and bailed him out of jail and tenderly cared for the cuts he'd won in a barroom fight, Hector never forgave her. He never would return to the cockfights, and when she ignored his order that she not attend either, he left her.

Small loss—Hector was just a man, after all. But Campeón! Week after week she had gone to see him fight, hiking alone the six kilometers to the pit at old Markus's worthless farm every Saturday night. She bet on her Campeón relentlessly, even when the odds against him were so long it was foolish to do so. Even when no one would take her bets, when Campeón was so feared and respected that no one would send a decent bird against him, still she went, just to see him dominate. Campeón's owner, Velente, kept the bird fighting long after he should have been retired, and when the inevitable happened, when a much younger cock slashed a spur through Campeón's left eye and closed the right with a series of sharp pecks, Juanita had stepped in between the two birds and offered a miraculous sum for the fallen champion.

Campeón had the run of her courtyard after that. Campeón would kill anything he could see, of course, but since he could hardly see at all and the chickens knew well enough to stay away from him, that hardly mattered. It meant keeping her nameless stud rooster in a wire cage out on the front porch—even a barnyard rooster would have sensed Campeón's weakness and killed him immediately—but the only alternative was caging Campeón himself, and that Juanita would not do.

She knew her neighbors thought her foolish, and shook their heads at the way she took her hens to the caged stud for service one by one. But they didn't know about her father, who had run off and left Juanita's mother to turn whore in Santo Domingo when Juanita was just a child. They had forgotten old Alverez, who found the orphaned Juanita sleeping on the beach, married her and brought her to Cielo Bay, only to drink himself to death and leave her with his worthless, used-up farm when his dreams of a great hotel died with the gold mine. They didn't think about Hector, or Antonio, or José, or any of the other men who had come and gone, all of them leaving, all of them taking a little more of her, all of them worthless. She needed them and hated them, all of these men who seemed so fine at the start but turned out undeserving of their own lives, much less of hers.

8

But Campeón never faltered, never failed. Even in defeat, one ruined eye oozing blood and water like a crushed grape, he had stood proud and strong, slashing at empty air in his blindness and anger. Campeón was all the strength of maleness without the foolishness of man. He was masculinity itself, strutting and scraping through his hard life, and he inspired her. Many times, when her bed was empty and her larder was bare, when the gentle waves slapping the shore out in the dark bay seemed to be calling her to come and join them, Juanita had turned to Campeón's memory and presence to find the strength to carry on. As long as Campeón persevered, so could she.

But now Campeón was dead. Dead, she slowly realized, at the hand of a drunken, crazy *yanqui* who fired bullets blindly through her own walls. Dead at the hand of an unseen enemy without the courage to even take Campeón face to face. Dead at the hands of one more rotten, lousy, stinking man.

Juanita let Campeón's broken body slip to the ground. She rose slowly and turned toward her bare ramshackle house. She wiped her bloody hands on her cotton apron, and looked up to the quiet second-story bedroom with murder in her eyes.

It was time to collect the rent.

The courtyard was quiet after Juanita's departure. Dust motes danced in the glittering sunshine, and a weathered wood shutter creaked slightly in the morning breeze.

Campeón the mighty lay where Juanita had dropped him, calmly awaiting ascendance or the ants, whichever came first.

The sound of a door slamming open suddenly sang out from the upstairs bedroom, followed by a loud and steady stream of expletives shouted in staccato Spanish. As if in response, the uppermost bale on the stack of hay Juanita kept in the barn for her goats began inching forward. It jiggled forward an inch at a time, stopped, and then moved again. Finally it reached a precipitous balance atop the other half-dozen bales, tottered forward, and fell.

Into the opening thus created came a very large, somewhat weathered hand, followed by a considerably larger and even more weathered face. Campeón, had he still breath to breathe and eyes to see, might have thought the man some sort of fantastic barnyard apparition, the ghost, perhaps, of discarded scarecrows long deceased. He had an angry shock of red hair tufted atop his huge head, beetle-eyes hidden far beneath his jutting brows, and a series of scars, scabs and fresh cuts mottling his road map of a face. His hands were big as plates, and his fingers, long and thick as immature plantains, were crisscrossed with star-shaped scars.

The figure pushed two more bales aside with an effortless sweep of his hand and strode out into the sunlight, six feet-six inches of ugly in a Brooks Brothers suit. He adjusted his blue silk tie, glanced up to where the angry Spanish tirade continued to blister the steamy air, and stood blinking in the bright morning sunlight.

He looked like Vulcan fresh emerged from his forge, a misshapen giant not quite sure of how to maneuver in this bright new world. The sunlight also seemed to spotlight his most extraordinary feature, that is, his mouth. It was not the bottomless-pit sort of a mouth normally found on a giant; it was, in fact, ludicrously small. It was a mouth intended for a face half this size, a mouth that would have looked at home on a child. That mouth would have been inadequate even on a small man; on this face, lost amid those acres and acres of weathered flesh, it was almost grotesque.

That joke of a mouth was the sole source of the shadowy giant's ill-fitting nickname. His real name, the name given to him by his youthful mother before she abandoned him in a Brooklyn orphanage, was Thomas Theodore Puglowski, but his friends all called him Tiny.

At least, Tiny supposed, they would if he had any friends. He didn't; not really. All he had was Big Al, who was more his boss than his buddy, and he didn't really think what Big Al called him was a nickname. He hoped not. "Big dummy" wasn't much of a nickname.

Still, Tiny knew that he was lucky to have Big Al to help him along. He needed guidance in life, and Al had been giving him that guidance for as long as he could remember. Well, not as long as he could remember, 'cause he could remember better than most people thought, but at least since that day up in Starke when Al had come up to Tiny in the exercise yard and told him he was gonna let Tiny be his bodyguard.

Big Al needed a bodyguard 'cause he was sort of a

little guy, and Tiny—well, like Big Al said, Tiny needed guidance. And it worked out okay for Tiny. Al always had some sort of scheme going, even in prison. Like when Al told people they had to pay a one-cigarette toll to go past his cell after 5 P.M. A toll in jail! Tiny liked that one. Even if he didn't smoke cigarettes.

They were a good team, that's what Al said. Tiny liked being on a team, which he had never done before, even if Al got mad and yelled sometimes. Al said he only did it because Tiny was so big and slow and clumsy, and Tiny sure couldn't argue with that.

Tiny got so used to Big Al telling him what to do that when the warden said it was time to leave, Tiny asked if he could maybe stick around until Al's sentence was up. But the warden said no, and Al said no, too. He said that he was making big plans for them, and that it was only gonna be a few more months, and that Tiny should get a job and lie low and try and save up a little money.

So that's what Tiny did. He got work as a fry cook at a Waffle Hut in Lakeland that was so small he kept banging his head on the pots hanging from the low ceiling. He cooked breakfast six days a week and dinners on Saturday nights, pancakes and sausages and grilled cheese sandwiches and sweet ice tea. And grits.

Tiny really liked that job. He liked the smell of bacon and butter, he liked the sleepy customers slurping coffee over morning papers, he liked how eggs looked like big yellow eyes when you fried them just right. But he still quit the day Al walked in and said he'd found work for them with a friend of a friend, even though the Waffle

Hut manager said Tiny made the best damn omelet in the history of Lake County and promised he'd find somewhere else to store the big pots. Tiny didn't even worry when Al said they had to fly to the Caribbean and then sail a boat back, even though he'd never been on a sailboat and couldn't swim. He knew Big Al would know what to do.

But then Al got sick. He got sick even before the big storm came and blew them into this bay with the dirty, smelly water and the strange black fishermen who would point and laugh at their boat hidden on the shore, but never ever wave. Big Al got *really* sick. He would lean over the side of the boat for hours at a time, puking his guts out, all the time yelling at Tiny about how to sail the boat, and Tiny would get all confused and do something wrong, 'cause he really didn't know anything about sailing, and that's how they ended up stuck in this dirty little bay.

That was almost a week ago, and Al was still sick. He wasn't throwing up much anymore, now that they weren't sailing, but he just laid in bed and didn't look real good. And he was worried too. He knew that they had to get the boat up to Miami soon, and that they were losing time sitting here, but every time he tried to get up to start sailing it just made him sick again, and he'd yell at Tiny for not being a good enough sailor to get them out of the bay on his own.

Tiny didn't know much about sailing, but he knew what Big Al needed. He needed a good meal. He especially needed fresh hot soup—chicken soup. But the only food they had with them was canned stuff, mostly Chef

Boyardee Beefaroni and Spaghetti-Os, and powdered eggs. Lots of powdered eggs, which weren't near as good as fresh eggs, but still Tiny doctored them up with everything he could find on the boat, and they weren't all that bad. Al liked 'em, liked 'em and kept eating 'em even after he got sick. But now Al was sick and needed more than just omelets, and still he wouldn't let Tiny go into the little town to get anything else. Al was real secretive.

So Tiny just made omelets, and Chef Boyardee, and omelets with Chef Boyardee in them. Big Al stayed sick, and they both worried more and more. Then, last night, Tiny had had a brainstorm. Al hadn't said he couldn't go off the boat, just that they couldn't let anybody see them. If Tiny could just find a chicken without having to talk to anybody . . .

So this morning Tiny got up very early, even before sunrise, and carefully dressed himself in the dark. He put on his best suit; Big Al always said you had to look your best in their line of work. Then he slipped off the boat and up into the hills above the bay. There were a few little farms there, shacks really, and Tiny thought they might have chickens.

He was right, too. The very first place he'd come to, hiding in the scrub pines and prickly mangrove bushes, he'd seen a big ol' black woman out in the yard feeding chickens from a plastic bucket. There was a little outbuilding behind the house that Tiny figured might be a chicken shack, and he was right about that too.

Trouble was, most of the chickens were out front getting fed, and the few that were in the shack, well, he just couldn't catch them. (David Tony, who was his manager in Brooklyn when Tiny was boxing as Gino the Giant, back before he got his ear problem and lost his balance, always used to say that Tiny's problem was that he was real big but also real slow.) Finally, though, he found one he could catch; in fact, it just stood there waiting for him. But when he reached down to grab it, it jabbed him, hard, with its pointy beak. Really hard, hard enough to draw blood; then it opened its wings, flapped real hard and charged right at him.

Tiny didn't know much about chickens, but he knew he didn't want to get pecked again. So he reared back and kicked that damn bird just as hard as he could. It went flying across the barn and slammed into the far wall. Then it bounced to the ground, stood up and took a few steps, even though any fool could see that its neck was broke and it was already dead. Finally it flopped its way out to the middle of the little barn, fell over on its side and stopped kicking. Tiny walked over to pick it up, already smiling about how much better Al was going to feel once he got some good hot chicken soup in him.

That's when he heard the gunshot.

Tiny figured the owner of the farm had seen him and was mad about the chicken. He ran to the back of the barn and got behind some hay bales, even though he wasn't real sure hay would stop a .38, and he knew that sound; it was a .38 for sure. He stayed there for a minute, and when nothing else happened he figured the farmer had the barn door covered and was just waiting for him to come out in the open.

He was still hiding behind the hay a few minutes later when the lady feeding the chickens walked in. He was peeping out real careful between the bales and saw her when she picked up that dead chicken and started crying. It made Tiny feel bad, like maybe the chicken was her pet or something, but when she ran out again he thought of poor Al puking his guts out and knew he had to have that bird, pet or not. So when he heard the lady upstairs yelling in Spanish, he figured he'd better make his move.

Now that he had a good look at that chicken, though, Tiny wasn't so sure. It was the ugliest damn chicken he'd even seen, and scrawny too. Tiny started to get an uneasy feeling that maybe he'd screwed up again, and maybe Big Al wouldn't be so happy after all.

Then he saw the row of nests back along the sidewall of the barn. There were eggs in some of them, and Tiny smiled in relief. He put the dead chicken in the coat pocket of his extra-extra-large gray flannel Brooks Brothers suit and loaded up his hands with eggs. Then he started out the barn door and—*wham!*—walked right into the doorjamb, headfirst.

Tiny bounced off the door, shook his head real quick a couple times, and smiled. That hadn't been such a bad one, and he hadn't cracked even a single egg. The manager of the Waffle Hut in Lakeland used to bet people that his fry cook could hold a dozen eggs in one hand, and he'd win, and Tiny was glad about that now.

'Cause maybe he didn't know much about chickens and he sure didn't know much about sailing, but Thomas

Theodore "Tiny" Puglowski made the best damn omelet in the history of Lake County.

Harry had just about gotten himself back to sleep, nestled there among the sticks and ticks of his straw mattress and the scratchy denim of his makeshift pillow, when the bedroom door slammed open and a furious figure charged in. His first instinct was to grab his gun and leap up into the shooter-ready position, both arms straight out, legs spread for balance, finger on the trigger. His second impulse was to collapse back into bed, grab his aching head and puke out as much of last night's rum and Red Stripe as possible.

He didn't get the opportunity to do either one. He had barely got to his feet when his landlady Juanita, completely mindless of the fact he was doing his best to point a loaded .38 in her general direction, whacked him hard upside the head with a plastic bucket swung by its curved metal handle. He abandoned the pistol in favor of raising both arms protectively above his throbbing head. Juanita's second blow caught him flat on his crossed elbows, sending him backwards onto the rickety bed. The bed in turn collapsed with a mighty crash, spilling him onto his knees before his furious, bucket-wielding attacker.

Harry didn't understand much Spanish at the best of times, and Juanita was peppering her diatribe with plenty of Cajun, a few choice words in English and a dialect or two Harry didn't even recognize. Still, it seemed to him that it more than likely involved money, so when Juanita stopped swinging and cursing to catch her breath, he scuttled across the floor, reached under the torn mattress and grabbed his wallet.

He flipped the wallet open, turned it to reveal his dwindling cache of bills and, still on his knees like a supplicant before a priest, offered it up to Juanita. But the sight of money did not have the pacifying effect on his landlady that Harry expected. If anything, it increased her rage.

"Money? Money?" Juanita sputtered. *"Le mata Campeón! Le mata mi querido Campeón!"* She swung the bucket in a murderous uppercut that missed Harry's head by inches but nailed the proffered wallet dead-on.

Harry watched in surprise as all the various parts of his life scattered upward in a multicolored explosion of paper. Money, credit cards, university ID card, brand-new plastic-coated P.I. license, all went knifing skyward and then came flipping back down again, captivating Harry's confused and bleary mind. All this paper, all his life, like so much confetti in the wind. Harry was entranced.

Then Juanita hit him with her backhand.

The bucket whacked into the side of Harry's head with a reverberating plasticized *thonk!* Harry spun around backwards, tried to rise and, holding his vibrating cranium, pitched forward onto what remained of the bed. The crippled cot fell over sideways, dropping Harry once more to his knees. It also catapulted the loaded .38, sitting on the far corner of the bed where Harry had dropped it, clattering to the hardwood floor.

Harry and Juanita both watched as the pistol skidded across the floor like a hockey puck on home ice. It rotated slowly as it slid, once, twice, and then came to rest four feet away from poor hurtin' Harry, right at Juanita's feet.

Both combatants stared at the gun for a moment, each contemplating in the sudden silence how this new development had changed things. Then Juanita looked at Harry and Harry looked at her—and Juanita smiled a wicked, wicked smile.

Harper, ol' buddy, Harry thought to himself, it's time for you to leave.

Things had not improved appreciably for Happy Harry Harper an hour later. His hangover had subsided only marginally, his bare legs and feet were scratched and bleeding from his flight through the mangroves around Juanita's boarding house, and his stomach was growling with hunger. He had fled wearing only what he slept in—a torn cotton undershirt and University of Michigan-Detroit campus exercise shorts—and the yellowflies were chewing him up. Worst—worst by far—Harry had had the time to translate some of the things his furious landlady had said, and he was deeply concerned.

Happy Harry Harper was beginning to believe he had committed murder.

"'*Le mata mi querido*'—'You murdered my lover,' right?" he wondered as he walked. "'You murdered my lover Campeón.'" Was it true? It was possible. He didn't remember doing anything brutal the night before, but then again, he didn't remember much of anything from the night before. He remembered drinking extra Red Stripes with that damnably hot chicken at supper. He remembered reading Mickey Spillane, re-reading, actually, by lantern light in his room, knocking back warm rum and dreaming of cold Cokes, and he remembered staggering down to La Bonita, which at least sold warm rum-and-Cokes. He remembered walking along the beach, singing, under a sliver of a moon. He remembered—

Harry came to a sudden stop, his feet digging into the hot white beach sand. He remembered this morning, those damn roaches, the .38 cold and angry in his hand. The bullet went right through that paper-thin wall, he remembered. If there had been someone outside, say down in the courtyard near Juanita's barn . . .

"I think I'm going to throw up," Harry said. And he did.

He felt a little better when he was finished, though in truth there hadn't been much in his stomach to begin with. But he was no less despondent. He'd killed someone, someone innocent and unsuspecting, some happy young islander in the prime of life. A young man, coming over to visit his lover for a morning tryst, shot down by a careless bullet striking like lightning from a clear sky.

How could he possibly live with that? And, come to think of it, how could he live at all? He was stranded in a foreign land far from home, with no friends, no phone, not even much clothing. All the money in the world was in the hands of the enraged woman whose lover he had just sent to an early grave, the woman who emptied his own gun at him as he fled from her home. Juanita was no doubt calling in the local constable at that very moment, that is, if she decided to call in the law at all. Maybe she'd just get together a lynch mob and come after him. Harry hadn't exactly made many friends in his time in Blue Bay, and none of those fishermen in La Bonita looked like they would balk at stringing up a murdering *yanqui*.

Harry groaned and held his head. After a minute, driven by guilt and the swarming yellowflies, he decided to walk a little farther.

Harry didn't know, of course, that Juanita had more menace than murder in her tired soul, and was no more capable of shooting him than he was of shooting her. The gunshots he'd heard as he dove into the thickets outside her home were simply her exacting her revenge on the only thing she knew Harry cared for. She fired point-blank into Harry's UM gym bag, reveling in the way each shot sent pieces of paperbacks flying into the air. But eventually the bits of torn pages drifting back to the floor reminded her of feathers, of Campeón's feathers, and Juanita gave up the shooting to collapse into her grief.

Harry also didn't know, couldn't know, that at that very moment a pair of white squirrels were happily nibbling away at the thick pulp oozing out of a gourd hanging from a vine twining through the tall mangrove tree fifty feet away from his bedroom window. There was a large hole on each side for the squirrels to nibble at, each large enough for the squirrels to stick their nimble paws into and extract more of the sticky goo. Nor could Harry know that when the sated squirrels left, the ants and beetles would move in, cleaning the inside of the gourd right down to the last syrupy seed.

Months later, after the gourd had dried and hardened in the steady Caribbean sun, a female doctor-bird hummingbird looking for a place to nest would find the .38 caliber holes a perfect doorway for her and her mate. Weeks later, the sight of the young hatchlings flitting around her courtyard, their colorful tails already much longer than their slight bodies, would help bring Juanita out of the months-long funk engendered by the loss of her beloved Campeón. Inspired by the energetic hummingbirds, Juanita would puncture, clean and hang nearly two dozen additional gourds of all sizes. When Walter K. Gentry Jr., insurance broker and vice-president of the Omaha Bird Watchers Association, awoke in Juanita's guest room a year later to find that his watch, his wallet and his Puerto Plata hooker were all gone, Juanita's courtyard would have become an avian rainbow. There were tall green cotica parrots, tiny manuelitos, sprightly querebebes, gaudy great hummingbirds, the doctor-bird hummingbirds, and a dozen more species and sub-species flitting back and forth among the bougainvillea vines and hand-carved gourds spidering through Juanita's courtyard. Despite his unexpected troubles, Walter would be entranced.

The trickle of middle-aged Nebraska birders who started drifting into Cielo Bay the following summer would be delighted to find that settling silt had made the once-brown water once more true to its name, and that their vice-president's somewhat dubious story of a hidden birders' paradise was not, as some small-minded gossips had suggested, merely a cover story. Walter would buy a new watch, convince his wife his wallet really had fallen overboard on a sightseeing cruise, and humbly accept his fellow birders' insistence that he take over as president.

Juanita, who would be delighted to learn that in Nebraska everyone pays in cash and in advance, would no longer have much time to mourn her murdered rooster. During the day there were meals to cook, gourds to hang, pottery to replace. And, judging from the way the handsome young carpenter who was adding on a second upstairs room kept looking at her, Juanita guessed her nights too would soon be busy.

Still, there were those moments, when the full moon glittered like a pitfire in the sky and the night heat sent sweat trickling down her brown arms like rivers on a muddy hillside, when Juanita would remember her fallen Campeón. She would think of that foolish macho bird who refused to stop, no matter what the odds, and then look around at her growing tourist empire and smile. Always, too, she took a moment to wonder whatever became of the crazy *yanqui* who sent Campeón to his final rest. Nothing good, she hoped.

That was, in effect, exactly what Juanita was thinking that hot September morning as she sat on the floor of her upstairs room steadily tearing each and every remaining paperback page into long thin strips while, miles away, a troubled and torn Harry Harper stumbled down the dirty beach. She was hoping, with all her saddened heart, that nothing good would happen to that murdering *yanqui*.

And she was getting her wish.

2

The first thing Billy Byars noticed about the scrawny teenager standing on the front deck of his bar, asking for work and sweating in the North Florida sun, was her electric-blue eyes. They were the summer-sky blue of the Gulf of Mexico on its best and brightest day, circled about with an almost-violet rim that made him think of the minutes just between sunset and full dark. Her face was sun-browned and thin; her stringy hair was unwashed and the color of old lemons. Her name was Jane Ellen Ashley.

Billy had seen Jane Ellen around often enough, peddling her battered old banana-seat bicycle down Highway 98 or walking gingerly along the oyster-shell–dotted shore of the bay. He knew from the way she kept every trash-fish and undersized crab she pulled from the Apalach that she was fishing for food, not for fun. And he felt sorry for her, sure enough, standing there in her dirty T-shirt, torn cut-off shorts and bare feet—but the truth is he hired her for those eyes alone.

As it turned out, it was maybe the best move of his entire business career.

Not just because Jane Ellen proved to be a steady and uncomplaining worker, or because she was happy to work for the lousy wages Billy could afford and was no more interested in social security and withholding than him. That was nice, sure enough, and so was the pleasant touch of having a woman around the place, even a woman as scrawny and scraggly as Jane Ellen. But the truth was, in the forty-seven tiresome years Billy had spent growing up in, on and near the oyster-rich Apalachicola Bay, Jane Ellen Ashley was the best damn oyster shucker he had ever seen.

Oh, he'd known faster shuckers. Wiry old women who could shuck a bushel without missing a minute of their soaps; thick-armed oystermen who could shuck for hours on end, attacking the knobby-shelled bivalves like they were bitter enemies. But Jane Ellen had an effortless grace he'd never seen before. She didn't so much pry as coax the oysters open. Her deft slender fingers found openings for the stubby oyster knives that veteran shuckers three times her age would have missed.

Billy had never seen Jane Ellen give up on an oyster, never toss one back into the bushel in hopes of better luck the next time, never try to sneak a stubborn shell into the garbage with the empty sauce-stained shells. He'd never heard her cuss even the toughest bivalve, or seen her jab herself with an oyster-knife blade. And even more surprising, since most serious shuckers had a constantly evolving road map of scratches and stabs and white-line scars on their hands, Jane Ellen's hands were as smooth as pearls, even though she often as not neglected to wear the thick shuckers' gloves Billy provided out of his very own pocket.

Too-Tall Jerry Jefferson once speculated that all Jane Ellen had to do was tickle the bottom of an oyster's shell and it would open up like a Blountstown whore on a Saturday night. Billy had to agree with that assessment, even though he had never spent much time in Blountstown and knew damn well that Too-Tall hadn't either. The point was, Jane Ellen had the touch.

Not so long ago, Billy's Oyster & Pool had been just one of the aging seafood houses scratching a thin living from the bay, a ramshackle old shack up on stilts out over the water right outside Eastpoint, one strong wind away from oblivion. It hung desperately onto the roadside of Highway 98, like an old sailor leaning his ass out over a boat railing to shit in the water. Still, Billy had worked hard for the O&P. It was all he had, that and the trailer that was really more Lurlene's than his, and he loved it.

But Eastpoint houses were dying steadily, fading like old pelicans, swallowed up by Langer Industries and the other big seafood distributors, or just driven into bankruptcy by one too many slim seasons. Billy had been headed that way, selling off more parking-lot footage or another boat every few months just to stay afloat. Then one bright Sunday afternoon a cousin of Billy's working part-time for the Marine Patrol pulled up to check a thirty-foot Morgan anchored in the lee of Dog Island and found a state beverage officer cutting lines of coke with a big-for-her-age cheerleader out of Panama City–Mosely

High. The cheerleader grabbed her shirt, Billy's cousin grabbed the coke, and eight days later the beer license Billy had routinely and hopelessly applied to the state for eleven years running came through.

Now he sold oysters on the half-shell when the bay was open and smoked mullet when it was closed. He'd buy oysters right off the boats in the afternoon, and in the evening the oystermen would come and spend the money he gave them on cold bottled beer. They'd bunch around the rickety pool table Billy put in where the ice chests full of fresh snapper and yesterday's shrimp used to be, bet on pool and try to get drunk on credit.

Because Billy occasionally did let a down-and-out fisherman run a tab, and because he still looked, talked and acted like one of them, the O&P gradually became the place most of the locals went for comfort and company when the weight of extra money was lightening their step, or the lack of it was crushing their back. Billy's the dying seafood house became Billy's the prosperous bar, and on weekends and Wednesdays the oyster-shell median along Highway 98 was lined with jacked-up Dodge pickups and ten-year-old wagons.

Business got so good, in fact, that when the skinny, barefoot, stringy-haired blonde came in lying about her age and looking for work, Billy decided to take her on. Six hours a night on weekends, and six more on alternate Wednesdays when the big packing house over at St. Joe cut its paychecks.

Jane Ellen came to work on a rusty old Schwinn that clicked like an outboard in bad need of a valve job and was so small that to get up any speed she had to poke her knees out sideways and pedal spraddle-legged, like a big gray gull hurrying down the beach. Rumor had it she lived in an old sharecropper shack back in the scrub pine on St. Joe Paper Company land with a mean drunk who was her father, or maybe her lover, or maybe both. She didn't talk much and she wouldn't let him screw her, but she worked hard and she was polite to the customers. Eventually, she became as much a part of Billy's Oyster & Pool as the chalky yellow goldfish crackers on the bar and the faded-neon Wurlitzer in the back.

Business was good, life was good, and Billy was a happy man. He loved his wife, he loved his job, he loved his bar—but still there were those occasional sleepless nights, lying there in bed next to Lurlene, listening to the steady whir of the window air-conditioning unit, when Billy just couldn't seem to stop thinking about those eyes.

Growing up in Franklin County, Florida, instilled two things in Jane Ellen Ashley, the first of which was a deep and abiding desire to get the hell out of Franklin County, Florida. That's why she took the job at Billy's Oysters & Pool, even though the pay sucked and Billy Byars spent more time chasing her around than serving beer to the weary oystermen and shrimpers who frequented his bayside dive.

Jane Ellen didn't mind talking to the customers, and certainly she knew all the locals, but she refused to think of herself as a resident. She made a strong distinction between people who were *of* Franklin County and those, like herself, who were simply *from* Franklin County. Billy and his oystermen customers, with their leather-brown hands and ever-present odor of fish, tobacco and sweat, were *of* Franklin County, as much a part of the place as the brown pelicans perching on every open piling in the bay. But Jane Ellen, despite her many and undeniable years in North Florida, was still only passing through. She could see a future, hazy and distant as it might be, in which her society friends would react in mild surprise when she admitted to having spent some time in Florida. "Why *cherie*," they would say, with only the barest hint of disapproval, "you have no accent whatsoever."

Being a temporary resident of Franklin County, Jane Ellen never could work up much passion for the conversations of those people who truly belonged there. She understood but didn't appreciate the constant talk of water and weather; local gossip to her was simply boring stories about familiar strangers. She kept Franklin County at a distance, and if that meant she kept to herself, so be it. It just gave her more time to read.

Reading was what Jane Ellen was. She didn't *do* it, like society people did lunch; she didn't take part in it like high school boys took part in whatever sport the season dictated. She *was* her reading. She was never without something to read, and rarely wasn't reading it. It didn't matter what she read, which was good, because she never had much of a choice. She just read.

She read the Tallahassee and Panama City newspapers left behind by the coffee-and-omelet crowd at Sarah's Breakfast Bin. She read sticky-paged porno magazines tossed out of cars at the high school parking spots back off of 98. She read romance novels that Lurlene gathered from her sewing-circle buddies and gave her out of charity. She read nature pamphlets about least terns and sea oats she'd get for free at the state park over on St. George. Every few weeks she'd pedal over to the realty places on the island and pick up a handful of paperbacks left behind in the cabins-for-rent by tourists, usually best-selling trash novels or how-to books for people who wanted to gain money or lose weight. She'd long ago worked her way through the small library at Apalach, even though they wouldn't give her a card because she couldn't produce an address or phone number. Jane Ellen read constantly, avariciously, mindlessly. If her hands weren't busy her mind was, always, always stocking up information for that day when her body as well as her mind could finally leave Franklin County.

If she wasn't reading—that is, if she needed to use her eyes and her hands for something else—Jane Ellen contented herself with daydreams. Sometimes, on good days, she dreamed of going home to the shack to find Nate waiting, sober, smiling, his arms outstretched. On bad days, she thought about finding Nate dead, broken-necked and cold at the bottom of those rickety front steps, Early Times bottle still clenched in one hand.

Mostly, though, she dreamed about her cities. Paris, New York, London. That was where Jane Ellen really belonged, and her dreams could get her there.

31

Her favorite was Paris. She'd torn a picture of the Eiffel Tower lit up at night from a *National Geographic* at the library annex in Apalachicola and kept it pinned above her bed. Sometimes at night, with Nate snoring like old engines and the North Florida rain rattling on the roof like marbles in a washing machine, Jane Ellen would put a quiet hand on that picture and feel herself soaring up and away, out of Franklin County and out of her life like an osprey rising from the waves. It kept her going when she wanted nothing more than to lay down and die, and sent her dragging back into Billy's three nights a week to smile and nod at the familiar strangers, shucking those goddamned oysters.

Now, Jane Ellen ate as many oysters as anybody in town, and there was no denying she had a special feel for shucking. But in her heart of hearts, she had come to hate the slimy little bivalves. Oysters were everywhere in Eastpoint; any store big enough to have a countertop sold them raw, the air around the packing houses kept a constant scent of oyster-funk in the air, the roads themselves were made of old shells. Eastpoint *was* oysters, and vice versa. Sometimes at night Jane Ellen could almost swear the salt-smudged sky was the inside of a giant oyster shell that kept everyone within sealed away from the real true world of the living, including her. Especially her.

And so she dragged herself to Billy's three nights a week, clacking along on her salvaged Schwinn, bouncing along the rugged oyster back roads and through the clouds of mosquitoes and no-see-'ems that thrived in the humid air. She gorged herself on pilfered oysters so she could save money on food, and kept the occasional tips she got hidden from Nate in a Mason jar tucked in a tree hollow near the shack, dreaming of the day she would have enough for a ticket out, to Paris, to Atlanta, to anywhere.

Then one night, quite by accident, Jane Ellen Ashley stumbled across her ticket to fortune.

It was a quiet Sunday night, with just a few of the regulars playing gin and debating the weather, when a group of fraternity boys from Florida State stopped off on their way back from the island. They were drunk when they came in, and got drunker over oysters lathered with Tabasco sauce and horseradish. When Jane Ellen stepped outside to dump a bucket of empty shells over the thin railing running around their deck, one of the boys followed her. He pinned her against the rail, pulled a ten-dollar bill out of his pocket and tried to convince her to go out to his car.

She raised her lips to be kissed, and put her hands gently on the drunken teenager's chest. She also quietly hooked one leg behind his, and when he leaned in for his kiss, she suddenly pushed with all her might. Jane Ellen managed to grab the bill out of his hands as he flipped backwards over the rail and into the cold black water eight feet below.

When the frat boy came storming into Billy's a few minutes later, soaked, suddenly sober and furious, even his friends laughed at him. When he demanded his money back, the smiling oystermen who were gathered around Jane Ellen suddenly grew very cold. He and his buddies left quickly, and Jane Ellen pocketed the single largest tip of her life.

It was a story the locals passed around and mulled over for weeks, enlarging it with each telling, worrying over details like sun-splashed hounds gnawing a favorite bone. Jane Ellen politely retold the story when she was asked, but mostly she just smiled and let other, more excited people tell it for her.

Now maybe she was already planning ahead, and maybe she was just quicker on the uptake than most folks gave her credit for. All anybody knows for sure is that, when Joe Duval made his move against the fat-assed car dealers from Atlanta a month later, Jane Ellen played her part like she'd been born to it.

It had all the inevitability of a train wreck. Four drunk businessmen, down from Georgia to troll for kingfish and dolphin, slipped away from their wives and kids out on the island to toss a few beers and laugh at the locals down at the O&P. They were playing the one Elvis tune on the juke-box over and over and sneaking shots from a hidden flask everybody knew they'd brought in, cutting into Billy's beer sales and irritating the living hell out of the pool players. They were telling hooker stories in ever-louder voices when Joey D. decided he'd had about enough.

Joe Duval was fifty-three and looked ninety. He had skin the color of old leather and about three teeth left in his near-bald head, but he still worked the oyster beds every day the weather and the law allowed, and was known to be the sort of guy whose poker bluffs and fishing lies you just didn't call. He got up from his stool overlooking the pool table—an event in itself—walked over to the tourists' table, spun a chair around backwards and sat himself down uninvited.

"Sounds like you boys got yourself a little action up there in Atlanta," Duval said. He took a long draw on his longneck Miller, knowing damn well it made his toothless cheeks collapse like he was swallowing his own mouth. The boys from Atlanta stared in silence for damn near a full minute before Jolly Jerry Johnson, who sold Caddys and used trucks out of six lots stretching from Atlanta to Thomasville, got himself together enough to answer.

"We got our share," Jerry Johnson said, and then, just to make sure this outback apparition was duly impressed, he leered companionably and added, "Nothing better than a Georgia peach, ya know."

"Oh yeah, oh yeah. Big city stuff just got to be good, way I hear. Wouldn't know myself." Joe Duval took another slow contemplative pull on his Miller, glanced around surreptitiously, and leaned forward to draw all four out-of-towners in with a conspiratorial whisper. "Of course, the best you'll ever get, anytime, anywhere—" He glanced around again, and all four businessmen turned to look at the plastic sharks and peeling paint adorning the walls of the O&P to see what he was looking for. "The best you'll ever get is right here in this very room."

Duval leaned back with a knowing smile. Jolly Jerry and his buddies looked around the room again, checked out Jane Ellen popping open oysters behind the bar, checked the room once more and then turned back toward Jane Ellen.

"Her?" Jolly Jerry said, trying gamely to keep the sneer out of his voice. "Sport, that may be prime-time here in surf city, but up in Atlanta she's strictly backroom. Girl's got no tits, looks like she ain't bathed in a month. Shit, I seen better tail on a redfish—and I sure wouldn't pay for that."

Jerry turned and gave a sloppy high-five to Aaron Whitman, who sold Buicks out of Gainesville and fancied himself heir to the Jolly Johnson automotive empire. Willis and Frank, long accustomed to laughing whenever Jolly did, threw in a forced chuckle or two.

Duval waited calmly for the boys to calm down. Then—"Right, no tits and no ass either. But boys—check out the lips."

Four stubby Georgia heads swiveled on four fat Georgia necks to take a closer look at the scrawny blonde sitting quietly on her faded-pine barstool. She was wearing a loose white T-shirt that promised "Two Fingers Is Enough" and hid her slender body well. Her hair was the color of old corn and clearly needed a good wash. She was staring not quite so much dejectedly as just disinterestedly at the rack of open-faced oysters she was arranging on a tray before her, looking like she'd just as soon be asleep and damn near was. Her lips were . . . well, they were lips. Functional, if not fascinating.

Still, there was something about those eyes. . . .

"It's like this," Duval said, not really quite sure what it was like but willing to give it a try. "See, Jane Ellen's dad was an oysterman, down near Carrabelle. Her ma died when she was little, and sometimes when her dad had to go out on the bay and couldn't find nobody to sit with her, he'd just lock her up out in his storeroom. Well, sir," Duval paused for a sip of beer, thought a minute and then pushed on. "Well, sir, one day Jane Ellen was crawling around in there and she knocked over a bucket of runt oysters her pa was saving for seed. Being a little kid, she just naturally popped one of those salty things in her mouth and started to sucking.

"Now those oysters had been outta water a while, and they was half open. Little Jane Ellen got to pulling and toking and sucked that poor damn oyster right out of its shell, *slurppp*, just like that.

"Now by the time her pa got home, Jane Ellen had sucked down about two dozen oysters, and never a one of 'em shucked. Her pa saw what she done, and figured she was bound to get sick, but she never did. So from then on he took to leaving her a bucket of oysters every time he went out, figuring they was cheaper than milk and Jane Ellen could serve herself.

"By the time Jane Ellen was fourteen, she could suck a full-grown, shut-tight oyster right out of its shell without ever opening it at all. I seen her suck out a scallop before it could even blink its eyes, and they say once she put out the candles on her birthday cake just by inhaling.

"Now boys—just imagine what a girl with that kind of talent could do for you—if she got a mind to."

The boys all turned to stare at Jane Ellen with newfound respect, all unaware the jukebox had gone silent and everyone in the room, with the sole exception of

Jane Ellen herself, was doing their level best to not laugh out loud at Duval and his new friends.

Jolly Johnson, who until then hadn't noticed how damn hot it was in this little redneck dive, pulled a red silk handkerchief out of his back pocket and wiped his considerable forehead. Willis and Frank, who were cousins by birth and fools by nature, watched Jolly closely to see what they should do next. And Aaron, who looked more confused than excited, leaned in to tap Duval questioningly on the shoulder.

"Scallops got eyes?" he asked.

"Yep. Lots of 'em. Bright blue ones." Duval answered without taking his eyes off Jolly, who looked like he might be heading for some sort of strange attack. "I made the mistake of French-kissing that girl one time, and she got all excited, and—well . . ." Duval grinned widely to show his impressive lack of teeth. Two of the Georgia boys looked like they were going to choke, but the big-mouthed one just stared at Jane Ellen all the harder.

At exactly that moment, Jane Ellen Ashley turned up her head, opened those lips in question as wide as she could, and let a fat juicy Apalachicola Bay oyster drop down into her waiting mouth. With her eyes closed in sensuous enjoyment, she brought the stubby oyster knife-blade to her mouth and ran it gently across her lips, savoring the salty-rich oyster taste. Then she opened her eyes, a gentle dribble of oyster juice running slowly down one soft cheek, and looked straight into the blood-shot gaze of Jolly Jerry Johnson.

Jolly Johnson could take no more. He let out his best

car-dealing war-whoop, pushed his considerable bulk to his feet and lit out after Jane Ellen, who in turn lit out the back door. Three generations of Eastpoint oystermen turned to watch, but nobody made a move to interfere.

"Hey, buddy. How many eyes?"

"What?"

"How many eyes? On a scallop?"

"Two, three dozen, I expect. Never counted."

"Two dozen bright blue eyes. Well I'll be damned." Aaron Whitman, who sold Buicks out of Gainesville and never, ever would take over Jolly Jerry Johnson's automotive empire, picked up his Miller Lite longneck, took a contemplative sip of slightly warm beer, and vaguely wondered what had caused that huge splash outside.

And so it went. Word of the great Apalachicola Bay dunk-your-buddy practical joke spread through the fraternity halls and state office buildings of Tallahassee, and among the amusement park owners and charter-boat captains of Panama City, Destin and Ft. Walton Beach. By the end of the summer, rarely a week went by when Jane Ellen didn't dump at least one randy victim into the cold blue bay. Her fame and that of Billy's O&P grew rapidly, and her stash of travel money grew right along with it. Jane Ellen began making serious inquiries into plane fares and travel dates; Billy started buying back chunks of his old parking lot and restocked the jukebox.

Her growing fame also brought a change in Jane

Ellen herself. She started wearing a better class of T-shirts, shirts that fit her better and revealed that she did indeed have a figure that was expanding beyond girlish. Her dishwater hair took on a golden shine; Billy eventually learned she was giving Mrs. Owens down at the Bayview Trailer Park and Campground two dollars a week to use her shower, and even washing her hair with lemon juice squeezed from the little quarter-lemon slices Billy gave out with each dozen oysters. Lurlene stopped bringing her romance novels and took to har-rumphing about Billy's hired help. Billy himself felt a responsibility to renew his efforts to get Jane Ellen in the sack. (Jane Ellen had got more interesting, but no more interested. She told Billy to fuck off and threatened to dump him in the bay. He threatened to start docking her pay for the lemon wedges, and they both relaxed and went back to work.)

The pace of life at the O&P picked up. So much so, in fact, that Billy was actually debating the cost of adding on room for a second and maybe even a third pool table that September Saturday night when two smirking fraternity boys led a slack-jawed friend up to Jane Ellen's perch behind the bar and suggested she take him outside. The rowdy crowd, both larger and more cynical than in months prior, took notice with a few elbow nudges and not much more, and Jane Ellen took her new charge in hand with the casual indifference of a weary prostitute. Sure he was stoned, that was obvious. That was also nothing different, at least not to Jane Ellen.

To Jerome Fitchett Langer III, however, the world

was most decidedly different. Fitchett had spent the morning gathering psilocybin mushrooms in a mist-cloaked cow pasture out near Lake Jackson, and passed away the afternoon tossing back the boiled-down purple-black liquid in larger and larger shots. When his more-sober friends suggested they all ride down to the coast it sounded like fun; when they suggested he leave with the slender bartender it sounded like paradise. He felt not in the least bit surprised when her kiss sent him tumbling on and on through the night skies, and the slap of cold water against his back seemed a caress from the gods. When Jane Ellen walked back into the bar, tucking a brand-new ten-dollar bill into her cut-off blue-jean pocket, Jerome Fitchett Langer III was sinking blissfully beneath the waves.

Jane Ellen acknowledged the applause in the O&P with a small smile, nodded at her victim's laughing comrades, picked out a dozen good-sized oysters and sat down to celebrate. She was about halfway through her fourth when she realized something was wrong. By the time she'd sent the sixth scuttling down her upturned throat, the whooping and laughing in the room had taken on the strained quality of fishermen eyeing a distant storm. She opened number eight with one eye on the door. Before number ten had completed its slippery journey down her esophagus, Jane Ellen had joined the suddenly urgent rush of customers and colleagues toward the back-deck door.

They used the loading lights still up from the O&P's seafood days, and a few strong-beam flashlights hurriedly fetched from nearby four-wheelers. They called and cried and, over the anguished protests of Fitchett's friends, they used a tri-pronged gaff tied onto a hank of leader rope to drag the water beneath the deck. But Fitchett was nowhere to be found.

"Fitchett. Oh my God, Fitchett. He's dead," moaned one of Fitchett's frat brothers, the fat one with the tortoise-shell glasses. He was near hysteria, he felt like he might throw up, and he was about to cry.

He was also dead wrong.

Jerome Fitchett Langer III was not dead, although even he was at that very moment giving serious consideration to the possibility. Had he not, after his miraculous fall through open space, felt himself carried away on the gentle currents of the heavens? Had he not, when forced to stand by the growing discomfort in his chest, found himself in this dark, ill-lit, tunnel-like space? And was he not, even now, hearing the distant and muffled voices of his dead relatives calling his name, welcoming him to this surprisingly wet but still not unappealing afterlife? Fitchett didn't exactly feel dead, but since he wasn't exactly sure what dead did feel like, he decided to stay where he was and patiently wait for whatever came next.

So Fitchett stood, chilled but content, underneath the wood-slat ramp running from the shore just east of the O&P out to a half-dozen old oyster skiffs moored in the dark bay, while thirty feet away friends and strangers alike mourned his untimely passing.

"He seemed like such a nice kid," Joey Duval said,

just to break the silence, even though he had never noticed the boy before Jane Ellen took him outside. He was hoping his voice might calm down the kid with the glasses, who looked like he was going apoplectic. It didn't. The boy gave yet another racking sob and buried his face on the shoulder of his stoic—or was it stunned?—frat friend.

The few oystermen still gathered on the deck of the O&P looked at each other wordlessly and turned to go inside. Leave the boys with their grief. Time to call the sheriff.

"Oh God. What'll we tell the Senator?"

The title stopped them cold. Those men who had always lived so far from power and privilege, they knew—knew without asking, knew from the way they could hear the capitalization of "Senator" in the boy's voice—just who he was talking about.

Billy was closest, so he was the one to ask.

"The Senator?" he said.

The more together of the two boys, the tall redhead, let go of his friend and took a step toward Billy. Even in the darkness, Billy could see that a touch of fear had joined the desperation in the boy's eyes.

"That," the boy said with a vague gesture toward the bay, "that was Jerome Fitchett Langer III. His daddy's Senator Langer. Senator Jerry Langer." The boy swallowed hard. "He'll kill us."

Billy put one hand against the O&P deck to steady himself. Jerry Langer. Senator Langer. "Banger" Langer, whose two-fisted rise to power was a legend and a nightmare all along the Panhandle coast, whose Langer Industries chewed up small businesses and spit out broken people from Pensacola to Cedar Key. Langer Seafood. Langer Shipping. Langer Bridge, for Christ's sake, six lanes over the Ohclockonee Bay up near Alligator Point that might see ten cars an hour on a good day, built just 'cause Jerry Langer told the Florida Senate he needed it there. Billy clutched the railing of the O&P hard, feeling like those beloved, rotten wooden rails were about to be ripped away from him.

The tall kid took a step toward the bay, toward where his fat friend was leaning far over the railing, stretching his arms toward the dark water and keening Fitchett's name over and over. Then he spun around and grabbed Billy by both arms.

"But it wasn't us, it wasn't our fault! It was that girl, she killed him! Where is she?"

The boy looked around frantically, then lunged toward the rear door of the O&P. The remaining oystermen, shocked into action by the Langer name, went after him. Even the fat kid roused himself from the railing and stumbled inside, leaving Billy Byars alone on the deck of his beloved O&P. Billy gave a deep sigh.

He knew the mob wouldn't find Jane Ellen inside, or anywhere else. Sounds carry far in the country air, and even above the steady slapping of waves against the O&P pilings, Billy could hear a steady clicking rapidly fading away down Highway 98.

Now some people might have mistaken that clicking for an outboard motor in need of new valves, or even an old Schwinn bicycle being pushed to its three-speed limit. Not Billy. He recognized it right away. It was the sound of a local legend on the run. It was the sound of money fleeing from the cash register of the O&P. It was the sound an osprey makes as she rises above the waves.

It was the sound of Jane Ellen Ashley, forever and ever getting the living hell out of Franklin County, Florida.

3

The yellowflies were still after Harry an hour later, and the morning sun was beginning to cook his barely covered skin, but at least now he had a goal—if only a very short-term one. Harry's recently emptied stomach had joined the chorus of unhappy body parts objecting to his recent treatment of them. Harry was starving. His stomach was growling and churning, he was feeling more than a little shaky; he was, in fact, starting to fear that he might actually pass out. Great, Harry thought, an angry lynch mob on my trail, and I'm going to conk out on the beach.

And then Harry's sun-scorched nose caught just a hint of an odor that doubtless had originated in Heaven. Better yet, in Heaven's kitchen. It was the smell of overladen breakfast bars in overcrowded American restaurants, the smell of quiet Sunday mornings with *The New York Times,* the smell of happy childhood breakfasts with his mother and father. It was the scent of refreshment, of relaxation, of redemption. It was the tantalizing, taste-tingling, tongue-tempting odor of fresh-cooked eggs.

Harry stood on the hot sand for a moment, his nose thrust into the air like a hunting dog, stomach growling and salivary glands spurting like fire hoses. Then he was off, scrambling down the beach in the direction of the wonderful odor, careless of what danger might be lurking ahead, desperate only to find and feast on the source of that delectable scent. He jogged until his weak legs and weary head made him dizzy, then he tromped on in a slow steady trudge through the sand, heading east, following his nose. He got weaker as the smell got stronger, and, as if put there solely to vex him, the sand dunes he had to climb on his excursion down the beach began getting bigger and bigger. Finally he stumbled up and over one room-sized dune, caught his foot on a chunk of driftwood, went tumbling face-forward down the dune's far side, too weak to stop himself, and came to a stop facedown in wet sand just above the waterline. He lay there for a minute, spitting sand, catching his breath, before he felt strong enough to raise his head and look up.

Right before him, to Harry's surprise, was the bright blue butt-end of a large sailboat, tied parallel to the shore and partially covered by branches and grass. There was gold lining around the railing, and gold lettering swimming along the stern in Harry's blurry vision; he concentrated for a moment and the letters sharpened into place and announced: *Miss Behavin'.*

Harry blinked, rubbed some sand out of his eyes and raised his head a little further. Standing there looking at him over the railing of the boat was the biggest, ugliest hulk of a man he had ever seen. He was immaculately dressed, he was staring at Harry in obvious surprise—and he smelled like an omelet.

"What the fuck you want?" the man said.

Harry swallowed, swallowed again, and said, "Breakfast." It was all he could think of to say, and it appeared to confuse the giant on the boat. He frowned, then disappeared for a minute. He returned accompanied by a second man, this one short and squat and unhealthily pale despite the blazing tropical sun. The smaller man was thoughtfully chewing something. He held a fork in one hand, and a cheap-looking plastic plate in the other. On that plate, Harry's quivering nose told him, lay the omelet of his dreams. Harry was hypnotized.

The small man stopped chewing, pointed the fork at Harry accusingly, and said something in Spanish. Harry shook his head and rose unsteadily to his feet.

"I don't speak Spanish," he said. "I'm lost, and I'm starving, and I'm sick, and I think maybe the police or maybe a lynch mob are after me. Can I have something to eat?"

The little guy stared at him, nonplussed, his giant friend looming right behind him. "You're American," he said.

"Uh-huh. And I haven't eaten in hours. And I'm thirsty, too."

"Oh. Oh, right, sure. Where is my manners?" The man leaned over the railing and handed Harry his plate. Harry surged forward, stumbling out knee-deep into the dirty bay to accept the offering. The little man wiped the fork on his shirt and started to hand that along too, but Harry was already attacking the half omelet left on the plate with his hands. He picked the entire taco-sized concoction up in his fingers, ignoring the sudden burn, and jammed half of it into his mouth. It was magnificent. He chewed frantically and swallowed a huge bite, anxious to get the second half into his mouth.

"American, huh?" the man said, watching Harry closely. "And you say the cops is after you?"

Harry nodded enthusiastically, not slowing his assault on the omelet. It really was, he'd decided, the best omelet he'd had in his entire life. Nothing fancy, just eggs, a little salt, some delicate spice he didn't quite recognize, a bit of yellow cheese, but all combined in exactly the right proportions, and cooked to perfection. He swallowed the last mouthful and started picking at the tiny bits of egg dotting the plate.

"You're looking for a way out of here then, ain't you?" the omelet man asked. Harry grunted affirmatively, swirling his fingers across the empty plate and then sucking the shine of grease off his dirty fingers. "Tell me—do you know anything about sailing?"

Harry stopped what he was doing, three fingers still stuck happily in his mouth, and glanced up at the strange little man on the boat. The man was staring at him intently, almost, Harry thought, predatorily. Slowly, without taking his eyes off the other man, Harry nodded.

The man smiled, slowly at first, and then allowed himself a full, hearty, grin. "Tiny," he said over his shoulder, "why don't you go fix up a pot of fresh coffee. And while you're at it, whip up another omelet for our new friend here." He turned back to Harry, smiling like a weasel, and put his hand out over the railing to help Harry on board.

The giant's name was Tiny. His coffee was as good as his omelets, Harry decided, and his name fit him perfectly. The little one was Big Al, he was very clearly in charge, and his name didn't suit him at all.

"The way I figure," Big Al said, stopping to cough violently into his hand and wipe it on his pants. "The way I figure, us Americans, we gotta stick together, especially down here in the fucking Third World, you know what I'm saying?" Harry nodded, concentrating on what was left of his second omelet. "I know you got some trouble with the law here, and that don't bother me none, that's your affair, and besides I know the cops down here'll jump on an American faster'n snake shit, just ta shake him down, I know that. But I figure, like you say, your best bet is to get on back to the good ol' U.S. of A. and get things straightened out from up there."

"Right," Harry said. "Once I'm there, I get a good lawyer, contact the embassy and—"

"Right," Al said. "Just right. But first you got ta get back home, don't ya know. Now me and the big dummy there, we got a problem too. We got ta get this boat back to the States, to Miami, but we're having trouble 'cause I ain't a well man, ya see, all the sailing we done is making me sicker and sicker, and Tiny there, he don't know sailing from shinola, if you know what I mean.

"Now we can take a plane back home easy enough, but we can't leave the boat behind 'cause . . . well, we

just can't. You can't take a plane, not if the local gen-
darmes are watching for ya. So it seems ta me—" Big Al
leaned over the table and waved his coffee mug at Harry
"—It seems ta me there is a logical solution ta both our
problems."

Harry nodded, frowned, and took a sip from his coffee. His eyes flickered past Al to the large box strapped to
a bolted-down table in the center of the boat's main
cabin. The box was long, bullet-shaped, luxuriously
carved out of a handsome hardwood. It would have com-
manded attention in any room, anywhere; here in the
cabin of a thirty-foot sailboat it was impossible to ignore.

It was a coffin.

"It seems you noticed our cargo," Big Al said. "That
there is the remains of a national hero, a heroic fighting
man of the Honduras Air Force, shot down in the war
with Panama, or Peru, I forget. His family has gone ta
great expense to find his body and ta bring it back home
for a proper burial."

"Back home to Florida?"

"Right, back ta Miami, which is where his bereaved
family is now residing and which they now consider
home. They had quite a bit of trouble with the government in the Honduras, ya see, which don't like the idea
of their national heroes getting dug up and moved to
another country, no matter what the hero's family says.
So the family went ta my boss, who is a high-up official
in the government back home, and he called some people he knew down in Miami, and they made some
arrangements with some people in the Honduras, and

next thing you know, boom, the body is all packed up and ready ta go."

"So why didn't they just put it on an airplane?"

"Now that's a very good question, a very good question indeed. Tiny, give me some more coffee." Al held his coffee mug out to his side carelessly and took off on another coughing fit. Tiny walked over and filled the bouncing mug slowly, careful not to spill any on the distracted Big Al. The look on the giant's face, Harry thought, was a strange and somehow touching mix—part fear that he would miss the moving mug and burn his boss, part motherly concern for his coughing comrade.

"Okay, where was I?" Al continued. "Oh yeah, it seems the paperwork in Honduras wasn't done exactly right, some red tape thing, and the coffin don't have all the clearance it takes ta get in through an American airport. So that's where Tiny and me come in."

"Ah-ha."

"Yeah. They got the coffin ta Colombia all right, 'cause Colombia don't care quite so much for regulations or for the Honduras if you follow me. And my boss hired a crew ta sail this boat down there, and flew me and Tiny down there to make sure the crew handled everything all right. But at the last minute it turns out that the crew has some immigration problems, and the Colombian officials want ta talk to them for awhile. So I call the boss, and he says we can't wait, and for me and Tiny to bring the boat on back by ourselves."

"Wow."

" 'Wow' is right. Now I done some sailing, back when I

was in the Navy, so I figure, all right, no biggie. We take off, and we're doing okay, but after about four, five days I start getting seasick. Seasick like I ain't never been before, seasick that just won't go away. I mean I'm tossing cookies dawn to dusk. So Tiny takes over, doing just what I tell him, usually me shouting at him from out the bathroom, and we're going okay, we ain't setting any speed records, but we're going okay. Then a few days ago we run into this big storm. Dummy there is doing his best, but he don't know shit about sailing, and I'm too sick to help. I'm thinking maybe we're gonna capsize and die, but instead we get blown inta this bay here, get shoved up right on this bank."

"Bummer."

"Right. So here we are. Tiny digs us out, once the storm stops, but I'm still way too sick to head back out ta sea. I'm thinking I got malaria or something, but I don't wanna go ta the locals 'cause I figure there ain't no doctors worth a squat out here in the sticks and I ain't even really sure what country we're in."

"The Dominican Republic."

"Right, that's what I figured, but what does the Dominican Republic think about Americans? Do they got real good relations to the Honduras? I don't know, see, so I'm like in a real quandary. I got that poor old war hero lying there, and his poor worried family waiting for him back home, and me too sick to move. I'm outta answers, so I start praying for a miracle. I'm thinking, 'Holy Mary Mother of God, I'm in a tight spot this time and even if you don't care about me maybe you could send me a miracle on account of that poor war hero in the coffin and his bereaved loved ones back home.'

"And then you shows up."

Harry stopped sipping and looked at Big Al over the lip of his coffee cup. "You want me to sail this boat up to Florida for you."

"Me and my boss and the family of that war hero and Mary Mother of God, yeah, that's what we want."

Harry put down his coffee cup and closed his eyes. He was tired, immensely tired, and spaced-out too, but the coffee and food had cleared his head up enough to know he was being lied to. God knows what these people are really up to, he thought, and who or what is really in that coffin. Not that he had any choice. So that's what happens when you become a fugitive, he thought. You find your choices get very limited.

Big Al apparently interpreted Harry's introspection as hesitance. Harry heard the man's fingers drum impatiently on the table. After a moment he coughed, quietly, and said, "Our boss would be happy ta pay you for your time and trouble, of course. When you get ta Miami."

Harry let his eyes ease open, not so much out of interest as fear he would fall asleep. Al leaned in toward him. "Say, five grand. For your time."

Harry suddenly realized Tiny was still standing just behind Al, listening carefully to every word his boss said. Tiny scowled hard at Harry; one catcher's-mitt–sized hand held the metal coffee pot exactly at the level of Harry's head. Harry felt a sudden heartfelt desire to not disappoint Al.

Harry's eyes flickered over to meet Al; he may have even nodded. At any rate, the weaselly smile returned to Al's face, and he slumped back into his chair, relaxed.

"Tiny," Big Al said, "I want you should start packing my stuff."

It took them a while to get going. Al spent some time walking Harry through the charts, outlining exactly where he needed to come into Florida waters and into Biscayne Bay; Harry, with a full belly and aching head, struggled to stay awake and pay attention all the while. Al showed Harry how to operate the *Miss Behavin'*'s recently rebuilt diesel engines and where the various sails and ropes and riggings were stored, stopping every few minutes to cough furiously. He fiddled with the radio for awhile, and then explained to Harry that it was out of order, but not to worry since the trip to Miami should be a milk run anyway.

Tiny stayed right behind Big Al the entire time, moping like a pet puppy who knows he is about to be left at home. The plan was for Big Al to fly to Miami while Tiny and Harry sailed the boat up—and Tiny did not like that plan at all. He argued, and he sulked, and then, too late, pretended he didn't understand, going so far as to pack his own bag and put it with Al's at the stern of the boat. It wasn't so much the idea of sailing with Harry that troubled Tiny, Harry quickly realized; it was just that he dreaded being separated from Big Al.

But Al insisted. He lectured Tiny, first loud and angry, and then in quiet undertones that Harry couldn't hear but still understood. Tiny listened silently, his rough features drooped in a caricature of misery.

Finally they got Al unloaded. Harry prodded the diesel engine uncertainly into gear, and the *Miss Behavin'* moved away from the shore. Tiny stood morosely in the stern, staring back at land and Big Al.

They hadn't gone fifty yards when Harry heard the splash from astern and realized he had lost his passenger. He popped the engine into neutral and trotted back to the stern. Big Al was on his hands and knees at the base of the first sand dune, coughing. Halfway to shore, swimming strong and steady despite still being in his formal suit and coat, was Tiny.

Harry returned to the wheel, engaged the engine and swung the boat into a wide circle. By the time he had the *Miss Behavin'* on track toward the bank, Al was sitting up, Tiny kneeling at his side.

Harry tried to bring the boat in parallel to the shore, close enough for Tiny to get back on board without wedging the boat up on the sand. But Tiny had other ideas. He glared out at Harry, then tried to wave him off. Finally, after a few words to Al, Tiny rose and waded out into the water. Harry slipped the boat back into neutral and went looking for the anchor.

"Suitcase!" Harry heard Tiny's deep voice booming over the water despite the steady thrum of the engine. He was waist-deep in the bay about twenty yards from the boat, which had slowed to a crawl and, nudged by the outgoing tide, was beginning to turn away from the shore. Harry walked to the back of the boat and called out to Tiny.

"I'll come in for you!" he said, but Tiny shook his head vigorously and pointed out toward open water. "My suitcase!" he shouted. On the beach behind him, Big Al raised one arm in an indecipherable gesture before collapsing in another coughing fit.

Harry picked up Tiny's suitcase uncertainly, looking back and forth between the giant in the water and Al on the beach. "I don't know," he began, "I think Al wants me to come—"

Harry never finished that sentence. Tiny, who apparently was not very big on talking, reached inside his coat pocket, pulled out a heavy black pistol, pointed it in Harry's general direction and fired. Harry heard the bullet whiz by and wondered briefly if it had been a warning shot or just a bad one.

Either way, he figured the argument was settled. He slung Tiny's suitcase as hard as he could toward the shore, then dropped beneath the boat's gunwales and crawled on his hands and knees back to the wheel. Without standing up, he spun the wheel toward what he hoped was open water and re-engaged the engine.

Harry stayed down on the deck of the *Miss Behavin'* for a full five minutes, steering by feel and guesswork until he figured he was safely out of gunshot range. When he stood up, Tiny and Big Al were just two dark figures on the distant and receding beach.

And Happy Harry Harper was on his way out to sea.

4

Boulder Baker carefully picked two more pecans out of the hand-carved mahogany bowl on the coffee table before him. He rolled them gently from side to side in the palm of one large and impressively muscled hand, clicking them like dice. Then he slowly, deliberately, closed his hand around the oblong brown nuts and squeezed. The nuts shattered, first with a loud sharp crack and then, as Boulder increased the pressure, with a long steady barrage of sharp little snaps and pops.

He kept it up for a long time, never once taking his eyes off the lanky young Cuban seated across from him. The Cuban, Joaquin, stared at Boulder's hand, mesmerized, then forced himself to look away. He took a quick little draw on his cigarette and glanced up at the third man, also Cuban, who leaned against the wall nearby, watching quietly.

Boulder gave the pecans one more good crack to make sure he had Joaquin's attention. Then he slowly opened his hand and let the pulverized nut-and-shell powder fall on top of the growing pile in the ashtray before him.

Joaquin couldn't take it anymore. "Hey, bro," he said, "why you smashing up all those nuts like that, bro?"

Boulder looked serenely at Joaquin, stolid as a stone. "Can't get at the nuts if you don't crack the shell," he said.

"But you aren't eating no nuts, bro."

"I don't like nuts."

"You don't like—ha!" Joaquin's laugh was sharp and girlish. "Hey, Rey, you hear? This man he breaks nuts and he breaks nuts, but he don't like nuts!" Joaquin leaned toward Rey, trying to draw the older man into his laughter, but Rey only shrugged. His eyes rose to meet Boulder's, and Rey reached for the inside pocket of his white blazer. He did so slowly, holding the jacket open with two fingers so Boulder could clearly see him pulling out a packet of Silva Thins cigarettes.

This one, this Rey, he's good, Boulder thought. Confident, calm, steady when trouble comes. But this other one . . . Boulder looked back toward Joaquin, who was shaking his head in overstated bewilderment, sucking hard on his cigarette. The ash on the cigarette's tip had grown long, too long, and Boulder saw Joaquin's hand move just slightly toward the ashtray. But the ashtray was right under Boulder's nose; when he made no move to move it, Joaquin stopped himself, smiled thinly, and turned away.

Boulder allowed himself a tiny, inaudible sigh. He wondered if perhaps Joaquin was a relative of his new employer; he could think of no other reason that a man like Carlos would have such a fool in his organization. Boulder wondered too if Joaquin were the reason Carlos had brought him here to Miami. He had taken care of such ticklish problems for other employers in the past.

Carlos had said this assignment would take several weeks, maybe even a few months. Longer than Boulder wanted to be in Florida, certainly longer than he wanted to be away from his garden. But Carlos had offered him more than Boulder was used to receiving—a lot more. Enough, if he managed it well, to retire for good, to sell off all his hardware and devote himself to his gardening—and so Boulder reluctantly accepted. He had spent two peaceful days tilling his frost-covered two acres, enjoying the horse manure smell of fresh-turned earth, and then boarded a plane for Miami.

Joaquin had met him at the airport, all white linen and gold jewelry, trying to look inconspicuous and dangerous at the same time. Joaquin had chattered nonstop during the limo ride to Carlos's Cape Coral estate, saying nothing at all and more than he should. With each passing mile, Boulder had wondered more and more if Carlos was as sharp as his reputation said he was.

Once at the estate, Boulder insisted on seeing Carlos right away, even though that meant waiting in his outer office while Carlos concluded an earlier meeting. That was all right—seeing Rey, seeing the difference between Carlos's errand boy and the men he kept close to him, had restored some of Boulder's confidence.

But then the door to Carlos's inner office came

flying open—and Boulder got his first look at Quiet Quiones.

Quiones burst into the room like a short hurricane, babbling enthusiastic greetings to Joaquin and Rey in an erratic mix of Spanish and English. He was a squat little man, thirtyish, Hispanic but as unlike the two whippet-thin Cubans already there as a basset from a greyhound. Quiones had a dumpy, baby-fat physique, the slight ridges on the sides of his nose suggested he had just taken off glasses, and Boulder suspected his jet-black hair had been dyed. He held a large mug of coffee in one hand; unlike Rey, who had sipped two cups of syrupy black Cuban coffee since Boulder arrived and still moved slow as a snake, Quiones was wired.

"Joaquin, my friend, *mi compadre, que tal?*" Quiones said. He bounced across the room in three quick steps, ignoring Boulder, to give the smirking Joaquin an enthusiastic slap on the back. The frenetic little man then initiated some sort of complicated handshake routine with Joaquin, a ritual of twists and snaps similar to what Boulder had seen among blacks in the northern cities where he did most of his work. Joaquin went through the ritual easily, lazily, smirking just a bit; Quiones, despite his light manner, was concentrating on every move. Boulder wondered if the little man had any idea that Joaquin was laughing at him.

"Mr. Baker." Boulder turned to face the man who had entered the room behind Quiones, and knew immediately that this was his new employer. Carlos was slender and fiftyish, his dark hair turning toward silver. He wore casual slacks, loafers, a light turtleneck—comfortable in his self-confidence, Boulder thought, unlike his overdressed employees. Boulder also noted, without surprise, that the moment Carlos entered the room, Rey moved to his side. Boulder was not offended that Rey watched him intently, or that he was poised to spring between Boulder and Carlos if the need arose. In fact, he approved—the man was simply doing his job.

"Thank you so much for joining us. I trust you had a pleasant flight?" Carlos took a half-step toward Boulder and extended his hand; Boulder was surprised to find the man's handshake was delicate, almost weak. But his eyes—gray, chill, emotionless as a shark. They studied Boulder's face intently, as if looking for a weakness, for a place to attack. Boulder met that gaze as steadily as he could. The world around him slipped into background—Carlos's light handshake, the constant ramble of Quiones's nonstop conversation—and Boulder remembered the words he had most often heard used to describe the man before him: Cold Carlos. Miami Ice. *Ruthless*.

"Quiet," Carlos said. He released Boulder's hand and turned toward the noisy little man still prattling on at Joaquin. Boulder realized that he had just passed some sort of test. He realized too that he had unconsciously been holding his breath.

Carlos told Quiones to wait, then gestured for Boulder to follow him into his office. Quiet Quiones fell silent at Carlos's mention of his name—Boulder understood now why Joaquin had laughed so when he told Rey who was in with Carlos—and nodded . . . fearfully? No, not exactly fear. Reverently. Quiet was already talking again when Rey closed the office door, but Boulder was sure Quiet would still be there, no matter how long a wait, when Carlos called for him.

Carlos's office was quietly luxurious. Heavy leather chairs, objects d'art resting on every tabletop, a painting so abstractly ugly Boulder knew it must be fabulously expensive. Too ostentatious for Boulder's taste, but pleasant just the same.

Carlos offered coffee and a cigar, both of which Boulder accepted, and the two men settled in to some companionable small talk—Boulder's trip, the South Florida weather. Joaquin, as Boulder had guessed, was a distant cousin. And Quiet Quiones—

"Quiet Quiones," Carlos said, "is the reason you are here. I want you to keep him alive."

Boulder pursed his lips and put down his coffee cup. "That is not what I do best," he said.

Carlos smiled. "Let me rephrase that. I want you to keep him alive—for a little while." Boulder nodded and picked up his cup once again.

"You see," Carlos continued, "I am working on a project, a project that is very special to me."

"I prefer not to know too many details of . . ."

"Of course, of course. You need to know only that Mr. Quiones is essential to this project, that he is, in his odd little way, really quite ingenious. But he is also—how shall I say this?" Carlos hesitated, studying the tip of his sleek cigar. "He is also a bit—unreliable."

Boulder nodded, and the two men exchanged small,

knowing smiles. Unreliability, in their world, was the most dangerous of all shortcomings.

"You have a dilemma, then," Boulder said.

"Yes. And there is more. Mr. Quiones has become quite active in the anti-Castro movement. He has made himself very useful to several influential groups here, some of them very public, some not. Some of the people in those organizations are aware that Mr. Quiones is in my employ."

"And if he were to suddenly disappear, and they felt you were involved . . ."

"Exactly. I have recently directed Mr. Quiones to keep a lower profile, and he has reluctantly agreed. He agreed in part because of a persistent rumor that he has been targeted by a violent pro-Communism radical group in the Miami area."

"I was not aware there were many pro-Communism radicals in the Miami area."

"There are none."

"I see."

"I have explained to Mr. Quiones that you are the best bodyguard available, that I have brought you here at great personal expense solely for his protection. He is quite flattered by this. Doubtless he has mentioned it to his political colleagues."

"Who will be pleased with your dedication to the safety of their friend."

"Yes. And a few weeks from now, when both Mr. Quiones and his vaunted bodyguard abruptly disappear, there will be no reason to question the anger and grief I display."

"A few weeks, you say?"

"At the most. Less, if the wind is right. More coffee, Mr. Baker?"

Boulder started to decline, stopped himself, and accepted with a gracious nod. A few weeks, he thought. He raised the fresh-filled coffee cup to his mouth, trying to find solace in the hot bittersweet contents.

If I'm going to be here that damn long, Boulder thought, I'd best get acclimated to the local cuisine.

5

In the summer of 1969, with most of the world distracted
by the tragedy of Viet Nam and the triumph of the
moon landing, the Central American nations of El Salvador and Honduras went to war over a game of football.

It wasn't, to be sure, just any game of football. It was
a World Cup playoff match between longtime rivals, with
the winner taking on Haiti for a spot in the finals. No great
surprise, then, that when El Salvador won by a single dis-
puted goal late in the match, disappointed Honduran fans
took their frustration out into the streets of San Salvador,
rioting and looting and generally raising hell.

Not surprising either that, when word of the riots
spread back to Honduras, many of the 300,000 Salvadoran migrant workers living in their neighboring country
decided to return the favor, and set off a series of their
own riots in Tegucigalpa. Honduras responded by order-
ing nearly a hundred thousand Salvadoran migrants back
to their own country, much to the chagrin of their over-
populated and underemployed neighbors.

Tempers flared; border disputes escalated. The two countries cut off diplomatic relations and accused one another of vague atrocities. At dawn on July 17, barely two weeks after the match, El Salvador sent an army of nine thousand men charging across the border into Honduras.

Three days later, with Salvador's vastly better-trained and equipped army kicking the living shit out of Honduras, the Organization of American States stepped in and negotiated a truce.

It didn't help much. The Football War lasted only seventy-two hours, but it left nearly four thousand dead, ripped apart the fledgling Central American Economic Community, and doomed the entire region to yet another generation of poverty, hunger and violence.

Such— thought Oscar Vicaro "Quiet" Quiones as he sipped his coffee and reviewed the lunch menu of Dario's Cubano Cuisine and Coffee for perhaps the twentieth time—such are the ways of love.

Not that Quiet thought of the Football War as an expression of love—though clearly the natives of both countries were blinded by passion for both their homes and their soccer. Nor did Quiet trouble himself with the idea of football as a metaphor for romance, despite all the obvious analogies of feint and attack, of defend and score.

Rather, Quiet saw in the Football War a clear analogy for the strange way in which the tiniest little thing could send an otherwise rational man teetering toward madness, toward war—or toward love. For some, it was the silvery tinkle of a lover's laugh, the sparkle of a soft brown eye, or the chance chemistry of a vagrant pheromone that sent a man tottering over the edge of that most passionate of maladies.

For Quiet Quiones, it was The Walk.

At first glance, The Walk didn't appear to be anything special. It was, in fact, so ordinary that had Quiet not had the fortune to look up from the *Wall Street Journal* he held carefully concealed in a tout sheet for the Hialeah Jai-Lai at exactly the right moment, he would have dismissed it as just another perambulation by just another pedestrian on the hot twilight streets of South Miami. But he did look up—whether by mere coincidence, as his friend and body-guard Boulder Baker insisted, or by an act of fate, as Quiet himself believed—and he was immediately captivated. The Walk was like nothing he had ever seen. It sent an arrow directly into his heart, and into his loins, this walk did, and right there on the corner of Seventh and Palmetto, amidst the blare of traffic and the sweet smell of palm trees and car exhaust, Quiet Quiones felt himself swept away.

The Walk started much like any other—a slight bend at the knee, the extension of a pleasant but unspectacular leg ahead of the rest of the walker's slender body, the unthinking and unremarkable transfer of weight from one set of muscles to another, immediately followed by the repetition of the entire process with the other leg.

But then came The Hitch. The Hitch was a sudden and yet smooth half-lift of one leg or the other, incorporated seamlessly into The Walk. The Hitch came apparently without thought or pattern, as if each leg had a mind and a mission all its own, a mission far more important than simply carrying this woman to her destination.

The Hitch occurred with the randomness of a winning lottery ticket. Sometimes there would be a half-dozen steps with no Hitch at all, followed by three quick Hitches from the same leg. The Hitch seemed to migrate from one leg to the other without reason, without cause, like a humming-bird dancing from one flower to another and then back again. Occasionally, the Hitch was accompanied by what Quiet came to think of as The Dip, an unconscious tuck of the shoulder and half-reach down by a slender brown arm, as if the walker herself were so enchanted by The Walk that she needed to reassure herself of her own humanity with an ever-so-brief brush of her fingers along her calves.

The Hitch spoke of mystery and magic, of exotic passions, of abilities and knowledge that far exceeded those of the normal human appendage. From that first moment, from the first serendipitous glance, The Hitch and The Walk slammed into Quiet's heart like a meat hook into a side of beef. He let the *Journal* slip from his unfeeling fingers, his jaw dropped like that of an imbecilic child, and, over the surprised protestations of Boulder Baker, Quiet Quiones took off in hot pursuit.

He had followed the woman for nearly five city blocks that night, trying to stay inconspicuous despite the complaining giant hustling along beside him, before he could pry his eyes off The Walk long enough to evaluate the walker. He estimated her age at about twenty, then seventeen, then back up to twenty-three. She was slender but not small. Starting at the bottom, Quiet saw ratty once-white boat shoes, legs so tanned that he at first dared hope she was Hispanic, and a smallish rump hidden beneath blue-jean cut-offs. She wore an ancient Tampa Bay T-shirt urging Buccaneer fans to "Dump MacKay in the Bay." Shoulder-length hair the color of faded lemons, curling in just a touch around her cheeks. Quiet couldn't see much of her face, following behind her as he was, but he thought she would be the sort who favored cleanliness over makeup. Judging from her body frame, and her posture, Quiet decided that her breasts would be smaller than he liked. Maybe much smaller.

Pero, no es importante, not important at all. Nothing mattered to Quiet, except that intoxicating and magical walk. It was a walk holding promise and denial, mystery and wonder. For Quiet Quiones, The Walk was a tantalizing mix of wantonness and innocence that brought back guilty adolescent fantasies of the Virgin Mary with no shirt on. It drew him on like a chummed shark.

In truth, it wouldn't have mattered much if the walker had the face of a dog and the body of a boy. To Quiet, this was the walk of a transformed mermaid adjusting to the earth beneath her new feet. It was the walk of a defrocked angel reluctantly submitting to a life without wings, of a harlot passing over sacred ground.

It was the walk of Jane Ellen Ashley, late of Franklin County, Florida.

Truth was, Quiet's fabulous fantasies notwithstanding, Jane Ellen owed her walk not to heavenly intervention or an overabundance of feminine sensuality but rather to the unkind, lifelong attentions of the Tabanidae chrysops, that is, the common deer fly. The walk was the second thing Jane Ellen had gained by having spent her youth in Franklin County.

There are few places in the world where the deer fly was more common than in Franklin County, and they were no strangers to Jane Ellen. Like their fatter and slower cousin, the horse fly, deer flies most often fed on the blood of their four-legged namesakes. But deer flies were by no means averse to sinking their needle-like proboscis into the flesh of other large mammals, especially those who wore little outer protection.

Such was the normal condition of young Jane Ellen Ashley, who never wore long pants, rarely wore shoes, and, until forced to do so by biology and society, eschewed even the lightest of T-shirts. Jane Ellen's incurable aversion to extra clothing made her a perfect target for the marauding Tabanidae.

Moreover, Jane Ellen's insatiable desire for the written word often forced her right into the deer fly's feeding grounds. Jane Ellen found it all but impossible to read at home, where the smoldering presence of Nate was a constant distraction and occasional threat. She had little patience for the teachers at her school, who felt obliged to drag her back from Narnia, from Middle-Earth, from springtime in Paris or fall along the Adriatic, just for algebra, civics or some other triviality.

Jane Ellen did most of her reading, then, in the one place where she was free from the constant interruptions and irritations of her fellow man—outside. For most of her childhood, Jane Ellen could generally be found curled up in the rough but welcoming arms of a live oak half a mile away from Nate and their crumbling shack, or sprawled unceremoniously on the dirty beaches of Apalachicola Bay, with whatever purloined paperback she had most recently acquired spread out before her.

But Jane Ellen was a restless soul, even with a book in her hand. While her hungry soul ached for the escape only her beloved paperbacks could bring her, her body simply ached. No matter how engrossing a particular text might be, Jane Ellen always found herself driven to motion, to rising for a run or a swim or just a brisk walk, after every few chapters.

Jane Ellen eventually found a solution for that distraction too. Walking with a book in her hand naturally evolved into browsing while she walked, and, eventually, reading with every step. With her mind engaged, her body in motion and her soul at rest, Jane Ellen was content.

She became a common sight in and around Eastpoint, carelessly striding along Highway 98 or casually picking her way through the rocks and oyster mounds along the bay with a new Harlequin or last month's *Esquire* in her hands. She would walk for hours along the overgrown timber roads behind her shack, a growing sixth sense warning her of unexpected obstacles and her leathery feet impervious to the sticks and stones of the woodlands. Best of all was when she could catch a ride out to St. George, or even convince a surly oysterman to drop her off at the otherwise-inaccessible Dog Island, where she could meander across the sugar-soft sand, book held before her like Demosthenes's lantern, to her heart's content.

The only irritant in those otherwise idyllic afternoons was the aforementioned Tabanidae. To the deer flies, Jane Ellen's warm-blooded and scantily clad legs were a moving feast. They honed in and struck at her from the sky like Zeros attacking the *Arizona*. And so, driven by the demands of self-defense, she developed The Walk.

In its early stages, The Walk was a simple stimulus-response reaction to the deer fly attacks. When she felt a deer fly light on her legs—of all the available unprotected skin, they seemed to most prefer the ankles and the meaty areas of the human calf—she would stop and swat it away. The deer flies, as persistent as they were pugnacious, would inevitably return almost immediately. Each attack would continue until Jane Ellen nailed the offender with a lucky swat, or the fly simply grew tired of trying to land on such well-defended turf and moved on. On a bad day, when there was no wind off the water and the warmth of the sand drew the deer flies like crabs to a corpse, Jane Ellen would spend more time chasing flies than reading.

But as The Walk evolved, with its peculiar gyrations and random jerks, the maturing Jane Ellen became all but impervious to the aerial attacks. She would twitch seemingly before a hovering deer fly could land. Her legs, with the frequent up-and-down jabs added to the constant back-and-forth of her steady stride, became to the frustrated deer flies what the rolling deck of a carrier in a storm is to a Navy pilot. If a deer fly were lucky enough to obtain a hold, in came The Dip, a flawless, simultaneous lift of the leg upward and swat of an arm downward that more often than not resulted in the death of the fly.

All this was accomplished without missing a step or losing a word of whatever volume she was perusing. A person watching from a distance might have thought the poor young girl afflicted by madness or epilepsy, but Jane Ellen had won her peace.

The Walk became an ingrained and natural part of Jane Ellen's walk, even on those occasional cold days or stormy nights when the deer flies were not present. Her Franklin County neighbors found The Walk no more remarkable than Bumby Jackson's nervous facial twist, or Fred Walker's habit of spitting loudly every time he passed a streetlight or fire hydrant. As for tourists and other strangers—well, until she developed her tumbling tourist trick, no one ever took much notice of the mousy little woman quietly cracking oysters in the back corner of Billy's Oyster & Pool, walking or otherwise.

The last thing Jane Ellen would have expected was that her ingrained little walk would drive an otherwise harmless little Bahamian accountant over the edge.

Yes, Bahamian. It was Quiet Quiones's greatest secret and greatest shame that he, who spent so much of his verbal energy cursing the *yanqui* and touting the courage and accomplishments of his Hispanic forefathers, should be able to trace his ancestry only to an island—a British island!—best known for its pink Jeeps and amiable policemen.

When he was young, Quiet's mother had calmed the angry tears he cried when their Des Moines neighbors branded him a "spic" by telling him thrilling tales of brave Hispanic explorers challenging the mysterious ocean and conquering entire nations of warriors. But it was from his father that he learned the disappointing truth: He was descended from a long line of hoteliers, and they had come to the United States only because Howard Johnson's needed a new midwest regional manager.

At college in New York, he had sought out the company of the fierce Puerto Rican gangs that haunted the subway exits uptown. But they laughed at his poor Spanish, at his Anglo mannerisms, and chased him back to NYU. In grad school, at Wharton, he pursued Spanish and Latin American studies far more diligently than the economics and math that came to him so very easily.

After graduation, with the Fortune 500 agents yapping at his quota-filling heels like so many Chihuahuas, Quiet had manufactured a false life story and headed south to win a place among the strongest, most fearsome Hispanics he knew of in the only way he knew how.

His first move had been a simple little stock transaction for the best friend of a fraternity brother's distant cousin. Then came a creative offshore transfer that brought him to the attention of Miami's hungry lesser players, who were always on the lookout for a fresh angle, for new talent. With a little capital backing him,

Quiet embarked on the breathtaking series of deal making, laundering and re-investments that had landed him a spot on the staff of the most respected player in all of South Florida, Carlos V. himself.

But even there Quiones wasn't happy. Carlos was polite enough, but Quiet knew his associates didn't respect him much. They saw him as an accountant, nothing more. The Anglos on staff—the Anglos who should have been fawningly grateful to even be acknowledged by Carlos's right-hand man—they were no better. Even Boulder Baker, who lately spent so much time with Quiet, even he sometimes seemed to be only half-listening to Quiet's lessons.

But what tormented Quiet most was that his Hispanic brothers, who believed he had ridden a patchwork raft from Cuba in the arms of his heroic and dying anti-Castro father, treated him with little respect. When Carlos was not around they bombarded him with regional dialects and odd colloquialisms, trying to expose his book-learned Spanish. They laughed at his weight problem, and they teased him constantly about his shyness around women.

And the women—yi! No matter how much power Quiet held, no matter how hard he struggled to put aside the unloved, out-of-place boy of his youth, Quiet turned into a mumbling, bashful fool any time a woman approached him. It was humiliating! And of course it did nothing to help him win the respect of his Hispanic peers.

Quiones understood the problem well enough. He had won a place among men of action but had not yet established himself as a peer. It was no wonder that such men were not yet ready to accept Quiet as a worthy heir of Cortez, of de Gama, and, yes, of Carlos himself.

For months, Quiet had waited for a chance to prove himself. He stayed as close to Carlos as possible, hoping for the opportunity to fling himself between his leader and some unexpected deadly danger, but so far, no luck.

And now this woman, this girl with the gait of a goddess. If his Hispanic brothers, his *hermanos*, learned that he was helplessly under the spell of a gringo, of a coffee shop waitress ... but he could not help himself. The woman asked him a simple question and he lost all sense, all control over himself. How could he possibly hope to impress his *compadres*, and win his woman, when he could not even control his own tongue?

Quiet sighed and took a sip from his coffee, then another, and another. Once it was gone he could signal for another cup, and his angel would come to him again. Maybe he could not speak in her presence, but still he needed desperately to be near her. She was the mistress of his heart, his vixen, his goddess.

Even if she did make a terrible cup of coffee.

6

Harry's first full morning on the boat was spent largely exploring his new home—not that there was much to explore. The *Miss Behavin'* was a beautiful craft, all hardwood and shiny brass, but not very large. She had a single central mast, a spacious back deck and a small main cabin dominated by the casket, a fold-down table and the galley. The second cabin was barely large enough to hold the double-size captain's bunk and a smaller mate's cot; there was a bathroom off the rear cabin just large enough to sit down in. The boat reminded Harry of a mountain cabin where his father had once taken the family on vacation—simple, small, yet well-crafted and, in its own way, really very attractive.

But she was starting to smell.

It was just a tiny smell, nibbling at the back of his nostrils, and at first Harry wrote it off to his imagination. As the day went on and the cabin got hotter, he decided the smell was nothing serious, and that he would no doubt get used to it. But by mid-afternoon, an afternoon Harry spent trying to make sense out of the *Miss Behavin'*'s indecipherable charts and the chicken-scratch notes Al had made, Harry could no longer deny the growing stench— and he could no longer keep his eyes off the coffin.

Harry was smelling rotten meat.

The images that began running through Harry's mind were—well, they were pretty bad. He wondered if he were really expected to sail all the way to Miami with such a thing on board, with the stench getting worse every day. No wonder Big Al got sick—if he really was sick at all. Maybe he just wanted to get off the damn boat before, well . . .

Finally Harry could stand it no more. He rose from his chair, stepped outside and took in a great lungful of clean sea air. Then he returned to the cabin, knelt beside the coffin, put his nose close to the thin line where the casket closed, and sniffed deep.

Nothing.

Nothing, at least, like he had expected. He could still smell the tang of decay, but, to his relief, it was not coming from the coffin.

Relieved, Harry started wandering around the *Miss Behavin'*, sniffing as he went. He'd already checked the tiny icebox and the cabinets in the galley; there was next to nothing there. The only thing remotely perishable he could find were the three or four eggs left in the icebox, and they were all right.

But the smell did seem to be strongest in the galley. Harry concentrated his search there, checking every pot and pan. The last place he looked should have been the most obvious: a large pot, big enough for boiling lobsters, with its top securely locked down. Harry popped the thin bar holding the pot cover in place—all the boat's cooking utensils were cleverly designed that way, Harry had noticed—and the stench of rotting meat caught him full in the face. He held his breath and looked inside. There was some sort of dead bird there, a chicken, he thought at first, and then he recognized the barnyard colors of a rooster, dead, but still completely feathered.

Now why, Harry thought, would someone put a dead rooster in a cooking pot? He could imagine Al and Tiny—especially Tiny—forgetting the rooster on the stove, but why have a dead rooster on board in the first place?

Harry shrugged his shoulders, relieved to know he was not sailing with an unembalmed corpse. He carried the lobster pot, rooster and all, out the cabin door and to the stern of the boat. He grabbed the pot securely by its handles and slung it outward as hard as he could, sending the stinking and stiffening chicken corpse sailing into the air behind the *Miss Behavin'*. He considered tossing the smelly pot itself overboard, but instead contented himself with leaning over to scoop up a gallon or two of salty water. That put Harry in a particularly precarious position, leaning over the butt-end of a sailboat with a potful of seawater. The boat rolled with a wave just as Harry was starting to straighten back up. The sudden tug of current against the pot jerked him headfirst toward the azure water, and he lurched back with a curse to fall hard on his butt on the boat's wooden deck. Harry managed to hold on to the heavy pot while doing so, which meant that when he fell he brought the potful of chilly Caribbean seawater over on top of him.

The accidental dousing acted as a sobering slap in the face for Happy Harry Harper. The shock, anger and fear that had kept him in a dreamlike state since Juanita jolted him awake that morning two confusing days ago dissipated like dew in the morning sun, and Harry felt himself growing calm. He sat there on the hard wet deck, rubbing his bruised bottom and contemplatively spitting out salty water, and asked himself just how in the hell he had come to be in his position.

The basketball game— he thought. As usual, it all goes back to that damn basketball game.

Now, this hadn't been just any basketball game. Not simply the sort of afternoon street-corner event that changes lives by sending screaming teenagers to hospitals with torn ligaments and blown knees, or provides athletic but insecure pimple-faced boys with the self-confidence to ask their future wives to the prom. No, this was a game whose importance was known long before it took center stage in Harry's own particular drama.

This was the regional semifinal between Harry's own Rosewater High and the hated crosstown rival Durwood Demons, a game that would settle long-standing animosities—at least for another year—and send one of the two top-ranked schools into an expected easy Dearborn-area championship game against a lightly considered rural upstart, and then on to the state tournament in Lansing. This game, as they say, was for all the marbles.

The Dearborn Civic Center was packed to the rafters

with rabid hoops fans, including media people from Lansing and Detroit and college scouts from as far away as the ACC and the PAC 10. It was projected as a too-close-to-call contest between Durwood's dominating inside game and Rosewater's phenomenal outside shooting. The wise money gave Rosewater a slight edge in coaching but conceded that Durwood had a deeper bench. Neither team could claim a home-court advantage.

But Rosewater had a special super weapon: Harry.

Harry was, at the time, a pretty typical high school kid. He had two sisters and a dog, a father who grumbled over breakfast and a perky mother who loved gardening. He drove a six-year-old VW Beetle he'd inherited when his oldest sister went off to Michigan State. He smoked Merit cigarettes because everybody else did; and whenever he could get it he drank beer for the high even though he hated the taste. He was reasonably sure that he was the only virgin left in Rosewater's senior class, but had high hopes that Angie Waterford, who let him get his hand a little further up her dress each time they went parking, was going to change all that fairly soon.

Harry was an average student who excelled in English and struggled with math. He got in trouble often enough to avoid being labeled a nerd—he was in fact widely suspected to be responsible for coating the keys of sixteen typewriters in Miss Willoby's Intro to Business Skills class with Vaseline—but all in all was the sort of kid that most teachers and classmates alike did not object to having around.

Truth to tell, Harry was also nothing special as an

athlete. He could run without falling down, but was never going to set any speed records. At five-feet-eleven-inches he could jump just enough to slap the bottom end of a basketball backboard, but dunking was clearly out of the question. As for his other hoops skills, Harry couldn't dribble behind his back, between his legs or around even the slowest opponent. His passes were about equally likely to find an opponent as a teammate, his leadership skills were pretty much negligible, and he couldn't play defense to save his life.

But Harry Harper never missed a shot. Never.

He couldn't explain it. Neither could his parents, or his coaches, or the UM motion sciences grad student who watched Harry hit 237 foul shots in a row one Saturday afternoon before deciding that a gender-focused study of attendance at Tigers baseball games would be easier to pull off.

Explainable or not, the undeniable fact remained: Harry Harper did not miss. In fact, if he could have dribbled, jumped or played defense worth a damn, he undoubtedly would have been a superstar. But he could not.

Fortunately, Harry's coach figured that out early on and had enough brains to design an offense that drew on Harry's strength. He would signal in a scrambling offense designed to screen off whichever guard had drawn the dubious honor of covering Rosewater's slowest yet deadliest player. Harry had to do nothing but run around the key until one of his talented teammates got the screen right and dumped him the ball. Then Harry would score. Always.

The problem, of course, was that with Harry playing defense, the other team generally scored with just as much ease. Still, even the hottest-shooting opponent missed sometimes, and Harry did not. Advantage, Rosewater. Even better, Coach Billy Haynes had early on realized that being beaten by a gawky klutz who could barely dribble without nailing his own feet drove other players bananas. The longer he could keep Harry and his invisible defense in the game, the more likely the other team's frustrated players were to bowl over a screen, or barrel into Harry himself. The opposing players got themselves into foul trouble—and Harry never missed a foul shot.

So it was no surprise that, with fourteen seconds left in the Dearborn regional semifinal and Rosewater trailing 59–58, Coach Haynes signaled in a complicated double-screen roll designed to put Gary Whittle's six-foot-five wide-body between Harry and his defender. Nor was it any great surprise that when Harry got the ball, a desperate Durwood forward peeled off his own man and lunged into Harry before he could get the shot off.

Foul. With three seconds left and his team down by a single shot, Harry was going to the foul line to shoot a one-and-one.

The crowd went wild.

Durwood's coach, sensing disaster, did the only thing he could do, which was call a time-out in hopes of somehow cooling off this inept but invincible killing machine Rosewood had sent to slay his championship dream. It was an old strategy, one that had been used against Harry many times before, and it did bother him. Not because he feared he might actually lose his rhythm and miss—Harry counted on his shot much the same as he counted on the sun rising, the tides rolling and the wind coming in from the north—but because it left him with so little to do with his hands. He was not oblivious to his own weaknesses, and was reluctant to pass the minute dribbling, for fear he would send the ball bouncing off his own feet while a breathless crowd looked on. And basketball shorts, for all their comfort and flexibility, did not have pockets. Harry didn't get nervous, he simply felt that those time-outs focused a spotlight on his own overlooked but undeniable klutziness.

Fortunately, Harry's astute coach had also figured this out, and had standing orders that in situations like this Harry's fellow Monarchs were to gather around him and keep him occupied with encouraging sports platitudes, brotherly high-fives and the like. It looked good to the crowd, and it kept Harry busy.

On this particular occasion, however, Harry was already occupied—preoccupied, in fact, with the possibility that he might be on the threshold of more than just the Dearborn-area regional finals. Angie, who was at the game not just as a fan and girlfriend but in her official role as a Rosewater cheerleader, had been acting mysteriously affectionate all day. She had insisted on holding his hand on the entire hour-long bus ride from Rosewater to the Civic Center, and had not once but twice asked if they would be going to their favorite parking spot hidden in the woods off of Dalrymple Road after the game.

So, while his sweaty comrades gathered around him

to murmur well-meaning lies about his athletic prowess and his opponents' ancestry, while thousands looked on, his school's pride hanging in the balance, Harry found he could not keep his mind—and his eyes—off of Angie. She was standing right before him, only a few yards away, helping the rest of the Monarch cheerleaders whip the Rosewater students seated in the cheap seats behind the visitors' goal into a frothing, screaming frenzy. She was facing the crowd, her back to him, her long brown hair bouncing up and down in gentle waves in time with her cheerleaderly leaps. Angie's short cheerleader skirt accented her athletic brown legs, and when she jumped up and down it fluttered just high enough to reveal her bright yellow shorts and the gold-and-black butterfly tastefully adorning one perfect cheek. Harry tried to swallow, and discovered that his mouth had gone dry.

The Marching Monarchs band hit a particularly dramatic snap in their enthusiastic rendition of the team's fight song, and the row of cheerleaders all spun around and gave a high-kick in the direction of the court. Angie caught Harry staring at her, smiled, and, in perfect syncopation with the less-than-perfectly-syncopated band, she raised her right hand and gave her black-and-gold pom-pom an enthusiastic shake in his direction.

The band crashed out with another energetic *ba-boom!* and Angie and the other half-dozen cheerleaders spun back around to face the crowd. While Harry watched longingly and the crowd roared, the cheerleaders began another routine, urging the fired-up Monarchs to fight on.

And then ...

... and then, without deviating even the slightest from her dancing partners, without missing a single beat, Angie turned her head just enough to look back at Harry. Without any expression at all on her face, and with her eyes locked on and burning into Harry's, Angie moved her head in a single, decisive and perfectly clear up-and-down nod.

Then "String" Sterling, the Monarch's six-foot-eight-inch center, stepped up to give Harry his own encouragement. Harry found himself staring directly into the faded-white "17" sewn onto the front of String's sweaty uniform, his view of Angie cut off by Sterling's hairy chest. It didn't matter. Harry had seen Angie's gesture, had seen that ever-so-expressive nod, and its meaning was as clear as a winter's night.

Harry was all but overcome. His overly active teenage libido took control and flooded his mind with images of Angie's nod, of Angie's legs, and of bright yellow-and-black butterflies flying free and unrestrained around the back of his moonlit van. He closed his eyes and had to fight to hold back a moan.

The screech of the referee's whistle brought Harry spinning back to earth. All the noises of the civic center came cascading back down on him, the claps, the cries, the rattle of the band. He felt a moment of disorientation, and was relieved when Stretch gave him a fraternal slap on the ass and a gentle nudge toward the foul line.

Harry raised the basketball chest high and focused his attention on the distant rim. This was his world, his zone, this place where distance, velocity, angle and success all effortlessly merged to become one and the same. Once again he felt the external world receding from him as his consciousness merged with that shining steel rim, the floor-wax sheen of the clear backboard, the whisk of white net. The cries of the crowd faded into the background to become a distant and unimportant thing, like the cries of birds on a beach. Slowly, confidently, he raised the basketball over his head to shoot.

And then Harry heard a strange thing. It was something he had never heard before, at least not while on the court. It was something so odd, so out of place, that it intruded on even his preternatural calm. He blinked, shook his head once, and tried to refocus.

And then that sound came again.

Someone was snickering.

Now Harry had heard just about everything in his years on the court. Pleas, cheers, threats, curses, questions about his ancestry, religion, upbringing, race and manhood, all that and more were a natural part of the foul-shooting experience and washed off him like rain on a rock. But snickering? This was something new.

It happened again. Another snicker—and worse, Harry was somehow sure this was a snicker from a different person. Then he heard what could only be described as a girlish giggle, followed by a definite chuckle, and then an outright laugh. And then another laugh, and another and another.

Harry dropped his hands and the basketball back down to his chest and stared in befuddled amazement as a wave of laughter, nay, of outright hilarity, moved through the crowd before him. He watched as laughter passed from person to person like a contagious disease, watched as face after face went from confusion to surprise to amusement to uproarious laughter. It spread through the crowd like ripples across a pond, spreading from the epicenter of students seated under the goal before him outward in both directions as person after person craned forward to get a look at whatever was causing the uproar.

Harry glanced around, turned full around in fact, thinking perhaps that someone had let an animal into the gym, or unfurled some sort of banner. But that did no good; it in fact confirmed an increasingly uncomfortable suspicion—they were all staring, and laughing, at him.

Suddenly feeling desperately alone, Harry turned toward his teammates standing along the key. They too were all staring at him. And they weren't staring at his face.

"Jesus, Harry . . ." he heard Sterling whisper. With a growing sense of dread, Harry lowered his head in the direction of their gaze. His eyes wandered over his own sweaty chest, past the upside-down number 14, over the wrinkled cotton covering his belly and the twisted elastic holding up his shorts. And there it was. Harry gulped and felt his face turn crimson.

There at the visitors' foul line, with hundreds of people watching including reporters from as far away as Detroit and Lansing, before scouts from the ACC and the

PAC 10, with years of tradition and the pride of his school hanging in the balance, Harry Harper was sporting the most dramatic and emphatic erection of his young life.

Now don't misunderstand. Harry was not the sort of genetic anomaly whose equipment causes strong women to faint and bold stallions to drop their heads in shame. But he was a healthy young man of better-than-average size, a young man beset by the twin demons of teenage hormones and a vivid imagination. This stranger in his pocket, this beast with a mind of its own, was not about to be restrained by the insignificant cotton strip of a jock strap or disguised by the thin nylon of gym shorts. This hungry animal had a statement to make—and it was making it, before the eyes of the world.

Horrified, Harry tried to bring the ball down to waist level to cover his excitement, but, typically, whacked the ball against his hip and sent it bouncing off down the lane. Gary T. Thomas, who thought he had seen everything in his nineteen years of refereeing high school hoops, grabbed the ball and walked back to stand directly in front of Harry, mercifully shielding him from the howling crowd.

"Here ya go, son," he whispered, handing the ball back to Harry. "Now for God's sake, shoot!"

And he did. Blindly, hurriedly, anxiously, Harry Harper, who never missed, Harry Harper, Rosewater's super-weapon and trusted savior, Harry Harper, who hit 237 foul shots in a row one Saturday afternoon before that grad student from UM gave up and went in search of easier A's, turned and fired the ball at the basket. It bounced off the backboard a good ten inches from the rim and into the arms of a surprised Durwood guard.

Three seconds fled by while Harry's stunned teammates stood in silent shock. The final buzzer sounded.

Durwood 59, Rosewater 58.

Half the arena erupted in pandemonium as Durwood supporters, most of them unaware of the biological imperative that had miraculously saved them from Rosewater's shooting machine, surged onto the court in victorious celebration. They slapped their players on the back and high-fived one another and hugged total strangers, just for the delightful hell of it.

But on Rosewater's end of the court, silence reigned.

Hundreds of Monarch fans, who moments earlier had been all but assured of a regional title and a year's bragging rights, were no longer laughing. They were still staring at Harry, but there was no humor on their faces.

Harry himself was in shock. He looked to his teammates for support, but it seemed as if they were the only people in the arena who were not looking at him. They stood silently along the foul lines, staring at the ground, and when "Stretch" Sterling turned to go, the rest followed silently behind him.

Harry turned toward the bench, to Billy Haynes, but his coach was sitting forlornly and alone with his head in his hands. Harry looked up into the crowd, trying to ignore the angry glares, looking for his parents, looking for his friends, looking for any kind of sympathy.

And then he saw something that broke his heart.

It was Angie, standing alone beneath the visitors' basket, already abandoned by the other cheerleaders. Her gaudy yellow pom-poms lay forlornly at her feet. She had her hands knotted into tight fists held up to her mouth, and there were tears running down her cheeks.

She was shaking her head steadily back and forth. No.

7

The best defense, Jane Ellen told herself as she carefully stirred a second teaspoon of chocolate-flavored Ex-Lax powder into the coffee cup of the twitchy little Cuban waiting at table nine, is a good offense.

She did feel just a little bad about what she was doing. She wasn't completely sure, after all, that the little man and his ever-present companion had any intentions at all of harming her. She wasn't even sure, for that matter, that the little guy was Cuban. There was a bewildering mix of Hispanics here in Miami, all of them fast-talking and quick to anger and dark as coals. Jane Ellen couldn't tell Jamaican from Colombian from Puerto Rican but, on the advice of her coffee shop coworker Darlene, had decided to think of everyone in the city as Cuban until proven otherwise.

But one thing she was sure of: The mismatched pair had been watching her, at least sporadically, for more than three weeks. It wasn't like they had been hard to spot, like they blended into a crowd. First off, this particular Cuban was, well, very small. He wasn't a dwarf, not exactly, but Jane Ellen figured that if they ever stood side by side she could easily slip his head under her chin. Even more noticeable was the silent walking mass of muscle that followed the little Cuban everywhere he went. Forty, maybe, or maybe fifty and in really great shape. Pale skin, close-cropped colorless hair, razor-thin lips that Jane Ellen had never seen smile. They were an odd pair—small and dark, big and light. It was like seeing a poodle throw the reversed shadow of a Rottweiler everywhere he went.

So of course she had noticed them that night she went out exploring her new Miami neighborhood. Hard to miss them. They had been close behind her for eight or nine blocks at least, sometimes walking together, sometimes whispering in obvious argument. Jane Ellen had thought maybe they were having a lovers' spat, had thought it funny, until she got a little worried and ducked into a busy nightclub. The next day they had come to her favorite bookstore, stayed there pretending to browse until Jane Ellen got nervous enough to go into the women's restroom and out a rear window. And the day after that they had followed her onto a city bus, the chubby little man trying to hide behind dark sunglasses and a copy of the Miami *Diario Las Americas* while his imposing companion stared unblinkingly at the passing streets.

That was too much. Once was paranoia, twice coincidence, but three times . . . Jane Ellen had ridden the bus five blocks past her usual stop, jumped off abruptly and splurged on a taxi heading back the way she had come. She'd quit her job from a corner pay phone, dashed into the YWCA long enough to retrieve her small bag of belongings, and set out walking. What she really wanted was a bus ticket out of there, way out, but there was no money for that. She settled instead for a bottle of cheap hair coloring and a seedy little pay-by-the-day room in Little Havana. The black hair dye was a total failure; she washed it out the following morning, vowing to die a natural blonde rather than live with blue hair.

Jane Ellen had bought a loaf of bread and a giant jar of peanut butter and hid in her new room for three days. When abject boredom and her dwindling funds drove her back out into the world, she'd been lucky enough to find a coffee shop with a Help Wanted sign in the window. The people at Dario's Cubano Cuisine and Coffee were nice, she had all the free coffee and donuts she could handle, and on a good day her tips covered rent.

But four days ago Jane Ellen had come out of the kitchen and found the little Cuban and his white shadow arguing over menus in a dining room booth. They'd both had the luncheon special, one fried ham and the other a veggie platter, then dawdled over endless cups of coffee while the big one grew obviously more and more impatient. Jane Ellen was nervously setting up for the dinner rush, growing more concerned with every passing minute, when they finally left.

From then on, the two came back every day. Usually they were sitting there when Jane Ellen arrived for her 10 A.M. to 4 P.M. lunch shift, never in her section, but always right there. Jane Ellen got to thinking of them as Quiet and the Giant, even though Quiet was never quiet and the Giant was not exactly a giant. Big, yes, six-foot-three or six-four and solid as a bulldog. He really was quiet, but there was something about the way he sat, about the way he always seemed aware of everything around him, that made him seem even larger than he really was. The Giant reminded Jane Ellen of the great blue herons she used to see hunting along the shores of the Apalachicola, of the way they would be so still, so tightly focused, and then *bam!* strike like snakes and come up with a flashing minnow or an incautious crab. That guy, the Giant, maybe he could be involved with organized crime. And if he were, and if he was after her, Jane Ellen shuddered. She remembered all the stories at the Oyster & Pool about Senator Jerome Langer and his mob ties, about a certain Port St. Joe labor leader who'd run up against Langer, disappeared, and shown up a week later in a shrimper's net, white and bloated, black empty gaps where the crabs had nibbled away his eyes.

But it just didn't add up. If the two men were stalking her, if they'd been sent by the Senator to exact revenge for the death of his son, then why was Jane Ellen still alive? If they were cops, then why hadn't they arrested her? It made her a little less concerned when one of the other waitresses told her the two men were actually semi-regular customers but only a little.

The little dude, the Cuban, they call him Quiet, and don't ask me why, Darlene had said. He goes to meetings with the anti-Castro people over at the New Havana hotel, and sometimes after he comes in here. The big dude, he's new, don't know much about him.

But I'll tell you one thing I know about 'em both. Darlene put down the silverware she was rolling in paper napkins and leaned forward to whisper in Jane Ellen's ear. Mafiosa, she said.

Mafia? Really? Jane Ellen blinked and pursed her lips, not quite sure what to make of the idea. She was also more than a little dubious.

Cuban Mafia, maybe. More likely Colombian or maybe even Jamaican gang. But they're cartel men, honey, sure as sugar's sweet. He's the brains, that little guy, that Quiet, and the big one's his bodyguard. I seen it before, seen it lots of times. And that little one's got it bad for you, girlfriend. You watch yourself.

Jane Ellen went back to rolling silverware, thinking. Maybe it did make sense, in a weird sort of way. The little guy, Quiet, he did stare at her every time she came out of the kitchen, quickly looking away whenever she looked at him. Could it be that what she had thought was murderous intensity was just a schoolboy crush? She couldn't rule it out. Ten years of living with the volcanic Nate and three seasons of quietly watching drunken oystermen in their natural state at the O&P had convinced her that all men were unpredictable at best and flat-out crazy at worst. The way she figured it, men carried their brains around in their balls, and years of being bounced around from thigh to thigh made them all a little crazy.

And it did seem pretty clear the big guy worked for Quiet, the way he stuck by the little Cuban's side constantly, even though he was clearly bored out of his mind. But Quiet a drug dealer? She just couldn't see it. She imagined drug criminals as dark, dangerous, ready as razors and bad to the bone. Quiet wore the Miami tough-guy regalia black jeans, sleeveless T-shirt, lots of gold but it looked as out of place on him as tits on a boar hog. Unlike his companion, who wore his sport coat and tie like a bear in a tuxedo, Quiet looked like he was born to wear suits.

If this guy is with the mob, Jane Ellen thought, he's their insurance agent.

But how could she tell, how could she find out for sure? If she could separate the two, see if the big guy still followed her if Quiet wasn't around. She racked her brain over it, tossing and turning all night, endlessly debating if she shouldn't just bolt and leave Miami, even if she had to walk. And then one night, after about the fourth time she'd rechecked to make sure her bedroom door was double-bolted and the windows latched down despite the sweltering heat, she remembered a story she'd read, a gothic novel in which the villainous step-sister had planned to get the poor-but-honest governess away from her brother by spiking her lemonade with hemlock.

Excessive, Jane Ellen had thought at the time. But now, it seemed to make sense. She didn't have any hemlock at hand, wasn't even entirely sure what it was. No problem—like any country girl who grew up poor and mostly on her own, Jane Ellen knew how to improvise.

The Ex-Lax hadn't affected the coffee's color much, Jane Ellen noticed, but she was a little concerned about the taste. She gave the fresh-doctored mug one more sprinkle of sugar, put on her best vacant-but-friendly waitress smile, and walked out of the kitchen.

The Giant sat facing the door, as usual, but somehow Jane Ellen was sure he was aware of her coming up from behind. Quiet was the one she surprised. He froze in mid-gesture, hand held high in the middle of making some emphatic point, when he realized it was Jane Ellen and not Darlene bringing his refill. His eyes opened TV-cartoon wide and his mouth actually dropped.

"How y'all today?" Jane Ellen said, trying not to laugh. The poor man looked all the world like a fresh-caught grouper, gasping in surprise in the hot afternoon sun. She thought of the poison waiting in his coffee and felt ashamed at her paranoid meanness. There just was no way this goofy little guy was any kind of threat to her. No way.

But then she turned and looked into the eyes of Boulder Baker.

Jane Ellen had seen death countless times in her years walking the beaches and back roads of North Florida. Raccoons, possums and armadillos scrunched and smelly on the hot tar of Highway 98, mullet and gar and redfish rotting at the high-tide mark, proud old pelicans tangled and strangled in discarded fishing line. Just last year she'd held a car-struck hound dog in her arms while it bled its guts out through its shattered ass. But Jane Ellen had never seen anything like the absence in this staring stranger's eyes. They were white as a surgeon's mask, brown as dirt from a grave, black as Jane

Ellen remembered once seeing a shark suddenly rise out of the water to engulf a commorant dozing on Apalachicola Bay. The shark locked its jaws on the terrified bird's wing and then slowly, lazily, rolled sideways and pulled it under. Jane Ellen had gotten a good look at the shark's eyes at that moment, empty as sea-foam, passionless even in the moment of the kill.

Standing in the suddenly still dining room of Dario's Cubano Cuisine and Coffee, looking at this silent man in the dark suit, Jane Ellen was seeing those eyes once again.

She staggered back a half-step, wanting to run, knowing she had no rational reason to, knowing the Giant could be on her before she took three steps. She couldn't even tear her eyes away from his face, from those eyes as cold and dead as last week's oysters.

And then he blinked. Blinked and turned his head away, like he was dismissing a lab specimen as unworthy of further study. Jane Ellen blinked herself, blinked like a deer suddenly free of the headlights. She felt the Naugahyde and neon world of Dario's Cubano Cuisine and Coffee come rushing back to her, and realized she was gripping her waitress pad so hard her fingers hurt, holding the six-by-four-inch pad in front of her like a shield.

"Uh," she said, and then, "well, uh, care for something to eat with those?"

Silence. The Giant did not turn back toward her, and Quiet—well, Quiet suddenly snapped out of his own trance and popped his mouth into gear.

"Well, yes, perhaps," he said. "Perhaps an omelet,

although it's late for an omelet isn't it? Perhaps a sandwich then, don't you think, Boulder? A sandwich or maybe the chicken steak, though of course we've just finished breakfast and the chicken steak would be—"

Two orders of toast, wheat bread. With jelly. You got peach jelly? It was the Giant, no, Boulder; Quiet had called him Boulder speaking in a voice calm as a churchyard. He gave an imitation of a smile, a slight movement of the lips that brought no warmth to those eyes. Jane Ellen swallowed hard, mumbled, I'll check, and hurried off toward the kitchen. Both men watched without comment until the swinging door into the kitchen closed behind her. And then:

"You see! You see, *mi amigo*?" Boulder turned to see Quiet beaming proudly, triumph rising in his squeaky voice. "She wants me!"

"Say what?" Boulder said. He had thought he was getting used to Quiet's absurd little fantasies, but this one surprised even him.

"The waitress, *la signorita*, this Jane Ellen, she loves me! Did you na see how nervous she is just to be near me, how she jumps like a colt when I speak? It is so clear, *mi amigo*, it should be so even to a cold gringo like you with no love in your soul!" Quiet paused long enough to sip from his fresh coffee; he grimaced, put the mug down and reached for a handful of sugar packets before starting again. "I should na be surprised, I am na surprised, it happen so much with the Anglo women. I tell you Boulder, *mi amigo*, I tell you it is a power we Cubanos hold over your women, over all women, but over your Anglo *chicitas* especially. Just as *yo digame*, just as I was telling you."

And telling me and telling me and telling me, Boulder thought. He leaned back in the booth, gave a little sigh, and let Quiet's nonstop monologue wash over him. When the little prick got started and hell, he almost never stopped, there was nothing you could do but let him go. Arguing only prolonged the conversation, and interrupting just made Quiet pout and turn from pontification to whining. Best to just close your eyes and ride it out.

The only one who could really shut Quiet up was Carlos. No surprise there; Carlos pretty much always got whatever he wanted. It was Carlos, Rey had said, who gave Quiet his nickname. Not intentionally. Carlos wasn't the sort who made jokes about names, or about much of anything else. It just happened. In his short time here, Boulder had already seen Quiet launch into his hyper act more times than he could count, in meetings or lunches or just hanging around the mansion, motoring his mouth like he had something to say, driving everybody up the fucking wall, until Carlos brought it all to an immediate stop with a simple, Quiet, Quiones. And Quiones would be quiet; he'd shut down like somebody had doused him with a bucket of water. Then, inevitably, somebody would ask the little shit for some important piece of information and off he'd go again, rambling on and on long after whatever he'd been asked had been covered, re-covered and covered again, until eventually Carlos would say, in his soft commanding monotone, Quiet, Quiones. And so Oscar

Vicario Quiones became Quiet. Quiet Quiones, the loud-est loser in Miami.

And now, something new. Part of Boulder's mind noted and filed for later consideration how Quiet's pidgin Spanglish had vanished when the girl's approach had flustered him, so more foolishness. But that was for later. Right now, Boulder was reevaluating his thoughts about the waitress.

Boulder had not until that moment understood Quiet's obsession with the girl. Okay, so she read a lot; that's great. And she did have fine lemony-blond hair, natural, which was a rarity here on Bleach Beach. But she was skinny, almost scrawny, and apparently got her wardrobe from the Goodwill. This walk of hers that so captivated Quiet looked to Boulder like she was having a fit, or at best constantly on the verge of falling on her face. An attractive face, maybe, but more cute than beau-tiful. Nothing special.

But then she had brought those drinks, and for the first time Boulder got a good close-up look at her eyes. Those eyes sapphire blue, blue like the eyes of Siamese cats, like the eyes of a newborn seeing the world for the first time. Boulder had looked into the eyes and been a boy again, lying on the hillside at his grandfather's farm, looking up into the clear clean endless Iowa sky. He was eight, nine, maybe ten, laughing and content. He was surrounded by the fertile scent of fresh-turned earth; he felt tall grass blowing against his body and the cool cleansing touch of a summer breeze.

Boulder snapped himself out of this spell, forced

himself back to the cheap, plastic, coffee-colored present, and told the girl to bring them food, seeing the fear on her even through his momentary confusion. He watched her stumble away and felt the cold self-assurance that always came when he saw the knowledge of mortality enter a target's mind.

But for the first time in a long time, in a very long time, that satisfaction did not put Boulder at ease. He shifted in his seat uneasily and ran one thumb along the table's edge till he found a chipped spot in the linoleum. He rubbed his thumb against that sharp edge, hard, using the small dose of pain to make himself focus, to draw his thoughts back to the task at hand and away from the girl with the electric eyes.

Nonsense, sheer nonsense, Boulder told himself. Baker, you are getting soft.

And that, Boulder Baker could not allow.

8

Harpoon Harrison ducked under the knife-thrust of his enraged attacker and swung a mighty uppercut that connected with the Chinaman's jaw. *Thwack!* Sing-po stumbled backward, then staggered, the steak knife he had grabbed from the restaurant table hanging loosely in his nerveless hand. Harpoon took one graceful step forward and grasped the knife as the Chinaman started to teeter forward.

"Didn't your mama ever tell you it ain't polite to take silverware from another man's table?" Harpoon said, eyeing the knife tip and stepping aside as his stunned attacker teetered and fell like a toppled oak. "But I guess you get the, ah, point."

Harpoon heard a slight noise behind him—Dr. Conrad, of course, trying to sneak off while his back was turned. Harpoon spun, bent his arm at the elbow and hurled the steak knife with barely a look. The knife buried itself in the restaurant wall inches away from Conrad's face, and the doctor, scowling, sunk back into his chair.

"Pull up a chair and sit a spell, Conrad," Harpoon said, an ironic sneer twisting his ruggedly handsome face. "You and me are gonna have a little talk about—"

"About . . . about what?" Happy Harry Harper pushed himself back from the *Miss Behavin'*'s galley table, dropped his pencil stub on the table and began massaging the thumb and forefinger of his writing hand. Cramping again. No small wonder, after writing virtually nonstop for . . . for . . . He didn't know. Harry glanced around for a clock, then remembered there wasn't one on board. How odd, he thought. He was a bit surprised to find himself still on board the *Miss Behavin'*, a bit surprised, in fact, to find himself anywhere at all. He felt detached, distant from the world and the waves and the walls of his aquatic home. Spacey, sort of, but in a good way, as if he had just stepped out of a matinee into the unexpected light of a bright afternoon and needed a minute or two to resettle himself in the real world.

"Odd," Harry said again. "I wonder if real writers feel this way all the time. That might explain a few things." He smiled at his own joke, aware on one level that he really shouldn't get too comfortable talking aloud to himself, aware on yet another level that he really didn't give a damn. If a professor babbles on the ocean and there is no one there to hear it, does he really make a sound? And, who cares?

Harry smiled at his own foolishness and stood up to fetch more coffee. He had awoken that morning bitterly aware that on top of all his other recent sins, in addition to gluttony and drunkenness, sloth and, yes—uninten-

tional or not—murder, he had lied. Lied to the two miraculous mystery men who had appeared in his hour of desperation and provided him a way off of Hispaniola, away,
at least for the moment, from angry mobs and filthy
Caribbean jails and the ultimate inevitable tightening of
the hangman's noose (assuming hanging was how they
did it down here). Lied, in short, to the two strange
Samaritans who had saved his undeserving neck.

Harry was fully aware that Big Al also had lied to
him, would have known it even without Tiny grimacing
and shaking his head all the while his greasy little boss
told his tale. Harry didn't particularly believe he had the
corpse of an airline-shy war hero strapped to the galley
table of his little craft, but he had not been in a position
to look this particular gift horse in the mouth, even
though he suspected he was adding smuggling to his
growing list of unexpected crimes. Harry simply felt that
he had no other choice but to play the fool, take the boat,
and run. That's why he had pretended to believe Al's
audacious story, why he agreed to take their cargo up to
Miami, why he was now out here on the open sea.

That's why he had lied to Big Al about knowing how
to sail.

Harry did know a little about boats. He knew how to
steer out of little Blue Bay, once the ponderous giant Tiny
had gotten the diesel engine going. He knew enough to
shut the noisy little engine off when the gas gauge
started leaning ominously toward empty. He'd even figured out how to get the main sail up and billowed out,
and, after two days of fiddling with the compass, sextant

and star charts, had managed to confirm that, as suspected, he was in fact sailing the *Miss Behavin'* in a large and impressively consistent circle.

He had tried consulting the *Beginner's Guide to Sailing* he'd found in the cabin, had read through it twice, in fact, and half a dozen times scrutinized the chapters on navigation and tacking against the wind. He had the knowledge there in his head. It was just that when he tried to put that knowledge to use, when he got out there with the huge flapping sails and the stubborn steering wheel, it all fell apart. The boat seemed to have a mind of its own, ticking when he wanted to tack, circling when he wanted a straight line, stopping dead when he wanted to catch what little wind there was.

What Harry needed, badly, was to relax. Take a deep breath, slow down, get his bearings. But how? There was not a drop of alcohol on board, he'd run out of cigarettes two days ago, and his one attempt at fishing had ended up with the line tangled in a knot that made "Gordian" sound inadequate. There was nothing on board to read except the *Beginner's Guide*—which only augmented his frustration—and a packet of permits from Colombia, Honduras and Haiti, permits that Harry really didn't want to look at too closely, and that were written in Spanish to boot.

And, of course, the blue book.

Harry had found the blue book his first night on board, when the lingering smell of Al's sugary cologne had driven him from the aft bunk to the bigger but less comfortable captain's bed. There was something under the wafer-thin mattress, something solid and square and hard. He'd sought it out, apprehensive at first, and then with growing excitement when his questing hand recognized the familiar, beloved feel of a book.

Harry had damn near kneecapped himself rushing from the dark sleeping area into the *Miss Behavin*'s moonlit main cabin. There, under the yellowish glow of the room's overhead light, he'd examined his new prize. It was big, navy-blue with gold filigree around the edges, thick and hefty as a photo album. There was no name on the cover or the spine. A logbook, he thought with a touch of disappointment. No great novel or saucy picture book, not Melville nor Miss May hidden beneath the bunk, but simply the captain's logbook tucked away for safekeeping. All right then. No long hours of pursuing adventure across the page, no sun-drenched afternoon reading beneath the *Miss Behavin*'s flapping sails, but perhaps the answers to a few mysteries. Maybe even a hint or two on how to keep this damn craft headed in a straight line.

He'd opened the cover, squinted at the blocky print in the dim cabin light, and read the first page with growing disbelief. There were no careful notations about wind and tide here, no comments on crew morale or battening down the hatches, not a word about trimming the sails or setting a true and stable course. This was no logbook entry.

It was a recipe for a Spanish omelet, with jalapeños and pepper cheese.

Page two was the same, or at least almost the same—a

recipe for western omelets, complete with Tabasco sauce, painstakingly spelled out in heavy, childlike block printing. Page three held similar directions for a French omelet, page four was potato-onion, page five Italian, page six spinach and sour cream. Sixteen pages in all were filled in, with sixteen different omelet recipes, all written in the same hand; three or four involved omelets made with some sort of caviar-like paste, the last was for a vile-sounding and yet somehow inevitable recipe for a Beefaroni omelet. Harry wasn't sure which of the gruesome twosome was responsible for the secret omelet recipe—his money was on Big Al—but he had realized right away that, other than torturing his deprived palate with visions of white sauce and fresh cheeses, the book could do him no good.

But that was two days ago. Two days filled with hour after hour of monotonous rolling blue water, blistering sun and the constant chips and chirps of a tightly rigged boat, two full days and nights far from land, with no alcohol, nothing to read, no music, no one to talk to. In desperation, Harry's mind had returned to the blue book, to that stash of nubby tooth-marked pencils. So what the hell—Harry decided to write a record of his journey, a sort of ship's log. Strictly nonfiction, no different from the student evaluations and critical papers he'd been churning out in his sleep at UM-Detroit for years. A diversion, nothing more.

But somehow, well . . . Once Harry put pencil to paper, an odd thing happened. Maybe it was embarrassment, or maybe just embellishment, but the character bearing Harry's name slowly started doing most un-Harry-like things. He somehow stood taller than Harry himself did, he acted directly and decisively; the dramatic moments he found himself in did not automatically deteriorate into comedies of errors. The more Harry wrote, the less Harry appeared in his pages. Eventually, he acknowledged the undeniable, went back through the three dozen pages he had at the time and carefully scratched through each mention of the name "Harry Harper."

Harpoon Harrison was born.

Harry felt a bit guilty about it, at first, as if by embarking on what was now clearly a work of fiction he was trespassing on territory where he had no right to tread. But it was not, he told himself, like he was actually pretending to be a real writer. This was just an exercise, a diversion for a desperately bored academic. He would never show his manuscript to anyone, never even finish it. Once he got within sight of land, he would simply drop it overboard and let the hungry secret-saving sea consume this hubris. Maybe even *before* he sighted land.

Harry leaned forward to pick up the thick stack of handwritten pages on the table before him. Amazing. He hadn't realized how much he had written—hadn't really felt like he was writing at all, at least not after he'd gotten his main characters on paper and in motion. Then the words had simply come from nowhere, gone right from the salt-sticky air around him through his arm and onto the paper, the characters simply doing and saying whatever it was that they had always been intended to do or say with little or no guidance from him. And Harry was having a blast.

"Now why haven't I ever tried this before?" Harry

said, knowing the answer even as he spoke. He hadn't tried writing for the same reason he hadn't tried snow skiing or archery or dating beauty queens or competitive backgammon—because he knew he would fail. Besides, he had too much reverence for the written word, too great a respect for those magical characters who had pulled him through so many miserable days after his humiliation at that basketball game, to think himself worthy of joining their ranks.

The basketball game. Harry rubbed his sore thumb and, in much the same way, rubbed once again at the one unhealable wound on his sore psyche. He closed his eyes and relived the cold silence of his teammates in the locker room, the unreturned phone calls to Angie, the heart-breaking sighs of his father and the excruciatingly chipper chatter of his mother at countless interminable family meals in the following months. He remembered the Dearborn sports writer who delicately reported that the infallible Harry Harper had been "too excited and happy" to concentrate on that one crucial foul shot, and arriving at school the following Monday to find "Happy Harry Harper" on his locker in scarlet spray paint.

Happy Harry Harper. It was his new name, and no amount of pleading or threatening or fighting could make it go away. Harry became resentful and then morose, and the few friends not too embarrassed to be seen with him drifted away. The inquiring letters from college athletic departments were returned unopened, and after graduation he enrolled early in a Missouri community college far away from Michigan.

But then, in a small bus station in south Illinois, waiting for a transfer on his way to school, Harry made the discovery that would salvage his shattered life. A tattered paperback copy of Dashiell Hammett's *The Thin Man* lay abandoned at the end of a bench right by the trash can. Harry picked it up out of desperate boredom, reading first a line and then a page and then chapter after chapter with growing excitement, the first real inspiration he had felt—perhaps the first real feelings of any kind he had had—since that night in Dearborn. Here was something he could grasp, something with meaning. Simple, strong men with honest problems, straightforward women who were either honestly good or thoroughly wicked, tough problems that could be solved with a shot of whiskey or a fistful of bullets.

Harry had finished the book and started over by the time they hit St. Louis, and his first stop in Meridian was not the college but rather a ratty newsstand three blocks down from the bus station. He had found salvation.

With his newfound allies, Harry found college at least tolerable. He had a hard time talking to anyone, especially to women, and his refusal to join any athletic event or even discuss sports added the brand of "eccentric" to his quickly earned label of "loner." Harry didn't really care. He had a whole new world of friends, friends he could depend on, friends who never laughed or got laughed at. They went by names like Nick and Dirk and Hammer, and lived in the pages of the paperback detective novels that went everywhere Harry did.

For Harry, the fantasies of men like Spillane and

Hammett, John D. MacDonald and Ian Fleming, were more real, more compelling, than the confusing and uncertain real life he drifted through. His natural inclination for reading blossomed, and he became the quiet star of English departments at community college and then the master's and doctoral programs at Iowa.

There were real-life adventures along the way, though few and far between. He wrote for the student paper at the community college, won reluctant praise for his series of trashy-but-inventive short stories, and helped edit the literary magazines at Iowa. He finally lost his virginity, to a drunken sophomore from Kansas who tasted like Purple Jesus and threw up both before and after the act. He broke a wrist slipping on the ice one January, and got mugged on a book-buying trip to St. Louis.

Mostly, though, Harry contented himself with his books. He was as much surprised as pleased when he finished up his doctoral work, and more than a little troubled when he realized it meant he would have to get a job.

He was particularly troubled when the only place that responded to his outpouring of résumés was the University of Michigan, Detroit campus. He postponed answering for weeks, hoping for another offer, and was secretly hoping UM-D might withdraw their offer when his dwindling student loan money forced him to actually make the call.

They didn't. Reluctantly, hesitantly, fearfully, Happy Harry Harper had headed home.

Harry shook himself out of his reverie and forced his

mind back to the present. "Enough already," he said. "Let's get that coffee." He stood and took the two steps to the galley stove, grateful once again that coffee at least was in plentiful supply on the *Miss Behavin'*. No alcohol, no cigarettes, and damn little in the way of food, but enough coffee to keep a small army awake and marching for a month.

Harry unclipped the cheap tin coffee pot from the clips that kept it from sliding off the galley burner—clever idea, that—and poured the last of the coffee into his mug. The over-brewed liquid was black and thick, almost syrupy, and Harry wished again for just a bit of milk. Harpoon Harrison, Harry thought with a smile, would take it with a shot of brandy—no, Wild Turkey. But of course Harpoon would not have bumbled his way into a situation like this in the first place. Harry looked out at the rolling sea, sipped his coffee, and slipped once again into his memories.

UM-Detroit, Harry thought, hadn't turned out nearly as bad as he had feared. He taught freshman comp, an introductory survey lit course, and a few other non-demanding classes with non-demanding students. His colleagues were friendly enough, and when he showed no interest in the usual faculty parties, politics and philandering, they left him to himself. Twice he had found Xerox copies of old newspaper clippings taped to his door, by angry students he supposed, and a few times he'd noticed other faculty smirking when he entered a room. He kept to himself, read his detective novels and was, if not happy, at least at peace.

Harry knew he was not exactly a star in the department, but that didn't worry him much. His student evaluations were generally at least average, and he published enough—usually overwritten analysis on the detective genre in obscure pop culture journals—to keep the tenure police off his back. So he was a little surprised when he returned to his office one day to find a note asking him to report to the office of the assistant dean for academic affairs.

"Well, Dr. Harper," Dean Miriam Conrad had said that rainy Monday as she ushered Harry to a seat before her imposing desk, "how good of you to come see me."

"Not at all," Harry said, wondering if he had in fact had any choice in the matter. He wondered too if he should tell Dean Conrad that the mascara under her eyes was smeared, and that there was a dark grainy streak running down her left cheek. Best not, he decided. Doubtless, the dean already knew that she had been crying.

Harry had seen the dean only once before, speaking at some unmemorable faculty function or another. She was fiftyish, slender, graying, with a handsome if somewhat sharp birdlike face. He couldn't remember what she'd said that day, but he remembered being impressed by her speech. Impressed too by a colleague's whispered speculation that she was in line for a university vice-presidency.

Her office, when he stepped into it that day, did nothing to dispel her image of power-on-the-rise—austere furnishings, dark wooden walls lined with hefty diplomas, citations and awards, a heavy steel-and-glass desk. Dean Conrad herself, however, seemed somewhat less than imposing. Nervous, even.

The dean reseated herself behind the desk, smoothed the perfectly unrumpled sleeves of her blouse, and gestured broadly toward the open windows behind her. "This weather," she said, and launched into a rambling diatribe against rain, snow, cold, ice and all the other universally despised but reluctantly accepted vagaries of Michigan weather. Harry murmured his agreement, added a good-natured complaint or two of his own, and quietly wished Dean Conrad would get to the point.

"Well," she said at last, and then again, "Well." She picked up a small stack of papers, tapped them into perfect alignment, put them back on the desk and carefully centered them before her. Then she impatiently swept them to one side and looked up at Harry.

"Dr. Harper," she said, "I need your help."

"Of course, Dean, anything I can do for the university . . ."

"This matter does not concern the school."

"It doesn't?"

"No," the dean said. She glanced down at her hands, and Harry saw that she was nervously twisting an ornate gold ring around one finger. A wedding ring. "Dr. Harper," she said, "I understand you are an expert detective."

"Pardon?"

"At the merit scholars' reception last week, I overheard Professor Garrington say that you couldn't attend because you were wrapped up in a case, that an expert detective like yourself couldn't spare the time for ceremonial activities."

Harry nodded and made a mental note to slip some

Wite-Out into Jack Garrington's coffee. "Dean Conrad," he began—

"I have need of a detective, Dr. Harper. My husband, you see . . ." The dean tentatively reached one trembling hand toward a framed photo standing on her desk. It showed a muscular, handsome man, several years her junior, gripping a football and laughing at the camera.

"Professor Conrad," Harry said. "John Conrad, is it? With the criminology department."

"Jeffrey Conrad, and yes. The chair of the department, in fact. Jeff consults regularly with the law-enforcement community, he knows everyone worth knowing, and everyone knows him. If I hired a professional detective, an established detective from anywhere around here, Jeffrey would know it within the hour."

"I see," Harry said. "And I'm quite flattered, Dean, but there's something I really must explain."

But he didn't explain, not then, not later. The dean at that moment put her head into her hands and began to sob. Harry found himself hesitantly moving behind the desk to pat her trembling shoulders, and then telling the distraught dean that things weren't as bad as they seemed, that everything would be all right, and that he, expert detective Harry Harper, would do all within his power to set the world right.

He hadn't meant to deceive her, certainly he had told her no outright lies. And what the hell, maybe he really could help. He did know every detective trick in the book—in all the books. And so, when the emergency leave papers arrived at his office, papers dramatically expedited by one Assistant Dean for Academic Affairs Miriam Conrad, Harry simply put down his pen, picked up his briefcase and walked to the door. He stopped there and took one hesitant look at the stack of ungraded midterms still sitting on his desk. Then he turned out the lights and quietly closed the office door.

Two days later Harry was on a plane bound for Miami and then on to Santo Domingo, Dominican Republic, where suspected philanderer Jeffrey Conrad was attending a conference on Third World law-enforcement techniques. And Harry was excited, excited, excited about something other than a new gumshoe novel or a late-night Bogart rerun for the first time in years. Harry was already envisioning a new life for himself, a life that did not include gossipy coworkers and unmotivated students, pitying looks and half-hidden smirks. A life that was as crisp and clean as a fresh-pressed trench coat, as clear and decisive as an uppercut to the jaw. A life where he would be respected.

But things had not gone well in the Dominican. Conrad was not at the conference, had not been there in several days, but a twenty-dollar bill slipped to a motel clerk quickly led Harry to Puerta Plata, a booming beach-and-casino tourist town on the Dominican southwestern coast. Jeffrey Conrad was there and, as his wife suspected, so was his lover.

The lover, however, was not the leggy blonde department secretary upon whom Dean Conrad had pinned her suspicions; rather, it was a bulky, balding brunette Harry recognized as the coach of the school's wrestling squad.

This troubled Harry to no end, knowing as he did that Dean Conrad was set on having her heart broken by an oversexed, underaged fellow female. The change in circumstances presented evidentiary problems for which Harry, to his great chagrin, was not at all prepared. He invested nearly half his ready cash in a 35mm camera, bought two rolls of film, and set about stalking his prey.

Unfortunately, Harry had not been able to afford a long-range lens for his new rig. Also unfortunately, Harry had no practice whatsoever at maneuvering through unfamiliar spaces with his eyes glued to a viewfinder. And so, when he found the two men in just the right pose, holding hands over cocktails in a dimly lit restaurant, it was all but inevitable he would trip over a table leg while trying to unobtrusively get within camera range. Harry sprawled headfirst to the floor at the surprised couple's feet, knees scraping but camera held high.

"Who the hell are you?" Professor Conrad roared, which under the circumstances, Harry had to admit was a more than fair question. And so Harry stood up, brushed his torn pants, and told all. Conrad turned white, said "Oh my God," and reached unsteadily for his drink.

Conrad's date was not quite so stoic. He leapt up with an outraged roar, smashed Harry's nose and his camera, and then collapsed into his lover's arms. He was sobbing loudly as an unsympathetic waiter hustled the bleeding, protesting Harry out into the steamy Dominican night.

Harry staggered back to his hotel and packed the nose in room-service ice. He called the dean, who adamantly refused to believe her husband was gay. She demanded pictures Harry no longer had, questioned his competence, questioned his sobriety and questioned his sanity, and abruptly hung up.

The next morning Harry found his expense account at the Puerto Plata Hilton had been canceled. He was asked to leave.

Harry made it as far as the hotel bar, where, cursing his fortune and bemoaning his future, he sat down and ordered six shots of dark Dominican rum. He awoke in the back seat of a taxi cab speeding down a narrow road to nowhere. The cab driver told Harry he had insisted on being taken to Cielo Bay—Cielo Bay?—and that he owed the driver seventeen dollars, American. In Cielo Bay he ordered more rum, found a room with a cantankerous local woman, reread his Spillane novels and, apparently, committed accidental manslaughter.

And that, Harry thought, was how he had come to sipping bad coffee in the tiny galley of an unfamiliar sailboat, far from land and far from safe. His brief career as a detective had been a spectacular failure. His fitness as a professor no doubt had been challenged by the outraged dean and confirmed by Harry's extended, unexplained absence. At thirty-one years old, Happy Harry Harper needed a new career.

Harry sighed and turned back to his writing. What the hell. Maybe he would do better as a smuggler.

It was full dark when Harry emerged from the *Miss Behavin'*'s cabin, driven from his writing by a coffee-laden bladder. He hated leaving his story even for a moment; even as he balanced precariously on the starboard rail and relieved himself into the phosphorescent deep, the vast majority of Harry's mind remained occupied with getting his new-born creation out of the latest deadly situation into which Harry had written him. Harry dedicated perhaps 1 percent of his conscious thought to the business at hand, and 2 percent more to keeping himself balanced there on the gunwale. His body was out on the deck of the blithely circling *Miss Behavin'*, but the bulk of Harry's mind was in a dingy bar in Rio, helping "Harpoon" Harrison stare down yet another opponent.

There was a tiny part of Harry's not-so-conscious mind, however, that transcended his writer's trance just enough to take notice of the dark, of the ocean, and of the stars. That restless, unsatisfied piece of Harry's mentality couldn't help but note the position of those stars and compare them with the charts Harry had pored over so unsuccessfully in the preceding days. While Harry's conscious mind composed, his subconscious computed.

Harry shook once, zipped up, and hopped down from the railing. He turned back toward the friendly yellow light of the cabin, detouring along the way just long enough to make a slight change in the pitch of his mainsail, wondering all the while if Harpoon Harrison should down his current opponent with an exotic karate move or simply nail him with a good old-fashioned American right to the jaw.

Back in the cabin, Harry spun his wheel six degrees starboard, poured another cup of coffee, took a quick sighting out the salt-spattered window, carved a new point onto his pencil, nudged the wheel one more degree starboard before locking it down, and returned to the table firmly convinced that a masculine-to-the-core fellow like Harpoon Harrison would choose a straightforward punch in the jaw over an effective and yet somehow effete karate chop any day.

Happy Harry Harper sipped his coffee, chewed his pencil butt, and leaned forward to send Harpoon Harrison's fist crashing into the hate-distorted face of his unfortunate opponent. Outside, the wind flowed into *Miss Behavin*'s eagerly awaiting sails. The boat settled contentedly onto her new course and drove on through the darkness, knifing steadily toward Harry's future and the distant glittering heart of Miami.

9

Quiet Quiones was even more miserable than most men would be after forty-five minutes on a toilet seat.

It was of course a most comfortable toilet seat—clean, padded but firm, top-of-the-line like everything else in Carlos's fortress home. The ceiling fan whirring steadily overhead managed to suck away most of the evidence of Quiet's gastrointestinal distress; the fat black cigar he had smoldering in the ashtray covered up the rest (the first time, Quiet noted with yet another bitter twinge of self-loathing, the first time he had gotten any real pleasure from one of the damned things).

The cramps seemed to be subsiding and, though his bowels still tightened and strained involuntarily every few minutes, Quiet knew without doubt there was nothing, absolutely nothing, left in him to be pushed out. The Kaopectate tablets Boulder slid under the door a half-hour ago were doing their job; Quiet knew that in a short time he would have no real reason to remain where he was.

And that was the problem. He was uncomfortable here in this well-appointed water closet in a drug dealer's mansion, locked in with his stink and his cramps and his misery—but those were all things he could deal with. But there were people waiting on the other side of that door, people waiting to laugh at him—and that, he could not.

Right now, with his pants around his knees and his dignity down the drain, with all the respect and influence he had struggled to create dissipating like the laughter he could still imagine echoing through the halls of his adopted home, Quiet Quiones could only think of himself as Oscar. Oscar, the fat, dark-skinned kid, so out-of-place on a midwestern playground, with snot on his nose and tears in his eyes. And laughter in his ears.

"Throws like a girl!" they laughed, and later, "Oscar is an egghead!" or "Quiones is a queer," and now *"Quiet esta lleno de mierda!"* From the playground through adolescence, through college and now here—the voices changed, the words changed, but the laughter was always the same. And the laughter always hurt.

It hurt how Joaquin had burst into laughter when Quiet came rushing in the mansion door, panic on his face and his pants already halfway down. It hurt how Rey and the rest of the men had gathered outside the bathroom door and hooted about the stench, about Quiet's potty training, until Boulder ran them off. It had hurt to see the undisguised disgust on Boulder's face when he realized that despite driving 85 over the Biscayne Bay Bridge they had not made it in time, that Quiet had soiled himself.

And it hurt to know who had caused all this misery.

Quiet sighed and rose unsteadily from the toilet. He reeled off a handful of paper and wiped his inner thighs one last time, then dropped the wad into the bowl and flushed. He walked gingerly to the sink, scrubbed his hands, then soaked a washrag in hot water and pressed it hard against his face.

Boulder had said it might be a stomach virus, or some food gone bad, but Quiet knew. This had been done to him twice before, once on a Boy Scout camp-out, again when he'd tried to join a fraternity at Wharton. He probably would've even recognized the mediciney-chocolate tang to the coffee had he not been so smitten by that mysterious woman, that distant, stunning, incredibly desirable woman.

Ah, that woman! Eyes like electric pinwheels, hair the color of the sun, a body in youthful bloom that not even that sandbag of a waitress uniform could hide. And the walk! The walk of an angel lost on Earth, the walk of a Bourbon Street hooker in a nun's habit. What mortal man could resist such a walk? None, of course.

No wonder Boulder Baker had slipped Ex-Lax into his coffee.

Oscar laughed ruefully and caught a flash of gold reflected in the mirror before him. He struck a pose, one eyebrow raised seductively, head dipped slightly forward, left upper lip pulled up as high as he could take it. It was more sneer than smile, but it showed the polished gold encasing his left upper incisor, gold cut to show an enamel silhouette of Cuba shining through.

Not so bad, he thought. Not so bad when I hold in my

gut, and turn my head like so. . . . He picked up the smoldering cigar and took a slow steady draw, careful not to inhale. He let the thick smoke out slow, watching it billow around the black eyebrows and dark complexion of the man in the mirror.

Not so bad. Almost piratical, like a sailor, like a warrior. Oscar knew, he *knew*, that there was indeed a warrior lurking behind that face, a warrior born to the heritage of De Gama, De Soto, and Roberto Clemente. But how to make the others see it, those colleagues who saw only the pudgy clown with the economics degrees? How to make the woman in the coffee shop see the fire and fury and danger that smoldered just below this sedate exterior? Oscar sighed deeply, and coughed lightly from the lingering cigar fumes.

And then it hit him. An idea, no, a plan, a full-blown plot so simple and so beautiful, so brilliantly crystalline perfect that Oscar laughed with delight. No, not Oscar, not Oscar the lonely little boy, but Quiet, Quiet the thinker, Quiet the warrior. Quiet Quiones, descendant of heroes and a man among men!

Quiet jammed the cigar into a corner of his mouth and bit down hard. He wrapped a towel sarong-style around his waist and boldly, proudly, stepped out into the mansion's hallway. Let them snicker, he thought, let *mi compadres* laugh while they could. He had a plan now, a brilliant and beautiful plan that would win the woman of his dreams and the admiration of his peers in one single daring act. Quiet Quiones was going to become a great lover. Quiet Quiones was going to become a great legend.

Quiet Quiones was going to kidnap the girl from the coffee shop.

"I look like a pimp," Quiet Quiones said. He wasn't entirely unhappy with that idea, and said it aloud in part to taste the sound of the word on his lips. Weasel Wofford, however, feared that Quiet's observation might be some sort of a complaint. The greasy little man straightened up from the Mariah Carey CD cover he was leaning over, pinched his nostrils together and snorted once, hard and quick, then hustled over to where Quiones was scrutinizing himself in Joaquin's full-length bedroom mirror.

"No, no, man, you look good, you look real good. And you should look like a pimp, that's good, man, cops see a pimp they keep going, there's lotsa pimps in Miami, man, they service the tourists and nobody cares much and what cop wants ta mess with that? So you blend in with your surroundings, man, like a deer in the jungle, man, like a chameleon, just like I toldja. Man."

"*Si, si, comprendo.* But still . . ." Quiet studied his image, and Weasel studied Quiet. The weird little dude was right, or at least half right, Weasel thought. He didn't look like a pimp; he looked like someone trying to look like a pimp. The full-length black leather coat was way too long for him, flapping over his feet, dragging a couple inches on the floor. Weasel remembered lifting the coat from the apartment of a six-foot-three New York

City brother who had worn it with a dignity Quiet could never have. What was cool on that man was clown on Quiet, and if Weasel had any integrity whatsoever he would have told him so.

But Weasel did not have any integrity, none whatsoever. What Weasel had was a two-hundred-dollar-a-day cocaine habit, a habit that rode him like a heat-mad jockey wearing razor spurs, a habit that had long ago destroyed Weasel's budding career as a promising young burglar and had brought him on the run when his occasional partner Joaquin called to say he had a pigeon lined up. A nice fat self-deluded pigeon who wanted to feel cool and wanted to hear lies and paid in coke and cash. And so—

"Look here, bro, you turn this way and you look," Weasel said. He put his long pale fingers against Quiet's left shoulder and pushed, gentle like but maybe harder than he should have, and when Quiet turned toward him Weasel drew back one dirty skinny leg and kicked him right in the nuts.

Quiet jumped back, eyes wide and mouth open, then stopped and looked down at himself. There was no pain. A dirty footprint was smeared across the jacket at crotch level, but there was no pain.

"You see, bro, you see? Coat like that, woman kick and kick but she don't get at you, can't get her foot past all that leather. It's like armor, see, like a beekeeper suit keeping the honeys off. You try and snatch a woman, and she get to kicking, you be thanking Weasel you got that coat, bro. And only three hundred dollars, man. A real bargain, bro, a real bargain, right, Joaquin?"

"*Si*, yes, a bargain," Joaquin said. He was coming back from the kitchen, carrying two bottles of beer and a glass of water. While Quiet preened before the mirror, Joaquin handed one bottle to Weasel, took a quick sip from the second, and put the water on his dresser beside the coke tray. He dipped two fingers in the water, brought them up to his nostrils and sniffed deep. Weasel did the same, joining Joaquin in the ritual cure for coke-dried nostrils.

Joaquin knew that Weasel had been in Quiet's coke again while he was out of the room, knew that each time he turned his back the dirty little junkie was digging deeper into their profits. Joaquin himself had already snorted more than he was accustomed to, foolishly trying to keep up with the Weasel and so get his fair share. Now he had to concentrate to keep from grinding his teeth, and the coke drip in the back of his throat was nauseating. Worse, Joaquin couldn't keep his hyper-speed thoughts from racing back to Boulder Baker. Boulder Baker, that dead-eye motherfucker who thought he was so tough, so cool, and damn him if he wasn't. Joaquin knew Baker's reputation, he knew Baker could kill him before breakfast and still sit down before the coffee was cold.

Boulder had left Quiet alone with Joaquin for just a while, for an hour or so while he ran his own errands, under strict orders the two of them not budge from Joaquin's apartment. Well okay, they were doing that, they hadn't gone nowhere—but Joaquin knew damn well that bringing in a certified high-risk loser like the Weasel was not exactly what Boulder meant when he said to be cool.

Joaquin wasn't sure what Boulder would do if he

knew Joaquin was taking this opportunity to skim a little extra spending money from the crazy accountant, but he was sure the story would get back to Uncle Carlos pretty damn quick—and that *really* scared him. He flashed on the slender silver blade that always sat on Carlos's desk—a letter opener, nowadays, but the 411 was that it was a souvenir of his very first kill, that when Carlos was fifteen he had used that very blade to open the belly of a competitor, and Joaquin knew for sure he still kept that fucking letter opener sharp as a scalpel. Joaquin shuddered and cast a nervous glance toward the apartment door. He didn't know why Quiet was so fucking important to his uncle, but he knew that if he took things too far with the little wimp, family or not, Carlos just might turn that blade on him.

"Yo, Weas, you got other stuff, right? Let's see what else you got, man." Joaquin reached over and picked up the coke tray like maybe he was gonna cut more lines, turning as he did to get his body between the coke and the Weasel. Weasel glared at him, sharp and shrewd, then jabbed one finger out and dragged it through the powder remnants still on the tray. He popped that finger in his mouth and worked it between his upper lip and gums, smiling crooked at Joaquin while he did it. That was one coke ritual Joaquin just couldn't get into—okay, coke is cool, coke is great, but who wants to go around with numb gums? Crazy people, that's who. Crazy from coke.

"You have everything I need, eh *compadre*?" That was Quiet, finally turned away from the mirror and sliding up to the Weasel like an earnest schoolboy. Weasel grinned, nodding, his powder-fueled enthusiasm catching and feeding on Quiet's own anxious energy.

"You betcha, *compadre*, you betcha. Now just look here . . ." The Weasel opened the battered black satchel he had brought with him and began taking out one item after another, describing each as they came—plastic clips for the arms, chamois cloth for the mouth, cotton wadding, ether. Most of it was legitimate for what Quiet had in mind; some of it wasn't. It didn't seem to matter. Crazy Quiet just kept nodding, kept peeling off bills and asking the questions. It was sort of flattering, really, probably the first time in years anyone had taken the Weasel serious. And so Weasel found himself responding in earnest, calling on everything he could remember from his gangster days that might help Quiet along, giving instructions, giving advice, issuing warnings. And Quiet just kept nodding and asking questions, and Joaquin just kept watching the door.

Quiet knew quite well that Weasel Wofford had ripped him off, badly, but he didn't care. With Carlos's contacts, coke was easy—information was not. Besides, Quiet was a man on a mission.

And Weasel was, after all, a true professional; Quiet could see that clear enough. And so, on Weasel's advice, he put aside his desire for immediate action and instead set out to learn everything he could about his intended. Quiet took to following Jane Ellen at a distance, forcing himself to concentrate on her movements and not, well, her movements. He bought a stubby pair of bird-watcher binoculars and a slender leather notepad for Boulder, who reluctantly followed along and recorded each movement Quiet dictated.

Quiones learned several things from his observations. First, that his beloved was a restless and energetic young woman. Not that she frequented the nightclubs and bars that sprouted on Miami's every street corner like mushrooms after a rainstorm; in fact, she worked overtime and even double-shifts at the coffee shop whenever possible. Daytimes, though, she never stayed in her room, spending most of her time instead out walking the streets. And she *read* while she walked, read incessantly, read anything. Quiet had watched one rainy afternoon, appalled, as Jane Ellen scrounged her way through a row of trash dumpsters behind a Walgreen's drug store. He had been considering breaking his discreet cover and sending Boulder to buy her lunch when Jane Ellen emerged from a bin smiling, clutching a tattered issue of *Rolling Stone* in one hand. Jane Ellen wasn't desperate for food, Quiet realized, but rather for literature. He fell even deeper in love with this enchanting, enigmatic creature.

Jane Ellen's favorite walking route, Quiet learned, covered nearly seven miles, from her dingy apartment through the steamy streets of south Miami to an old newsstand tucked away between two heavily barred pawn shops, then on to a used book store in a strip mall on the fringes of the better part of town. She would spend no more than ten or fifteen minutes in either place, usually huddled around the ten-for-a-dollar unwanted paperbacks or torn-cover magazines, and then emerge with her plastic Burdine's department store bag bulging with new reading material. She made that trip every three or four days, always returning to the used book store with a bagful of whatever books she'd managed to scrounge up in the meantime.

Quiet was also surprised by the trip Jane Ellen never made—or at least, almost never. She was young, healthy, white, and in Miami—but she never went to the beach. It was Quiet's experience that the beach was why people, especially healthy young white people, came to Miami in the first place. The one time Jane Ellen did make it to the beach, riding a bus through the deco and pastels of South Beach to the white sand and blue waters of Biscayne Bay, left Quiones with only another mystery. She had gotten off the bus, with Quiet and Boulder following in a taxi behind, and marched straight across the beach and out into the water. She wasn't wearing a bathing suit but kept going anyway, until she stood nearly chest-deep in the quiet surf. She'd stood that way for nearly a half-hour, barely moving while the overdressed Quiet and Boulder sweated and stewed up on the beach. Then she'd suddenly spun around and walked quickly back to shore, emerging like a Venus in cut-offs. She had, much to Boulder's relief, gotten, dripping, right back on the first bus to Little Havana. But Quiones had had his binoculars locked on Jane Ellen when she came out of her reverie, and he was troubled. Jane Ellen was a stoic, but when she came out of the surf that day, there were tears in her eyes.

Mostly, though, Quiet was worried about Jane Ellen's other frequent walking route. She would ride the bus again, twenty minutes through the diesel fumes and angry horns of mid-day Miami traffic, to a somewhat upscale business district in Coconut Grove. There she would carefully visit each of a half-dozen or so travel agencies scattered throughout the Grove, sometimes spending just a few minutes leafing through the gaudy pamphlets and travelogues on display in each agency's outer office, sometimes spending an hour or more in animated conversation with an agent. Three times, Quiet had sent Boulder into those agencies to buy information, and each time he had emerged with the same story: Jane Ellen was meticulously researching the costs of flying to Europe—Paris, in particular, though she had also made inquiries about London, Milan, Rome, Athens and, once, Tokyo.

Clearly, his beloved Jane Ellen was not staying in Miami for long. The woman of his dreams was right there, just beyond his reach—and he was running out of time.

Quiones had learned that Dario's Cubano Cuisine and Coffee closed at midnight on Tuesdays and Thursdays. Jane Ellen would stay for an extra half-hour, cleaning the last few dishes, wiping off dirty ashtrays and coffee-stained tabletops, filling the cheap ceramic creamers with half-and-half for the following morning. Most of the walk home was along well-lit Centro Avenue, usually crowded even in mid-week with sleek young executives spilling out of the discos and nightclubs, reeking of imported beer and too much cologne. Jane Ellen would even stop sometimes and dawdle, reading a bit in the sodium glare of a streetlight or just staring at the yuppies on parade. Eventually, though, she would have to turn off Centro onto Baker, and then down Bryan. Two and a half blocks of few lights and fewer people before she reached her apartment in an old converted warehouse, five bedrooms and a common bath and kitchen, two rooms vacant and the others locked and dark long before she came home.

Quiet knew that Jane Ellen did not dawdle along that dark stretch of road. She never seemed scared, at least not to his admiring eyes, but she did keep up a pretty good pace. She did slow down, right as she got to the door of her building, just long enough to dig into the pockets of her tight shorts and find her door key, the only key she carried. There was a light there, a single bare bulb suspended above the door frame, but that could easily be taken care of. Better yet, the door was right at the far corner of the building, and around that corner there was nothing but an empty alley.

And so it was, that hot Tuesday evening in the middle of yet another sticky South Florida summer, that Quiet Quiones found himself hiding in the shadows of a piss-stained alleyway, nervously checking his bag and his watch, listening for footsteps and thinking of the Football War. Such, Quiet reminded himself, are the ways of love.

Quiet listened closely for footsteps coming down Bryan Street, then decided to risk a quick glimpse down the quiet road. He dropped to his knees before looking; the Weasel had said people don't expect to see faces at knee-height and, unless they happen to be staring right at you, are likely to dismiss any glimpse of motion as a cat or dog or some such. He moved his head sideways around the corner, one eye closed, until just enough of his head cleared the brick to give him a one-eyed view of the street. Nothing.

Quiones sighed and struggled back up to his feet, once again cursing the ankle-length black leather coat Weasel had pressed on him. It made him look like a pimp and sweat like a pig, but the Weasel was right; it helped him blend with the night, and the broad button-down pockets on either side easily held all the materials he would need. Weasel's other admonition had made sense too; in the few seconds it would take the ether to work, his target was likely to flail about pretty enthusiastically. The thick leather might be uncomfortable now, but it might just save him from a debilitating kick in the nuts later.

Quiet listened intently. He heard a distant step, then another. He pushed himself tight against the alley wall, back first, and strained to identify the oncoming steps. It was almost certainly her, he knew; no one else used this street at this time of night. But he had to be sure. He closed his eyes and focused all his attention on his hearing. One step, then another, and another, slight, quick, definitely feminine and coming right toward him. Then there was a brief break in the pattern, a pause that no one other than Quiet Quiones would have recognized. It was the Hitch, that sweet pause in his beloved's sensuous walk. Quiones pressed tighter against the brick and shivered in delicious anticipation.

The footsteps drew closer, and Quiet went into the

motions he had practiced so many times in preparation for this very moment. He reached into his pockets and pulled thick cotton wadding out with one hand and the ether bottle with the other. Quietly, using Jane Ellen's footsteps to gauge his timing, he unscrewed the ether cap and poured a generous splash onto the cotton.

Quiones held very still, not breathing, picturing Jane Ellen's every move from the sound of her movements. He heard a quiet curse, no doubt aimed at the absent landlord who had let the only light bulb at this end of the alley burn out once again. Now, just a few steps more, slowing down as she approached the doorway. Then she stopped, right around the corner, fewer than five feet away, all unsuspecting. In his mind's eye he saw her poking her stiff fingers into those skin-tight cutoffs, struggling to find her door key.

He heard the crinkle of plastic—her bag of books, no doubt—and then the sound he was waiting for—the slight metallic scratching of Jane Ellen inserting her key in the door. Her attention would be fully engaged now, one arm held out toward the door, the other busy with her book bag. She was as vulnerable as she was going to get.

Fighting back the sudden urge to let out a war whoop, Quiet Quiones made his move. He sprang around the corner, adrenaline surging through him and a ferocious grin on his face. He had just a quick glimpse of Jane Ellen's shadowed face in the dim alley, more surprised than frightened. Then he thrust the ether-soaked wadding dramatically toward her, leapt forward, tripped over the leading edge of his ankle-length black-leather pimp coat, crashed past Jane Ellen and slammed face-first into her securely locked apartment door.

Stunned, Quiet dropped to his knees on the doorstep there beside Jane Ellen. He heard her surprised "What the hell . . . ?" and swung his left arm wildly in her direction. He caught the bottom of her T-shirt and latched on desperately. He pulled himself up, pulling her down at the same time, and once again thrust the cotton wadding toward her face. He felt a muffled thump near his groin and knew that the damned jacket had in fact saved him from a solid kick in the crotch. The adrenaline cleared his head and he grinned wolfishly, knowing he would be victorious, that he would not fail, that he, Quiet Quiones, was about to capture the woman of his dreams.

Then Jane Ellen Ashley swung her book bag with all the strength in her oyster-opening, Southern-bred and waitressing-strengthened left arm and caught Quiet Quiones upside the head with six pounds of recycled paperbacks and a hardbound copy of Henry Miller's collected works. Stunned, Quiones dropped like a stone.

Quiet fell to his hands and knees on the sidewalk, veering toward unconsciousness, knowing his nose was bleeding and probably broken. He dimly registered a metallic ting and Jane Ellen's "damn!" and realized she had dropped her door key. He also registered, there at the edge of his fading consciousness, the sound of squealing tires and the sudden flash of oncoming headlights.

The cops, he thought. Busted.

The car screeched to a halt right beside the reeling Quiones. The driver's door flew open; a giant figure jumped out and effortlessly stepped over the kneeling Quiones. Quiet heard the sudden sound of bone slamming into flesh, and Jane Ellen fell senseless to the sidewalk beside him.

Quiet dropped face down on the cold cement. He tried to rise but managed only to roll over on his back, warm blood streaming down his cheeks and over his ears. The menacing giant stepped over the fallen Jane Ellen to stand astride him, one thick leg on either side of Quiet's waist, huge dark head haloed by the stars in the distant South Florida sky.

"Damn you, Quiones," he said.

Quiet recognized the familiar gravelly voice of Boulder Baker, smiled peacefully, and passed out.

10

Jane Ellen lay on her back on the biggest, softest damn bed she had ever seen, bathed in the soft afternoon—or was it morning?—light filtering through the thick gold curtains, and tried to figure out just what the fuck was going on.

She had been kidnapped, that was clear enough even without the gag in her mouth and the heavy plastic binders pinning her hands uncomfortably together behind her back. She even had a good idea of who had done it, judging from the voices that had been arguing out in the other room for the better part of a half-hour now. The high squeaky voice with the Hispanic accent, that was Quiet, the one she had been so sure would never do anything to hurt her. And the stronger, bass voice, the one that seemed to carry menace without ever revealing anger, that had to be the big guy, Boulder, the one who had jumped out of the black limo and cold-cocked her the night before.

What Jane Ellen couldn't figure out was the why.

Why her? It wasn't money, obviously. Last night's limo alone probably cost more for a night's rental than she had in all the world. And, yes, the little guy had a crush on her, but this seemed a little extreme. Besides, Miami was packed with women far more desirable than she, jammed, in fact, with the most beautiful women in two hemispheres. Jane Ellen knew that she wasn't unattractive, but she just couldn't believe that anyone would pick her out of a city of beauties to shanghai in the name of desire.

That left only one alternative, an alternative that chilled her to the bone. They were the Senator's men after all, they had to be, sent to fetch her for the drowning of his son. That meant she was going to die.

Jane Ellen struggled against the bonds chaffing her tired wrists and cursed herself for carelessness. She should have kept going that night six weeks ago, when she'd fled Franklin County and the Senator's vengeance with the clothes on her back and barely six hundred dollars in her pockets. She should have jumped off the bus at the first opportunity, Jane Ellen realized now. Got out at Gainesville or Ocala or a dozen other Podunk stops and caught the first thing heading west, through Alabama and Mississippi and on to Texas and Mexico. But she didn't want west, not then, not now, didn't want a life of shitty jobs in dirty little towns in dank little counties. Miami wasn't Paris, wasn't anywhere close, but it had an international airport, and it had places she could work in quiet anonymity, saving every cent and watching for any sign she'd been found.

She'd changed jobs three times in her first month here, and apartments twice more. But there was never any sign of trouble, no strangers asking after her, no one waiting for her in the darkness, not even any mention in the paper of Senator Jerome Langer's tragic loss. She still grieved over that young boy's drowning, but Jane Ellen found herself starting to relax.

She'd had a few bad moments when the little Cuban started trailing her, but Jane Ellen just couldn't believe that anyone so obvious, so inept, could be in the employ of the legendary—and legendarily murderous—Senator Langer. Now, too late, she realized the truth—it wasn't the little Cuban at all. He was just some sort of assistant, a thug-in-training or something. Her real enemy, the one she could see working arm-in-arm with Langer, was the big guy, the one with the dead-shark eyes and the wicked right hook. The one Quiet called Boulder.

Jane Ellen was actually as worried as anything by the fact that she was still alive. Her imagination ran wild with possible explanations, with gory images of tortures and starvation. A thousand cruel scenes from hundreds of scavenged horror and spy novels went racing through her head. She could see Boulder doing it easily enough, inflicting excruciating agony with glittering sharp implements and no change of expression. She shuddered in the darkness and tried once more to wriggle free of her bonds.

Jane Ellen thought she might wet herself when the door finally cracked open. She felt a rush of relief when she saw not Boulder but the little Cuban poking his head solicitously into the room, smiling happily, his eyes swollen half-shut and two large pink Band-Aids criss-crossed over his flattened nose.

"Ah, my sweet senorita, awake at last," he said. "May I come in?"

Jane Ellen tried to sit up, failed, and fell back on the bed. She tongued aside as much of the soft cloth in her mouth as she could and said as clearly as possible, given the circumstances, "Uh habb po tee."

"There, there, *mi amora*, don't try to talk. Just let me look at you," Quiet said. He sat on the edge of the bed and did just that, taking Jane Ellen in as if she were a fine piece of art, or maybe a fresh piece of grilled grouper. It didn't exactly thrill her, this fawning gaze of his, but for the first time since awakening bound and gagged in this amazingly rich room, Jane Ellen felt a slight stirring of hope. She tried to smile beneath her gag and raised her eyebrows in what she hoped was a friendly gesture.

Quiet met her eyes and smiled with obvious pleasure, and Jane Ellen felt the first whisper of a plan stir in her mind. She tried once again to speak through the wadded cloth in her mouth. "Pees, why habb po tee."

Surprise and delight burst across Quiet's face. "Oh my darling, *mi amora, quiero tu tambien*, I love you too! And I knew you would return my love, knew that once you saw the warrior in me, saw the lion in my heart—but no, *pero* no, I talk too much, no? Here, let me take that off you; let me show you my love."

Jane Ellen nodded meekly, doing her best to smile around the gag, and wondered if it were a good thing or a bad thing that her kidnapper was so obviously a total nut case. Quiet put his arm behind her back and helped her to sit up, shivering with delight whenever he touched her. She felt him fumbling with the cloth tied behind her head. Then the cloth came tumbling free, and Jane Ellen delicately spit out what had to be a twenty-dollar silk handkerchief. Quiet leaned back and looked at her expectantly.

"I have to pee," she said.

Quiet looked taken aback, then he gave a quick little high-pitched laugh. "*Si*, of course, of course. Right through there." He pointed toward a door off to the right of the bed. Jane Ellen nodded, then turned around and extended her bound hands as far toward Quiet as she could. She looked at him over her shoulder and frowned.

"You don't expect me to go like this, do you?"

Quiet looked at her dubiously, staring from her hands to her face and back again. Jane Ellen hopped from one foot to the other and did her best to look desperate. "Oh, please please hurry! I really have to go!"

Quiet frowned, then seemed to make up his mind. He reached out and took her hands; she felt him working the security latch on the plastic binders. "*Si*, all right," he said. "But you must promise—"

"No."

Quiet stopped his fumbling with Jane Ellen's bonds, and they both looked toward the bedroom door. Boulder stood there, calm as a clam, his huge bulk nearly blocking the light streaming in from the living room windows.

"No," he said again. "You let her loose and she'll just whack you again."

"Oh, but that was just because you scared me," Jane Ellen said, careful to address Quiet and not the grim giant in the door frame. "I didn't know it was you." She felt Quiet hesitate behind her, and did another little dance. "Please Quiet, I have to go right *now*." When he didn't respond, she gave an exasperated snort and said, as girl-ishly as she could manage, "You don't think I could really hurt you now, do you? A little thing like me?"

Quiet gave a derisive snort, and Jane Ellen felt his hands return to her bonds. Boulder glowered at them both, but turned without comment and walked back into the living room.

Jane Ellen felt the plastic bindings slip free. She rubbed her wrists for a moment, then turned, bounded into the bathroom and closed the door.

She leaned back against the door and closed her eyes. She was exhausted, more drained from stress and fear than in pain. She wanted desperately to be outside, to feel the sun on her arms, maybe to jump into the clear cold sea. She wanted to be anyplace but here, anyplace. Out on the hot Miami streets, back in Eastpoint, far away in Paris . . .

Jane Ellen shook herself and forced her eyes back open. "No daydreams now, Janey girl," she whispered. "Right now, you got to *think*." They hadn't hurt her yet, not really, but she had no idea how long that would last. They were waiting for something, obviously, maybe for the Senator himself to arrive. Jane Ellen repressed a shudder.

She drew in a deep breath, then took careful stock

of her surroundings. There was no window in here, that was hardly a surprise. But she had not been prepared for the sheer opulence of the place. The bathroom was larger than her whole apartment uptown, all sparkling chrome and snow-white marble, and the air smelled delicately of lavender. The bathtub was big enough for three or four people and had metal jets on the sides that she figured had to be for a Jacuzzi. It was like nothing she had ever seen, maybe like nothing anyone in Franklin County had ever seen. Under different circumstances, Jane Ellen thought, she could spend all day in a tub like that, relaxing, reading, letting the warm water soothe her cares away. She ached to slip into that tub and into the pages of a book, any book, or to just close her eyes and retreat into the familiar comfort of her daydreams. She felt herself teetering between reality and fantasy, wanting nothing more than to slide away from her current circumstances.

But that was just not possible. She stepped up to the sink, splashed a little cold water on her face, and studied herself in the ceiling-high mirror. Her shirt was torn at the collar and splashed with crimson at the bottom, but the blood didn't seem to be hers. Her jaw ached and there was a bright pink bruise on her left cheek, but nothing felt broken. As for the rest of her, well, she looked—

She looked like shit. No denying it. Her hair was tangled and disarrayed, there was a streak of dirt across her forehead, and she needed desperately to brush her teeth. Normally Jane Ellen wasn't too preoccupied with her appearance—rarely paid it any attention, in fact—but right now, she knew, her looks were about all she had going for her. The little one, Quiet, he had it for her bad, had it for her worse than any of those drunken horny idiots who'd chased her out onto the deck of the old O&P. That was all she had right now, and she had to work with it.

There was a bright silver brush on the bathroom counter, and a comb, an assortment of makeup still in the wrappings, and a new toothbrush. Jane Ellen brushed her teeth, swept the makeup aside, and set to work clawing the tangles out of her wispy blond hair.

She tried to plan while she brushed, but her thoughts kept drifting back to the old O&P, and to dear toothless Joey Duval. She remembered Joey D. telling one of his favorite stories, about how he'd been cornered by a group of angry shrimpers in a bar outside Pensacola. The local fishermen were already tense, divided as they were between lifelong residents and an unwelcome batch of Vietnamese immigrant newcomers. The last thing they wanted was a Franklin County shrimper leaving the abundance of Apalachicola Bay to raid their turf.

"Well, now," Duval had drawled, "it's just that those boys over there"—and he paused to point out a table of Vietnamese shrimpers quietly sipping their cold long-necks—"those boys said it was all right once I paid them my five-hundred-dollar visitor's fee. What, ain't they given you your share yet?" Duval had quietly slipped out the back door and out of Escambia County during the ensuing ruckus.

Jane Ellen gave her hair one last desultory tug and

looked herself over in the mirror. All right, Joey D., I'll try it your way, she thought. Divide and conquer.

Jane Ellen marched through the empty bedroom and right on out into the living room. The elegance of the place once again struck her. Thick white carpet, fireplace, a chandelier dangling crystals delicate as icicles, wallpaper of red velvet patterned with golden fleur-de-lis—it could have come right out of her vision of Paris, could be a mansion in the city or a palace in the countryside, and Jane Ellen wanted desperately to just stop and drink it all in. She paused half a moment in mid-step, aching to simply reach out and caress the velvet walls, then shook herself mentally and walked on. She strode past the startled Quiet and stopped a few inches away from the taciturn Boulder, who, she noted, was pointedly standing between her and the front door.

Jane Ellen pointed an accusing finger right in Boulder's face and did her best to look outraged. "You," she said angrily, "you got blood all over my favorite shirt. Now just what the heck am I supposed to wear?"

Boulder looked back at her, unblinking, unemotional, and Jane Ellen felt her resolve start to buckle. Then she heard Quiet cough gently behind her, and she spun around to face him.

"I, um, I picked up a few things for you," he said, and gestured toward a stack of packages on the coffee table. "I wasn't exactly sure of your size, but I, uh . . ."

"Well, wasn't that sweet of you." Jane Ellen shot a dirty look at the unconcerned Boulder, gave Quiet a quick peck on the cheek, and walked over to the table. All the boxes, she quickly noted, were from the same place—Frederique's of Miami—and they all contained the same thing. Lingerie.

"Why, Quiet," she said demurely, "you naughty boy." She picked out the least revealing of the purchases and walked toward the bedroom. "I'll just try this one on for us to have a little look-see—but only *us!*" She shot an angry stare at Boulder and then ducked into the bedroom. She heard their voices raised in argument almost as soon as she had closed the door.

Jane Ellen slipped out of her bloody T-shirt and, after a moment's hesitation, let her torn cut-offs slip to the floor. She didn't like it, didn't like it one bit, but she had decided to use her unfamiliar femininity as a weapon just like a thousand different brave heroines had in a hundred different novels. They were the only role models she had, those fictional femme fatales, and if following their lead meant waltzing around in the altogether, well, so be it.

Even so, her determination almost wilted when she got the lingerie on. It was worse than she had feared; a Valentine-red nightie and matching panties that barely covered her crotch. Quiet had indulged in a bit of wishful thinking; the nightie had been purchased with at least a D-cup in mind. Still, if she pushed her chest out like this, and pulled the nightie tight in the back like so . . .

Jane Ellen listened for a minute to the hushed argument going on outside, then picked up her discarded clothing. She cracked the bedroom door open and stuck her head out, careful to allow just a little bit of bronzed bare leg to show as well.

"Quiet, dear, do you think the hotel could get these stains out for me? Maybe you could send your *boy* out to get them done." She smiled at the suddenly slack-jawed Quiet coyly, tossed her pants and shirt at his feet, and retreated to the bedroom once more.

Jane Ellen leaned against the door, holding her breath, listening intently for Boulder's reaction. She couldn't help remembering Too Tall Thompson's story of the day one of the Senator's political enemies had come out of the bay on the end of a grappling hook, feet knotted to a cement block, eyes and ears chewed away by crabs and pinfish. She could easily imagine Boulder doing that, wrapping heavy wire around dead feet, slipping a cold corpse off into the bay with no expression on his face . . .

Jane Ellen took a desperate look around the room. If I have to, she thought, if he comes after me, I'll go right through that window, glass be damned. It occurred to her that she had no idea how high up she was—and then that it didn't really matter. If she were wrong about Quiet, if she had overplayed her hand and Boulder came after her, falling to her death might just be the easiest way out.

Jane Ellen kept one eye on the window and one ear pressed against the bedroom door. Finally, she was rewarded by the sound of the front door clicking open. She poked her head back into the living room just in time to see Boulder closing the door behind him, her soiled clothing tucked under one arm. She heard a sharp click and knew that he had locked the door behind him, from outside. Well, she thought. One problem at a time.

Jane Ellen took a deep breath, pulled the unfamiliar silky outfit tight around her, and swept into the living room. Quiet welcomed her with an audible appreciative gasp.

"My, what a pretty day!" she exclaimed with her very best dumb-blonde smile. She strode past Quiet and stood before the large picture window. She raised her arms toward the golden sunlight, knowing from a thousand fashion magazine photo layouts that it would silhouette her figure almost naked against the sheer nightie. She heard Quiet's intake of breath behind her and smiled grimly.

Jane Ellen twirled around and favored Quiet with her most coquettish smile. "Can we go outside for just a minute, can we, please?" Without waiting for an answer she spun back around, threw the sliding glass door open and stepped out onto the balcony.

It wasn't what she had hoped. They were way up, seven or eight stories at least, much too far for a leap to safety. There was a magnificent view of Biscayne Bay stretching out sapphire blue before her, and a bright clean swimming pool in the courtyard far below. The courtyard was crowded with people, sunning, sipping drinks, oblivious to her plight, too far away to hear her scream.

Jane Ellen leaned on the balcony railing in despair, her escape plan shot to hell. It was just too much—the weeks of hiding, her brutal abduction, the hours of silent terror lying in the hotel bed, this degrading charade in this ridiculous outfit. She felt her frustration turning to anger, felt herself getting royally pissed off despite all her years of rolling with the punches and keeping her emotions under control. Jane Ellen didn't know whether to curse or cry, so she slapped at the balcony angrily, making the metal ring dully and sending a burst of pain stinging through her hand.

And then, slowly, a smile crept across her face. The railing, she realized, was new and steel and strong, but it was really no higher than the rotting wooden railing around the old O&P.

"Quiet dear," Jane Ellen said, with her eyes still on the courtyard far below, "could you come out here a moment please?" Then she turned, gave him a radiant smile, and opened her welcoming arms.

11

Boulder Baker did not want a soda water, extra ice, with lime. He did not want to be sitting in the lobby of the Biscayne Marriott, drumming his fingers on the stiff plastic chair, holding Jane Ellen Ashley's bloody and smelly clothes. What he wanted, wanted with the sort of distant wistfulness usually reserved for weeks in the country or a quiet night with a good book, was a scotch, straight up, his worn canvas sneakers, and his garden. Especially his garden.

Boulder missed the thick black soil of his Michigan home, where corn and beans and flamboyant sunflowers burst from the cool ground as if they knew their days in the sun were numbered. He missed rain that came in honest infrequent thunderstorms, instead of the every-afternoon-at-four twenty-minute showers that Miamians hardly noticed. He missed cornworms and root rot, weevils and weeds, and seasons. Boulder had been in the land of eternal summer for almost six weeks. Up north, the earliest touch of spring would be in the air;

he ached to breathe it deep into his salt-air–saturated lungs.

More and more, it seemed to Boulder that everything in Miami was watered down. The soil was thin and scratchy, more sand than dirt. The air was so moist that he was always coated with a thin layer of water, either from the humidity or his own sweat, and he was constantly wiping a thin sheen of moisture off his bald pate. Even the people here were watered down, gaudy and bright, certainly, but under it all as thin and inconsistent as azalea petals.

Boulder sighed and sipped his watered-down soda. It was just too easy here, he thought. Easy money, easy women, easy living. Easy weather—you didn't even have to put on shoes, or hardly even dress, if you didn't want to. Easy living made easy people, soft, shallow, empty people—and it was happening to him. Boulder resisted it every way he could—he kept his regular workouts in the gym and the shooting gallery, he stayed away from the cocaine and the smoke, he avoided the beach and the hookers and the nightclubs. He forced himself to dress immaculately in suit and tie and vest and shoes every day, knowing that in routine there was strength, knowing, like the British World War II prisoners of war who continued inspections even when their uniforms were rotting off their bodies, that precision was the only way to hold back the tide of inertia. Boulder expected weakness in others but could not abide it in himself, and so he fought every way he could, every waking moment, against the ease and sloth around him.

But it wasn't working. Here in Miami, the sun and the salt and the water worked on people like rust on a knife blade. Despite his efforts, despite his legendary willpower and iron self-control, Boulder Baker knew he was losing his edge.

And he was tired, tired as he could ever remember being. Not physically tired; Boulder was approaching fifty but knew he could still out-lift, out-last, out-drink and out-fight 95 percent of the gym-rats half his age. But mentally . . .

Not Alzheimer's, or ADA, or any such pop-psychology pap. His memory was fine; his faculties were sharp as ever. He was reading Melville again, one hundred pages before bed every night, and had found that he still knew Ahab's soliloquy just before sighting the white whale almost word for word: "What is it, what nameless, inscrutable, unearthly thing is it; what cozening, hidden lord and master, and cruel, remorseless emperor commands me; that against all natural lovings and longings, I so keep pushing, and crowding, and jamming myself on all the time; recklessly making me ready to do what in my own proper natural heart, I durst not so much as dare?" Beautiful, my poor doomed captain, beautiful.

But when it came to his work, Boulder found it increasingly difficult to concentrate. His ridiculously loquacious charge Quiones could bore the balls off a brass monkey, of course, so it was no wonder that Boulder's mind wandered a bit now and then. Wandered, most times, back to the Indiana farm of his childhood, back to hot sweet summers working side-by-side with his father in the endless rows of jade-green young corn, fighting a continual battle against borer worms, against brain fungus and black mold and too little rain or too much rain or no rain at all, but always coming to the end of a row, to the end of a season, he and his father, with fresh golden ears of midwestern corn held high and another year safely behind them. His hands and feet back then were dirty, always caked with fresh wet earth or dried gray dust, but looking back at it now, Boulder was sure that he had never felt quite so clean.

But Boulder had been bored before, been nostalgic before. None of that was an excuse for sloppiness, something Boulder had never allowed himself in a lifetime of assignments. Sloppiness was something a bodyguard could not accept, something an assassin could not afford.

Boulder sighed and raised the soda water to his mouth, throwing his head back to let the ice clink against his teeth. Perhaps, he thought, perhaps it was because of the inescapable uncleanliness of his current assignment. Always before he had gotten in, done his job and gotten out, quick and clean. He'd never before gotten to know a potential target, rarely had more than the briefest of contacts with his employer. But this time he was immersed in it, right up to his unsmiling eyes. Quiones more and more treated him like an old friend, like a trusted comrade, and Carlos called him in for cognac and conversation several times a week. Being with Quiet brought Boulder into regular contact with Joaquin and Rey and the rest of Carlos's crew and clients, not to mention losers like the Weasel and the odd young woman Quiet had up in his room right now. It all left Boulder feeling slightly unclean, as if he were wearing a thin coating of sleaze as omnipresent and unavoidable as the Miami humidity.

Boulder pulled a thick linen handkerchief from a vest pocket and dabbed the sweat off his bony skull. Sweat, even in an air-conditioned hotel lobby. He needed to get out, to get away from this place and these people. He wouldn't break a contract, wouldn't go back on his word, but after the fiasco with Quiet and the girl, perhaps Carlos would want to dismiss him. Carlos was on his way here now, angry enough to come take personal control over a situation Boulder should never have let get so out of hand. Angry enough, perhaps, to send Boulder packing. He had never been fired before; it would hurt his reputation, but he was thinking more and more of retiring anyway. Money would be tight, but he had a little socked away, a few investments here and there, and the farm. . . .

Boulder was feeling better about himself, quietly wondering if he could still get in a late crop of summer squash, when he noticed the commotion around the swimming pool outside. Some faux-sophisticated European woman had taken her top off, or a child fell in the deep end, he thought, but he knew without knowing how that it was more than that. Keeping one eye on the elevators, he half-turned toward the pool and the growing crowd milling around it. The glass windows of the lobby kept him from hearing what they had to say, but there was no way he could ignore the geography of the situation.

The swimming pool, Boulder realized with a sudden sinking feeling, was directly beneath the balcony of the Marriott's tenth-floor penthouse.

Boulder charged across the lobby like an angry bear. He stormed outside and shouldered his way through the excited crowd around the pool, his trim dark blue suit a sharp contrast to the bathing suits and bare skin around him. He finally pushed his way to the pool's edge and saw, sure enough, two burly college kids pulling a soaking wet Quiet Quiones out of the deep end.

At first glance Boulder thought Quiones was dead. Then the little accountant rolled his head from one side to the other, coughed, and spit out a mouthful of red-tainted water. Quiones's mouth was bloody and it looked like he might have lost a few teeth, but he was alive—and Boulder wasn't sure how he felt about that. He did know, however, what needed to be done next.

Boulder turned away from the pool, nodded curtly to the people staring at him, and walked back into the lobby. He got in the elevator, punched the button for the penthouse, and reflexively ran one hand over the familiar weight of the .38 tucked inside his belt.

Enough was enough.

Jane Ellen Ashley was pissed off. Pissed off, in fact, like she had never been pissed off before. She was by nature and circumstance a very accepting person; when life gave her oysters, well, she made oyster stew. Hard times with Nate, hungry days and cold nights, pitying looks from tourists and neighbors alike, she had always managed to shrug it off and retreat into the comfort of her daydreams. Life went on.

But somewhere in the last few weeks, it seemed to Jane Ellen, the world had gone too damn far. Maybe it was that night at the Oyster & Pool, when someone else's practical joke had turned her into a frightened fugitive. Maybe it was, though she hated to even consider it, being so long separated from the gentle waves and funky stench of her bayside home. Maybe it was just living in her ratty little South Miami room, serving coffee and eggs with Tabasco sauce to all these loud-talking, ill-tempered strangers. Certainly being assaulted on the doorstep of her apartment, bludgeoned into unconsciousness, carried off in the night and forced into this ridiculous little outfit had done little for her outlook on life.

At any rate—Jane Ellen was pissed off. So pissed off that she dumped crazy Quiet over the balcony railing even though she was not 100 percent sure he would in fact hit the swimming pool glittering so far below. And if she paused just a moment after turning from the balcony, if she held her breath and strained her ears a bit until she heard the reassuring splash of displaced water from far below, well, that was no indication that in her moment of resolve she was still weakened by the familiar tug of compassion. Force of habit, nothing more.

And right now, Jane Ellen knew, she had more important things to do than worry about Quiet's health.

She had no idea where Quiet's intimidating companion was, or for that matter if there were a dozen other of the Senator's men right outside the door, all itching to exact bloody vengeance for the careless drowning of their employer's son. For that matter, everyone in this hotel might be on the Senator's payroll, employees and guests alike. From the stories she had heard all her life, owning a hotel full of henchmen would not be beyond the Senator's reach.

Jane Ellen forced herself to take a deep breath and calm down. First things first, she thought, and the first thing was her clothing. The lipstick-red nightie Quiet had provided her with barely covered and certainly did not conceal her private parts. Near-nudity wasn't exactly uncommon in Miami, but if Jane Ellen did manage to make it out of the hotel alive, she did not want to be attracting the attention of every street-corner gawker. Besides, she felt ridiculous.

But big bald Boulder had her clothes, and the other items Quiet had purchased were no better than what she had on. The only other clothing in the room was the absurd full-length black leather coat Quiet had been wearing when he kidnapped Jane Ellen; she scooped it up and slipped it on. Something banged against her thigh; she reached into a deep pocket and pulled out a heavy .38 pistol. She spun the cylinder one quick time and then thrust it back into the pocket. The gun was not loaded.

Next, the door. Jane Ellen grabbed the handle, planning to rip it open and dash down the hallway before anyone who might be standing guard outside could react.

She ripped at the handle like a terrier at a rat's nest, twisted it, yanked it, pounded and pleaded, with no effect. Finally she let out a frustrated sob, closed her eyes and, with one hand still wrapped tightly around the heavy brass doorknob, let her forehead droop wearily against the door.

Suddenly she missed the familiar beaches of St. George Island, the heavy smell of fried mullet and the click of pool balls on the warped tables of the O&P. She missed the sad gray pelicans, she missed Billy, she even missed all those damned oysters. Trapped here in this fancy hotel room, surrounded by the luxury she had hungered for all her life, Jane Ellen wanted nothing more in all the wide world than to just go home.

While Jane Ellen was thinking all this, while she dreamed of Eastpoint and fought back the tears, a small miracle was taking place. Her hand, the hand that had coaxed open a million reluctant bivalves, the hand that held secrets unknown to safecrackers and surgeons, the hand that could outshuck any hand in a dozen generations of Apalachicola oystermen, was still on the knob of that locked door. And that hand was not at rest. While Jane Ellen dreamed on, overcome by frustration and fatigue, that restless hand took on a life of its own and did what it knew best. Fingers that could find the single weak spot on a hoary oyster shell without the aid of eyes or intelligence worked their magic on that brass door handle, poking here, prodding there, applying pressure this way or that. Like a relentless starfish straining at the sealed shell of a captured clam, Jane Ellen's hand worked steadily away, searching for the one weak spot on that impervious lock.

Sought, searched and found. There was a slight click, the door popped open, and the surprised Jane Ellen tumbled out into the hallway.

The corridor was just as alien to Jane Ellen as the room had been—red velvet wallpaper, brass and crystal light fixtures, white carpet as thick and soft as springtime deer moss. There were two elevators catty-cornered across from her room door; the indicator above them, she noted, showed one elevator was already on the way up. To her left, almost at the end of the hall, a bright red exit sign glowed above a doorway she figured had to be a stairway. She bolted toward it.

She passed a third, smaller elevator just before the stairs, marked "Employees," and slapped the call button without thinking. She hit the stairway at a full run, jammed the "open" bar with both hands and slammed hard into the unyielding door.

Jane Ellen frowned, shoved the bar down and put her weight into the cool metal door. It opened about three inches, far enough for her to see clearly the chain looped around the door handle on the other side. The chain was bolted tight by something out of her sight. Boulder, she thought. No exit here.

She took a single step back toward her room, then stopped, frozen by the *ping!* of an arriving elevator. She heard the door *shoosh* open, and Boulder stepped into the hallway. He glanced once at the door to their room—stupidly, Jane Ellen realized now, she had left it open. Then he turned his gaze down the hallway and spotted her. He looked her up and down, clinically, without appreciation, and a cold smile crossed his face.

"Nice outfit," he said.

Jane Ellen glanced down at Quiet's black coat, dangling half-open almost to her ankles. Bits of the scarlet nightie showed through where the coat gaped open, like bright blood beneath black skin. She shuddered and pulled the coat closed around her.

Boulder was putting on gloves, dark, soft-looking, like calves-hide leather. Part of her distractedly wondered why. Then he slipped a hand into each jacket pocket, pulled them out again, and she stopped wondering.

Jane Ellen had never seen a silencer before, but she had read enough spy novels to figure out what it was—especially since the giant was screwing it carefully, almost delicately, onto the end of the largest goddamned pistol she had ever seen. He was moving gently, almost lovingly. His preparations had a fascinating grace to them, like a rattlesnake coiling up for the strike. Jane Ellen knew she was going to die.

And then the freight elevator beside her pinged open.

Boulder's eyes moved, nothing else, shooting up to catch her in their milk-white glare. For a moment they both stood there, frozen, hunter and prey, charming snake and hypnotized sparrow. Then he swung his right arm upward, and Jane Ellen dove sideways into the elevator.

She heard a sharp *whiff!* of air behind her, as if someone had been slugged in the stomach and exhaled suddenly, and something jerked hard at her coat. She fell hard to the floor of the elevator, bounced up, and slapped frantically at the row of buttons beside the door. She heard heavy footsteps thudding down the hallway and wondered if she were going to die after all.

The door finally, agonizingly, began to close, just as the giant got there. Jane Ellen got a quick look at him, face expressionless but eyes on fire, and the door eased closed. Jane Ellen let out the breath she hadn't realized she was holding—and then gasped again. The door wasn't quite closed, and there, just about head high, four cigar-thick fingers protruded through the black plastic seal on the double-doors. She saw the fingers whiten with effort, and knew the giant was going to force the doorway open.

Jane Ellen threw herself against the door and pounded those terrifying fingers with all her might—with no effect. The door opened a crack wider, and the fingers slipped all the way in, an entire angry hand intruding into her sanctuary. A second hand thrust into the opening, this one holding a gun, and the two began pushing the door apart. Jane Ellen looked around the elevator frantically, searching for something, anything, she could use as a weapon. Then she remembered the unloaded pistol in her pocket. She jerked it out, grabbed it by the barrel and swung the handle down, hard, on the giant's right wrist.

The hand winced but did not withdraw. She swung again, and again, aiming at the fingers clenched tightly around that night-black gun. The third time she thought she heard something crack. The hand jerked back, withdrew, and the door snapped shut.

Jane Ellen leaned hard against the door, sobbing for breath, the gun barrel clenched tightly in her right hand. She felt the elevator drop, slow, steadily, like an oak leaf in the forest. After a moment she realized her left leg was on fire; she looked down and saw she was standing in a puddle of blood.

Jane Ellen pulled the coat back as far as she could. Bending backwards, twisting hard at the waist, she could see a bright red gouge running three inches long and perhaps an inch wide just below her left butt cheek. The bullet had hit her just below the top of the skin, ripping a crimson rivulet through her thigh as if somebody had carefully run a fat round oyster knife through there. The damage, she figured, wasn't all that bad, but it hurt like hell and there was lots of blood.

She slipped the gun back into one coat pocket and searched through the others until she found one of Quiet's perfect silk handkerchiefs. She twisted it around into a tight rope, then tied it over the bloody wound as best as she could.

Jane Ellen leaned back against the rear wall of the elevator, putting her weight on her right leg, and watched the floors slowly click by on the overhead indicator. Her angry assailant, she knew, would be coming down on the regular elevator at that very moment, maybe traveling faster than her, might even be waiting for her, gun cocked and ready, when she reached the bottom floor.

Jane Ellen clutched her aching leg and wished she was back in Eastpoint. There wasn't much to do there, but then again there were precious few cold-blooded assassins living along the Apalachicola shoreline, no kidnap-crazy Cubans, no inescapable high-rises, no elevators to doom. No elevators, in fact, at all.

Then she closed her eyes, leaned her head back against the wall and let out a quick sharp laugh.

Whattaya know, she thought. My very first elevator ride.

12

If a rooster falls in the ocean and is too dead to notice, does he make a sound? You betcha.

When Happy Harry Harper tossed poor funky Campeón over the side of the *Miss Behavin'*, sending his own ass to the slippery deck and his mind off into deep reverie, he was not merely tossing a smelly corpse into a sterile trash dump. The Caribbean is alive beneath its calm surface, alive and jumping with activity, a salty stew of life, packed with fish and crustaceans and planktons, humble sandworms and wise old leatherbacks, common blue crabs and rare Ridley's turtles, sharks and snook and snails, living on the sand, under the sand, in the sand and in every different depth of the sapphire-dark water. Life from the microscopic to the magnificent, from sea slug to stoic shark. The Caribbean that seems so calm above the waves below them teems with millions of members of thousands of species, each of them frenetically alive, going about the business of life, each in its own way seeking companionship, procreation, love.

And, of course, lunch. If there is one thing all species share in common, it is the universal desire for a free meal. Whether it be a corporate kingpin suppressing a smile as his host pulls out an American Express or an Atlantic blue crab contentedly ripping strips from the week-dead corpse of a rotting mackerel, there is something about feeding at someone else's expense that makes even the most fetid food taste like filet mignon.

For Happy Harry Harper, sprawled there on the hard cold deck of the *Miss Behavin'*, nursing his bruised bottom and picking at his psychic scabs, that rotten rooster vanished from consideration as soon as it sank beneath the waves; sooner, in fact, for when Harry hit the deck he was below the level of the boat's gunwales and out of sight of the sea's surface. In Harry's world, the rooster was already insignificant history, yesterday's news, a Tarzan-movie spear carrier who, having appeared on-stage just long enough to take a bullet from bwana's rifle, expires and is forgotten. Incident over, case closed.

But in the world on the other side of those gunwales, down beneath those waves, Harry's rooster was quite the topic of interest. Ninety feet below the *Miss Behavin'*'s fiberglass bottom, a barrel-backed, ham-fisted stone crab recognized something un-lifelike in the vibrations of Campeón's splash and scuttled over into position, eyes waving giddily on the end of their extended stalks, waiting eagerly for whatever delicious detritus might be winding its way down to his sandy dinner table. Nearer the surface, a jittery school of pinfish minnows whipped five feet to the left, a single silvery entity reacting as one to whatever new threat was coming its way this time, each inch-long individual member relying on the time-tested tactic of species preservation through outrageous overproduction—that is, they hid in the crowd and hoped it was the other guy who got eaten. And a quarter-mile away, cruising casually through the mid-level waters of his marine kingdom, a sleek and arrogant dolphin noted the *ploosh* of poor Campeón's final exit from the world of air and sunshine. Driven, as always, by the unceasing demands of his rapid metabolism and constantly complaining stomach, the dolphin turned to check it out.

Consider the dolphin. Not the mammal, the air-breather, the beloved and smiling star of Greek vases and Hollywood fantasies; no, the other dolphin. The dolphin the fish. The dolphin of the half-moon tail, of the canary-yellow skin, of the deliciously flaky white flesh. The dolphin who by sharing a name with one of nature's most cuddly performers has inspired a nation of frustrated restaurant owners tired of trying to convince bawling children that they have not been served Flipper-on-a-platter to begin a massive re-naming campaign, trying to teach the eager appetites but balking brains of America's eaters that they have in fact been served the exotic-sounding and most un-cuddly Hawaiian delicacy, mahi-mahi. *That* dolphin.

Consider the dolphin. Out of water, flailing helplessly around the bottom of a charter boat or hung dead and undignified at the dock, he is an ungainly, in fact, an ugly creature indeed. The body of an algebraically extended triangle. A giant, black, blunted forehead right out of an *Aliens* movie. An eerily human face, pinched and tucked low on a huge head large enough for three such faces. On a human head, those dull eyes, pinpricks-nose and fat lips would signal mongoloidism, and force other, more complete people to turn away with the ill-concealed disgust compassionately reserved for cripples and multiple Super Bowl losers. Ugly as sin, ugly as cancer, ugly as the guy your girlfriend used to date.

Ah, but in the water. In the water the dolphin is a tiger and a terror. That bullet-shaped body and a tail thick as a marathoner's calves give dolphins the maneuverability and power to be superb hunters, difficult targets for other carnivores and magnificent fighting game fish. In the water the dolphin is a flash of gold with tiger's teeth, a voracious, omnivorous swimming appetite. Its tenacity and strength, along with its coloration and willingness to attack and consume damn near anything, have earned the dolphin yet another nickname. To the sailors and sportsmen who know and respect him, the dolphin is also known as the Golden Goat.

This particular goat, this multi-named, bullet-shaped battlefish, responded to the sound of Campeón's splash-down with the arrogance of a barracuda. He knew the sound of crippled prey—there was no mistaking the absence of sound after that splash, the lack of vibration that told of an able-bodied fish still able to duck and dodge. He knew that sound would quickly attract other carnivores—scavengers and hunters alike—some of whom might be large enough to trouble even the mighty mahi-mahi. And so he rocketed toward his prey with all the speed he could muster, zeroing in on the distant sound with time-honed accuracy. He shot through the aqua depths like an Olympic sprinter, darting unseen beneath the bow of the *Miss Behavin'* and the lost-in-thought Harry Harper. The dolphin burst onto the scene like a comic-book superhero, scattering a trio of opportunistic squirrel fish gathered around Campeón's corpse, and slammed into the rooster like a ravenous cannon ball.

The dolphin sank his teeth deeply in Campeón's feathery side, carrying the rancid rooster with him deeper into the water and away from the *Miss Behavin'*. He meant to get his meal quickly away from the echoes of its fall before any competing predators moved in to challenge him for the precious piece of flesh. The dolphin raced on for fully a minute, aware now that there was no life, no struggle left in his prize. Finally the dolphin slowed and prepared to make the savage sideways rip of his head that would tear a convenient bite-size strip of flesh from his prey. He would do that again and again, as he had a thousand times before, slashing at Campeón's corpse until the sound of his own feeding caught the attention of a shark, a marlin or some other larger predator and sent the dolphin back on his never-ending search for supper. It was a ritual the dolphin knew well, as deeply ingrained in his life as an advertising executive's three-martini lunch. It was what he did; it was what he was.

What, then, led this particular Golden Goat to slowly, almost gently, release his prize and back off, watching, unblinking, as Campeón drifted downward toward the ocean floor? Did he realize, somewhere down in the murky depths of his ichthyoan brain, that what he really wanted was a light lunch of squirrel fish? Was he confused by Campeón's unfamiliar feathers, or disgusted by his putrefying flesh? Or had he perhaps sensed, sometime between locking in that death grip and his uncharacteristic release, that this funky flotsam, this rotting rooster, was also a warrior, a fellow predator and champion, deserving of, if not mercy, at least respect?

For whatever reasons of his own, the dolphin did release Campeón, and then remained where he was, hovering like a watchful father, as Campeón completed his journey downward. The dolphin's presence kept away the lesser predators that normally would have moved in on the descending corpse. The dolphin and the rooster were well away from any sheltering rocks, reefs or wrecks now; with no place to hide and nothing to eat, this section of the sandy ocean floor was as barren as any dry desert. There were no crabs waiting to welcome Campeón when he finally settled into the sand, no fingerlings to pluck out his blind eye. There was only the eternal sand and the gentle current, already combining to cover Campeón just a bit, a few grains here, a few more there. There would be no desecration of Campeón's corpse, just a slow, gentle burial far from the dry world of sun and earth.

And where was Campeón during all this? Was there any spark of his true essence left in that battered body to silently witness his own interment? Or was he perhaps residing in the Hindu Well of Souls, patiently waiting for the day he would be reincarnated as a different, higher predator—as a dolphin, perhaps, or a tiger, or a welterweight prizefighter? Or had he instead ascended to a roostery heaven, to stomp proudly through a celestial barnyard crowded with fat juicy grubs and plump compliant hens, happily crowing his challenge to a morning sun that never, ever stopped rising?

The sole mourner at Campeón's burial, the mahimahi, did not concern himself overmuch with such thoughts. Nor did he dwell long on his own uncharacteristic actions regarding this corpse. His thoughts turned instead to his continually complaining stomach, and to the squirrel fish he had seen earlier. They had been drawn out from whatever cover they called home by the sound of Campeón's splashy entry, by the noisy promise of an easy meal. If the squirrel fish had lingered in their disappointment, if the dolphin could get back to them before they returned to their protective nook among the undersea rocks . . .

He could and did, slashing into the fattest and slowest of the squirrels just before she reached the safety of an undersea rockbed, ripping her mottled skin from her bony carcass even before she had stopped her frantic piggish grunting. Squirrel fish, the dolphin knew, were usually not much of a meal, cartilaginous and small. But there was a bonus here. This fish was pregnant, and the dolphin fed on her bloated eggs and unborn children as consciencelessly as he did on her own flesh.

Close, the saying goes, only counts with horseshoes and hand-grenades. But here, in the tightly knit, intricately interdependent world of Mother Nature, close can be catastrophe.

Had that pregnant squirrel fish made it into the rocks in time to frustrate the darting dolphin, she may well have stayed there long enough to give birth to the several hundred children she carried in her belly. She would have eaten a few of them herself, of course, and the squirrels she traveled with would have eaten many more. But some of those young fish would have survived, to grow and breed and make more squirrel fish, all of whom would have been naturally accustomed to the relative safety of that small rock pile. Their activity would have drawn other life to that undersea oasis. Algae would have taken root on those rocks, fertilized by the squirrel fish's excrement. Then snails and pinfish would come to feed on the algae, and crabs to feed on the slugs and scoop the bottom clean of the squirrel fish detritus. Snapper and trigger fish would come to eat the crabs, dancing in to tear off powerful claws and then feed at their leisure on the scuttling, defenseless crippled crustaceans. Wandering amberjack and contemplative grouper, come to suck unlucky pinfish into the sudden vacuum created when they popped open their massive jaws. The major predators, sharks and barracuda and, yes, more dolphin, all drawn to the growing community of undersea edibles clenching tightly to life around the undersea rocks.

But it didn't happen. Without the pregnant squirrel fish to act as catalyst, without the smallest life to beget larger life, the rocks remained just barren rocks. Without the steady whir of a thousand fins in constant motion around them, with no eels, octopus and crabs to tunnel out careful homes in the sand at the rock's base, with no giant jewfish and gag grouper hollowing out huge egg-nests in the sand, with nothing at all to hold it back, the ocean floor would slowly, steadily bury those rocks, putting an end to one of the few safe spots for traveling fish in this chunk of the Caribbean. The solemn seafloor, already barren as a desert, would become that much more desolate. Life would go on—but not here.

For want of a squirrel fish, the kingdom was lost. All because Harry Harper picked that ill-chosen moment to toss Campeón overboard, all because a wandering dolphin found himself unable to tear into the inviting flesh of this alien and fallen warrior. All because even here, far from the busy buy-and-sell, seduce-and-abandon, divide-and-conquer world of the restless human race, actions have repercussions.

Miles away now, speeding steadily north on the deck of the full-under-sail *Miss Behavin'*, oblivious to the ecological catastrophe he had set in motion, Happy Harry Harper was considering his own recent actions—and waiting, with more than a little concern, for their repercussions.

13

The quiet thump of the elevator coming to a stop startled Jane Ellen, and she wondered if she had, just for a moment, passed out. The elevator doors pinged softly and, with no idea what to expect and no other options, Jane Ellen put her back up against the far wall, extended the heavy pistol before her and aimed straight at the opening door in what she hoped was an effectively menacing stance.

It was. Patsy Middleton, a fifty-five-year-old semi-retired beautician from Sioux Falls who was enjoying the best darn vacation of her entire life right until the moment that elevator door opened, got one look at the bloody, half-naked gun-pointing specter in the elevator, screamed, dropped her Tropical-Hurricane-light-on-the-rum-and-extra-lime-please-drink, and fainted dead away. Jane Ellen blinked in surprise and slowly lowered the gun.

True Miamians would have looked at that scene—one woman down and another dripping blood—and resignedly headed for the nearest exit (there was, in fact, a notable absence of hotel employees in the lobby within moments of Patsy's collapse). Most of the people in that lobby, however, were not Miamians, and had not yet had ingrained in them the South Florida survival instinct that screams mean guns, and guns mean danger, especially for innocent bystanders.

The people in the lobby were by and large tourists, and by and large more inclined to gravitate toward a woman in obvious need than to run away from her. That is what people do in Sioux Falls, Iowa, in Pastatuket, New Jersey, in Greenville, Mississippi, and in the thousands of other hamlets and habitats that annually send millions of glassy-eyed, paunchy-stomached, obsessively hopeful people either too young for children or too old to care skittering south to the fading, sun-splashed glory of South Florida. Those are the people who came to poor Patsy Middleton's rescue, and those are the people Jane Ellen saw as she gazed out of the elevator in uncertain consideration of just what to do next.

Clearly, Jane Ellen realized, this was not a hotel full of mobsters and thugs in the employ of the Senator or in league with the little Cuban and his trigger-happy aide. This collection of blue hair and white bellies, of polyester suspenders and yesterday's sunburn, was curious and concerned and closely watching her, but they were not a threat. She eased a sigh of relief, slipped the pistol back into a sweaty leather pocket and took one unsteady step toward the exit.

Then three things happened at once, or at least in rapid succession. Jane Ellen heard a startled protest from the back of the crowd surrounding the fat lady on the ground, the granite visage of Boulder Baker appeared over the shoulders of two gawking Boise boys wearing Disney World T-shirts, and Jane Ellen jumped to frantically slap at the first elevator button she could reach. Boulder surged forward and stumbled over the sprawling body of the fallen fat lady; Jane Ellen heard the heavy thud of his weight slamming into the elevator just as the doors swished shut.

Jane Ellen felt the elevator drop downwards and glanced at the lit-up control panel. "P." All right then. She wasn't exactly sure what "P" stood for, but anywhere away from Boulder seemed like a good idea at the moment. She inched toward the door and resolved to take off running as soon as it opened, regardless of who or what might be in her way.

The elevator came to a halt sooner than Jane Ellen had hoped. The door slipped open and she rushed out into a large, dimly lit room, wincing at the pain in her leg. There was no one there to meet her, no one there at all. She stopped to get her bearings, letting her eyes grow accustomed to the dim light. She was in an underground garage, packed with Cadillacs, Oldsmobiles and Buicks sporting license tags from all over the country. "P" for parking then, of course.

There were two heavy metal doors about twenty yards away, illuminated by the promising red glow of an overhead exit sign. Jane Ellen hop-skipped over to the doors, making the best time she could on her gimpy leg. One door was marked with a large red "D," the other a "B." "D" for deck, she hoped, and pushed her way through the door. She heard the ping of an arriving elevator behind her as she did so, and forced herself to climb the stairs she found waiting for her as quickly as she could.

At the top was another door, this one stenciled "members only" in heavy black paint. Jane Ellen heard the sound of heavy footsteps slapping across the garage behind her, resigned herself to whatever the millionaires no doubt basking on the deck beyond would think when she came busting in, and pushed through the door.

She stopped, blinking in the late afternoon sunlight, and wondered just what deity she had managed to offend lately. "D," it seemed, was for dock. Big, long, private dock, dotted with a dozen or so cigarette boats and small sailboats that no doubt cost more than the combined annual income of any ten Eastpoint residents. A private luxury dock thrusting out into Biscayne Bay, reserved for the rich; so private, in fact, that it was surrounded on both sides by a ten-foot-high hurricane fence, designed to keep beachwalkers from jumping up onto the rich folks' dock.

Unfortunately, it also worked in reverse. There was no way Jane Ellen could jump off the dock and, judging from the footsteps pounding up the stairs behind her, no way she could turn back.

Forward, then. The dock was about ten feet wide and looked to be about forty or fifty yards long; the fence ran about half that length. If she could get past the fence before Boulder caught her, she could jump into the water and hide under the dock. The phrase "shooting fish in a barrel" came unwanted into her mind; she shrugged it off and began lurching down the dock. No Boulder yet; maybe she would have time to try hiding on one of the boats moored out before her. And maybe, she thought with a sudden tingle of hope, maybe there's still time for the cavalry to arrive. . . .

There was a boat coming into the dock, a thirty-foot Morgan with her sails folded, cruising in on diesel. As she lurched down the dock, Jane Ellen saw for the first time that there were two men watching that sailboat arrive, one even larger than the behemoth on her tail, the other a greasy little man who looked almost dwarfish beside his huge companion. Maybe they would help her; if nothing else, Boulder might be less likely to shoot in the presence of witnesses. And if they were associates of Boulder's—that seemed likely, given that they were dressed more like pimps than sailors—well, she was no worse off. Jane Ellen pushed herself onward, trying to ignore the growing pain in her hip.

The two men were concentrating on guiding the incoming boat, and hadn't noticed her yet. Jane Ellen raised her arm and started to cry out, allowing herself to believe, for the first time since waking up bound and gagged in that beautiful hotel room, that she might live through the day.

Then she heard the door slamming open behind her.

Big Al was not having a good week. The *Miss Behavin'* was a full three days overdue, his stomach was still acting up, and spending hours each day waiting on the hotel dock had given him the worst case of sunburn he had ever had. Worrying about what the boss would do to him and Tiny if he ever found out they had entrusted his cargo to a stranger, much less what he would do if that stranger took the boat to Rio or some such shit, was giving him a migraine, and the damn salty smell of the bay was bringing up disturbing memories of his recent hellish bout of seasickness. The whole damn city smelled like the ocean, in fact, even in the cheap room they had rented far from the waterfront Al was certain he could hear the slap of the waves and feel the constant roll of that goddamned boat. The whole damn thing was stressing him out so much he was starting to lose his hair. Not that he had that damn much left to lose in the first place.

And Tiny was driving him nuts. The big man had been deliriously happy ever since they got back to the States. He'd invested a small fortune in spices, vegetables and eggs—eggs!—and spent every moment cooking omelets, rushing into the living room of the two-room kitchenette every fifteen minutes with a bite of some new variation for Al to sample. Once Al had forbidden him to do any more cooking—he was feeding the leftovers to stray cats, for God's sake; Al couldn't go out for a paper without stepping in cat shit—the big idiot took to happily scribbling away in a new recipe book, interrupting Al's game shows every few minutes wanting to know how to spell this or that. Even if Al had been able to spell worth a damn, it was downright irritating. Al was going through two bottles of Pepto a day, and still spent half his time feeling like a knocked-up newlywed with morning sickness.

Now, though, things were looking up. The *Miss Behavin'* was here at last, and looked none the worse for the trip. The guy at the wheel, that Harry guy, was waving and grinning and, judging from the way he was slipping the big boat right in toward the dock, he really did know what he was doing. Al forgot about his stomach for just a moment and allowed himself a smile.

Al turned toward Tiny to make some encouraging comment on their good fortune. To his surprise, the big guy wasn't watching the incoming boat at all; he was turned back toward the shore and the hotel with a look that was half confusion and half delight.

Al turned to see what Tiny was looking at, and felt his stomach twist.

There was a woman running down the dock toward them, a heavy black leather coat flapping around her like the wings of a giant bat. She was wearing something tiny and transparent underneath, and one of her legs was slick with blood. The woman was waving.

Okay, it was Miami, and Al had seen stranger things. He had seen worse things too—and one of them was the sight of the big bald man standing twenty feet behind the fast-approaching woman. That man had both his hands extended, and one of them was holding a very, very large gun.

Al hit the dock about the time he heard the first shot. The girl did, too; he wasn't sure if she was shot or had just dropped when he did. He rolled to his left, raking jagged splinters through his brand-new slacks, $14.99 on sale at

Big K, and came to a halt behind a tree-trunk thick piling at the dock's edge. Al rose to a half-squat, pulled his own seldom-used .38 out of its shoulder holster, and took a deep breath.

Then Tiny started shooting. The great ox was walking straight down the middle of the dock, both pistols out and blazing away like a gunslinger in a bad Western. *What the fuck, Tiny,* Al thought, and then had just the smallest twinge of guilt. Tiny, he knew, was walking straight into a hail of bullets without a second thought because he wanted to protect Al. The dumb shit.

The strange gunman had ducked behind a piling of his own, all but eliminating any chance that Tiny, who couldn't hit the sky with six shots and a road map, could actually do him any harm. Okay, fine. Tiny couldn't hurt the guy, but for the moment, the guy was pinned down. Trouble was, Al knew that Tiny was going to run out of bullets any second now, and he figured the hidden gunman must know it too.

He's after the boat, Al thought. He's got to be.

That thought made Al swing around and take a look at the incoming *Miss Behavin'*—and he was not happy with what he saw. The guy at the wheel, that Harper dude, was gazing open-mouthed at the commotion on the dock, his delicate docking procedure completely forgotten. The *Miss Behavin'*, without a steady hand on the wheel, was charging right toward the dock at collision speed.

Al flashed on a brief image of what the boss would do if the *Miss Behavin'* and her cargo were to go under fifty feet off the Miami shore. He let out an injured yelp, and then, trusting to the tall piling and the more tempting target of Tiny to keep the gunman off his back, stood up and began waving his arms.

It worked. Harper snapped out of his trance, glanced at Al and then at the dock itself, and reached down to throw the lumbering diesel engine into full reverse. The *Miss Behavin'* shuddered, cut sharply to the right, and dropped her speed in half.

Even that, Al could see, was not going to be enough to prevent a shattering collision with the damn dock. He shot his eyes heavenward and raced forward to ward off the decelerating sailboat with one out-thrust leg. The impact almost knocked him down, but he managed to prevent the boat from slamming into the dock, even managed to send it sluggishly turning back away toward open water.

That put him frighteningly close to the edge of the dock. For one terrifying instant, given the way his luck had been running lately, Al felt certain he was going to slip off and drop into the disgusting, chilling water five feet below. He danced backward, keeping low as he could out of respect for the momentarily quiet gunman, and turned toward the safety of his piling.

Then something hit him square in the center of his back, hard. Al lurched forward, toward the edge of the dock. He spun around and clawed desperately at the empty air, looking for something, anything, to keep him from falling over and into that damn ocean. He caught a fleeting glimpse of black leather and bare skin darting past and realized, in that fatal moment when he hung suspended between the dock and dark oblivion, that the crazy woman with the bloody leg had pushed him. And, prisoner to the twin forces of momentum and gravity, cursed by his own bad luck and doomed to his own worst nightmare, Big Al flipped over the edge and dropped into the dark salty waters of Biscayne Bay.

When she was eleven years old, a group of Jane Ellen's classmates led by the obnoxious Fatty Wingo had run across her while she was out reading in the woods not far from her house. They were delighted to find their odd classmate alone so far from adult intervention, and had started in teasing with the relentless cruelty only children are capable of. They called her bookworm and trailer-trash, egghead and freak, and when she tried to run away they chased her, pelting her with pine cones and monkey-pod fruit.

Jane Ellen had run straight for her dilapidated little shack in the forest, knowing that if there was anyone in the world she could count on to save her from her tormentors, it was Nate. She bounced through the woods like a frightened deer, slashing her bare feet and tender legs on blackberry thorns and fresh-fallen acorns, with Fatty and his gang in hot pursuit. Finally she burst into the clearing behind her house, panting in exhaustion, tears of fear and frustration streaming down her face.

Jane Ellen didn't have enough wind left to call out for Nate, and feared her pursuers might catch her right in her own backyard, within a few yards of safety. But then she saw Nate, napping beneath his favorite live oak, snoring gently with his head slumped forward on his chest. She sprinted up to him, gasping for breath, and roughly shook his shoulder.

Nate mumbled grumpily, shook his head and half-turned to his left. A fifth of Smirnoff, drained down to the final few drops, slipped out from under his arm and rolled to a stop right at Jane Ellen's tattered feet.

Nate was dead drunk.

Fatty and the boys came crashing out of the woods, howling like dogs on a deer's trail. Buoyed by the sight of their prey, they came sprinting across the yard with arms cocked and ready to throw. Then, almost as one, they registered the unexpected sight of an adult, and all but tumbled over one another in their sudden hurry to halt and retreat.

It was Fatty, whose own father had a seemingly endless thirst for Early Times and Pabst Blue Ribbon, who realized just what was going on. He stood up and stared, first at Nate, and then at Jane Ellen, and smiled viciously.

"He's *drunk*!" Fatty said. "He's stinking passed-out drunk at ten o'clock in the morning!"

The other boys took a moment to let this novel realization sink in, and then, as usual, turned to Fatty for guidance. Fatty Wingo, with a characteristic sneer distorting his pudgy little fifth-grade face, strode right up to Jane Ellen and poked a fat little finger right into her face.

"You're a *drunkard's* girl," he said.

So Jane Ellen picked up the empty Smirnoff's bottle and whacked him upside the head.

Holding that hard cold bottle that autumn morning, watching as the bleeding, howling Fatty Wingo and his frightened henchmen retreated through the woods, Jane Ellen Ashley realized three things. First, that with perhaps a very few freakish exceptions, people are just downright mean. Second, that sometimes whacking somebody upside the head is a good thing. Third, and most important, Jane Ellen finally fully understood that if she were going to make it through elementary school, much less through all of life, she was going to have to do it entirely on her own.

And so it was, that muggy Miami morning nearly a decade later, that when Jane Ellen found herself pinned between the murderous Boulder Baker and three strangers who might or might not be coming to her rescue, she instinctively put her faith in the only person she knew she could trust—herself. While the giant she knew and the giant she didn't occupied themselves with their gun battle, Jane Ellen took the sudden opportunity to dump the smaller stranger into the bay. Then she jumped into the back of the arriving sailboat and pointed her unloaded but still menacing pistol at the surprised pilot.

"Shove off," she said.

"What?" he said, and Jane Ellen wasn't exactly sure how to respond to that. Fortunately, at that instant the cabin window just to the right of the pilot exploded into a thousand eloquent pieces. Jane Ellen dropped to the deck, below the gunwale, and the inspired pilot frantically slammed the engines into reverse.

Jane Ellen heard three more quick shots and then,

except for the rumble of the straining engine, nothing. She raised herself up gingerly and peeked over the railing.

The man she had pushed into the water was clinging tightly to one barnacle-encrusted piling, sputtering and splashing far out of proportion with his circumstances. On the dock, the big stranger had dropped to his knees, empty pistols hanging forgotten at his side, staring blankly at a bright red spot blossoming on the middle of his crisp white shirt. And Boulder Baker was sprinting down the dock, his face unimpassioned, immaculate blue suit not so much as ruffled. When he saw her peeping over the gunwale he stopped and thrust his arms out in the policeman's shooting position. Jane Ellen noticed with grim satisfaction that he was shooting left-handed, and that the index finger on his mangled right hand was pointing off sideways at a most unnatural angle. She dropped back below the railing just as a chunk of the gunwale three inches to her right exploded into splinters and sawdust, and realized just how lucky she was that Boulder could not use his stronger hand.

The next two shots slapped into the cabin wall next to the wheel, and Jane Ellen realized Boulder was shooting not at her, but at the visible and vulnerable pilot. The pilot realized it too; he yelped and dropped to the deck. The driverless boat chugged backwards, taking Jane Ellen in a graceless, steady arc away from Boulder Baker.

"What the fuck is going on?" yelled the pilot; Jane Ellen ignored him and forced herself to stay down and be patient. She counted to sixty, then to sixty again, and then slowly inched her eyes up above the gunwale.

The dock was receding in the distance. Boulder Baker was standing at its very end, hands in his pockets, staring dispassionately out at her. The big stranger had collapsed face-first onto the dock behind Boulder; the smaller one had found a dockside ladder and was pulling himself out of the bay. Farther back, two black limousines had pulled up beside the hotel and dark men wearing suits and sunglasses were spilling out of them. They didn't look like police.

She crawled forward to where the pilot was lying face-down on the deck, hands folded defensively over his head, and poked him in the side with her foot.

"Okay," she said. "Stand up."

The man raised his head and glared at her angrily. He had deep brown eyes and a ragged, new-grown beard. He was sunburned-turning-to-tan, and the pale outlines of sunglasses around his eyes gave him an owlish look.

"Are you crazy?" he said. "That guy is shooting at us!"

"Not any more. We're out of range."

"Then why don't you stand up?"

"Maybe I just don't want to stand up."

"Well, I'm not standing up if you don't stand up."

"You have to stand up; you have to steer. We're going backwards and starting to circle, and if you don't steer we might go right back to the dock and he will shoot us."

"Right, that's another thing. Why's he shooting at you in the first place? And why the hell is he shooting at *me?*"

"Look, are you going to stand up or not?"

"Not until you do."

Jane Ellen grimaced in frustration, unsure just how far Boulder's pistol would carry. Then she remembered her own gun, clinched but momentarily forgotten in her right hand, and pointed it at the stubborn sailor.

"Up," she said. "Now."

The stranger frowned but did as he was told. Jane Ellen let him stand there for a minute and, when no bullets went whizzing by, slowly rose up beside him.

They were farther from the dock than she had thought, clearly out of gunshot range. Boulder had walked away from the end of the dock and was talking with an elderly, distinguished-looking Hispanic man. Two others were pulling the soaking wet white guy out of the water, a third was kneeling beside the fallen giant. Jane Ellen thought she heard the sound of a police siren in the distance. She swung back around to face her silently waiting prisoner.

"Okay," she said. "Let's go."

"Go? Go where?"

"Anywhere. Away from here. That way." She gestured in the general direction of the open sea, trying not to let her uncertainty show.

"I can't do that," the sailor said.

"Yes, you can. You have to. I have the gun."

"Look, I don't know about that guy who was shooting at us—shooting at you. But those other two, they own this boat, and they aren't good guys. If they think I'm stealing this boat, if I don't get it back to them, they'll kill me."

"Yeah, well, if we go back, that big guy will kill *me*. And I got the gun, so I get to decide. That's the rule."

"What rule?"

"The rule about guns! Don't you know nothing?"

"Anything."

"What?"

"Anything. It's 'don't you know *anything*?'"

"I know we're both gonna die if you don't get us out of here!"

"Okay, okay, how about this—I put you ashore downstream a ways, and you just call the police, and then I come back here."

"I can't call the police," Jane Ellen said, and something in the way the sailor looked away made her suspect he couldn't either. Funny. He didn't strike her as the kind of guy who spent a lot of time dodging the police. Or gangsters, for that matter.

"I've got a little skiff here," he said. "How about if I put you off in that, and then I can go back."

"Sure, and while I'm bobbing around in your little life raft they'll get another boat and come fetch me. Nope. Sorry, but we have to go."

The sailor frowned, looked back at the shore and then back at her. "And what if I refuse?" he said.

"Then I'll shoot you, dammit! God, you are a stubborn son of a bitch!"

The sailor stared at Jane Ellen, and then looked down at the pistol. Jane Ellen tried to keep her hand from shaking. Suddenly his face lit up in a broad grin.

"You can't shoot me," he said. "The safety's on!"

"What? It is not!"

"It is, too. That's a Colt .45, and the safety lever is

pointed down, and that means the safety is on, and you can't shoot me."

Jane Ellen didn't know if he was right or not; she did know the gun was empty and she wasn't especially sure she could shoot somebody anyway. But the sailor didn't know that. What mattered was that he *thought* she could shoot him. She raised her right hand to toggle the safety switch, and the sailor jumped toward her.

So she whacked him upside the head.

Later, as she worked with the unfamiliar steering wheel and guided the sailboat out toward the darkening open sea, Jane Ellen found herself thinking of that morning so long ago when Fatty and his boys had chased her through the Franklin County forest. All these years, she thought, and there were still people chasing her, trying to do her harm, for reasons she couldn't completely comprehend.

She had been right back then, Jane Ellen thought. People are just downright mean. As for the rest of it—well, given her current circumstances, she had to admit she wasn't doing all that good of a job of taking care of herself.

But she was getting pretty darn good at the whacking people in the head part.

14

Happy Harry Harper's head hurt.

It hurt bad. Throbbed, in fact. That was the first thing Harry noticed when he woke up. He also noticed that he was in bed, and, judging from the familiar rocking motion of the world around him, still on board the *Miss Behavin'*.

The next thing Harry realized was that he couldn't seem to move his hands to his head to massage the pain. In fact, he couldn't seem to move his hands at all.

Harry was sure that all this meant more trouble, and he was about fed up with trouble. He thought about trying to go back to sleep, to seek his refuge in the darkness, and hope that the world was less troubled when he came to again. But his head hurt too much for that, and besides, his nose was starting to itch. The world was demanding his attention and, like it or not, Happy Harry Harper was going to have to open his eyes.

Reluctantly, he did.

He was, as he had assumed, in the captain's cot in the

Miss Behavin's small sleeping cabin. It was full daylight; he had to blink his eyes to adjust to the bright glare. When he opened them again, he saw that the crazy woman who had jumped on board and shanghaied him, the woman who had slugged him with the butt of her gun, had pulled the ship's lone chair into the room and was sitting in it backwards so that her legs straddled the backrest, and was staring at him. She was wearing a T-shirt long enough to serve her as a short skirt—his T-shirt, he realized, and the only thing to wear on board other than his shorts. He wondered briefly what had become of her crimson underwear; a glance sidewards told him that she had sacrificed her silks to secure his arms to the side-beams running behind the cot. He turned back to glare at her.

"Pervert," she said.

"What?" Harry wasn't sure what he had been expecting, but that wasn't it.

"You heard me. Pervert."

"I'm not a pervert."

"You were trying to smuggle a coffin into the United States. With a body in it."

"That doesn't make me a pervert," Harry said, feeling flustered. "Besides, I had to. He's a war hero."

"Normal people don't go around smuggling bodies. Which one?"

"Which one what?"

"Which war. You said he was a war hero."

"Who?"

"The guy in the coffin. The war hero."

"Oh."

"So?"

"So what?"

"What war?"

"I don't know, exactly. It was in Central America. Or maybe South America. I'm not sure."

"You're smuggling a corpse in a coffin and you don't even know what war he's from? That's crazy."

"Yes . . . I mean, no. I mean, that's all I know. He belongs to the people who own this boat. The very angry people who no doubt are looking for it right now." Harry's head was throbbing worse than ever now, and his nose felt like ants were creeping along it. He wanted to scratch, he wanted to sneeze, he wanted an aspirin. Mostly, he wanted up.

"Are you going to let me up?" he asked.

"Why should I?"

"Because . . . because I have to go to the bathroom!" Harry said, and in saying it realized it was true. It was so true, in fact, that Harry wondered for the first time just how long he had been unconscious.

"All night," the woman replied when Harry asked. "And all morning too. I was starting to think I'd killed you."

"All night!" Harry groaned and tried to sit up; his bonds put a quick end to that. "Then where are we?" he asked.

"Damned if I know. Out at sea somewhere. And don't ask which sea; I don't know that either."

"You sailed us out to the middle of the ocean and you don't even know where we are?"

"I didn't sail us. Who said I sailed us? I didn't say that."

A fresh new worry arose in Harry's mind to take its place alongside his complaining bladder and irritating nose. If she hadn't sailed them . . .

"I just pointed it away from land and revved the motor up as high as it would go. We had to get out of there quick, you know."

"But . . . but there wasn't much diesel left. . . ."

"Tell me about it. I'll bet we didn't go more than an hour before the motor conked out. We've been drifting ever since. But that's all right, see, 'cause I figure if Boulder and Quiet were out looking for us they'd be listening for the motor anyway, so it stopping was a good thing. I kept the lights off all night too, so they couldn't see us."

Harry thought about nighttime traffic through the Straits of Florida and closed his eyes. He pictured the *Miss Behavin'* being nailed amidships by an incoming freighter, himself waking up to the sound of splintering wood and incoming water, going down to the bottom of the sea with his hands securely strapped to the sinking boat with gaudy red underwear. . . .

"Hey, what's the matter? It's no problem, right? You're a sailor, and we got sails, so all you got to do is get up and sail. Right? Right?" Harry looked at the girl again. She was trying to look confident, he realized, but she was chewing on her lower lip and twirling a loose strand of her long blond hair around one slender forefinger. For the first time, Harry realized that she was just as troubled and confused as he was.

"Sail where?" he asked.

The girl sat up straight and released the lock of hair. She brightened visibly, folded her hands confidently in her lap, and smiled.

"France," she said.

"France."

"Right, France." Harry didn't say anything, didn't, in fact, show any reaction at all, and the girl's confident smile slowly faded. Her eyebrows knitted together in concern and she leaned over toward Harry solicitously. "That's in Europe," she said helpfully.

"I know France is in Europe," Harry said quietly.

"Well you act like you never heard of it. 'France,' I said, and you said—"

"I know what I said, I know where France is, I'm not stupid!" Harry exploded. "I know every damn country in Europe, and their capitals, and—"

"Prove it."

"What?"

"Prove it. Every country in Europe, and the capitals. Betcha can't."

"Lady, please! My head is killing me and I *really* have to go and somewhere out there two very angry thugs are no doubt renting a boat and carving my name on their bullets at this very moment. I am not going to recite countries and capitals for you!"

"I *knew* you couldn't. But that's okay, I don't think I could either. Let's try just the countries."

"Jesus H. Christ."

"England, Ireland, Scotland, Northern Ireland, Belgium, France . . ."

Harry sighed heavily and let himself flop back on the cot. "Wales," he said.

"Oh right, Wales. Then what? The little one, Luxembourg. Switzerland. Spain and Portugal, they make up that peninsula. Italy."

"The Iberian Peninsula."

"No, it's 'Iberian.'"

"What?"

"Iberian. You said Why-berian. It's the Iberian Peninsula."

"I know it's the Iberian Peninsula!"

"Then why did you say Why-berian?"

"I did not say Why-berian, I said Iberian. Spain and Portugal, it's the fucking Iberian Peninsula!"

"I bet you say 'Caribbean' wrong too. And 'tomato,' and 'potato.' Go ahead, say 'tomato.'"

"I am not going to say 'tomato,' dammit! This is—"

"Ha! You did say it!"

"What?"

"Tomato! You said 'tomato'! You said it right though."

"I—" Harry stopped himself, took a deep breath and scrunched up his desperately itching nose. "Look," he said. "That's not the point, Whyberian or Iberian or tomato or potato, that's not the point. The point is, we can't go to France."

"Why not? And what's wrong with your nose?"

"It itches, dammit, and I can't scratch it! And we can't go to France because you used up all the fuel."

"What do we need fuel for? This is a sailboat."

"Right, but what do we do when we get becalmed out there in the middle of the Atlantic Ocean?"

"We just sit there and wait for the wind to come again. It's not like we're in a race or something."

"Uh-huh. And what do we eat while we're sitting there waiting for your magical wind?"

"There's seventeen cans of Chef Boyardee Beefaroni in there," the girl said triumphantly, "and six boxes of instant macaroni and cheese and about a half gallon of powdered egg mix—and two fishing rods! We'll use macaroni as bait and catch all the fish we need!"

"And what do we drink?"

"Drink?"

"Right, drink! What do we drink while we're drifting around there, eating all that salty fish and dry Beefaroni?"

"There's two big jugs of water out there . . ." the girl said, but she was hesitant. She starting biting her lip again.

"That won't be enough for two people, not for an Atlantic crossing. Especially if we get becalmed." Harry knew he had her—but for some reason, instead of enjoying his small victory, he felt a little mean. "Look, I'm sorry, but it just can't be done. We don't have enough water, we don't have enough food or fuel, we don't have a radio, we don't—"

"You are a very negative person," the girl interrupted. "No wonder nobody wants to sail with you." And then she jumped up and stomped out of the cabin.

Harry stared after her, not quite sure what he had said wrong—or, in fact, what he had said at all. For a

moment he actually felt guilty—the poor woman seemed
so disappointed—and then he remembered that he was the
one tied up and suffering.

Harry tried unsuccessfully to scratch his itching nose
on first one shoulder and then the other. He thought
about trying to reach up with a foot or a knee. He even
remembered an ex-roommate who used to win bar bets
by touching the tip of his nose with his tongue, and
wished for a moment that he too had the tongue of an
anteater. Finally he swallowed his pride, took a deep
breath, and called out to the girl.

"Hey!" he said. "You can't just leave me here!"

"Why not?" she answered almost immediately. Harry
couldn't see her, but from her voice he could tell she was
out in the small main cabin, just outside the door.

"Because I'm dying! My nose is itching like crazy,
and I have to piss!"

"You shouldn't say 'piss' in front of a lady. Didn't
your mother ever teach you about how to behave with a
lady?"

Actually, Harry was having a hard time thinking of
his captor as a lady. Not that she was unladylike—despite
the whack she had applied to his forehead—or even
unfeminine; it was just that she didn't seem to have any
of the fussy prissiness he associated with that word. Even
"woman" didn't seem quite right. She reminded him of
an enthusiastic young animal, a colt, perhaps, or maybe a
sea otter. Girlish, he thought, but managed to keep that
thought to himself.

"I'm sorry," he said. "You're quite right. It's just that I

am in, um, a bit of distress here. Do you suppose you could let me loose?"

"Why should I?"

"Because if you don't I'll piss all over the damn bed!" Harry exploded.

"So what," she said, ignoring the second piss. "I'm not the one who's going to be sleeping in it."

"You wouldn't!"

"I might."

"But . . . but . . . you have to let me up to sail the boat!"

For a long moment there was no response, and the worried Harry thought his captor was going to ignore him. Then she poked just her head around the edge of the doorway and glared at him.

"I'll let you up on one condition," she said.

"Anything, anything. Just hurry!"

"Okay then." The girl stepped into the open doorway. The sunlight streaming in from outside outlined her T-shirted, slender figure there in the door frame, and Harry distractedly realized that "girlish" wasn't exactly the right word either.

"Okay," she repeated. "Then you have to tell what happens to Harpoon Harrison after he finds the stolen diamonds and then learns that his brake lines have been cut while he's driving down the steepest mountain in all of South America."

Harry blinked in surprise. "What?" he said.

"I said you have to tell me how Harpoon Harr—"

"You read my book," Harry interrupted softly. And then, much louder, "You read my book!"

"Well, sure. I had to, there's nothing else on this boat to read, except that boring sailing textbook, and I—"

"You're not supposed to read my book! Why did you read my book?"

"Look, I'm sorry, I didn't know it was such a big deal. I just thought it was funny that a smuggler wrote a book."

"I'm not a smuggler!"

"A sailor, then."

"I'm not a sailor either."

"Well you're sure not a writer!"

"I'm not a writer, I'm not a smuggler, I'm not a sailor! I'm an English teacher!"

"A what?"

"An English teacher. College English. Dr. Harry Harper, associate professor, University of Michigan, Detroit campus. I teach freshman English."

"You're not a smuggler?"

"No."

"Not even a sailor?"

"Nope."

The woman frowned delicately and pulled on her hair so hard Harry thought she must be hurting herself. Then she nodded her head sharply, just once, as if she'd made a final decision. She stepped forward and reached one hand out toward Harry.

"Jane Ellen Ashley," she said. "Soon to be from Paris."

"From Paris."

"Soon to be."

"Ah." Harry nodded thoughtfully. He reflexively tried to offer his bound hand and realized that, of course, he couldn't do that. The woman stood there, gazing at him, one hand still extended expectantly, her gaze slightly unfocused. Finally, Harry raised his left leg and extended one bare foot in her direction. The woman smiled and, without hesitation, grasped his foot and shook it enthusiastically.

Strong grip, Harry thought. "Jane Ellen Ashley," he said.

"Yes?"

"You are wearing my shirt."

"That's okay," Jane Ellen said. "You're wearing my underwear." Then she threw back her head, closed her eyes and laughed—and Happy Harry Harper's world changed forever.

Harry wanted to humor this strange person, wanted to laugh right along with her, wanted to open his mouth and let all the tension of the last two weeks explode outward in uncontrolled manic hilarity. But something was happening to him, something strange and unexpected. Later, Harry would attribute it to hunger and emotional exhaustion, to stress, to the whack on the head Jane Ellen had given him. But at that moment . . .

At that moment, Jane Ellen's childish laughter echoed through the small cabin like the delicate splashing of a waterfall in a mountain forest. Her bright teeth rose along her parted lips like ice-glazed snow, and her electric blue eyes shone like sapphires under running water. Her hair flowed over her shoulders like molten gold,

Harry's T-shirt melded to her slight figure like the petals of a flower, and the light spilling through the cabin's open door sparkled around her like the golden lighting in a medieval religious painting.

Harry was enthralled. He was captivated, he was mesmerized, he was entranced. And he was staring.

"Harry," Jane Ellen said, "you're staring."

"What? What?" Harry shook his head, blinked his eyes twice, and looked back at Jane Ellen. She had stopped laughing, that peculiar lighting effect seemed to have faded, and the T-shirt had reacquired its traditional dinginess. Her eyes still had the electric glitter of distant lightning, but Harry managed to keep his gaze off them. "Sorry," he said. "I was just thinking."

"About what?"

"About how bad my nose itches, and how bad I have to—"

"Okay, okay. Hang on just a second." Jane Ellen stood up and walked across the cabin, then stopped and glanced back at Harry. "Don't go anywhere," she admonished. Then she laughed again and bounced out the cabin door.

She reappeared a moment later, carrying her gun in one hand and a large galley knife in the other.

"Not that I don't believe you or anything," she said, waving the gun casually. Harry grinned ruefully and nodded. Jane Ellen sat on the bed beside him, pointed the gun in the general direction of Harry's stomach, and set to work sawing away at his knotted bonds.

"You're ruining your underwear," Harry said.

"This stuff? It's not my underwear, not really. I wouldn't wear this junk if my life depended on it." Jane Ellen stopped and frowned reflectively. "Okay, maybe if my life depended on it. But I'm sure not gonna wear it now."

"Then why—"

"That's a long story. How come you're out smuggling corpses if you're not a smuggler?"

"That's a long story too."

"Good. We'll have plenty to talk about on the way to France." Jane Ellen leaned in to put her weight into the knife and frowned in concentration. "I found some rope later, while you were asleep, but I had already tied you up with this stuff. I didn't know how long you would be out, so I was in sort of a hurry, ya know?"

Harry grunted noncommittally, his eyes closed. Truth was, he was fading away again, lost in the delicious onslaught of olfactory images that had enveloped him when Jane Ellen moved in to work on his bonds. He caught a delicate, feminine musk, and again he pictured wild animals—a fawn, perhaps, rising from its grassy bed on a dew-soaked summer morning. There was also a hint of the sea, of salt and blue water. He pictured rainbows and rainbow trout, oak trees and orange groves, warm sand beaches and—

"Hey."

Harry's eyes popped open and he came crashing back to reality.

"You're free."

"Free . . . oh yeah." Harry raised both hands to his nose, scrunched his eyes shut and scratched furiously. He felt Jane Ellen shift her weight on the bed beside him, and heard her laugh.

"What's funny?" he asked without stopping his scratching.

"You. You look like a muskrat."

"A what?"

"A muskrat. They lie on their backs in the water and groom themselves sometimes, and when they do they use both their front paws to really work over their faces. Like you."

Harry stopped scratching his nose and turned his attention to restoring circulation to his fresh-freed hands. "Where'd you see muskrats?"

"In the lakes back in—back where I used to live. There were lots of 'em. Sometimes I'd see otters too, but they were real skittish. You couldn't hardly get close enough to really see 'em good."

"Oh." Harry remembered his other pressing business and started to stand. Jane Ellen jumped backwards quickly and swung the gun up to center it on his chest.

"Easy," Harry said, raising both hands before himself protectively. "I just got to go to the bathroom, remember."

"The head."

"What?"

"The head. On a boat it's called a head."

"Right. The head." Harry eased himself off the bed slowly, Jane Ellen watching his every move. He strode quickly across the room to the closet-sized head at the rear of the cabin, turned sideways to squeeze through the tiny door and pushed his way inside. He pulled the door halfway shut, glancing back at Jane Ellen sitting on the bed as he did so. She had lowered the gun but was still watching him closely.

"Um, well, I'll be out in a minute," Harry said.

"Okay."

"I just have to go. I'm not going to try and escape or anything."

"Okay."

"Um. Well, then . . ." Harry looked at Jane Ellen, who looked back at him. He swallowed deeply, forced himself to break eye contact, and backed into the tiny head.

Once inside, Harry pushed the little door closed and leaned his forehead up against it. "Oh my God," he said quietly. "What the fuck is going on?"

Just outside that bathroom door, sitting still and stunned on the rumpled cabin bed, Jane Ellen Ashley was thinking pretty much the same thing.

15

If she hadn't known better, Jane Ellen would have thought it was love. All the classic symptoms were there, or most of them anyway, just like in *Heart of the South* and *Woman of the West* and a thousand other Harlequins Lurlene Byars and her sewing circle had sent Jane Ellen's way over the years. Her knees were weak, she was getting delicious little rushes in her stomach, and she couldn't seem to stop herself from talking—talking!—about nothing, babbling on like a raving idiot.

She'd never experienced it firsthand before, not even close, but all that sure sounded like love to Jane Ellen. And of course she did believe in love at first sight, believed in it fervently, hopefully, desperately. . . .

But love at first sight with *this* guy? Not likely. He was skinny, he was scruffy, and she wasn't completely sure yet about his intelligence. No doubt she was just impressed by the fact he was writing a novel—even though it really was pretty bad—and that he was a college professor, or at least claimed to be. As for the rest—well, she was still recovering from a gunshot through the leg and, except for the half-can of Beefaroni she'd had last night and what she'd spooned down this morning, Jane Ellen hadn't eaten anything in, what, forty-eight hours? No wonder she felt funny. No wonder too, considering all that she'd been through lately, that she found herself overwhelmed with nervous energy the first time she'd found a sympathetic ear.

But then there were those hands. . . .

They weren't special hands, at least not at first glance. But she'd gotten a good look at them when she was tying him up the night before, and now, in the sharp light filtering in through the *Miss Behavin*'s portholes, she couldn't seem to keep her eyes off them. They were strong without being muscle-bound; long slim fingers, forest-patch of sandy-brown hair growing from the backs. They didn't have the weathered and worn look of the hands Jane Ellen had grown up with, the thick gray calluses of the oystermen or the always ready-to-strike tension of Nate's clenching fists. They weren't fat and pallid, like the Cuban accountant's hands, or dead white and sinewy-cold like Boulder's. The sailor's hands, Harry's hands, had a kind of supple, unassuming strength to them, strength that was there but didn't have to be displayed. They were the sort of hands she expected to see on a writer, or maybe a musician or a surgeon. When she closed her eyes, Jane Ellen saw those hands cupped gently around the face of a child, or dancing fluidly along the neck of a guitar, or even moving knowingly down the length of her—

Jane Ellen heard the head door opening and popped her eyes back open. She sat upright on the bed and thrust the gun out protectively. The safety, she noted with satisfaction, was clearly in the "off" position.

Harry Harper emerged from the bathroom, frowning, scratching at his half-grown beard thoughtfully. He glared right at Jane Ellen, right into her eyes, ignoring the gun entirely.

"What do you mean, I'm 'certainly not a writer'?" he said.

"What?"

"That's what you said; you read my book and you said, 'You're certainly not a writer.' How can you say that when you just read two hundred pages of my writing?"

"Oh. Well, you're right."

"Good, then."

"What I should have said is, 'You're certainly not a very good writer.'"

"Ah. Much better," Harry said. "And for that you're going to shoot me?"

"What? No, of course not."

"No, no, don't apologize. There's too damn many bad writers out there anyway. Maybe if we shot a few early on it would discourage the others."

Jane Ellen grinned, but did not lower the gun. "Right, just like Shakespeare said. Kill all the writers."

"Lawyers."

"Even better."

"And *then* we could kill all the writers. And maybe telemarketers and people who sell insurance, too."

"And people who ride Jet Skis on quiet lakes."

"Or play car stereos designed to shatter windows."

"Or spit tobacco in cups and leave them for someone else to toss out."

"Tow-truck drivers."

"TV preachers."

"Office politicians."

"*Any* politicians."

"Critics. Got to kill all the critics."

"Right. And people looking for a plot in *Huck Finn*."

Harry grinned. "'Persons attempting to find a motive in this narrative will be prosecuted,'" he quoted.

"'. . . persons attempting to find a moral will be banished . . .'" Jane Ellen continued.

"'And persons attempting to find a plot in it will be shot,'" Harry concluded. "Hey, is that coffee I smell?"

"Yeah, there's still some left out in the . . ." But Harry was already gone, headed out to the main outer cabin, scratching his fuzzy cheeks all the way, oblivious to the gun centered on his back. Jane Ellen started to say something, then looked at the gun, shrugged, and got up to follow him.

She winced as she stood, then walked gingerly across the room. Harry was standing at the small stove that passed as a galley on the *Miss Behavin'*, pouring coffee into a battered tin cup.

"God, I would kill for some fresh cream," he said. "Even some skim milk, or some of that fake powdered stuff."

"No kidding," Jane Ellen said, though she had long

ago learned to drink it black and strong, working all-day, all-night Saturday shifts at the O&P. "How do you make the macaroni and cheese without milk?"

"You just mix seawater with the powdered cheese mix. All the extra salt helps."

"Ick."

"No kidding. I used to mix it with vanilla ice cream, back when I was an undergrad and couldn't seem to keep fresh milk around. That was pretty bad too, but it beats the hell out of this stuff."

Jane Ellen nodded noncommittally, trying to hide her amazement at how easily, how nonchalantly, Harry talked about going to college. Like everybody did it, like it was expected or something. She felt a twinge in her sore leg and hobbled over to the small table to sit down.

Harry poured coffee into Jane Ellen's abandoned mug without asking, then brought both cups over and sat down across from her. He put her mug in front of her, took a tentative sip from his own cup, and raised both eyebrows expectantly.

"Well?" he said.

"Well . . ." Jane Ellen said, and thought, here we go. "It's hard to explain, really. See, I was working as a wait-ress, in a coffee shop up in Little Havana, and this little Cuban guy kept coming in and looking at me funny. And he always had this big guy with him, the guy you saw back there on the dock, and—"

"No."

"No?"

"I mean, well, what about my novel."

"Your novel."

"Right. What's wrong with it?"

"You really want to know?"

"No, but tell me anyway."

Jane Ellen sipped her coffee and studied Harry closely. He was looking right back at her, at her eyes, waiting for her to speak. He wasn't waiting for her to fetch him a cool one or crack a dozen oysters, he wasn't trying to sneak a peek down her shirt or grab at her bare legs, he wasn't smoldering like Nate, like a volcano hoping for an excuse to erupt. He was simply, honestly, waiting to hear what she had to say.

Jane Ellen noticed for the first time, there in the full light of the outer cabin, that Harry's eyes were green, vibrant emerald green, like fresh-budded live oak leaves in the North Florida springtime. His wonderful hands were cupped protectively around his coffee mug, holding it close to his mouth so he could blow across the steaming liquid. He closed his eyes to take an appreciative sip, and as he raised the mug his index fingers, twined together around the mug, pointed heavenward like an upside-down V, or maybe an inverted heart.

Jane Ellen swallowed and looked away. "Well," she said, "I'm not sure exactly where to start."

Harry smiled in a gentle, self-deprecating way that Jane Ellen liked immensely. "You know what I tell my students when they say that? 'Start at the beginning, go on until the end—'"

"'—and then stop,'" Jane Ellen finished for him. Then she smiled too.

"Lewis Carroll."

"*Alice in Wonderland.*"

"You've read it?"

"Twice, and *Through the Looking Glass,* too. There was a copy of it in the library when I was, I don't know, about 7 or 8."

"That's pretty young for Carroll."

"It is?"

"Sure. I've had plenty of students, even English majors, who never read any Carroll, and hated it when I required them to."

"Really?" That was news to Jane Ellen. She'd seen enough drunken FSU and University of Florida students showing their asses at the beach, or tossing their cookies over the railing at the O&P, to understand that college students weren't necessarily the most intelligent creatures under the sun. Still, she had an innate respect for anyone who could pack that much education into their head, and regard for English majors that bordered on reverence. After all, they were going to get a degree, and make a living, just by reading books. To hear that she had done something that many of them hadn't, that she had exceeded the intellectual accomplishments of the wealthy and blessed, that was heady stuff to Jane Ellen. It gave her the courage to say what she had gradually realized while reading Harry's book the night before.

"Actually, the writing in your book is pretty good," she said. "But you don't know nothing about people."

"Anything."

"What?"

"It's 'anything.' I don't know anything about people."

"Oh. Right, anything." Jane Ellen didn't mind being corrected by a college professor. It was considerably better than what she had expected. She had figured Harry would get upset again, defensive and huffy like he had earlier. But he didn't. He just put down his coffee and then sat studying his hands for a minute, like he was seeing something there that she couldn't. Then he got up and walked over to the coffin, where he had apparently put the novel down before pouring his coffee (it still bothered Jane Ellen, dominating the main cabin like it did, but Harry treated it just like any other piece of furniture). Harry brought the heavy gold-gilded book over to the table, sat down, and slid it over in front of Jane Ellen.

"Show me," he said.

Jane Ellen looked at Harry, hard, watching his lips to see if he were smiling, watching his eyes to see if he were going to crack and laugh out loud. But he didn't. He wasn't teasing. There was no trickery there, no malice. He really wanted to know.

So, what the hell—she told him.

Jane Ellen told Harry all about his characters' lack of easily recognizable physical characteristics while they finished off that pot of coffee, brewed up a second, and knocked it off, too. When they went outside so Harry could take a solar sighting and get a rough estimate of where they were, she told him about her unwillingness to accept Harpoon Harrison's allegedly tough upbringing at the Catholic orphanage. Later, while Harry taught her how to trim the mainsail and they set a course due east,

Jane Ellen gently criticized Harpoon's appalling ignorance about women—Lady Gifala might forget the combination to her husband's safe, certainly, but she would *not* forget her sister's dress size—knowing all the while that it was Harry himself who was completely clueless about the fairer sex. At some point, without either of them really noticing, Jane Ellen put the gun down.

And all the while, Harry listened. He listened quietly, interrupting only to ask an insightful question now and then, never defensive, never angry. He kept on listening when she showed him how to rig the heavy fishing poles in the *Miss Behavin*'s cabin for trolling, and how to set the hook when a marauding triggerfish jumped on the soggy Beefaroni squares they used for bait. Harry listened quietly when Jane Ellen questioned Harpoon's ability to deduce the murderer based on the scant evidence he'd provided, he listened when she pointed out that Brazilians speak Portuguese, not Spanish, and when she somehow found herself talking about Wakulla County, about oysters and nights at the O&P, well, he listened to that, too.

Eventually, as Jane Ellen wound down, Harry Harper started doing his own share of the talking. While she cleaned the fresh-caught triggerfish, slicing it into fillets thin enough to fry in their own juice, Harry talked about his love for reading, for books, about his newfound ability to utterly submerge himself in the act of writing. Over succulent fish, cool water and a side dish of macaroni (without cheese) they discussed the books they had in common, and laughed out loud over a game of the-worst-thing-I-ever-read. When it got dark enough for Harry to take a star sighting, they sat side-by-side on the deck of the *Miss Behavin'*, bare knees almost touching, and he talked about his rootlessness, his lack of feeling for academia, even his anguish about the accident in the Dominican.

Mostly, though, they talked about the book. They talked about plot while Harry did the dishes—he insisted—after their salty supper. They discussed character motivation while Harry battened the boat down for the night, and argued individual word choices through the closed bathroom door as each prepared for bed. They talked as they each settled into a bunk, Harry in the captain's bed, Jane Ellen across the small cabin in the mate's. They talked lying there in the moonlit darkness, they talked over the quiet creakings of the *Miss Behavin'* at rest, they talked and they talked and they talked, right up until the moment Jane Ellen surprised Harry and astonished herself by getting out of her bunk and padding quietly across the room to stand silently beside his bed.

Part of Jane Ellen thought she had surely lost her mind, standing there in the cool moonlight while Harry's T-shirt billowed down across her bare feet like a falling cloud. But another part of her, a calm and steady and cooling voice deep down inside, was as sure as she had ever been that she was doing the right thing. She stood there motionless listening to that inner voice, a slight sea breeze blowing across her skin through the open ports, feeling the slow roll of the boat beneath her legs. Then Harry wordlessly reached out his hand, his wonderful, gentle, welcoming hand, and Jane Ellen stepped forward to take it.

She was a hundred miles from shore and a million miles from her childhood, slipping into the bed of a stranger. And yet, somehow, when Harry closed his arms gently around her there in the cool dark interior of the *Miss Behavin'*, Jane Ellen Ashley felt, for the very first time in her whole entire life, as if she were coming home.

16

They might never have come ashore if Jane Ellen's leg hadn't started tasting funny.

Harry wouldn't say "bad." "Funny," he insisted, and conceded even that only reluctantly. Still, he had spent a lot of time over the past three days getting acquainted with Jane Ellen's legs—and other points both north and south—including (though of course not limited to) their taste. They had a slightly salty tang that was part sea-spray and part sweat and part just general Jane Ellen. The taste wasn't as wild-animal musky as her middle, as giggly-soft as her stomach, as blueberries-and-cream feminine as her snowy-soft breasts, but it was a wonderful, erotic, gentle-but-firmly-Jane-Elleny taste all its own, and, like every other taste, touch, smile, sight and sound of her, Harry loved it. So, naturally, when the taste changed, he noticed it right away.

"What do you mean, 'funny'?" Jane Ellen asked. She sat upright and twisted around so she could look down at Harry and the leg in question. The sheet that had been draped across her midsection slipped off when she did so, but Jane Ellen felt no inclination to cover herself. Her natural modesty, maybe even over-modesty, had evaporated over the past few days in the blazing light of Harry's open admiration. In fact, with only one change of clothing each and no one other than the occasional passing dolphin or curious sea turtle anywhere in sight, Jane Ellen and Harry had both adopted a laissez-faire attitude toward clothing. The result, on Jane Ellen's case, was a nicely developing all-over bronze tan; in Harry's a bright red and distractingly sensitive ass.

Harry had, in fact, taken to wrapping a square of bed sheet sarong-like around his waist whenever he ventured out into the sun. At the moment, however—the moment being that deliciously drowsy time between first waking and first coffee—the only thing between the two of them and complete nudity was the three-fingers-wide strip of torn sheet wrapped tightly around Jane Ellen's injured thigh. It was to that thigh—specifically, to that very injured bit of flesh—that Harry was directing his attention.

"Not 'funny,' that's not exactly the right word. It's just—" Harry paused and gave Jane Ellen a long gentle lick just below the homemade bandage. "Just . . . different. How long since you changed the bandage?"

"Not long. Last night, after you fell asleep." Jane Ellen remembered rolling over on her side, half-asleep herself, and wincing at the stab of pain from her thigh. She had slipped quietly out of bed and changed the dressing in the dark, tearing a bandage wide enough to cover the dark greenish bruise she knew was spreading on her leg. The pain wasn't really that bad, and the bruise didn't bother her—she'd grown used to bruises over the years with Nate—but she couldn't stand the idea of Harry seeing her at anything less than her best.

Harry was prodding at that bandage now, gently undoing the securing knot with those long sinuous fingers. Jane Ellen murmured a complaint, but Harry was insistent, in his quiet way. He worked steadily away at Jane Ellen's inexpert knot, tugging here, pulling there, always responding with a quiet "sorry" when Jane Ellen winced even the slightest. Finally the knot gave way, and Harry slipped the bandage off Jane Ellen's thigh.

They both sat staring in silence for nearly a full minute before Harry opened his mouth.

"We have to get you to shore," he said.

"No, wait, there's still some aspirin in the first-aid kit. Couldn't I just take a few of those..." Jane Ellen's voice trailed off under Harry's unflinching stare. He wordlessly dropped his gaze to her thigh again, and Jane Ellen, reluctantly, let her eyes follow. The greenish-yellow bruise had expanded; it was now a hideous circular blotch the size of a coffee cup. The blotch was bisected by an angry red line, scabbed over at the very edge. A thin line of whitish pus ran along the edge of the path left by Boulder's bullet, like egg white escaping from a badly undercooked omelet. Jane Ellen turned her head away and bit her lower lip in despair.

It wasn't the wound itself that upset her, or even the frightening implications of the undeniable infection. Rather, it was the unwelcome but unavoidable end of their fantasy cruise that made Jane Ellen want to bury her head in her pillow and retreat into sleep. She and Harry had recklessly, foolishly, happily spent the last few days sailing through a fragile dreamland, passing their time making love, working on Harry's novel and talking, endlessly talking, while Boulder and Quiones, Harry's smuggler contacts, the Senator and his cronies, and God knows how many law-enforcement agencies were no doubt focusing all their malignant energies on finding and crushing the tiny *Miss Behavin'* and her blissful crew.

Foolish or not, they had been the happiest days of Jane Ellen's life, learning to love her new man and, maybe even, just a little, herself. If that required ignoring the storm clouds gathering just over the horizon, well, so be it. Harry had told her about a line of graffiti he had seen somewhere—"As long as we're skating on thin ice, we might as well dance," it had read—and it had become the watchword of their time together. Now Jane Ellen could feel that beloved ice cracking beneath her feet, and she didn't know what to do.

"There should be some sort of ointment in the first-aid kit . . ." Harry began, but his voice trailed away even without Jane Ellen having to shake her head. She had found the emergency kit that first night, with Harry unconscious and bound in his bunk. Someone had rifled through it mercilessly, leaving wadded-up seasickness-pill wrappers and torn sunburn-ointment tubes scattered carelessly inside the box. There was a half-tube of insect repellent, a few bandages and a scattered handful of aspirin left. Nothing else.

"Okay. Okay then," Harry said, and Jane Ellen could hear the anguish in his voice. "Try washing it in seawater, lots of it, and then put another bandage on it. I'll be outside." He started to say something else, and Jane Ellen looked at him hopefully. Then he shook his head and, without looking at her, stood and walked out of the cabin.

Jane Ellen was miserable. She frowned and ran her thumb roughly along the red line on her thigh, relishing in the self-inflicted pain. Harry was blaming himself, she knew that—as if it were his fault that her leg was rotting off!—and he needed some time alone. But Jane Ellen didn't want to be alone; she wanted Harry with her right now, wanted to nestle in the safety of his arms. Suddenly, it seemed that there was a great clock ticking away the time they had had together, and the only one who could slow that ticking down, Happy Harry Harper, had marched off to be stoic. Damn.

Just like a man.

Jane Ellen stood, careful not to put too much weight on her gimpy leg. She hopped over to the mate's bunk, which she had appropriated as her sewing table (she was still skittish about using the coffin, even though it was the only good solid working surface onboard). She stripped off a good thick bandage from what was left of the mate's top sheet, taking as much time as she could. Then, slowly, she hobbled through both cabins and out into the bright morning sun.

Harry was standing in the rear of the boat, studying a chart spread out along the stern railing. He had forgotten his sarong; the crimson splotch that was his sunburned butt stood out like strawberry jam on burnt toast. It reminded Jane Ellen of Harry's careful lecture about Shakespeare the other night, when she had asked him about the bitter end of *King Lear*. How had he put it? Oh yes—the tragic flaw in an otherwise noble character. Jane Ellen suppressed a giggle and walked across the deck.

Harry must have heard her coming—Jane Ellen saw him raise his head, just a little—but he didn't turn to face her. She stopped just behind him and put one hand on his browned shoulders, feeling without wanting to the tension running through his tight muscles.

"How could I let this happen to you?" Harry said. His voice was as flat as the quiet Gulf, but Jane Ellen could see white where his knuckles gripped the railing.

"You didn't," she said. She put both hands on his waist and gently forced him to turn toward her. "You didn't. I did. I knew it was getting worse and I kept it hidden from you."

"But—" Jane Ellen put a hand over Harry's mouth.

"I didn't want to worry you. I didn't want our trip to end," she said.

Jane Ellen saw the edges of a smile peek around her clasped fingers. Harry pursed his lips forward exaggeratedly and slurped the inside of her palm. She smiled and dropped her hand to his shoulder.

"Nothing's ending, not yet. Not without a fight anyway. First thing though—" Harry half-turned to look back at his map, keeping one arm draped around Jane Ellen's waist. "First thing is, we've got to get you to a doctor and get that leg treated."

"Are we far from land?" Jane Ellen asked. The sea gulls dotting the sky around the *Miss Behavin'* had already given Jane Ellen the answer to that one, but she liked the confidence returning to Harry's voice, and wanted to hear it again.

"Not far, not far at all," he said. "With this wind, and the quiet sea, we should be able to see Tampa within an hour."

"Oh," Jane Ellen said, disappointed. She leaned in to press her breasts solidly against Harry's bare back. She wrapped both arms around him and slid her hands gently down his chest, down his abdomen, down past the sharp knobs of his hipbones. "Do you suppose we could make it two?"

In fact, it took them closer to three—but Harry didn't mind at all.

According to local legend, the bloodthirsty pirate Jose Gaspar once sailed an armada of ships into Tampa Bay and vowed to raze the booming coastal town of Tampa if he were not immediately given a hefty ransom. The ransom was paid and Gaspar sailed peacefully away, an event now celebrated annually with a raucous city-wide party honoring the pirate for his excellent manners.

In fact, Gaspar probably never did any such thing; truth is, Tampa's adopted patron pirate may have never actually existed. Certainly he never came close to burning the city to the ground.

And that, Jane Ellen Ashley thought, really was a pity.

Part of her was glad the city still stood, of course, thankful that there were hospitals and clinics and doctors all just waiting to work their medical magic on her infected thigh. But the rest of her, the part of her that was ruled not by intellect but by heart and soul and instinct, felt anything but grateful. In fact, with each step she and Harry took toward the concrete and steel heart of the city, each step farther away from the *Miss Behavin'* and the clean clear Gulf, Jane Ellen grew more and more unhappy.

She knew she was being silly. Tampa was actually smaller than Miami, and she had never experienced this sense of being overwhelmed there. But it was different . . . Miami was spread out, spread out over miles and miles of homes and shops and businesses and slums stretching from Biscayne Bay north into other cities, into Lauderdale and Hollywood, Delray Beach and West Palm and on and on, all independent communities linked by a river of concrete. Tampa was all right *here*, all jam-packed into one tight area wrapped close around the bay.

And Tampa was tall. Miami, accustomed to regular poundings from hurricanes sweeping north out of the Caribbean, was built low to the ground. Tampa, largely protected by the bay at its doorstep, had fewer such reservations. The city center here towered upward, glittering skyscrapers reaching toward the heavens in silent testament to Tampa's audacious claim to be "the newest world-class city." The buildings cast long chilly shadows even in the tropical heat; they formed a steel canyon herding people ever onward into the city's interior. Worst of all, the buildings cut off the wind coming from the sea. The air around Jane Ellen smelled of car exhaust, of garbage and tight-pressed people. And that, Jane Ellen realized, was the real cause of her uneasiness. For the first time in her adult life, she could not smell the sea.

Jane Ellen shivered despite the heat, and leaned close up against Harry. He slipped an arm around her and patted her back automatically, lost once again in the city map he had scrounged at the marina.

Harry was troubled too, Jane Ellen knew that. Worried not about some nebulous claustrophobia, but about real-world things, things like her injured leg and their lack of money and the loose assortment of lunatics and lawmen who might be closing in at that very minute.

And worried, no doubt, about the frequent stares and smirks they drew from the people around them. Harry was too nice to say it, but Jane Ellen knew their outfits didn't exactly inspire confidence. Harry had his cut-offs and T-shirt, not too uncommon in Tampa, and she had managed to stitch together a passable if flimsy skirt and T-top from a spare sheet. But the only shoes they had were baggy moccasins she had sewn from spare sailcloth, already gone ragged from wear. Add in her limp, Harry's obvious discomfort from his scorched crotch and the rolling stride they had both acquired from so many days at sea . . . all in all they stood out like two plums in a pea patch, just when attention was the last thing they wanted.

Even getting into the city hadn't exactly been easy. It had taken them nearly two hours to find a marina that would even let them tie up without paying in advance, and that only because Harry agreed to leave the *Miss Behavin'*'s fish-finder as collateral. Then another hour or more walking the city streets in search of the Hillsborough County Health Clinic, Harry carrying the boat's to-be-pawned electric depth-finder and Jane Ellen feeling more skittish every minute.

Jane Ellen bit her lip and watched Harry struggle with the map. She had a pretty good idea where they were, knew that they should have turned west instead of east three blocks back. But she knew too that once they got to the clinic Harry would leave her, would take off in search of a pawnshop. The idea of being all alone in this suffocating city . . .

"Harry?" she said. He "ummm?"-ed politely but didn't look up from the map, so Jane Ellen poked him gently in the ribs. He turned to her with raised eyebrows and a forced smile.

"Harry, is Paris like this?"

"Like what, hon?"

"Like, I don't know, like *this*. Big and close and crowded."

"I think all big cities are like that, mostly, and Paris is a lot bigger than Tampa." Harry looked back at his map, too distracted to notice Jane Ellen's worried eyes. "Prettier, maybe, but a lot bigger. And there's no ocean there, of course . . . Ah-ha! Got it. We should have turned left back there, not right." And Harry was off, his street-blackened moccasins slapping quickly against the dirty sidewalk, with Jane Ellen in troubled pursuit.

Jane Ellen was horrified. The Hillsborough County Health Clinic reeked of despair and cheap disinfectant, and the people waiting in the overcrowded lobby looked like all the life had been leeched out of them long ago. Jane Ellen knew what it was like to be poor, knew the feeling of no heat and not enough food and no paper for the outhouse. But for Jane Ellen poverty had always been just another fact of life, like the weather or the tide or the day of the week, something she could put out of her mind with a simple walk in the Franklin County sunshine. For these people, old and young and black and white and Hispanic and every conceivable mix thereof, all coughing and sniffing on the cold metal chairs of the Tampa clinic, poverty seemed to have tunneled down inside their guts, taken root and rotted. Bitterness was in their posture, in their angry pinched faces; Jane Ellen could swear she smelled it coming out of them like sour sweat. She watched a young woman swat a toddler hard on the rump, passing anger from one generation to the next, and wished desperately there was a window in the room.

She sat in that sad waiting room for nearly two hours before she got to talk to anyone, twisting her hands and reading the same drug abuse and venereal disease pamphlets over and over. Finally her name was called by a weary receptionist who just couldn't accept that Jane Ellen didn't have an address or a phone number or a social security card. The poor woman just got more and more flustered, and brought out more and more forms for Jane Ellen to fill out. Eventually Jane Ellen figured out that all the lady really wanted was some numbers to scribble down, so she pretended to remember an aunt in St. Petersburg, made up an address and guessed at a phone number. It took her three tries to get the phone number right, but the receptionist gave her plenty of hints, and eventually they settled on a number that satisfied them both.

Then came a nurse who weighed her and measured her and asked about her medical history. Jane Ellen had learned her lesson from the receptionist, so instead of saying "I don't know" to everything she'd never heard of, she mostly just said "yes." The nurse frowned a few times and once she asked if Jane Ellen had ever had a vasectomy. Jane Ellen knew she was being made fun of, so she just stared, and eventually the nurse went away.

Then she had to sit for a long time, reading wall charts about setting bones and helping people who were choking. Eventually a different nurse came, told her to hike up her dress, and peeled off Jane Ellen's makeshift bandage. She was washing the wound with alcohol when the doctor finally arrived.

He was young, black, skinny and already half-bald, and he didn't look Jane Ellen in the face the whole time he was there. He looked at her injury, asked a lot of the same questions the first nurse had, and finally said, "Bullet wound."

Jane Ellen had been expecting that. "No," she said. "See, I fell on this metal thing, over near where I live, and—"

"I'm supposed to report bullet wounds," the doctor said. "When did this happen?"

"Six days ago, but it's not a bullet wound. See—"

"Allergic to penicillin?"

"Excuse me?"

The doctor finally looked up and stared at Jane Ellen. He needed a shave and his tired brown eyes were blood-shot, and Jane Ellen wondered how long he had been working in a free clinic. Suddenly she didn't feel like lying anymore.

"I don't know. I've never had penicillin before."

The doctor frowned, then took his forefinger and thumb and rubbed the bridge of his nose, hard. "Wound like that, you don't treat it right, it could get infected. You could lose your leg, maybe even die. You don't want to lose your leg."

"No sir."

"How old are you, girl?"

"Twenty-one," she said, and then, "Twenty."

"Your man do that to you?"

"No!" Jane Ellen said, shocked. "He'd never do something like that to me; he wouldn't hurt me."

"Okay, good then." The doctor took a pad out of his pocket and began scribbling. "Nurse, run a blood check for penicillin allergy; if it checks out okay, you give her this. You get these pills, hear me, and you take 'em three times a day till they're all gone, and you wash that wound every morning and night, with rubbing alcohol or good strong antibacterial soap. You hear me?"

Jane Ellen said yes, and started to thank the doctor, but he was already gone, mumbling, out the door and down the hall, already reading another chart. The nurse produced a needle and a rubber hose, wrapped up Jane Ellen's arm and began rubbing her with an alcohol pad.

"Why'd he ask that?" Jane Ellen said.

"About the penicillin? Just wanted to make sure you wouldn't have a bad reaction."

"No, I mean about my ... my boyfriend. Why'd he think my boyfriend would shoot me?"

The nurse looked up at Jane Ellen and stared at her a minute, lips pursed. Then she looked back down at Jane Ellen's arm. "You see that roomful of patients out there, waiting to see the doctor? You see how many were women, women with kids? Half of them, their husband hurt them, or hurt the kids. Or maybe their boyfriend or their pimp or their father or brother did it. You never heard about nothing like that?"

Jane Ellen didn't answer. She was looking away, at the wall, like she couldn't stand to see the needle go in. Truth is, she was thinking about Nate.

"Never again," she promised herself. "Never again."

Harry was sitting in the waiting room when Jane Ellen finally got through. She grabbed his arm and pulled him up, not wanting to answer his questions, not wanting to hear his news, wanting nothing but to get out of that terrible gray building and back into the open air. She half-dragged him down the hall and outside, then she ran a little ways down the sidewalk, let out a whoop and ran back to wrap her arms around him. Jane Ellen felt like she had just been let out of a cage, like she had just escaped death. She was excited, and it took her a minute to notice that Harry wasn't happy.

"Fifty dollars," he finally said. "The pawn shop guy said it was an old model, and not worth much, and the guy in the next pawn shop said the same thing. That's a three-hundred-dollar depth-finder, easy, and all he would give me was fifty dollars."

"But . . . but fifty dollars is a lot of money!"

"No it's not, not really. It may not even cover your prescription, and if it does, there sure won't be much left over for food, or fuel, or to fix the radio. I'm sorry, honey, but fifty dollars just isn't enough."

Harry jammed his hands into his pockets, turned and dejectedly strode off down the street. Jane Ellen had to hustle to catch up with him, silently cursing herself all the way.

"Okay, okay. Harry, here's what we'll do," she said. "We'll just get a few pills for now, okay, and we'll get some more later. And we'll spend the money on just enough fuel to get us out into open water, and back in again if we need to, and really essential food, like bread, and maybe some milk, and more coffee. We'll just catch more fish, and we don't really need a radio, we've done all right without one so far. We'll be all right, Harry, we will."

Jane Ellen realized she was rattling on again, talking fast because she was scared, trying to convince herself. She made herself shut up, and shot a sideways glance over at Harry to see what he was thinking—but Harry wasn't there.

Jane Ellen stopped, suddenly frightened, and spun around. Harry was about twenty feet back, standing still and quiet, staring into a storefront window. Jane Ellen called his name, and when he didn't respond, walked back to stand beside him.

The place that had captured Harry's attention wasn't a storefront at all, Jane Ellen realized—it was a bar, a dirty-looking dive called Pigskin Paul's. For just a moment she was afraid Harry had given up, that he was going to go inside and blow their precious fifty bucks on booze. Then she noticed that Harry really wasn't staring into the bar itself, but rather was intently studying a bright red sign posted inside the window. She looked at the sign, then at Harry, and then back at the sign.

"Pool Tournament Tonight," it said. "Cash Prizes."

17

Once upon a time, a very long time ago, the great god Dionysus got himself in a spot of trouble on a Greek island known as Kerkira. Harry couldn't remember exactly what sort of trouble Dionysus was in, or why, being a god, he couldn't get himself out of trouble with a blink of his eyes or a twitch of his godly nose. All he remembered about the legend was that a local satyr named Priapus had come to Dionysus's aid and gotten the god out of whatever trouble he was in. The grateful god had offered to grant any wish Priapus might have. Priapus, being obsessed with the one thing that obsessed all satyrs—sex—had asked for an eternal and extensive erection. He got it.

Time went on. The Romans came, the Christians came, Dionysus and his Olympian colleagues faded into myth. The Turks came to Kerkira, then the British, then the tourists. Kerkira became known as Corfu, and, in a brilliant move that both embraced its mythic past and encouraged its tourist-dependent future, adopted the nickname of "The Island of Love."

The Turks left, the British left, the tourists kept coming—and Priapus became the island's official symbol and mascot. The greatest depiction of him—a larger-than-life, classic-era jade-green statue, complete with Priapus's happy leer and python-sized perpetual erection—was spirited off to a museum in Athens, but imitations both exact and whimsical sprouted up on the island like hardons at a stag party. Drawings of Priapus decorated every restaurant menu and shop awning. His image was etched onto belt buckles and shoe soles; carvings of him could be found in wood, glass, metal, stone, big, small, medium, costly, cheap or in between. Imitations of Priapus's three-foot member spouted forth in a Corfutown fountain, served as coat racks in the best hotels, pointed directions on city street signs. The first sight greeting tourists arriving in Corfutown harbor, sailing east from Brindisi or west from Athens, was a marble depiction of Priapus playing sailboat, lazing along on his back, blowing the panpipe, a taut sail attached to the satyr's mast-sized hard-on.

Harry hated him on sight.

His trip to Corfu was both college graduation present and a last-ditch effort by his parents—his mother, at least—to break Harry out of the funk he'd been in since his humiliation at the Rosewater basketball tournament. Harry had liked the idea, had even entertained thoughts of losing his curse among the new places and strange faces he would encounter. He had flown into Athens with high hopes, spent a day prowling the Acropolis, and enjoyed the starlit overnight cruise to Corfu. He had arrived with the rising sun, left the ferry in an early morning fog and, while searching for a taxi and someone who spoke English, had stumbled across and nearly into the Priapus sailing statue. Things went downhill from there.

Priapus's image haunted Harry at every turn. How could he possibly forget his troubles when everywhere he looked there was this mythic character enjoying, embracing, *flaunting* his very own curse? He couldn't go to a restaurant without seeing Priapus's engorged member rising from a flower planter, couldn't go to a museum or gift shop without having a hundred phallic images thrust in his face. He couldn't enjoy Corfu's nude beaches for fear some wrong move would turn him into a human caricature of the island's mythic mascot (contrary to expectations, there are few things more inappropriate on a nude beach than an erection). Harry retreated to his room and spent most of his vacation reading and rereading the detective novels he had brought along.

But one night, overcome by cabin fever, he had wandered the streets of Corfutown, looking for a bar that might be poor enough to not have invested in any decor at all. He took a chance on a dingy little dive far from the usual tourist haunts, a small little bar whose only outward decorations were a sign proclaiming "Taverna" and a flickering Amstel Beer light.

Inside, the tavern was all Harry had hoped for. Dim, cramped, three or four locals lounging at rickety wooden tables, a tired white-haired man behind a short wooden bar—and absolutely no decorations, of any sort, anywhere in sight. Harry ordered an ouzo and water and sat down to celebrate.

Thirty minutes and three ouzos later, Harry was tipsy but bored. He'd been aware for some time of a familiar clicking emanating from a back room of the tavern, and decided that the hand-lettered Cyrillic sign above the entrance to that room spelled out "pool." Or maybe "billiards." Harry really wasn't sure what sort of games they played in Greece—hadn't pool been an early Olympic sport?—but he was willing to investigate. He couldn't play, of course, but it wouldn't hurt to watch for a while.

He stood up and stumbled toward the back room. Inside, as he had expected, two men were standing beside a faded green pool table; three others lounged on stools against the wall, watching. They all nodded to Harry, surprised but cordial. Harry nodded back, happy to find something so familiar so far from home. He wondered absently how many drachmas it took to operate a quarter pool table.

And then Harry glanced up at the wall behind the table, and his world came tumbling down.

There was a tapestry hanging there, big as a bedsheet and immaculately stitched. Someone had spent hundreds of hours, maybe thousands, sewing an image of Priapus at a pool table, perhaps this very table. He was leaning over the table, his erect member clutched in both hands, bright pink head positioned just behind the cue ball. The dirty old satyr was lining up a shot with his own swang.

And he was laughing.

Harry had bolted from the room, knocked back what

was left of his ouzo as he crossed the outer bar, and stumbled out into the hot Mediterranean night. He had left Greece the next morning, resigned to his fate.

There is just no escape, he thought.

And now, ten years later and half a world away, standing at Pigskin Paul's with a beer in one hand and a pool cue in the other, Harry was once again thinking pretty much the same thing.

Not that he was afraid of losing at pool. Hardly. Harry had been banned from every pool hall in Kalamazoo by his thirteenth birthday; could rarely even get a game in Detroit by the time he was old enough to drive there. Harry never missed, *never,* and it pissed people off. Scared them sometimes too, for reasons Harry had never understood. There was nothing scary about it, nothing magical. It was the same principle as basketball, as baseball, as marbles or football or any other activity that involved moving an object from one point to another. Harry simply looked at the ball, *saw* which way it had to go, and then moved it that way. Nothing to it.

Nothing, that is, until that terrible, terrible day at the basketball tournament, when his entire Clearasil-coated, fantasy-fueled high-school world had come tumbling down around him. Since his humiliation at the state tournament, just about all sports had been off-limits for Harry. Basketball was out, baseball, football, darts, all impossible to play without invoking that damnable, unwanted gentlemanly reflex. Even nondirect projectile games, like tennis, croquet and, yes, pool, would immediately initiate the phenomenon. Thoughtlessly tossing a wadded-up paper into a classroom trash can had once caused hapless Harry a half-hour hard-on, to the whispered amusement of his sharp-eyed students.

Not that Harry was monstrously overendowed; he wasn't. He had measured himself in a burst of teenage curiosity one night, and found himself to be a comforting one-quarter inch above the Masters and Johnson-proclaimed national average. The problem was, when Harry's pubic problem manifested itself, it went all out—and straight out. His pants became home to a rock-hard self-inspired tower of exhibitionism, an immovable, inconcealable five-inch flagpole.

It was humiliating. Harry had tried everything he could think of to cure the problem, consulted doctors, dieticians, psychiatrists and sports psychologists. He tried every form of clothing and contraption known to man. Some were uncomfortable, some were unfashionable and some just downright hurt—but none were successful. Masturbation didn't necessarily make the problem go away; the problem, one understanding but unhelpful specialist had told him, was emotional, not erotic.

It seemed a horrible addition of insult to injury when the few friends he had left after blowing Rosewater High's play-off began shying away from him—but he could hardly blame them. Who, after all, wanted to spend time with a guy who couldn't toss a football around, who couldn't play Ping-Pong or tennis, who couldn't even throw a Frisbee without becoming a public spectacle? In college, he had drunkenly confessed his problem to several of his fraternity brothers, who were beginning to suspect his refusal to participate in sports meant he was gay. They thought it was hilarious, and took to tricking Harry into throwing things just to watch the effect his inevitable reaction had on their blushing dates. Soon enough, the novelty wore off, and once again Harry's "friends" began treating him with the polite coldness usually reserved for cripples and other people's parents. Branded by his peculiar difference, Harry was alone.

Harry had been alone—except for his beloved books—for so long that he thought he had grown used to it, accepted it as the normal course of his life; but the last few days had changed that. In Jane Ellen, he had found a true partner, a soul mate whose scars seemed to match his, a friend and lover who had filled the unfillable void in his heart. How ironic that the only way he could think of to keep her, to provide the money they needed to keep on running, would invoke the curse that had kept him alone for so long.

Harry shook his head and signaled the bartender for another beer. They had splurged on two cold longnecks with the money left over after filling Jane Ellen's prescription and paying the tournament entry fee; Harry had meant to make his last at least until the tournament started, but his nerves were getting the best of him.

"Harry," Jane Ellen said. She placed one delicate hand on his knee and, without facing him, gestured down the bar to where a small crowd had gathered around a pale, scraggly man wearing combat fatigues and a dingy T-shirt bearing the familiar anchor-and-fishhook logo of Langer Seafood. The man was picking up a fresh-poured pitcher of beer; Harry expected him to begin pouring mugs for the semicircle of people gathered around him. Instead, he raised the pitcher up above his head, and, at a signal from a watch-bearing waitress, poured the beer into his open mouth.

Harry had seen people drink beer before, of course, had seen shotgunning and funneling and just plain-out hard drinking—but he had never seen anything like this. The beer flowed into the bearded man's open mouth and out of sight as fast as he could pour, vanishing down his open gullet with no sign of a gulp or swallow. He may as well have been pouring a pitcher of water down an open drain.

The man finished the beer with a flourish, slammed the empty pitcher down on the bar and looked expectantly at the waitress. "Nine seconds," she said, and the group gathered around the drinker groaned. The drinker laughed, coarse and loud as a seal's bark. He wiped a dribble of foam from his beard with the back of one hand and scooped a handful of bills from the bar with his other. He jammed the money into his pocket, said something unfriendly to his victims, and staggered off toward the rear of the barroom.

"Got no throat." Harry looked up to see the bartender standing beside him, fresh bottle in one hand and a long black clipboard in the other. He put the bottle on the table in front of Harry and gestured toward the drinker with his chin. "Name's Gush. Claims he was in Central America a few years ago, Nicaragua or El Salvador or some such, got himself shot through the neck. Says they had to replace his whole damn throat with a big plastic tube, and now he makes his living off bar bets like that. He pours the beer straight down, doesn't even get his throat cold. Can't feel nothing, doesn't even know he's drinking until it hits his stomach."

"Wow," Jane Ellen said. "Doesn't he still get drunk?"

"Shit-faced, all the time. Calls it an occupational hazard. He's going back to the bathroom now to puke so he can make another bet. Does it four, five times a night, got his stomach muscles built up so good the beer comes up near as fast as it goes down. That's why they call him Gush."

"Yuck." Jane Ellen took a ladylike sip from her own bottle and frowned thoughtfully. "What about, I mean, doesn't he get like disability and stuff from the Army?"

"Who knows? He says he was doing top-secret stuff, poking around where he wasn't supposed to be, and now the government won't even admit he ever worked for them. Me, I figure he's making it all up, except for the bit about his throat. Hey, your name Harvey?"

"Harry. No, uh, that's right, Harvey. That's me."

The bartender looked up from his sign-up sheet without comment, then back to the sheet. "Tough break, bud; you drew Jackie C. He wins more of these things than he loses. Table three, right there in the middle." He pointed toward the phalanx of pool tables dominating the back half of the barroom, tucked his pencil over one ear and turned away.

"Great," Harry said under his breath. "Show time."

"Don't worry, honey. You'll be great," Jane Ellen said. She gave his arm an affectionate squeeze and smiled.

She was trying to understand, Harry knew, and that helped. He had told her about his problem—told her about his loneliness and his childhood and his wanderings and damn near everything else in his life, and then laid there listening in rapt attention while she did the same—and she had been supportive and understanding. She hadn't joked, she hadn't questioned him, declined his offer to toss something and give her a demonstration. "Frankly," she'd said with a perfectly straight face, "I'd rather do it myself."

But that had been out on the *Miss Behavin'*, out there in their own private nautical fantasy world. Now they were back in the real world, in the steamy smoky neon lights of reality, and more than anything in all the world, Harry was afraid of how Jane Ellen would react to what she was about to see.

Jackie C. had greasy black hair, bad teeth and a tattoo of a blood-dripping knife on his muscular upper shoulder, but despite it all was pleasant enough, even friendly. Trouble was, he had brought his own audience. An adoring girlfriend, a trio of darkly looming Cubans with identical knife tattoos, and a growing circle of unattached bar patrons familiar with Jackie's reputation for brilliant pool. A dozen or so of them ringed the table, at least half of them women, perched on bar stools and other tables like Romans come to watch the lions at play. Harry wiped his sweaty hands on his shorts and took a long draw on his Budweiser.

Jackie C. broke with a sharp snap of his wrist, scattering the nine balls and dropping the 4-ball into a corner pocket. He sank the 8-ball with a nice combination off the 1, then rattled the 1 into the side before leaving a long shot at the 2 just a touch wide. Harry licked his lips and stepped up to the table.

He stood for a minute looking down at the familiar green felt. The 2-ball was an inch off the wall, just short of the corner pocket—an easy shot, even for someone who hadn't picked up a cue in nearly ten years. Harry didn't really need the "magic" vision that had carried him through so many victorious Michigan afternoons; but there it was. He saw, faint but undeniable, a narrow path of lighter green running along the felt from the cue ball to the 2, like the first stripe of mown grass through a long-neglected field. All he had to do, Harry knew, was send the cue ball sliding along that path. Simple.

Harry knelt over, sent the tip of his cue slipping through the circled "O" of his left forefinger a few times, and then lined it up behind the cue ball. He hesitated a few seconds, letting the old feeling return to him, then slapped tentatively at the cue. It rolled quietly down the table and clicked into the 2-ball, dropping it neatly into the corner pocket.

Harry walked around the table, watching his magic line appear between the cue and the 3-ball. He would have to cut it fairly sharply to send it sideways into a side pocket, being careful not to put enough force into it to send the cue on down the table and into the far corner pocket. He studied the shot carefully for a moment, then leaned over and lined up along the cue. Just a delicate touch, that's all, careful but not too light, and then—

Someone giggled.

Harry heard it without wanting to, like a soldier hearing the distant *whomp* of a mortar being launched. He swallowed hard and then sent the cue ball into motion, watching intently as it slid down the table and nicked the 3-ball just enough to cut it nicely to the right into the side pocket. It was a nice shot, a fine shot, but even as he stood up, Harry knew the rising tide of whispers growing around the table was not about his game.

"Hey, dude," Jackie C. said, "what you bring the extra stick for?"

The group of people surrounding him exploded into laughter, and Harry felt all the blood drain from his face. He turned and walked, as dignified as possible, to his next shot, but he couldn't keep himself from letting his eyes drop down to below his waistline. Sure enough, it was there. His treacherous cock was jutting forward like the lone tree on a bald mountaintop, tepeeing Jane Ellen's hand-made shorts like sails stretched taut to a mainmast. His curse was back, back and strong as ever.

Harry tried to tell himself it didn't matter, tried to focus solely on the game. That was the only thing that mattered, the only thing that was important. Winning the tournament meant winning money, winning time for him and Jane Ellen to be alone again. If she still wanted to be with him, that is; to spend her time with a laughingstock, with a walking freak. He knew she was right there, sitting on a bar stool just out of his view, but he wouldn't let himself look at her. He forced himself to raise his stick and to focus on the table, to tune it all out, but the crowd was growing now as more people came over to see what the fuss was about. The laughter was rolling over him in stinging waves. He tried to line up his shot, leaned in to stare at the cue and the 5-ball, but his magic line wasn't there. Then it was there, but crooked, then gone, then back and swaying like loose fishing line. Harry felt the laughter rising up around him like an incoming tide, thought for a moment he was back in the Dearborn Civic Center with the basketball title on the line, felt like all the sad and lonely nights he had ever spent on his own were rising up to overwhelm and claim him for their own, felt like he was drowning.

And then Jane Ellen was there.

She was right beside him, her hand on one arm, her face impassive. She stared right into his eyes, her own the color of the Gulf in the morning. Then she put her hand on his cheek, rose up on her tiptoes and very gently, very lovingly, kissed him softly on the lips. She drew back and looked right at him a moment more, totally oblivious to the hoots and howls all around them. She turned and walked back to her barstool, sat, looked at Harry expectantly, and smiled.

Harry watched the corners of those beloved lips turn up and felt like he was being enfolded in the arms of an angel. There was no mocking in that smile, no pity or humor. There was only warmth and quiet confidence. That girl loves me, Harry thought. He had thought it before, out there on the boat, but it had been sort of an abstract, fantasy-world sort of thing. Now, with that gentle smile cutting through the humiliation like a laser through the fog, Happy Harry Harper knew without any doubt, knew right down to the tips of his toes, that he was loved.

He looked back down at the pool table, where the white cue ball and the distant 5 were connected by an emerald-green line straight as a stick. He leaned over, swung his cue into position and without hesitation sent the 5 rocketing into the corner pocket. The riotous crowd responded with sarcastic applause. Someone said something about his sense of direction, but Harry paid no attention. He walked halfway around the table, distantly aware that there was no longer any tension in his pants, and executed a complicated combination that dropped the 6-ball flawlessly into a side pocket.

There was little applause and no laughter for that one. When Harry smacked the 7-ball in with a quick bank shot there were appreciative murmurs, when he dropped the 8 with a table-length drive several people commented on the nice leave, and when Happy Harry Harper dropped the 9 in with a simple shot to the corner, Jackie C. himself nodded in appreciation, slapped Harry on the back, and said, "Good game, dude."

Harry hardly heard him. He had eyes only for Jane Ellen, who was still sitting there, smiling solely at him. He walked up to her and cupped his hands around her face. "Jane Ellen Ashley," he said, looking directly into the most beautiful eyes in the world, "I think I'm in love with you." Then he kissed her, and the two dozen strangers who had gathered around to laugh at Harry's affliction burst into enthusiastic applause.

Harry didn't mind the attention, didn't mind it at all, but he could feel Jane Ellen smiling self-consciously beneath his kiss. He drew back and she buried her face in his shoulder, blushing furiously. Someone made a joke about his plans for the night, but it was friendly, and then Jackie C. slipped a fresh cold beer into his hand. It was wonderful, it was intoxicating. Harry knew it was only the first round, that he had half a dozen games to go to win the tournament and the money, but he had no doubt it would happen. He was on top of the world, his arms around his beloved, surrounded by happy supportive people, his curse apparently cured.

Harry was so happy that he never even noticed when throatless Gush, who had been standing right behind Jane Ellen through much of the game, abruptly spun around and walked away. Had Harry not been so preoccupied with his own problems, he might have noticed that Gush, who had already tossed down and then tossed back up four or five pitchers, had been drunkenly taking in the whole affair right up until Harry called Jane Ellen by name; and that he then suddenly became very awake. Harry might have even wondered what had sent drunken Gush so determinedly staggering to the back of Pigskin Paul's, where he shakily dropped a quarter into the hallway pay phone and slowly punched out a number.

But Harry *was* preoccupied. He didn't know, couldn't know, that even as he moved to the second round of Pigskin Paul's Greater Tampa Bay Area Friday Night Pool Challenge, his number was already up.

They should have left as soon as the tournament was

over, or at least after buying that first comradely round for Jackie C., his girlfriend Carla, Jackie C.'s two quiet cousins and Jerry the bartender, who kept the bar open for their little party long after most of his paying customers had headed on home. Harry knew that, knew that Jane Ellen knew it too. But it just felt too damn good, these easy relaxed beers with friendly company. Leaving Pigskin Paul's would mean returning to the fray, going back out onto the battlefield where God-knows-who might be waiting for them around the next street corner. So they stayed, tempting fate, Harry listening to stories of the Tampa barrios and telling lies about his student days while Jane Ellen and Carla quietly traded confidences in a corner booth.

When they did leave the bar Jackie C. insisted on playing taxi driver, driving them halfway across town and then making out with Carla in their red Fairlane while Jane Ellen and Harry shopped their way deliriously through the aisles of the neon-lit all-night grocery. Then he took them to the docks, where they passed another fifteen minutes or so saying their goodbyes; Jackie sternly advising Harry with one arm draped over his shoulder, Carla and Jane Ellen tearfully hugging, breaking out in laughter and then hugging again. When their new friends finally departed, their aging Fairlane huffing out greasy clouds of carbon monoxide into the late summer air, Harry and Jane Ellen stood on the deck arm in arm until they were long out of sight.

It was nearly 5 A.M. when they finally stepped onto the familiar deck of the *Miss Behavin'*. That was good,

Harry figured. A couple hours' sleep before the dock master opened for business, then they could get their radio out of hock and leave Tampa Bay on the morning tide. He yawned heavily and put his arms on Jane Ellen's shoulder, guiding her sleepily through the open door and into the boat's main cabin. He remembered too late that the door should have been closed; realized there was already someone in the cabin just as something hit him hard above the ear and drove him off into blackness.

Jane Ellen gasped and dropped to the deck beside Harry. She pulled his head up onto one knee, feeling something warm and wet roll over her fingers. She pushed her hands down over his chest, terrified, and didn't relax until she felt him take a strong breath. Then she looked up.

There was someone standing just inside the door of the boat, his face covered by shadow. One hand was out before him in a strip of street light shining through the open door, and Jane Ellen could see that he held a thick, short blackjack. He stood there a moment, watching her from the shadows like death itself, before stepping out into the open light.

"Hey, Jane Ellen," he said.

Jane Ellen felt like someone had just kicked her in the stomach. She let out a heavy sigh, dug her fingers into the thick sailcloth of Harry's shirt, and dropped her gaze to the floor.

"Hey, Nate," she said.

18

Now Harry liked an occasional bit of déjà vu just as much as the next guy, but this was getting ridiculous. He had managed to pass thirty-one reasonably active years without once finding himself tied up, much less tied up to a bunk in a rapidly moving sailboat, and now it had happened twice in barely a week. It was enough to make a man swear off women. Or at least swear off sailing.

The only advantage to waking up tied up more than once, Harry figured, was that you learned a little from experience. This time, instead of simply popping his eyes open and cursing at whatever happened to be waiting for him, Harry was letting himself ease back into consciousness slowly, eyes closed, breathing steadily, savoring and thoroughly considering each new bit of information as it came to him.

First, and most important—his hands were definitely tied. Tied much more securely and much less gently than the last time. And no silky undergarments this time; judging from the scratchy itchiness ringing both wrists, his assailant had gotten into *Miss Behavin*'s storage bins and found the spare sail ropes. Not good—not only did it hurt, but it meant that Harry had been out long enough for his attacker to make himself—or herself, or themselves—right at home.

Second—the *Miss Behavin*' was chugging along, judging from the regular slap of waves against the bow, at a pretty good clip. And she wasn't running under sail; Harry could feel the steady rumble of the aft diesel engine pumping away. Also not so good—his attacker had been anxious to get away from land, which implied he was not associated with the police. It also meant he had been confident enough to refill the boat's near-depleted tanks. Before or after we came back from the bar? Harry wondered. Good God, how long was I out?

Last, Harry was not alone in the *Miss Behavin*'s cabin. He could sense, with the near-radar sense of the even-temporarily blind, someone sitting on the bunk across from him, level with his head, about three feet over. But who? Even if he was ready to open his eyes, Harry wouldn't be able to see the other bunk without turning his head, and he couldn't do that without alerting whoever was sitting there that he was awake.

A dilemma. Harry listened hard for any give-away sounds, but whoever was there was sitting quietly, without even the simple decency to sneeze or cough or quietly mumble his name. Harry held his breath and focused hard on listening, but got nothing other than the normal sounds of the boat in motion. Finally he gave up and took a deep breath. He breathed through his nose, steady but slow, trying to avoid making any give-away snorts. The act brought the familiar scent of spice and sunshine to his nose, and Harry grinned widely and opened his eyes.

Jane Ellen was there.

Harry turned his head and, sure enough, his beloved was sitting just a few feet away. Her eyes were closed, and she was not crying—Harry got the unmistakable impression that Not Crying is exactly what Jane Ellen was doing—but she had twirled a thick strand of her sun-yellow hair into a long cord, draped it into her sweet mouth and was chewing away at it timidly. She had her legs drawn up protectively onto the bunk before her. In all the troubles they'd been through together, Harry had never before seen Jane Ellen looking so much like a scared little girl.

"Hey Janie," he said. He hadn't meant to whisper, but somehow that's how it came out, soft and gentle, as if he were in the library back at UM-Detroit.

Jane Ellen's eyes popped open. She dropped the hair, gave a relieved little sob, and threw herself on top of Harry. Harry instinctively tried to wrap his arms around her, but couldn't, of course, because of his bonds. He contented himself with covering the top of her head with kisses, reveling in the touch, the sound, the scent of her closeness. Ropes be damned, Jane Ellen was there and that was enough.

"Jane Ellen. What the fuck you mean loving on that dirty smuggler like that?"

Harry felt Jane Ellen tense up against him. Together,

they raised their heads to stare at the dark figure standing in the cabin doorway. He was about Harry's height and age, slender, almost skinny, but wiry and strong-looking. He had dark hair, cut just a shade longer than a military crew. He wore fatigues, black boots, an Army-green T-shirt. He had a thin red scar running across most of his forehead, and his eyes were sharp black marbles.

"Harry," Jane Ellen said, "that's Nate."

Nate. Harry felt his world teeter a bit more. Not the gangsters then, either his or Jane Ellen's, and not the police. Nate. Jane Ellen had talked about him only the slightest bit, only enough to let Harry know that he was someone from her past she did not want to revisit, not even in conversation. And now here he was, in the flesh, in control. Harry wasn't sure what to think, but he could feel tension running through Jane Ellen like an electric current.

Nate just stood there, glaring at him silently, and Harry felt threatened and confused and uncertain all at once. Jane Ellen didn't move, but somehow her body language had gone from seeking comfort to providing cover. It was she who finally broke the heavy silence.

"Harry, guess what," she said. "Nate told me I didn't kill that guy after all, the Senator's kid? He just drifted under a dock and stayed there all night, high or something. Nate said he came out in the morning wrinkled as a raisin, hung over, and scared the shit out of all the cops there looking for his body."

"That's right," Nate said. His gaze shifted from Harry

to Jane Ellen, and Harry could hear the anger in his voice drift away into . . . what? Affection? Tenderness? Love? Whatever it was, it made Harry's heart sink.

"They aren't after you anymore, Jane Ellen. Never was, really. There was no reason for you to leave. No reason you can't come home."

"Is that why you kidnapped me then? Why you hit poor Harry and tied him up? Because there's no reason why I shouldn't come home?"

"Don't be like that, Jane Ellen. It's gonna be different now, I swear. I've changed. I haven't had a drink since you left, not a drop. I got your old job at the O&P; I been saving a little money. Billy let me have an old oyster skiff on credit; I been fixing it up some. I figure once I got enough money for a seafood license I can start up oystering, and you can go back to Billy's, and—"

"And you can go to hell, Nate. Straight to hell. I'm not going anywhere with you. I'm with Harry now, and I'm staying with him."

"Jane Ellen." Jane Ellen and Nate both turned toward Harry, surprised, almost like they'd forgotten he was there. But he was there, and he was hurting, and what he had to say next almost killed him.

"Jane Ellen, maybe he's right."

Jane Ellen looked at Harry like an injured animal, and this time there were tears in her eyes. "Harry . . . ?" she said.

"Janie, darlin', listen to me. You can go home now, you can go anywhere you want. You're free. But me . . . I'm still wanted, Janie, the police will be after me for killing Campeón Razon. And the guys who own this boat, they'll be after me, too. I can't ask you to be part of that, not now, not when you can have a normal life again."

"But Harry, I don't want normal. I want you!" Jane Ellen buried her face in Harry's shoulder and wrapped her arms around his neck (or at least as much around them as she could, with the ropes in the way). Harry tried to say something, found he had an immense lump in his throat, and simply closed his eyes to better appreciate the feeling of his heart breaking.

Nate snorted. Harry opened one eye just a bit. Nate was glaring at him again, but this time he looked as much confused as angry.

"A chicken?" he said.

"What?" Harry replied, somewhat inanely. He didn't know if he was being insulted or not.

"A chicken. A rooster. You're going to give up my sister because of a rooster?"

"Your sister?" Harry said.

"A rooster?" Jane Ellen added.

"Yes, my sister, and yes, a rooster. A champion rooster. *Campeón razon.* That's what you said. In Spanish."

Harry didn't say anything. Jane Ellen looked at him, confused as Nate, and then let a little smile creep onto her face. "Harry . . . ?" she began, but Harry didn't answer. He was thinking, thinking hard, trying to push back through the surreal hangover-tainted weirdness of that morning in Cielo Bay, trying to remember the village and Juanita's little farm through the alcohol-induced haze. There had been the house, and the little barn, and the chickens, and the goats . . .

. . . and every morning he had awakened early to the sound of a rooster crowing . . .

. . . and the hole he'd blasted through the wall was right out toward the barn . . .

. . . and Juanita had said, "You bastard, you *yanqui* bastard, you killed Campeón, you killed my Campeón razon."

You killed my champion rooster.

"Oh God," Harry said, and grinned.

"Oh Harry," Jane Ellen said, and sighed.

"Oh Christ," Nate said, and left.

He wasn't gone long, though—not long enough to suit Harry, anyway—and when he came back he was holding a long bare knife from the *Miss Behavin*'s galley. Harry swallowed hard and wondered if there was any chance at all he could land a good hard kick in Nate's crotch before he got slashed up, and he could tell by the way her muscles flexed that Jane Ellen was thinking along the same lines. But Nate didn't hesitate. He walked right past Jane Ellen, grabbed the rope holding Harry's left arm and sawed through it with a few deft strokes. He repeated the maneuver on the right rope, then stuck the knife into his belt and stepped back.

"Get up," he said. "I want to see you explain *this* to my sister."

Harry sat up, rubbing his wrists, and Jane Ellen helped him to his feet. They walked out into the boat's main cabin to find Nate standing beside the coffin dominating the center of the room. He had the knife out again, and was working diligently at the brass clasp holding the coffin lid shut.

"Nate!" Jane Ellen said. "What are you doing? You can't–"

But he could. A muffled click came from the sprung coffin lock, and Nate, eyes glittering above a wolfish grin, swung the coffin lid open. The lid swung up toward Harry and Jane Ellen, blocking their view of the coffin's contents. Eerily, a rush of white fog billowed out of the coffin, briefly hiding Nate in a smoky blanket. When it cleared, Nate was peering at them over the lid, Dracula playing Kilroy, one eyebrow raised quizzically.

"No way!" Jane Ellen said. "No way, Nate. You may be out of your head, but I don't want to see no dead body, now or never. You close that damn lid!"

But Harry, somewhat to his own surprise, did want to see. He had sailed with that coffin for nearly a month, evaded it, ignored it, learned to live with it, alternately wondered about it and tried his best not to think about it, and somewhere, deep down inside, had wondered maybe just a tiny bit if it did in fact contain the charred and crusty remains of a Central American war hero. He took a few steps forward, walked past Jane Ellen and around the corner of the raised lid. Then he looked down into the coffin, frowned, and looked up into the expectant face of Nate.

"That's not a body," he said.

"No," Nate replied. "It's not."

"It's not?" Jane Ellen said. She too walked around to

stare down into the coffin. The three of them stood there a moment, gazing down at the dozens of heavy plastic bags nestled in the black satin lining. Finally, Jane Ellen poked at one bag and broke the silence.

"That's dry ice," she said. "That's where the fog came from."

Harry nodded, more perplexed than ever. "But why would anybody pack a coffin full of dry ice?"

"Right, like you don't know," Nate said, sarcasm thick in his voice. He dug through the top layer of bags, most of which had melted into just ponderous bags of water, and pulled one out of the middle. It was just a heavy duty freezer bag, Harry realized, maybe a foot square, clouded with frost. Nate rubbed the frost off with a corner of his T-shirt and held it up for all to see.

"Crabs," Harry said. "Little green crabs."

"Pregnant little green crabs," Jane Ellen added. "See those orange clumps attached to their butts? Those are eggs."

"Little green momma crabs," Harry said. "There must be dozens in there."

"In just that bag," Jane Ellen added. "And look, here's another just like it. And another."

"And another, and another—no, wait, this one's only got eggs in it. This one, too."

Harry and Jane Ellen kept at it, digging their way into the coffin like ghouls at a body buffet. They stacked bag after bag at one end, then reversed the process, counting all the while, while Nate glowered in silence behind them. Eighty bags in all, most packed tight with crabs, or eggs, or both. Two dozen more ringed the edges of the coffin; once frozen solid but now only flaccid balloons of chilly water. Two bags were empty of all but a few smears of orange crab eggs; another was half-full.

"Seventy-seven bags of eggs," Harry said. "In five-pound freezer bags."

Three hundred and eighty-five pounds of frozen crab eggs, Jane Ellen wondered. "What would anyone want with three hundred and eighty-five pounds of frozen crab eggs?"

"Well, not quite that. Remember, some of them are just crabs."

"Right, but there's also the two empty bags."

"OK, and maybe, what, fifteen bags are crabs only? So sixty-five five-pound bags of frozen crab eggs."

"Three hundred and twenty-five pounds of eggs. How many hundred, how many thousand, to a pound? And some of the crabs may have been pregnant."

"I thought when they were pregnant the eggs were on their butts."

"No, that's only after the eggs are fertilized. They carry them inside till they're ready for that."

"If they're pregnant but not fertilized, then some of the un-egged crabs must be boy crabs."

"Right, sure. So, say seventy-five pounds of crabs, with and without exterior eggs."

"And say half have got eggs showing."

"Thirty pounds of eggless crabs. Maybe half are male."

"So that means—"

"Enough!" Nate exploded. "God dammit, who cares how many god damn pounds of god damn crabs are in there! That doesn't matter. What matters is *this*." He grabbed Harry by the shoulder, spun him around and pinned him against the coffin. Before Jane Ellen could react, he drew his knife-hand back, waist high, and slammed it forward as hard as he could.

Forward, that is, into the coffin, right through a bag of eggs and deep into an interior casket wall.

For a moment, the room was quiet except for the sound of water dripping off the two freezer bags in the surprised Harry's hands. And then—

"Um, Nate," Jane Ellen said. "Why did you just stab the coffin?"

"Smuggler-boy here knows, don't you, Smuggler-boy?" Nate glared at the taller but much lighter Harry, one hand braced steady against Harry's chest, the other drawn back, ready to strike.

"Um . . . well, no," Harry said.

"God dammit!" Nate said. Harry felt Nate's hand tense against his chest, and decided he was about to get his ass kicked. But not just yet—Nate drew back just a little, keeping that one hand hard in Harry's chest. With the other hand, he fumbled about in the coffin, eyes locked on Harry, until he found the knife hilt. "OK, smart guy, explain this!" He yanked the knife hard along the inside of the casket, ripping through the silk lining. Harry saw something white and feathery spill out of the lining wherever the knife cut. Nate, though he was staring non-stop at Harry, clearly got a glimpse of it, too.

"Ah ha!" Nate exclaimed. "So what do you call that, Smuggler-boy? Cocaine? Heroin?"

"Styrofoam," Harry said.

"What?"

"It's styrofoam, Nate," Jane Ellen said gently. "See?" She dipped one hand into the coffin and brought it up to where Nate could see. Slender fingers, wet with cold water, smeared with gooey orange crab roe, dotted with a dozen or so little white balls. Styrofoam.

"What the hell . . ." Nate said. He let go of Harry, reached into the coffin and ripped loose a long stretch of the black-silk lining. There was just a little padding there, a half-inch or so of beige fabric. And under that—styrofoam.

"I'll be damned," Harry said. "That stuff must be six, eight inches thick."

"God dammit," Nate said, voice dull as dirt.

"Have to be," Jane Ellen said, "to keep those eggs cold this long."

"God dammit," Nate said, louder this time.

"Of course," Harry added, "they didn't know it was going to be at sea this long."

"God dammit. God dammit God dammit God dammit!" Nate suddenly grabbed the coffin lid and slammed it down, hard, and spun on Harry, knife in hand. "Where's the fucking drugs?" he demanded.

Harry frowned, torn between fear and his growing exasperation. "There are no drugs, Nate," he said. "The first couple days I was aboard, I was going nuts with boredom. I tore this boat apart looking for something to read, something to write on. I searched every inch of this place—and there are no drugs here."

"Then why is there a coffin full of ice here?"

"To keep the crabs and eggs cold, Nate," Jane Ellen said. She sounded like she was talking to a slow child.

"You keep eggs cold in a cooler. In a freezer. Not in a coffin. Now you tell me," Nate said, menace shining in his voice like mercury in moonlight, "you tell me, why is there a coffin on this boat?"

"Nate," Harry said. "I honestly don't know."

"God dammit."

"It was supposed to be a body, a soldier," Harry said. "A pilot in the Honduran Air Force. I was bringing him up here to be buried."

"Uh-huh. And you were hired by these two guys down in the Dominican, these two strangers, to sail this dead pilot up here?"

Harry looked at Jane Ellen, who shrugged. "That's right," he said.

"And these two guys, strangers you met on a beach, they just gave you their boat and let you sail off into the sunset?"

"Right."

Nate glared at him for a moment, stoically, then raised one hand to rub the bridge of his nose between thumb and forefinger in exasperation. "All right," he said. "If you wanna do this the hard way." Nate raised his knife again, parallel to the deck. The eight-inch blade gleamed like quicksilver, shiny as sunlight, except for where a few clumps of crab roe sat on it like orange marmalade on a spoon. Harry stared at silver death and wondered inanely if crab eggs would infect a freshly opened wound. The world hung frozen for a moment, frozen like crab eggs frozen like knife blades frozen like ice in a casket, and then Nate took one determined step toward Harry—

And Jane Ellen was there, stepping between Nate and Harry like a momma bear defending her cub. She swept Harry behind her, holding her arms out like spread wings; when Harry tried to push her aside she would not budge. And Nate was frozen too, stopped in mid-stride like a marble carving of an ancient warrior, staring down at the slender woman before him.

"No," Jane Ellen said. "I love him, Nate, and I swear, if you touch him, I will never speak to you again. I will jump off this damn boat and swim to shore, and if you catch me again and again and again I swear to God you will never ever hear my voice. I mean it, Nate."

Nate twitched, intensely focused, taut muscles unwilling to relax. Harry saw the angry light in his eyes slowly dim, and Nate lowered the knife. "All right, Jane Ellen," he said. "All right. But this ain't over yet. Not by a long shot." Nate wiped the knife on his pants, then carefully moistened his fingers and ran them lovingly along both sides of the blade. He slipped the knife through his belt and, catlike, licked his fingers clean. He stopped suddenly, fingers still on his lips, and shot Harry an intensely curious look. That deadly fire surged back into his eyes for just a moment, and just as quickly disappeared.

Nate kept Harry locked in the stateroom the rest of the

day while he and Jane Ellen worked the sails. He let Harry out not long after sunset and the three of them ate a quiet meal of fried pork chops, corn on the cob and fresh salad Jane Ellen had assembled. It was easily the best meal Harry had had in weeks, but he barely noticed it.

After dinner Nate locked Harry and Jane Ellen in the stateroom once again—"I got some thinking to do," he said, "and I can't be worrying about you two knocking me in the head"—and went to work on the *Miss Behavin*'s faulty radio. Harry could hear him clinking tools around, occasionally muttering to himself or slamming around the outer cabin in frustration. Jane Ellen sat on the captain's bunk, watching in silence as Harry stood listening, ear pressed against the cabin door. Finally he gave up and joined Jane Ellen on the bunk. Harry lay on his back and gratefully let Jane Ellen slide halfway atop him. He slipped his hand up under her T-shirt and started massaging her tense back muscles. After a few minutes, without any prodding from him, Jane Ellen finally told Harry Nate's story.

"I was only three years old when Daddy died," she said. "He got cancer. He worked in a paper mill outside Jacksonville, and Momma always swore it was the chemicals he was around that did it to him. I don't know.

"Momma said it took Daddy a long time to die, lying in his bed, too weak to stand. The mill gave him a little money but not enough, so Momma had to go to work waiting tables. Sometimes she worked two jobs at the same time, worked one restaurant at breakfast and lunch and then tended bar someplace else at night.

"Nate tried to get work, but he was only about fourteen, and besides, somebody had to stay home and take care of me and Daddy. So he quit school, and he'd spend all day changing my diapers and making lunch and cleaning the house, all the stuff Momma was just too tired to do. Mostly, though, he sat and listened to Daddy talk. Even when the cancer was real bad, when Daddy was out of his head with pain and the drugs, Nate would sit there and listen to him for hours and hours. Nate told me once Daddy told him all about his own life, about meeting Momma and falling in love, and how Momma and Nate and me were all he ever had or ever wanted. Mostly, though, Nate said, Daddy talked about how Nate was now the man of the house, and how we were all gonna be his responsibility once Daddy was gone.

"Momma tried to make Nate go back to school after Daddy died, but he wouldn't do it. He took any kind of job an underage kid could get, delivering newspapers, mowing lawns, and God knows we did need the money. One day he went down to the recruiting center in Jacksonville, lied about his age and joined the Army.

"Momma was never happy about that, but it kept us all off welfare. Nate had a steady check coming in, and when he got assigned to Fort Bragg, up in North Carolina, he packed up me and Momma and took us with him. We lived in a little apartment right off the base; I remember I would stay with a neighbor lady while Nate was on-duty and Momma was out waitressing.

"Nate never had the education to go for officers' school, but he was always looking for ways to upgrade his pay. One day he joined the Special Forces. He got good at it, real good, and one day some government men came and told him they wanted him to go on a special assignment, off overseas. Nate didn't really want to go, but they offered to make him a sergeant, and give him combat pay, and more on top of that besides. I was starting school then and Momma was assistant manager at a Shoney's, so we were doing all right, and Momma told Nate to go ahead and go.

"Nate was gone for nearly three years, and we barely heard from him that whole time. We didn't know it then, but he was in El Salvador, helping the government fight off the rebels. He wasn't supposed to be there, not in combat anyway, so it was very hush-hush. Momma and I wrote him all the time, but he said he never got any letters. Partly it was because he was out in the jungle for months at a time, really out of touch. Partly I guess they just didn't want him getting distracted.

"So they never even told him when Momma got the cancer, too."

Harry moved his free hand up to where Jane Ellen was knotting her fingers distractedly through the thin thatch of hair on his chest. He took her hand in his, raised it to his mouth and gently kissed her palm. Jane Ellen let her hand linger there for a moment, balanced delicately on Harry's lips, before taking up her story again.

"When Nate got back to the U.S., I was off living in a youth home in Raleigh. The Army said the CIA had told them he was dead, and besides, I was Momma's dependent, not his, so they turned me over to the social-services people. Nate stormed out and came up to Raleigh to get me, but the state people said he couldn't adopt me 'cause he wasn't married, and I wasn't his legal dependent, and that was that.

"Nate tried talking to lawyers for awhile, and even went to court. But he had gotten strange in El Salvador, mean and violent, and he was drinking all the time. The judge said no.

"One night about a week after that I woke up to this scratching on my window, and there was Nate. We packed up my stuff and lit out for Florida.

"I was happy to go with him, but the state said Nate was a kidnapper. Not only that, but he was AWOL too. We moved around for a year or so after that, Nate getting odd jobs wherever we went. Finally we sort of settled in Apalachicola, where he could work most days at a fish house or on one of the boats, for cash, and nobody bothered much with last names or social security. I even started going back to school a little.

"But Nate was sick, sick with something he'd caught down in the jungle, sick with paranoia about the Army and the CIA and the government, and I think sick too from feeling he'd let down Daddy and Momma and me too. He started drinking more and more, at first for medicine, then out of habit, then 'cause he needed it. After a while he couldn't get work anymore, 'cause the fishermen all knew he'd show up drunk or hung over or not at all. We couldn't get welfare or food stamps or nothing 'cause we were fugitives. Mostly we lived off what people gave us out of sympathy, or what Nate could beg or shoplift.

But I learned how to fish and catch crabs and cook polk salad, and Nate found us an empty house out in the woods, so we got by.

"But living out like that, with no heat or running water, Nate just kept getting sicker. He had nightmares a lot, and he'd drink to make them stop, and that made him mean. He hit me sometimes, when he could catch me, and then later he'd apologize and cry and beg me to forgive him and swear I wouldn't ever leave him. But I knew I would."

"And then you got the job at the bar."

"Yeah, then I got the job at the O&P, and ran away, and then I met you. And now Nate's here and he's dragging me back to all that, and I'm scared he's going to hurt you."

"I can take care of myself, Janie."

"I know you can, Harry, but you don't understand. Nate's Green Beret, and he did all that jungle fighting, and I think maybe he's a little crazy. Oh, Harry, what are we going to do?"

Harry started to say something, something comforting, but nothing came to mind. So he just wrapped himself around Jane Ellen as tight as he could. Then he kissed her, and then he kissed her again. After a minute Jane Ellen sat up and pulled off her T-shirt, and then her shorts, and Harry's shorts too. She kissed him and straddled him and guided him inside, and they made soft quiet love to the gentle rhythm of the waves. Harry lay on his back looking up at Jane Ellen, her eyes closed and head cocked slightly back, soft blond hair flowing down between her breasts, and thought for sure his heart would break if ever he lost her.

But all the while, Harry could hear the muted sound of Nate's voice through the locked cabin door—and the insistent crackle of the *Miss Behavin'*'s radio answering back.

19

From his office on the twelfth floor of the Florida State Capitol, Senate Dean Jerome M. Langer could see the very spot where a handful of cold and hungry Spanish explorers celebrated the very first Christmas Mass held in the New World.

Langer liked that. Not that he was a particularly religious man, or that he was big on history; he was neither. But Langer knew the whole story of that first mass, had heard it from a nervous assistant state archeologist trying to pry a few dollars from the Senate Appropriations Committee, and there was something about it he liked.

The first mass, held back in December of—what was it, 1538? 1539? Something like that—had been celebrated by Hernando De Soto and his men, one of the first groups of luckless Spaniards to come tramping through Florida in search of gold and finding only mosquitoes, fever, Indians and alligators. De Soto had made his camp in an abandoned Miccosukee Indian village, right there off to the side of what was now the Apalachee Parkway, just across the street from Bennigan's fern bar and the Parkway Shopping Center. The village was abandoned, freshly abandoned, because the Indians living there had heard that the devil De Soto was coming. By that time the frustrated gold hunter had acquired quite a reputation for enslaving, killing and casually mutilating any of the locals who got in his way, and the Miccosukees weren't stupid.

And *that*, Langer thought, was power. The kind of power he liked, power so strong that it didn't even need to be used to be useful. At that stage of his career, before the mutinies and the malaria and his slow sad death cursing his strange new world, De Soto was so strong that he didn't actually have to *do* anything; he just had to show up, and things happened.

Langer had spent his lifetime acquiring just that sort of power. That was, in fact, why he had arranged for his office to be on the twelfth floor, eight stories above his Senate and House colleagues, eleven floors above the governor's ground-floor office and his transparent fiction of accessibility. What bullshit. You got power so you could get *away* from the common people, so that you didn't *have* to spend your time kissing asses and looking humble. And once you got power, you flaunted it, you put it in people's faces and in their minds. When you had enough power, the right kind of power, like De Soto, and like Langer, then things got done for you without you having to ask. Just being in the neighborhood was enough.

That philosophy had brought Langer a long way.

Brought him up from backwater Bay County, where he was the dirt-poor son of a dirt-poor fisherman, ignorant and scrappy and mean as a snake. Langer had been a big kid, and strong, and just smart enough to realize that that was all he had and that he had better damn well make the most of it. So he bullied all the kids around him into doing what he wanted, stealing lunch money from weaker kids and eight-tracks out of unlocked cars. Later on he and his lieutenants had forged a coalition of East Bay fishermen, set prices with the Panama City restaurants and fish houses, and run off anybody who didn't play along. That had given him the collateral to form Langer Fisheries, and the clout to put himself on the Bay County Commission.

There Langer had learned his next important political lesson—that money breeds money, and power feeds on power. Langer Fisheries became Langer Industries, and the county commission seat took him up to the state House and then the Florida Senate. Along the way he'd left a trail of battered and bankrupt opponents, some of them broken legally and some of them, well, just broken. Eventually his reputation started feeding on itself, and Langer got credit for things he didn't do. When a business rival got drunk, fell off his boat and drowned, people figured Langer had done it, and the lack of evidence just meant he had done it well. Langer didn't raise a finger to discourage that thought.

In the Senate, Langer used the same tactics that had always served him so well. A favor done there, a threat carried out here, rookie senators intimidated into line and opponents pushed over the edge. Senators who supported him found pork-barrel bonuses in the state budget; those who didn't found they couldn't get bills out of Langer's Rules Committee and unexpected opposition at re-election time. Eventually, Langer became a legend, and, like most legends, rarely had to *do* anything. He just let it be known what he wanted done—and it got done.

That was all well and good—but it was also why he found his current dilemma so noxiously galling. It had been years since Langer had stirred himself, years since he had allowed himself to become directly involved in any but the most important projects. Now he had himself involved right up to his neck, right up to his head, and things were not going well.

It had been a gamble all along, Langer knew that, and normally he wouldn't have touched it. But the potential rewards were so great, so very tempting—and besides, Langer was ready for a new challenge. He was at the top of his mountain, with no opponents willing to tackle him and no more hills to climb. He'd thought about buying himself a congressional seat, but going from number one in Florida to a rookie role in the House didn't have much appeal. He'd toyed with the idea of a run at the governorship, but, despite all his power inside state government, Langer doubted that he had the money or the public appeal to carry a statewide election.

And so he sat in his deluxe twelfth-floor office like a fat old spider, shooting down bills just for the fun of it, promoting colleagues he knew he could control, playing kingmaker in both the House and Senate and laughing when the liberal lawmakers and downstate newspapers railed their impotent criticism. It was a simple game, one he'd run for a long time, and, truth be told, Langer was pretty damn tired of it. Absolute power might corrupt absolutely, he figured, but first it bored the piss out of you.

Langer sighed and took a sip of twenty-year-old bourbon from the cut-glass crystal he held in one hand. "Did you ever feel that way, you old Spanish bastard?" he said aloud, surprised even after all these years at how his voice sounded so small in his ludicrously huge office. "Did you ever get tired of having them all lay down before you, ever wish one of those poor terrified Indians would just stand up and take a swing at you? Just so you could swing back?"

Langer raised his glass in mock salute toward De Soto's long-ago campsite. Sunlight shining through the window lit up the fine crystal, casting a rainbow of reflected light on the Senator's weathered brown hands. There were scars on those hands, lots of them—but they were old scars. Langer could barely remember the days he'd come home with hands slashed and swollen from twelve hours of gutting sharp-finned snapper, or knuckles scraped raw from loading crate after crate of oysters or crab claws. It had been years since he'd had even a decent political battle. And the last time he'd actually duked it out with another man, fists knotted tight and fire dancing through his belly—well. A damned long time.

And that, Langer knew, was the real reason he'd agreed to a meeting when he got the phone call from an old colleague he hadn't done business with since the early days, a colleague he had no business even acknowledging. That was why he'd sat there and listened to that quirky, oddball little Cuban accountant, why he'd let himself get wrapped up in the whole crazy project—he badly needed somebody, something, to take a swing at.

That was also why he was on his way to this damn meeting today, a meeting that would take him far from his familiar arena in political Tallahassee. Things were in a mess; the project was apparently shot all to hell. If it was going to be salvaged at all—and Langer had his doubts about that—he was going to have to step in and take some direct action himself.

Damn it all. It had seemed like such a wonderfully balanced plan, one careful step leading inevitably to the next like dominoes falling in a line, every possible option considered and accounted for.

And then that damn fool Al had started eating crab-meat omelets.

It had been an unsettling two weeks for Quiet Quiones. First, his amateurish attempt at kidnapping (he had botched it from the beginning; Boulder and Carlos and every half-grown hood on Carlos's payroll had made that abundantly clear). Then his near-death when he was thrown from the balcony by that crazy, treacherous vixen in the red underwear. The utter collapse of the most important scheme in his life when Jane Ellen had hijacked—amazing!—the very boat that played so crucial a role in Quiones's plan. Then Carlos's unexpected fury at Quiones. He should have been proud, proud that Quiet was trying to live up to their common Hispanic heritage, but instead the Iceman had cracked wide open, broken into a furious rage that left Quiet fearing for his life and devoid of respect for the man who had long been his role model.

Then his best friend Boulder, himself fallen from Carlos's good graces, angrily announced that they were friends no longer; said, in fact, that they never had been. Then all those days locked up in a back room of the mansion, wondering if he would see the sun again, and the sudden long drive up the entire length of the state, knowing all the while that he was on probation with Carlos, his very life depending on salvaging something of the great plan. Quiet Quiones had lost his self-confidence, his only friend and his faith in Hispanic brotherhood all at once, and still might lose his very life. It had all shaken poor Quiet right down to his bones.

And then he had found God.

Well, maybe not God, not exactly, but at least religion. Maybe not even religion even, certainly not the down-on-your-knees-and-beg-forgiveness sort of church religion Quiet's devoutly Catholic mother had dragged him to every Sunday and Wednesday of his childhood, but at least—at last!—something great and wonderful and beyond himself. Something to believe in.

It had happened the third day they were here on St. George Island, nearly a week ago. They—Quiet, Boulder, three of Carlos's gunmen, the injured giant named Tiny and his horribly ill partner Al—were all staying in a huge house belonging to Carlos's silent partner (Quiet was the only person other than Carlos who knew that partner's identity; he knew too exactly what would happen to him if he let it slip). The house was on the bay side of the island, away from the beach and the tourists. The oddly matched little group had settled in, secluded and safe and secured away while they waited for Carlos himself to arrive.

Quiet wasn't a prisoner, not exactly, but he knew better than to try and wander off. When he did go out, for a walk over to the beach or to the only store on the island that sold a decent newspaper, one of Carlos's henchmen would always be there, a little behind but always in sight. Usually it was Rey, quiet as death, lean and sharp as the switchblade he constantly used to pick at his shark-white teeth. Quiet had no doubt that, if Carlos allowed it, Rey would happily put that knife to work on him.

Rey had been standing out on the end of the house's private dock that momentous afternoon three days ago, crabbing. He had become obsessed with the hobby since a friendly clerk at the St. George Bait and Breakfast Shoppe had explained it to him; now he would stand out there in the blazing Gulf sun for hours at a time, trailing a rotten chicken neck into the water at the end of a long thick cord. Every now and then he would feel a steady tug on the string and, laughing hysterically, reel in a fat Atlantic blue crab. The crabs, either too stupid or too stubborn to let go, would hang onto the rancid bait even when they were pulled out of the water, through the air and onto the dock. Rey would then punt them as far as he could with his sharp-toed black-patent shoes, or casually slice them up with that switchblade, humming and chuckling all the while.

Quiet should have known to expect Rey out on the dock that day, but he was preoccupied with his own troubles. He had come down the sandy path from the house, eyes down to spot the prickly sand spurs that seemed to jump up at anyone passing by. He hadn't noticed Rey until he raised his head and took that first step out on the dock. Rey felt the dock vibrating beneath Quiet's step from thirty feet away and had turned to stare at him, teeth bared in a hungry smile, eyes dead and dark.

What to do? No way Quiet wanted to walk out onto that long slender dock with Rey, but he didn't want to just turn around and give the man the pleasure of knowing he had run Quiet off. He glanced back toward the house; already, he could hear the footsteps of whoever was assigned to follow him that day coming down the path. To the east the shore was an impenetrable tangle of eelgrass and oyster shells, but to the west a slender sandy beach ran down about forty yards or so toward a pine-covered point jutting out into the bay.

Quiet turned around and dropped down to sit on the beach-side end of the dock, doing his best to look like that was what he had planned all along. He pulled off his shiny black loafers—he had returned to dressing like an accountant when he realized just how tired Carlos was of him trying to be one of the tough guys—and then rolled off his skintight black nylon socks. His feet were pale white in the bright afternoon sunshine, white as a

Caucasian's feet, and Quiet wondered momentarily about the last time he had gone barefooted.

Quiet felt the vibration of Rey walking down the dock toward him. Without turning, he stood and jumped down to the beach, surprised at how soft and warm the sand was. He rolled up his pants legs and walked a step or two out into the bay—also pleasantly warmer than he had expected—before turning to wander off casually down the beach.

He heard Rey's footsteps come to a stop on the dock behind him, then a low greeting in Spanish as Rey hailed whoever had come down from the house—Pinto, probably, or maybe Juan. He could barely make out their low conversation over the steady slapping of the bay's small waves beneath his feet. They were arguing, no doubt, about who would have to follow Quiet on his walk. It didn't really matter much to him; Quiet did not want to share the narrow dock with Rey, but he knew full well that he wasn't really going anywhere.

He rounded the little point, momentarily behind a stand of pines and out of his guardians' sight, and stopped. Before him stretched a little half-moon inlet, perhaps thirty yards long, lined with more scrub pine and a few spindly tall mangroves. The steady lapping of the bay had eroded the beach down to a red clay base sloping sharply downward. He put a foot hesitantly on the cool ruddy clay; it was slick and wet, and would make treacherous footing. Behind him he heard the heavy scrunch of a shoe in sand and decided to push on a bit farther.

Quiet took a tentative step forward out onto the clay,

then another. On his third step he slipped and went scooting down the slope toward the water. He waved his arms frantically, trying to keep his balance, and came to an abrupt stop once his feet were barely submerged. He could feel sand between his toes again; obviously, the beach was only eroded where it was above the water line. Quiet sloshed on along the shoreline toward the next bend, smiling to himself at the thought of Rey trying to follow along the clay slope in his fashionable Miami street shoes.

Around that bend was a fairly long straight stretch of dirty sand. Quiet knew he was pushing his luck, getting this far ahead of his paranoid pursuers, but he decided to push on long enough to see just around the next bend. He was distantly aware that he had put several turns between himself and the bridge connecting St. George to the mainland; the regular swoosh of crossing cars had faded out entirely.

The sand here was striped with dark wet dirt; in spots it was almost muddy. There was an aerial map of the region on one wall of the house he'd left behind; Quiones figured the dirt was silt brought down from Georgia and dumped into the bay by the Apalachicola River.

Quiet heard a heavy thump and a muffled curse from behind him. Wonderful, he thought. Serves the bastard right. He jogged off over the sand, circumventing another small half-moon beach toward the next point.

Here Quiones ran into a bit of an obstacle. There was a tall pine tree right on the tip of the point; apparently it had once been back away from the water but erosion had worn away the ground until it now stood barely a foot above the high-tide mark. The waves had removed the soil from around the tree's arm-thick roots, leaving them exposed and reaching out toward the bay like arthritic old fingers.

Quiet moved up to the tree and carefully slipped one leg over the largest root, leaning on it for support as he went. He brought the other leg over, then moved on to the next root, balancing carefully on an exposed rock. Then up and over the next root. The sand here didn't look like sand at all; it was brown and wet-looking, dotted all over with little black lumps. Quiet raised his back leg to bring it up over the root, and—

What was that sound?

Quiet froze, leg still in the air, holding his breath, and the noise quickly subsided. It had sounded like paper rustling, perhaps, or the wings of a thousand insects folding all at once, or fields of dried brown corn rattling in a strong wind. Quiet suddenly became intensely aware of just how far he was from anything manmade, realized in fact that he was probably as deep into the untamed wilderness as he had been in his entire city-bred life. He had vague flashes of rattlesnakes and poisonous insects and other unimaginable threats from the wild kingdom.

Quiones glanced slowly around him, trying to move his eyes without turning his entire head. He could see nothing unusual, and the mysterious clacking noise had not reoccurred. Still, he suddenly wished that whichever bodyguard was following him would hurry up.

Ten seconds passed, ten more, and nothing happened. Quiet decided there was nothing to worry about, not really, he simply needed to turn around and head back toward the house. No problem. First thing he needed was to get both feet on the ground, then swing around and head back over the roots. Quiet went back into motion, swinging his raised leg carefully out before him.

And the ground ahead of him stood up and moved.

Moved, not like a man moves, or an animal moves, or even like the earth moves in an earthquake. The muddy beach before him shimmered and rolled like a black sheet twisting in the wind, moved like a wave of long black hair flipped over milk-white shoulders, moved in a thousand separate pieces all sliding together, like choppy animation from an old movie cartoon.

Quiet stared, blinked his eyes and stared again. The moving earth stopped and separated itself into a thousand black spots on a bed of brown muck, each spot waving a thick blunt arm in front of itself protectively.

Crabs. Hundreds of them, maybe thousands. Some small as a fingernail, others as stubby and plump as Quiet's thumb. They were black as road tar, and had bulbous little eyes raised high on short stalks, all of them still and watching him as if he were center stage at a rock concert. Each one had a single small claw extended upwards, and a disproportionately large claw, nearly as big as the rest of the crab's body, held in front of itself like a fat black shield. Quiet raised one hand and they all moved again, darted backwards a few inches in perfect coordination. The thousands of crusty legs skittering across the sand sounded like dry leaves rustling in a high wind; their bodies dancing sideways in perfect unison again created the momentary illusion that the beach itself was moving.

Quiet blinked, let out a breath he had not been aware he was holding, and swung his raised foot out and down onto the soft black muck before him. The ooze squinched up thick and cool between his toes, soft and squishy. Quiet flashed on childhood afternoons running barefoot through the wooded lots and muddy construction sites of urban New Jersey; wondered briefly how long it had been since he had felt mud between his toes. He felt a rush of dizziness and let himself drop down onto the heavy pine root behind him. The bark underneath was rough and stringy and wet with salt spray, and felt more vital and alive than anything he'd felt in years.

Quiet heard a splash out in the water ten feet away from him. He looked up just in time to see a long slender fish pop up out of the water, hang suspended and shining in the open air for a brief second, and then splash back down into the waves. The same fish reappeared a moment later, and then again. A few feet behind, a second fish exploded out of the water, then a third, and a fourth. Mullet, Quiet remembered. Pinto had said the jumping fish were doing the mullet dance when he pointed them out to Quiones that first day at the bay, but now, to Quiet, their performance seemed much more than a simple aquatic ballet. It was a circus, a celebration, a vibrant, brief embrace of a world just slightly beyond their reach, a whole school of living, breathing beings struggling together to push beyond their limits. They were courage and desire personified.

Quiet was watching for more mullet when he saw a shadow pass over the slight waves. He looked up to see a large hawklike bird hanging suspended out over the bay. The bird hung almost motionless some forty feet up, eyes glued on the water below, wings moving ever so slightly to maintain its balance against the wind. Then it folded its wings and knifed straight down into the water, from the sky to the sea in a dazzling few seconds. Almost immediately the bird slapped its wings against the water's surface and rose up again, holding a sleek silvery mullet tightly in its talons. It flapped enough to get a few feet above the water, then stopped flapping long enough to shake its body dry like a dog fresh from a bath. Shining drops flew off the bird's tail feathers and caught the sun, prisming the late summer rays into a thousand separate rainbows.

Quiet Quiones was transfixed. There was beauty here, yes, beauty that he had somehow missed seeing for years. But more than that, Quiet sensed a wonderful unity, a common, perfect purpose. The fish, the bird, the crabs, the sand and water and waves, all of it existed in a perfect and wonderful balance, each playing its perfect part without complaint, without thought. It was exactly the sort of belonging that Quiet had searched for all his life, in the neighborhood gangs of Trenton, in college, in Carlos's group, in his incessant, obsessive search for a unifying Hispanic identity. And here it all was, spread out before him on nature's canopy. He rubbed a tear from his eyes, wiggled his toes happily in the soft brown muck, and wondered at the thought that he too just might have a place in this amazing united world.

He was still sitting there, happily squinting out at the dazzling dancing bay, when Rey came stumbling around the bend. Rey's black leather shoes were soaked and ruined, his pants were spotted with seawater nearly up to his waist; red mud streaked across both hands and one cheek. He was in a foul humor, and clearly intended to take it out on Quiet. He strode up to where the mousy little accountant sat on an exposed tree root and raised his hand ferociously up to his head, fully intending to backslap the silly bastard right into the sea.

And then he stopped. Rey looked down at Quiones and felt all the anger seep out of himself, felt himself grow confused, and then almost embarrassed. He dropped his arm, muttered something about Carlos wanting them, and, with Quiet following serenely behind, turned and walked back toward the house.

Later, Rey would dismiss it as a momentary lapse of will, as a temporary softening of his iron-hard heart. It would never happen again, would not, in fact, have happened in the first place if he hadn't been so taken aback by the look on Quiones's face.

But how in the name of Jesus, Joseph and Mary, Rey thought, could he possibly have hit someone who could smile like that?

Senate Dean Jerome M. Langer hitched up his sleeve and checked the time on his two-thousand-dollar Rolex for the third time in the last ten minutes. Time to leave for his meeting. Past time, and still he found himself reluctant to leave the familiar comfort of his Tallahassee office. Instead he poured himself another finger of bourbon and gazed out the window toward De Soto's old campsite. Langer knew the ending of De Soto's story as well as the beginning. He thought once again about the terrible old explorer in his final days, his search for El Dorado ended in total catastrophe, cursed and abandoned by the few crewmen still alive, feverish and dying in a strange land full of enemies who thought him part god and part devil. I wonder, Hernando, Langer thought, at what point did you look up and realize you'd lost control? You crazy old son of a bitch—did you ever realize it at all?

Langer stared out his window and sipped at his bourbon, wondering why it never seemed to taste as good as it used to.

20

The way Billy Byars figured it, things had been going pretty steadily downhill since Jane Ellen Ashley left.

It hadn't taken long for word to spread that the quiet girl with the strange smile and the wicked trick had gone, and that what little entertainment could be found in Eastpoint on a Saturday was no longer at the ramshackle fish shack out on Highway 98. The tourists and college boys and charter-boat captains had vanished, vanished like sea foam stranded high on the beach, and even the regulars had taken to complaining of boredom and leaving early. Billy knew too that they weren't too fond of the bartender he'd hired to replace Jane Ellen—and he couldn't blame them. Not that the guy was rude, or mean, or even unfriendly. He just went about his job, did all that was asked of him and no more, and when that was done he'd settled in leaning against the bar, arms folded, keeping to himself. It was hard to say why—but the fact was, he gave people the willies.

Billy hadn't ever really meant to hire him in the first place. Like most folks along the Apalachicola, he knew Nate's reputation, and Billy was not inclined toward hiring drunks. But he couldn't help feeling sorry for ol' Nate the first few times he'd come around the O&P, asking after Jane Ellen. He looked as hurt and forlorn as one of the unwanted kittens and lame hunting dogs that got abandoned pretty regular in the natural forest, and sooner or later ended up run-over and stinking out on 98. Billy didn't expect Nate to wander out in front of an eighteen-wheeler, but he pretty much figured Nate would end up about the same way.

So Billy was surprised when Nate showed up early one morning, painfully sober, asking for work. Not surprised enough to hire him, of course, but surprised nonetheless. He was also pleasantly surprised at how Nate took his refusal. He just kind of nodded his head, frowning down at the ground, twisting his worn old baseball cap in his hands. Then he'd walked next door, to Fizer's Fishery, and talked to Fizer for awhile before leaving there too. It was the talk of the O&P that night, how the crazy drunk hermit from out in the forest had gone up and down the whole mile-long stretch of 98 that was Eastpoint's main street, asking at every fish house, oyster boat, convenience store and service station, looking for a job. Everybody figured he was just in shock over losing Jane Ellen, and he'd retreat to his woods and his bottle soon enough.

But Nate was at Billy's door again the next morning, and the one after, and the one after that, looking more human and less like a burned-out torch every day. Billy got to expecting him about the same time each morning, and got tired of hearing his customers deride the man. He was some kind of kin to Jane Ellen, after all, and Billy was missing that woman a lot more than he would have expected. So what the hell—after eleven straight days of saying no, Billy decided to give Nate a job.

It wasn't entirely altruistic on his part. The crowds were still coming in then, and even though they always asked for the dunking lady, Billy still had hopes that they might keep coming for, well, the atmosphere, maybe. At any rate, on Wednesdays and weekends things were still so busy that Billy had to beg Lurlene to come in and shuck oysters, and neither one of them was too happy about that.

And then, Nate worked dirt cheap. Not that Billy was taking advantage of him or anything; he wouldn't do that. But Nate had insisted from the very beginning that he only wanted cash, and that he didn't care for social security or withholding or anything of that sort. Billy tried to talk him into it at first, but somehow Nate just wasn't the sort of guy you kept after once he said no. Besides, the revenue agents rarely got to Eastpoint.

So Nate worked steady, and he worked cheap—but he bothered the customers. He never smiled, he never laughed, and somehow he made other people reluctant to do so either. Nate was a one-man wet blanket, a dour black hole who could suck the life out of a room just by entering it—and to a bar, that was death.

But even the naysayers who had laughed when Billy hired him had to give Nate credit—sometimes he seemed to sweat a bit much, handling all those cold beers and double-shots, and if you looked close enough you could see his hands still trembled every now and then, but Nate hadn't touched a drop in weeks. How could you fire a man like that just for not being the life of the party?

Eventually, Billy decided to go to Plan B—*B* for breakfast. Opening the O&P for breakfast was an idea he had been toying with for some time now, but when Jane Ellen was around he didn't have the energy or the need to do so. Now, with his customers disappearing like sea foam in the sun, with Nate often as not getting paid to just stand around and maybe crack open two or three beers in an hour, Billy decided it was time to reallocate his resources.

Billy had heard the local oystermen complaining for years about the lack of early morning sustenance available in Eastpoint. You could microwave a frozen sausage biscuit over at the Majic Mart, or get up a half-hour earlier to drive over the bridge to Mary's Morning Mess over to Apalach, but for men who hit the water before sunrise and might not come back till dark, neither was a satisfying option. Most oystermen badgered their wives into getting up to make a 4 A.M. breakfast, or made do with a handful of beef jerky or tin of Vienna sausages. But they weren't happy.

Unhappiness in some, Billy had learned long ago, could mean opportunity for others. So he'd used his fresh-earned credit to stick a big griddle back behind the bar, stocked up on eggs, bacon, sausage and instant grits, and opened the O&P for sunrise breakfasts.

It was an instant hit, and, happily, Nate was a perfect

fit for it. Tired fishermen who didn't want the grim bartender looming over their late-night drinking appreciated Nate's quiet nature when they came in barely awake and grumpy for coffee and the three-egg special. Nate wasn't a great cook, but he was quick, and he didn't mind coming in at 4 A.M. to heat up the griddle and pack up fresh-made sausage biscuits for the oystermen too rushed for a sit-down breakfast. Nate was so good, in fact, that after a week of running himself ragged trying to tend bar at night and scramble eggs each morning, Billy decided to make Nate his morning manager. He gave Nate a fifty-cent raise and a spare set of keys, and gratefully went back to sleeping till noon.

The breakfasts weren't as lucrative as the beer-and-booze crowd of the O&P's heyday, of course, but they sure helped take the sting out of Jane Ellen's disappearance. His nighttime business missed the tip-happy tourists, but at least his pre-Nate customers were staying around till closing again. The money was unspectacular but steady, and Billy figured that once he'd paid off the new griddle, he'd be able to get himself back in the black.

And then Nate disappeared.

It had been three days ago, on a Wednesday. It was the second Wednesday of the month, so Billy had Nate come in to handle the St. Joe Paper Company workers who wanted to celebrate payday somewhere other than in Port St. Joe. The phone had been ringing, which usually meant a hassle from somebody's pissed-off wife, so Billy had signaled Nate to answer it and had gone back to work on the stubborn top of a pickled pigs' feet jar he was struggling with. Fifteen or twenty minutes later, with customers backed up at the bar and getting rowdy, Billy had noticed Nate's neatly folded apron sitting beside the cash register.

Billy tried to tell himself Nate had just got sick and run off to puke or something. When Nate never showed, Billy figured he'd gone off on a bender and would be back in a day or two, contrite and hung over. But three days of working both shifts had burned out Billy's patience, and so today he had given Fatty Wingo five bucks and a six-pack to lead him to Nate and Jane Ellen's shack out in the woods. There was no one there; judging by the pregnant possum curled up on the mattress in the cabin's main room, there hadn't been for some time. Billy halfheartedly ran the possum off and trudged back to the O&P.

Now, normally Billy kept the O&P closed from 10 A.M. till 7 P.M., but he was hot and tired and wanted a beer, and damned if he'd pay retail. He got back to the bar at about noon, and was surprised to find a customer sitting on the front steps, patiently waiting for him to arrive.

He was an out-of-town fella, a salesman or maybe a bureaucrat, judging from his blue suit and black shoes. He was carrying a suitcase, though, a fat shiny aluminum-looking thing, so Billy allowed himself a moment of hope that the stranger was the advance guard of a new wave of tourists that would once again find their way to the O&P. He smiled his best smile, unlocked the door and invited the man in for a drink.

Billy was disappointed that the stranger only wanted ice tea, extra sugar, but he was determined to be sociable. He got the man his tea and a beer for himself and sat down to chat a spell.

"Well, now," Billy said. "Hot enough for ya?"

The stranger didn't answer. Instead, he held one finger up for silence and took a tiny taste of his tea. Then, apparently satisfied with the flavor, he tossed his head back, raised the glass and poured the entire thing down his throat. Literally poured. As far as Billy could see the stranger never swallowed, not once, just let the tea flow straight down until the ice cubes clinked against his teeth. It was the damnedest thing Billy had ever seen.

The stranger opened his mouth wide enough to let in exactly one ice cube, and crunched down on it hard enough to make Billy wince. Then he carefully put his empty glass down on the table, glanced at Billy's untouched beer, then looked up at Billy and smiled.

Billy knew without doubt that he had just been challenged. Challenged, in his own bar, by a total stranger. Well, so be it. Billy might not be able to inhale tea without swallowing, but he could damn sure shotgun a beer. He took a deep breath, raised his Bud longneck and bubbled it down to the backwash. Then he put his bottle down and returned the stranger's wry smile.

"You know, it is a bit warm," the stranger said. "I could use another glass of tea. More sugar this time, if you don't mind."

"No problem," Billy said, though he knew damn well the tea had just the right amount of sweetener in it. He went to the refrigerator behind the bar, poured a glass and added a spoonful of sugar. Then he headed back to the table, grabbing another longneck along the way.

"So," he said as he settled into a chair facing the stranger, "what brings you to Eastpoint?" But the man raised that damn silencing finger again, nipped at his tea and then once again tossed the whole glass down his throat, a nice big sixteen-ounce glass of tea, drunk and gone without benefit of a single swallow.

"Needs just a little more sugar," he said. And then he looked at Billy's beer, and then at Billy, smiling that insipid little smile. Billy wanted nothing more than to just reach over there and swat it right off the man's face; what he did instead was raise his Budweiser and chug it dry.

"In Eastpoint," the stranger said, "in Eastpoint, I'm looking for a boat."

Billy nodded, whipping a bit of beer foam off his mouth with the back of his shirt sleeve. "Lots of boats in Eastpoint," he said.

The stranger nodded, staring forlornly into his empty glass. Billy reluctantly stood up and went for more drinks, feeling that he had somehow gotten drawn into a contest whose rules he didn't know and could not win. This time, he added three spoons of sugar.

"I'm looking for a very particular boat," the stranger said. "A Morgan sailboat, thirty-eight feet, sky-blue hull, polished teakwood railings. Seen it?"

"We get lots of sailboats too, coming out of Apalach, but I don't think I recall . . ." Billy's voice faded away in mid-sentence. He stared, all but hypnotized by the sheer weirdness of it, as the stranger effortlessly knocked back his third glass of tea.

Billy picked up his beer, tossed his head back and went to work on draining the bottle. This one took some time, took some work, and he closed his eyes to better concentrate on each chilly swallow. When Billy put the empty bottle down and opened his eyes again, the stranger was up and behind the bar, helping himself to another glass of tea. He scooped in four spoons of sugar and brought back another beer, smiling all the while.

The afternoon took on a quiet surrealness after that. Billy lost track of how many teas his companion tossed back, though he was distantly aware that he hadn't drunk so many so quickly in quite some time. And all the while the stranger asked Billy questions—about the bay, about the local folks, and again and again about that damn sailboat. Billy had the uneasy feeling he was being pumped for information, but since he had nothing to hide, he kept on talking.

And then, quite abruptly—"Where's your bathroom?" the stranger asked. Billy aimed a thumb in the general direction of the gents, and the tea drinker rose and strode off. Billy sat in the silence for a moment, blinking unsteadily at the suddenly empty chair before him, and then decided he could do with a little fresh air. He stood unsteadily, walked to the door leading to the O&P's back deck, and stepped out in the bright afternoon sunshine.

The sun was so bright, in fact, that Billy, emerging

from the dim interior of the O&P, was temporarily blinded. So it was, staggering across the deck dazzled and drunk, that he collided headfirst with his brand-new deluxe tourist-trap-type telescope.

The telescope was heavy brass, mounted about shoulder high on a metal stand right in the center of the deck. Billy had picked the damn thing up second-hand from the man who supplied the big fishing piers at P.C. and Ft. Walton, figuring the tourists—who for some crazy reason seemed to like eating their oysters and boiled shrimp out in the hot, sticky, bug-infested open air—would pump the thing full of quarters, paying fifty cents a shot to squint out over the bay at passing oyster boats and the ever-present pelicans. Unfortunately, by the time the telescope had arrived, the tourists had departed. The only person pumping quarters into the brass-and-glass white elephant now was Billy himself.

Billy had, of course, seen enough beat-up skiffs and broad-beaked birds to last a lifetime, but every now and then he would spot a bikinied passenger on a passing sail-boat, or zero in on a passing pod of dolphin. Even after his forty-seven years at, by or on the ocean, Billy still never tired of seeing those always grinning rascals at play.

Lately, too, he had had something new and a bit puzzling to turn his glass onto. The telescope was strong enough to bring the cottages on the bay side of St. George Island, a half-mile or so straight out across the bay, into fairly sharp focus. Most of those houses were pretty well hidden away behind gangly scrub pine and stubborn live oaks, but a few of them—the best of them—

had sunning decks and even private fishing piers that were easily viewable.

Take, for instance, the bay-front home of Senator Jerome Langer II.

Langer's house was often a center of discussion around the bay. Not that Langer himself ever went there— or, as far as Billy knew, anywhere else in his sprawling district outside of Tallahassee. But Langer often loaned the place out to lobbyists, or other legislators, or big-shot party money men. Those sort of men never showed up without about a two-to-one ratio of beautiful, young, barely dressed women who seemed to spend entire days sunning out on the dock. When Langer's house was occupied, boat traffic by his property just about doubled.

Even when there were no people around, sometimes Billy would turn the telescope on Langer's place just to stare at the beautiful bright-red powerboat Langer kept tied there. It was a semi-cigarette boat, long and fast as those South Florida hot rods used for racing and running dope, but with a bigger passenger area, big enough for, Billy figured, a captain, three mates, fishing gear and a good size icebox. With a boat like that, Billy knew he could pick up three of the richest visitors to St. George Island, get 'em out to the offshore fishing grounds, loaded up on snapper and grouper, and back in time for lunch. But Langer, damn his eyes, mostly just let it sit there for show. A damn crime.

Things had been jumping over at Langer's for the last few days though. Everyone knew about the half-dozen or so out-of-towners who'd been staying there the last

week, about the short fat one who had trudged all over
the island in a three-piece suit, trying to find a copy of
the *Wall Street Journal*—the *Wall Street Journal*, for
Christ's sake!—with the skinny, evil-looking one never
more than a few steps away from him. Everybody knew
about the slow-talking giant with the bad arm who had
gone into the Sunrise Grocery and bought a loaf of bread,
two pounds of cheese, an armful of spices and six dozen
eggs, and paid for it all with a crisp new one-hundred-
dollar bill. Everybody knew too that not one of the group
was a woman, or ever went swimming, or took the cigarette boat out for a run, or, except for the skinny guy who
apparently had a bottomless appetite for crabbing, even
went fishing. But nobody really knew what the hell they
were doing there.

Standing on his deck now, the slight buzz of a beer-
and-sunshine headache already blooming in his head,
Billy realized that there was some sort of activity on the
Senator's dock at that very minute. He pulled two quarters out of one pocket, slid them into the twin metal slots
on the telescope base, and scrunched down to take a look.

The first thing he noticed was that the boat was
gone. Then he spotted two men standing at the railing at
the end of the dock, hands covering their eyes and staring out into the bay. He focused in on the pair, but
couldn't quite see their faces. They were both well-
dressed, middle-aged men, one stocky and silver-haired,
the other slender and dark-complexioned, but that was
about all he could make out.

One man turned to face the other—talking, Billy

figured. Just as he did, the other raised his arm and pointed out toward the bay. Billy raised up from the 'scope and looked in the direction he had pointed. There was the sleek crimson cigarette boat that usually was tied up to Langer's dock, moving slowly down the bay's center, with a single driver on board. About twenty yards behind it a slender sailboat was coming in, her sails limp in the still air. That was why the cigarette boat was putting along so slow then—it was towing the sailboat, or at least leading it in. Billy turned back to the sailboat; drunk as he was he recognized the distinctive lines of a Morgan despite the unusual blue hull. And Billy knew immediately that the tea drinker's ship had come in.

The sailboat was about midway between him and Langer's place, so when Billy turned the telescope on it he got a pretty good look at the people on board. He counted six in all, though there may have been more in the cabin. One man was up on the bow, watching the cigarette boat. Three others were standing just outside the cabin, one steering while the other two watched. Amidships, Billy could make out two pair of legs, one in jeans, the other clearly feminine and in something short. The people belonging to those legs were on the far side of the boat's sail, apparently trying to ease the sails down. The main sail was coming down like a theater curtain in reverse. It dropped the last few feet all at once, and Billy got a sudden clear look at the couple on the far side.

"Holy shit," Billy said. He rubbed his eyes and ducked back to the lens for one more look. Then he stood up, turned toward the back door and nearly collided with the tea-drinking stranger, who had quietly come out and was staring out at the sailboat.

"It's the *Miss Behavin'*," he said. "Teak rails, blue hull, gold stripe along the railing, just like he said. About time."

Agitated, Billy took the stranger by the elbow and guided him back inside the O&P, stopping to lock the deck door behind him. "Listen, buddy, I hate to be unsociable and I sure enjoyed the conversation, but we're closing, closing right now. You be sure and come back, come back tonight and bring all your friends, but I got to go, right now."

"You've got a boat?"

"Well, yes, not much of one but good enough to catch a sailboat, I reckon. Not that that's any of your business, but—"

"I'll be going with you."

"You what?" Billy stopped, his earlier suspicions flaring to life, and glared at the unblinking stranger. "Now just what makes you think I'm gonna take you anywhere, friend?"

"Why, this does," the stranger said. He pulled his suit-coat forward with his left hand and reached into an inside pocket with his right. For one frightening moment, Billy thought the tea drinker was going to pull out a gun.

He wasn't much relieved when the man instead produced a badge.

21

Jane Ellen didn't think she had ever seen the waters of the Apalachicola Bay look quite so perfectly blue.

Maybe it was because the bay was abnormally calm, so there was no Apalachicola River silt stirring around to turn the water its usual brownish-green. Maybe it was just a reflection of the sapphire-blue North Florida sky. Maybe it was because her beloved Harry was standing there beside her with his arm snaked over her tanned shoulder, or because Nate had not had a single drink or said a single cross word and had even cracked a smile or two over the last two days. Maybe—although she refused to consider this idea, even for a moment—maybe Jane Ellen was just a little bit happy to be home.

It had been, after all, nearly six months since she left Eastpoint, including five months in Miami and two weeks more on the *Miss Behavin'*. Miami hadn't really impressed her all that much, and she was a little less driven to get to romantic Paris when she already had all the love she could possibly want right here beside her. Not that Jane

Ellen was reconsidering her desire to see the world—not a chance!—but still, there was something about the feel of the wind off the bay, of the smell of saltwater and the familiar silhouette of the St. George Island bridge, that set butterflies to flitting around in her stomach. She spotted the Oyster & Pool off to starboard, its rickety old deck jutting out into the bay, and started to point it out to Harry. But something seemed to be caught in her throat, and rather than trying to explain, she just pulled his arm tighter around her and nuzzled in close to his sun-warmed chest.

Harry had started giving Nate sailing lessons mid-afternoon of their first full day out of Tampa, skittering Nate forward or astern to tighten this sail or trim that line. To Jane Ellen's surprise, the two men had quickly formed a good working relationship. Nate seemed hungry to learn about sailing, and patient Harry was more than willing to show off his own new skills. The ominous coffin in the cabin still cast a pall over everything they were doing, but for now talk of crime and conspiracy had been replaced by the comradely conversation of sailors working together to catch the wind.

Things were going so smoothly, in fact, that Jane Ellen was beginning to let herself hope that everything would work out. Nate would accept that the egg-filled coffin was just some sort of prank, let it go, and go back to work at the O&P. Harry could call his gangster contacts in Miami, explain to them that it was all a big mix-up and tell them to come get their boat. She and Harry could spend a day or two visiting in Eastpoint, she could show him the beaches at St. George and the best places to catch flounder along the causeway and the lakes back in the woods where you were most likely to see otter, and then they could go ... go wherever it was that they decided they wanted to go. It was all a bit precarious, Jane Ellen knew that, but still, it was the first time in weeks that she had seen any possibility at all of a happy ending.

And then the men in the racing boat pulled alongside, pulled evil-looking pistols out of their ridiculously inappropriate three-piece suits, and ordered the *Miss Behavin'* to heave to.

So much for clear blue waters.

Quiet Quiones couldn't believe his eyes when he realized that the single-masted, blue-hulled sailboat cruising right down the center of the bay was in fact the *Miss Behavin'*.

He was sitting on the dock, meditating and trying not to think about the meeting going on in the house behind him, when he first noticed the boat's distinctive hull. Rey was sitting just a few feet away, keeping a closer watch on him than usual now that Carlos was here. The wispy Cuban was listlessly tossing his ubiquitous knife into the splintery wooden dock, prying it out and tossing it again, and Quiet hoped for just a moment that he wouldn't notice the oncoming *Miss Behavin'*. But then the steady *thock!* of knife-into-wood broke rhythm, Rey let out an under-his-breath curse in Spanish, and Quiet knew he was screwed.

"*Madre de Dios*," Rey said. "That's the boat! That's the boat the whore stole!"

"No, no it's not, it can't be, what would that boat be doing here? And she's not a whore, she's—" But it was already too late. Rey had retrieved his knife and was sprinting up toward the house. He ran up the trail through the weeds, careless for once about his precious shoes, darted past where Boulder and Tiny were sipping lemonade in their usual place on the house's outside deck, and disappeared into the house. Thirty seconds later the doors flew open and Carlos's henchmen came boiling out like ants from a disturbed nest. Rey, Pinto and Juan pounded out onto the dock, jerked the cloth cover off the waiting cigarette boat, and jumped in. They got the boat started and went roaring off just as the Senator and Carlos himself reached the dock, walked past Quiet without so much as a glance, and positioned themselves along the dock's railing to watch.

Quiet turned to watch too, despite the sinking feeling in his stomach. There was no way the *Miss Behavin'* could escape that powerful launch, and he could already see sunlight glinting off the gaudy silver-plated .45 that Pinto always carried. The shit had unmistakably, undeniably, hit the fan.

And Quiet knew what he had to do.

Boulder Baker was really quite surprised at how much he had come to enjoy the company of the gentle giant sitting beside him. Sometimes he thought it was just that Tiny was one of the few people in the world who could make him feel small, and that, unlike virtually everyone else he dealt with, Tiny never showed any sign that he was intimidated, or threatened, or challenged, or for that matter even noticed, that Baker himself was such an imposing figure.

Part of it too was that Tiny was so unlike the people that Boulder had been associated with for . . . for longer than he liked to think about. The people in his line of work, and the people who hired people in his line of work, were always a little edgy, always a bit tense. They had a frantic underpinning to them, a rats-in-a-cage tension that never quite went away, even when they were drinking or screwing or fucking themselves up in whatever manner they preferred. Even Carlos, possibly the most self-possessed man Boulder had ever met, had a hidden edge to him that made Boulder think of razor blades in apples.

But not Tiny. Tiny was as relaxed and mellow and forgiving as anyone Boulder had ever known. Despite their current circumstances, he was as tranquil as a summer night. If he'd had just a little ambition, Boulder thought, Tiny could have made a fortune as one of those phony Eastern hippie-dippie guru guys. Or maybe even as a real one.

But Tiny had no ambition at all. The only things he seemed to care about at all were his cooking and his sick friend, Big Al, still stretched out and looking like death warmed over in the loft bedroom upstairs. If Tiny knew that he was as much prisoner as guest, that Boulder had been assigned to keep a close eye on him and Big Al, it didn't bother him a bit. He didn't seem to resent the hole Boulder had put in his arm that day back in Miami either, even though he still had the arm in a sling, and in fact seemed surprised when Boulder had uncharacteristically apologized for shooting him. Tiny had just nodded and said, "Oh, okay," and gone to get them both more lemonade.

The lemonade was Tiny's current obsession. He was intent on creating the perfect glass of lemonade, refining his recipe with every fresh pitcher he made, and Boulder had to admit each time he thought it couldn't get any better, it did. The two of them could go through a lot of lemonade, especially spending as much time as they did out in the blazing Florida sun. Tiny made breakfast for the whole mixed crew each morning—delicious omelets dripping with cheese and white sauces, fresh-baked biscuits, bacon so crisp it snapped like cheap glass when you tapped it against your plate—and afterwards the two of them would settle in out on the deck. Tiny had found gym shorts and several touristy T-shirts big enough to fit them during one of their visits to the Island Inlet Store and Sandwich Shoppe for more lemons. Boulder had felt ridiculous the first time he put them on, and had done so only to avoid hurting Tiny's feelings, but the more he wore his new beachwear the more he came to resent the stiff black suits he had always worn on the job. Black suits, because that was what he was wearing when he made his first kill. A black suit at his father's funeral, and when the praying and the burying was done, fifteen-year-old Boulder had walked from the church to the county hall, marched upstairs and into the tax assayer's office. In the pocket of that suit was an old Army-issue .45, the very gun his father had used to take his own life when the county came to take his farm.

A lifetime of black suits, a lifetime of guns, Boulder thought, and still his father was dead. Enough.

And so Boulder sat with Tiny on the deck each morning, looking like beached manatees in their garnet-and-gold FSU Seminole shorts and "I got mine on St. George Island!" T-shirts, Tiny's copper-red thatch a crimson contrast to Boulder's stone-bald scalp, sipping their lemonade and discussing Tiny's current recipes or Boulder's future garden. Tiny watched the birds, and Boulder watched the oystermen out working the bay. He liked these distant sunburned men, who spent hours every day tonging for oysters from their little skiffs, thrusting the long double-poles with the heavy metal scoopers on the ends deep into the water, clenching the scoops together, hauling the whole mess in and then starting over again. They reminded him of farmers, the way they were out there every day, in broiling sun or drizzling rain, patiently trading their sweat and skin and muscles for whatever Mother Nature had to offer. Watching them, Boulder felt increasingly distant from his old colleagues, from the itchy-twitchy Hispanic gunmen and their constant directionless energy, and more and more comfortable with the sluggish golem at his side.

When Carlos had arrived that morning, cold and distant and as focused on his upcoming meeting as a circling barracuda, Boulder had felt even more like a stranger among distant acquaintances. It all added up to something he had never felt before.

For the very first time in his long and distinguished career, Boulder Baker was not at all sure what he would do when his employer gave the order to kill.

Truth is, Tiny was just about as happy as he had been in his whole life. Sure, Big Al was still sick, but he wasn't throwing up near as much as he used to, and now sometimes he could get up and walk to the bathroom by himself. And Tiny didn't mind nursing him. Al didn't yell near as much as he used to, partly because he'd been sick so long, but partly too it was because for once he needed Tiny to get by, and not the other way, and Tiny thought maybe that was making Al think about his attitude a little. 'Cause, to be honest, sometimes Big Al was a little grumpy. Sometimes.

And Tiny really enjoyed spending time with his new friend Boulder. He loved sitting on the deck, listening to Boulder talk about the difference between radishes and rutabagas, and growing up on a farm, and how you can make some plants grow more by cutting them down. He liked cooking for a houseful of people, and he thought maybe he was getting pretty close to having his lemonade recipe just the way he wanted it. He had been thinking lately about starting to work on iced tea, but Boulder loved the lemonade so much Tiny was reluctant to put it aside.

And Tiny loved the weather here, and he loved the bay and all the birds you could see in it. One of the guys who really liked Tiny's Cuban omelets had brought him a camera, a fancy new Canon with a great big telescope lens on it that he said he found on the beach, and Tiny would spend hours just watching birds through that big lens. Quiet, the only one of the Spanish people who didn't always go around looking like he'd been drinking Tiny's lemonade without putting the sugar in it first, bought a book on birds and was helping Tiny learn the names of them.

Quiet was teaching Tiny how to play cards, too. Sometimes at night they would sit up in Big Al's room, Al and Boulder and Quiet and Tiny, and they'd pull a card table over to the bed so Al could join in, and they'd play Hearts and Spades and even Bridge, even though Tiny wasn't real good at that one yet.

Tiny knew that he wasn't the smartest guy in the world—Al had told him that, and before that the guards in the joint, and before that his boxing coach, and before that, well, he just knew. But now he knew too that being smart didn't matter all that much, because Boulder told him that. Boulder told him some of the smartest people he knew did really dumb things, and that none of them could cook near as good as Tiny.

And Tiny knew too that he could learn things when he wanted to. Like how to cook, and how to name birds, and how to play Hearts and Spades and everything about Bridge except the bidding part. His trouble, Boulder said, was that he had a hard time concentrating on stuff that didn't interest him. Tiny figured that was right, but then why would he want to concentrate on something that didn't interest him? Like now, for instance.

He and Boulder had been sitting on the deck, enjoying their lemonade and guessing what all the fuss out on the dock was about, and Quiet had came up, looking all serious and worried. He started into telling a long story about the boat Tiny and Al had sailed up from Colombia, and Quiet's boss the mobster, and Tiny's boss the Senator, and something about a coffin, and Tiny had lost interest and drifted off into thinking about maybe just a quarter-teaspoon more lemon juice, and then Quiet said something to Boulder that got his attention back real quick.

"You have to stop them," he said. "They're going to kill the bay."

Now that made Tiny mad. He sat up and made Quiet go through his story again, more slowly this time, and the more he talked the madder Tiny got. After a minute Boulder got up and went inside, and Tiny figured it was because he'd already heard this part of the story before. By the time Boulder came back out a few minutes later, Tiny was about as mad as he'd been in his entire life. He turned around to tell Boulder about how mad he was, and what he saw chilled him so sudden and so bad that he almost forgot to be mad.

Boulder wasn't smiling like he did most of the time now, and he wasn't drinking lemonade, and he wasn't wearing the garnet-and-gold gym shorts or even the T-shirt that said "World's Most Beautiful Beaches" and had the smiling girl in the little yellow bikini. He'd changed

into the black suit with the black shoes and the white shirt
and the skinny black tie he'd been wearing the day Tiny
had first seen him down on that pier in Miami.

Boulder Baker had his working clothes on.

There hasn't been this much activity on his dock, Senator
Jerome Langer II thought, since the day the Manufactur-
ers Association lobbyist hired a stripper to swim up out of
the bay dressed as a mermaid and invited the whole
damn Subcommittee on Workers' Compensation to come
down and scale her.

But here they were, gathered like ants around a pic-
nic pie. Him and his partner Carlos, who he trusted about
as far as he could throw him. One of Carlos's skinny gunmen, grinning like a cat and tying his launch up to one
side of the dock. Two more pencil-thin Cubans, guns
drawn, watching close while their three prisoners secured
the *Miss Behavin'* to the end of the dock. Those three
prisoners, formerly the crew of the *Miss Behavin'*. The
pretty young blonde figured to be the wild woman who
had bewitched Carlos's accountant and then hijacked the
boat. One of the two men with her had to be the sailor his
two bumbling henchmen had hired to bring the *Miss
Behavin'* up from the Dominican; the other, well, who
knew? And coming down the path from the house was
that damned accountant, followed by two of the biggest
men the Senator had ever seen not dressed in football
pads. One of them he recognized as Tiny; the other figured

to be Carlos's notorious hit man. He didn't see his other man, Big Al, but from what Carlos had said he deduced that Al was inside the house somewhere, busy dying.

Langer figured no odder, more mismatched and out-of-place crew had ever been assembled on the shores of the Apalachicola, and that made him unhappy. The whole reason he had insisted on holding this meeting here in the first place, a hundred miles away from the baying hounds in the Tallahassee press corps, was so they wouldn't get noticed. Get things done, get himself disentangled from Carlos and his accountant and the entire out-of-control nasty mess, nice and quiet. And now here he was, hosting a goddamned multicultural circus on his bay-house dock, out in plain view of God and the Devil and any blasted boater who happened to cruise by. Thank God there were no photographers around.

"Okay, look, there's obviously been a big misunderstanding here, but I'm sure we can work it out if we just talk about it for a bit." That from one of the two men on the boat, the skinny one who looked like he hadn't shaved in a month. He took a step toward Carlos and the Senator and one of Carlos's men swatted him from behind with his gun barrel—not really necessary, Langer thought. The man dropped to one knee holding his head and the girl was beside him murmuring condolences immediately. Okay, so that was the girl's boyfriend—Harry, she called him. The other sailor hadn't moved, not a muscle, but there was something about the way he stood, and the cold anger in his black eyes, that made

Langer's hackles rise. He had an immediate suspicion that that one wouldn't go down quite so easy.

"All right, that's enough. I don't want any killing on my property," Langer said. In fact, he didn't want any killing at all. Despite his ferocious and shady reputation, despite the half-dozen or so deaths attributed to him over the years, the truth was that Langer had never killed anyone. Hospitalized a couple in his younger days, sure, but he'd never been involved in an actual murder. Judging from the practiced confidence of the gunmen around him, and from the razor smile on Carlos's face, that was about to change. Langer felt his bowels tighten, and wondered if he had at long last put himself in a situation he could not handle.

But if there was one thing twenty years in the Florida Senate had taught Jerome Langer, it was how to take control of a chaotic situation. Another one was that he who looked like he was in control usually became the one in control—and Langer was used to being in control.

But before he could follow up on his momentary advantage, before he could bark out the orders that would get all these people moving toward the house, out of the open, the giant Boulder went striding by him, ignoring him completely, and walked right up to Carlos. Carlos's other three henchmen shifted their attention noticeably, from their prisoners to Boulder, and Langer wondered briefly just how much control Carlos had over his own hired gun.

Carlos looked up at Boulder looming above him, cool as a cucumber, and raised one eyebrow questioningly. "Yes, Mr. Baker?" he said.

"Quiet says you're going to kill the bay, that you're going to destroy the oysters and drive all the people out. Is this true?"

Carlos gazed at Boulder and blinked, slowly, like a thoughtful cat. He reached into the jacket of his bone-white linen coat, took out a silver cigarette case, and casually lit a slender brown cigarillo before answering.

"Yes, Mr. Baker, that is exactly what I am going to do. And it is going to make me very, very rich."

Carlos stared impassively up and Boulder stared impassively down, and Langer found himself wondering which one would blink first. As it turned it, it was one of the sailors—the unnamed, stocky one—who broke the silence.

"The crabs," he said. Several heads turned toward him, and when no one spoke, he continued. "The crabs and all those eggs. You're going to plant them in the bay."

"That is correct, young man," Carlos said. "And you are—?"

"Nate Ashley. Major Nathaniel Ashley. But why? There's not enough radiation in those crabs to pollute a bay this big, probably not even enough to be noticed. What's the point?" The two other prisoners, Harry and the girl, looked at Nate in surprise. *He's figured it out, at least partly, but he hasn't told them,* Langer thought. *Interesting.*

"The radiation isn't the point. The point is the crabs themselves." This time it was the little accountant who'd spoken. He was standing at the end of the ramp, where the dock ramp widened out into a large rectangular docking area, and every head swiveled to look at him. Langer felt like he was watching a tennis match.

The accountant lowered his head in shame, and Langer remembered it was this odd little man who dreamed up the whole scheme in the first place. And now he's showing remorse? Langer wondered briefly what had changed his mind, and just as quickly dismissed it as unimportant.

"Quiet?" the blonde said. "The crabs?"

Quiones looked up, glanced at the girl and then looked away. "They're not just crabs," he said, almost in a whisper. "They're European greens."

The girl gasped audibly, her companions just looked at Quiet quizzically. OK, the girl knows, but the boys don't, Langer thought. Big deal.

"European green whats?" Harry said.

Quiones started to answer, but the blonde pre-empted him. "European green crabs, Harry," she said. She had one hand on the skinny sailor's arm, seeking support or maybe comfort, but her bright eyes glared back and forth between Carlos and the Senator. Langer mentally upgraded his assessment of her a notch. "They're native to the northern coasts of Europe, to the Baltic, to Denmark and Scandinavia. They're ravenous eaters—and their favorite dish is oyster spat."

Quiones nodded. "An invasive species," he said. "In Europe they're a minor problem, because they have natural enemies to keep the population down, and the shellfish there have evolved natural defenses against them—faster growth rates, thicker shells when they're young. But here—"

"Here they're an oysterman's nightmare," the girl said. "A small batch of them turned up out west a few years ago, in Oregon or something—"

"Washington state," Quiones injected.

"In Washington, and it almost destroyed the whole industry there. The oysters were being eaten before they could grow, and the government put all kinds of restrictions on where harvested oysters could be shipped for fear of spreading the crabs. They spent millions and millions getting it all under control, and that was a small population of crabs, spread out over a lot of water. In a closed system like the Apalach, enough green crabs . . ."

"Like, say, three hundred and twenty-five pounds of eggs, give or take a few," Harry mused. "But why the adult crabs?"

"Because," Carlos said, "the whole point here is to let people know their precious bay is doomed. Obviously."

"They give the eggs a few weeks to hatch, to establish themselves," Quiones picked up. "Then they start salting the bay with the adult corpses. A few wash ashore, a few show up in oyster tongs, word gets sent anonymously to the newspapers. State fisheries people get called in, and then national officials."

"And the bay gets shut down," Harry finished. "And everybody who lives here is out of work and starving and desperate." Quiones just nodded, looking thoroughly miserable.

"But—that would destroy every oysterman here!" That was the girl. Passionate, Langer thought. Too bad she's so scrawny.

"And why?" Harry said. "You bankrupt an entire region, and then what?"

"And then he steps in, the local senator, the local hero," Quiet raised an accusing finger at Langer, "and saves all his poor hungry constituents by buying all their land along the bay, and on this beautiful island. All of it, at cut-rate prices, at great personal sacrifice, using money he borrowed from a misunderstood Miami millionaire with a shady background who's trying to go legitimate." Carlos closed his eyes and nodded his head forward in a modest little bow.

"So that's why the eggs have been irradiated." Not so dumb as he looks, Langer thought.

"I noticed it on the boat," Nate said in response to Harry's quizzical look. "When I cleaned off my knife that time, the roe had this funny tang to it, like some experimental k-rations I had once. But I couldn't figure why anybody would radiate crab eggs. I thought you were smuggling in radioactive material, plutonium maybe, built into the sides of that casket.

"But damn," Nate said, and then "Damn" again. "You really were innocent all along, weren't you?"

"Yep. Still am," Harry said, and then, to Quiones. "So why irradiated eggs? Are you saying they won't hatch?"

"Oh no, they'll hatch," Quiones said. "But the young will be sterile. They won't be able to breed. Just one generation of European green crabs, one generation to ravage the industry and bankrupt all the landowners—temporarily. And then the crabs will all vanish, and the oysters will reappear. But by then all the oystermen, all their families and friends and the businesses who depend on them, will be long gone. And most of the Apalachicola Bay will be in the hands of one heroic, heavily indebted public servant."

"And that's me," Langer said. "The old oystermen will have all taken the money I gave them and relocated, to Alabama and Louisiana and Texas and who knows where else, so the only way I can eliminate my debt is to turn over my holdings on the island to my silent partner, Carlos. With no oyster industry to protect, Carlos will have no problem getting the construction permits he needs to become the largest individual hotelier on the Gulf Coast. He gets the legitimacy he wants and still gets to continue living in the style he prefers. And when the oysters do come back, Langer Seafood has a virtual monopoly on the richest oyster bay in the entire world, not to mention docking rights and a nice chunk of real estate on the island itself. I'm a rich man, and a hero—and soon enough, a United States senator."

"Why, you nasty old son of a bitch."

Langer stopped, surprised to see that it was the blond woman who had spoken; passionate or not, she had been so quiet so long that he had all but forgotten her. He was even more surprised when she strode forward, past the smirking Cuban guards, and slapped him resoundingly across the face.

"You would kill my beautiful bay, you'd destroy all these people who trust you, just so you can go off to Washington and be a fatter cat than you already are?" the woman accused. "You go to hell!"

Langer raised a hand to his reddening face, feeling the group's eyes on him much more sharply than the sting of the slap. He had to act quickly, had to prove his strength now or lose his partners' respect forever. Langer took a step closer to the woman, closer to this sun-bronzed wild-Indian slip of a girl, feeling the old glorious surge of adrenaline fire in his belly. He raised his clenched right fist over his head—and suddenly things started happening all at once.

The half-dressed sailor, Harry, leapt forward and grabbed Langer's arm before he could bring it crashing down on the girl. All three Cubans swung their guns toward Harry. Someone shouted "Now!"—Boulder, maybe? Tiny stepped forward and drove a meat-hammer right fist into the chin of the nearest Cuban, who dropped to the deck and did not move. Boulder Baker spun a stiff elbow into the midsection of the henchman beside him, then chopped a forearm down on the doubled-over man's neck. The accountant pulled a heavy pistol from under his T-shirt and put it up against the head of the surprised Carlos. The third Cuban, Rey, immediately swung his pistol up and took a step toward Quiet, only to be slammed full in the chest with a perfectly executed karate back-kick from the major that sent him staggering backwards into and over the dock's railing.

Rey dropped his pistol as he went off the dock; Langer lunged forward, scooped it up, and then felt his whole world explode into crimson agony. The gun slipped from his nerveless fingers as he dropped onto his knees and rolled over, groaning, into a fetal position. Pain laced through him, starting from his crotch and shooting directly into his paralyzed brain. Langer looked up through the pain, saw the blonde bitch grinning down at him savagely, and realized that she had, with great accuracy and greater enthusiasm, kicked him squarely in the Langer family jewels.

The great and powerful Senator Jerome Langer II lay on the creaky wooden dock, feeling like he might vomit, or pass out, or both. Pain burned through him like a malarial fever, and from somewhere far off he thought he heard an old Spaniard laughing.

Now this— Langer thought, just before he passed out—this is what happens when things get out of control.

22

"Well," Jane Ellen said. "Now what?"

Most of the clearly recognizable bad guys were unconscious, under guard or, in the case of the skinny one with the bad teeth, floundering around helplessly in the bay. On the other hand, the crazy accountant who had kidnapped her in Miami was holding a very large pistol and, while he didn't look especially pissed off, he couldn't have forgotten how she had thrown him off the balcony of that hotel. Nate had scooped up one fallen gunman's pistol, and she figured that was all right, but the giant assassin had grabbed the third Cuban's gun, and now the two were staring at each other, unblinking, like two stiff-legged dogs debating whether a fight was winnable or even worthwhile. She glanced over at Harry, but he shrugged his shoulders, clearly as confused as she was.

It was Nate who broke the silence. "Now," he said, "we wait." He very slowly clicked the safety of his gun into place and slipped the pistol into his belt, keeping his eyes locked on the Miami hit man the whole time. The hit man engaged his own safety and slipped his pistol into a coat pocket. "Wait for what?" he said.

Nate turned toward the open bay and searched the water for a moment before pointing out a single oyster skiff gamely fighting its way toward them. "For that," he said.

Jane Ellen had been aware of the drone of the skiff's overtaxed motor, but that was hardly an uncommon sound in the Apalachicola. She followed Nate's extended finger, put a hand over her eyes to block out the glare of the sun, and then broke out into a happy grin.

"It's Billy!" she said. She climbed up on the lower railing of the dock and waved her arms enthusiastically, calling out "Hey, Billy Byars! Billy!" as if there were nothing else on her mind at all. A hundred yards away, the man seated in the rear of the boat returned her wave; the formally dressed man in the stern remained unmoving until the little skiff had pulled alongside the dock and was being tied off.

"Hey, Jane Ellen, welcome home," Billy said. "You know you got a half-drowned man hanging onto the other side of the dock over there?"

Jane Ellen grinned even wider and nodded her head happily. She helped Billy stagger up onto the dock, and then jumped into her surprised ex-boss's arms and gave him an enthusiastic bear hug. She could smell the fish on his clothes and the beer on his breath, and wondered why she had never noticed before what a wonderful combination that was.

The second man in the skiff, who looked familiar somehow, had meanwhile gotten himself and the bulky suitcase he was carrying out of the boat and onto the dock. He straightened his jacket fussily, coughed loudly to get everyone's attention, then pulled out a leather wallet and held it high above his head, letting it flop open to reveal a shiny silver badge.

"All right, give me your attention," he said, though everyone was already staring at him. "I am with the Nuclear Regulatory Commission, and you are all—"

"Forget it, Gush," Nate said.

"Gush?" Jane Ellen echoed.

"Uh, and all of you are hereby ordered—"

"I said forget it. Just get on inside the sailboat there and check it out."

"But . . . but Major, I got this badge and I bought a suit and—"

"Just check out the boat, Gush. Especially that coffin in the main cabin."

"Gush," Jane Ellen said. She was mentally adding a tangled beard, bloodshot eyes and ragged clothing to the man standing before her, and, sure enough, it added up. "From the bar in Tampa."

"Right," Nate said. "But before the bars, he was Sergeant Leo Gaspaldi, Special Forces. We served together. Back then, he was the best explosives man I ever saw."

"Still am, Major," Gush said. He had opened his heavy suitcase, pulled out a wadded-up white jumpsuit and was putting it on.

"That's who you radioed from the boat that night. You told him to meet us here," Harry said.

"That's right. And before that, he was the one who

called me from Tampa and told me he'd just seen my kid sister. I hit the road for Tampa, and had him eavesdrop on you two long enough to find out about the boat. He was waiting for me when I got to Tampa, and I was waiting for you at the boat."

"But why—?" Jane Ellen began, but Harry interrupted her.

"Because plutonium is more precious than gold," he said.

"That's right," Gush chimed in. "Me and the major is gonna be rich." He put on a pair of heavily padded white gloves, and pulled what Jane Ellen figured had to be a Geiger counter from his suitcase. Then came a metal tool kit, filled with who-knew-what. Gush walked past Jane Ellen, Harry and Nate, reached over his shoulder to pull a protective cowl over his head and, looking like a lost beekeeper, stepped onto the *Miss Behavin'.*

"But there's no plutonium on that boat," Harry said. Nate looked at him, glum, and then turned to stare after Gush. He didn't say a word until Jane Ellen slipped around Harry to stand beside him.

"I was doing it for you, Jane Ellen. Gush has some contacts who'd pay well for plutonium, real well, and I thought with my half I could buy us a house, maybe an oyster skiff or maybe even a charter boat. We'd be a family again, Jane Ellen, and I could make it all up to you. Just like I promised Mom."

Jane Ellen didn't say a word—but she took Nate's hand in hers and stood beside him, quietly gazing at the *Miss Behavin'* and the bay beyond.

"Well, this is all very touching, but I don't really see why I need to stay. If you'll excuse me—" Jane Ellen turned around; it was the older, distinguished looking Hispanic man, the one who still had Quiet's gun pressed against his temple. Jane Ellen tried not to smile; Quiet looked ridiculous, so short and squat he had to reach high and go up on tiptoes to keep the gun at the man's head.

"Quiet, you," Quiet said. "You'll leave when I say you can, not before." He glanced over at the big man standing beside Boulder, and, just for a moment, Jane Ellen could have sworn he smiled.

"Um, hey, Jane Ellen. It's real good to see you again and all, and you, too, Nate, but could you maybe tell me just what the hell is going on around here?" It was Billy, looking a bit beer-buzzed and confused.

"Of course, Billy, of course," Jane Ellen said. "First off, I want you to meet the best man in the whole world. This is Harry, my . . . this is Harry. Harry, this is Billy Byars."

"Well. Pleased to meetcha, Harry."

"You too, Billy. Janie's told me a lot about your bar."

"It's a restaurant now. Got tables and everything."

"Right, your restaurant. Anyway, nice to meet you."

The two men shook hands, as honestly open and friendly as they sounded, and Jane Ellen looked on, enjoying a feeling she had never known before. She was sure she'd introduced people to each other before, at least in grade school or back when she was a kid, but she could not remember ever having taken such pride in it.

"And you know Nate, of course." Jane Ellen had Billy by the arm and was walking him around the circle of strangers and friends assembled on the dock. What the hell. Jane Ellen didn't really know what to do in circumstances like this—she had never even heard of circumstances like this—but she read "Miss Manners" whenever she could get a newspaper, and she by God knew her etiquette.

"Hey, Billy," Nate said. "Sorry about taking off on you with no explanation like that. I had to go get Jane Ellen."

"Aw, that's okay, Nate. I knew you was coming back. I told everybody that, too, you ask around and see."

Jane Ellen could see that Nate was pleased by that, and she wondered again at the change he had put himself through since she took off. She stepped up to the next person there on the dock, pulling Billy along with her, and stopped.

"And this is, um . . ." she said.

"I'm Tiny," Tiny said.

"The hell you say," Billy mumbled, but he stuck out his hand and the giant happily took it. Jane Ellen introduced herself too, and hesitantly accepted the handshake Tiny offered. She smiled after a moment, half pleased and half amazed that someone so big could be so gentle. She eased her hand out of Tiny's, thinking he could easily have held both her hands and probably a foot, too, and moved to the next person.

"And this," she said, the disapproval in her voice evident, "this is Quiet Quiones."

"It's wonderful to see you again, Jane Ellen," Quiet

said. "I know you probably won't believe this, and I know you'll never forgive me, but I want you to know that I'm very ashamed of all that I did in Miami, and I am very, very sorry."

Jane Ellen glared at Quiet, frowning, but he looked so shamefaced and hangdog that she couldn't keep it up. "It's okay, Quiet. I guess it all worked out for the best."

"Yes, I see that," Quiet said, glancing at Harry. "And I'm happy for you. I really am."

"Well then," Billy said. "My name's Billy Byars." Billy thrust out his hand. Quiet stared at it, frowned, and then carefully switched gun hands so he could shake with Billy and keep the pistol pressed against the tall Cuban's head at the same time. Jane Ellen thought back to the day she had hijacked the *Miss Behavin'* and wondered if Billy knew, if the Cuban knew, if even Quiet himself knew, that the gun's safety was on.

"My name is Carlos, Miss Ashley, and I am pleased to make your acquaintance. Yours, too, Mr. Byars." Carlos shook Jane Ellen's hand gently; safety or not, she was impressed by how cool he was, with Quiet sweating and trembling right beside him. She took a step to her right, and then stopped still. Out of the corner of her eye she saw Billy shake Carlos's extended hand then take a step over to stand uncertainly beside her, but she kept her eyes locked on the familiar figure in front of her.

"Boulder Baker," she said.

"I'm pleased to meet you, Billy," Boulder said, though he was looking directly at Jane Ellen. "I'd shake your hand, but as you can see I'm still recovering from a recent injury." He raised his right fist, palm inward, to chin level and slowly unfolded his fingers. The index and middle fingers seemed fine, but the ring finger was striped with scabbed-over cuts, and the last knuckle on the pinkie slanted outward at an unnatural angle.

Jane Ellen stared at the hand, and then flicked her eyes sideways to look at Boulder's face. For a moment he was absolutely impassive, still as a statue. And then, quickly but unmistakably, he winked.

It was like seeing a shark smile. Jane Ellen wasn't sure if she should feel relieved or not, so she hurriedly stepped back to her original place in the circle, beside Harry, pulling Billy along with her. "And those two, I don't know who they are," she said, waving at Carlos's two men still unconscious on the dock. "And the guy on the boat, that's Gush. Gush is—"

"Gush is getting off the boat, is what Gush is doing, because there ain't nothing on the boat worth being on the boat for." Gush came striding out of the *Miss Behavin*'s cabin, agitated, his hood already pulled back. "Shit, Major," he said. "There ain't no plutonium on that boat."

"Gush, I'm sorry. Did you find anything at all?"

"Just real low levels in all those plastic bags in the coffin, like what you'd find in irradiated food if somebody was doing a real sloppy job and not too worried about getting caught. That's it, Major."

"There's nothing in the walls of the coffin?" Nate said hopefully.

"Nothing. Just a coffin. Worthless."

"Well, shit. Gush, I truly am sorry to drag your ass all the way up here, and we'll figure some way to pay back all your expenses. I guess what's important, for right now, is that we're all okay, and the bay is safe."

"Is it?" Harry said. "What's to keep these jerks from getting another boat, and another group of suckers, and starting all over again next week?"

"I'm glad you asked that," Boulder said, and for a moment Jane Ellen feared he might pull out a gun and start blasting people. Instead, he raised one arm and pointed up at the house fifty yards away. Jane Ellen and everyone else followed his gesture, and after a moment spotted a man leaning out of an upstairs window, smiling. The man was pale and thin, almost gaunt. He was using one bony hand to support himself on the window frame.

The other hand was holding a camera.

"Oh my God," Langer said.

"Like it?" Quiet said. "That's a Canon AE-1, with a 200-millimeter telegraphic lens. Our friend Al has been snapping pictures of everything that's been going on out here for the last fifteen minutes. We told him to be extra sure to get lots of nice pictures of you, Senator."

"That won't prove anything," Langer said. "I can say I was here against my will, kidnapped by armed men."

"Yes, you could do that—if you really want to testify in court that Carlos here conspired to kidnap you. But I don't think it would matter much. I suspect nice clear pictures, on the front page of every newspaper in Florida, of a state senator meeting in secret with a known narcotics dealer will have all the impact we could possibly hope for."

Langer glared at Quiet, then looked at the impassive Carlos, and up at the distant photographer. When he finally turned back to Quiet, squinting in the sun reflecting off the bay, Jane Ellen thought he seemed to have shrunk somehow.

"All right," Langer said softly. "What do you want?"

Quiet smiled, and Jane Ellen thought that, for once, his smile seemed honest and confident, rather than just fatuous. "First of all," he said, "our friend with the camera is going to need a place to stay while he recovers from the deadly diet you people inadvertently put him on. Someplace large enough to also accommodate his friend Tiny." Tiny beamed at the mention of his name, and then, remembering the circumstances, did his best to glower menacingly at the Senator.

"All right," Langer said. "I could arrange to set you up in a nursing home I own part interest in, over in Bay County."

"Actually," Quiet said, "Al tells me he's grown to like it right here."

"Here?" Langer said. "But . . . that's a four-bedroom house, my four-bedroom house, just for two people—"

"Three, actually, since I'll be staying here with them. And I'll be using the bottom floor for my new office."

"Office?"

"That's right. I've decided to open an accounting firm, right here on St. George Island. It seems to me all these small-business owners, the fishermen and the hoteliers, could use some help with their businesses, with their taxes and investments. I can do just about everything they could need from right here, with a nice computer and modem. And with Langer Seafood as my first client, I'll have a nice solid foundation to get my business started."

"I already have accountants," Langer said.

"Fire them."

"I'm not going to just give you my house!"

"Of course not. I was thinking of a long-term lease, at a fair rate. Say in return for a percentage of the increased profits I'll be providing Langer Seafood."

Langer looked at the distant cameraman, then at Quiet, and then again at the house. Finally he gave one slow, sad nod.

"Excellent!" Quiet said. "We can go up to the house and draw up an agreement right now, and then you can be on your way."

"Not just yet," Nate said. He took a step forward so that he was standing directly in front of the Senator. "I've been handling those damned irradiated eggs for days, slept on the deck right next to them for three nights, thanks to you and your rotten little scheme. Now what the hell do you think that's going to do to me?" Gush opened his mouth like he was going to say something, but Nate silenced him with a glance. He glared at the Senator for a moment, and then turned and walked toward where Langer's cigarette boat sat tied at the dock.

"The way I figure it," Nate said, "the money I saved up over the past few months ought to cover my medical bills. But I had planned to use that money to buy myself an oyster skiff, or maybe even a little charter boat. Of course," Nate looked down at the cigarette boat and rubbed his chin thoughtfully, "of course, with a boat like this I would be the hottest charter captain in the Apalachicola basin."

"That's a twenty-thousand-dollar boat!" Langer exploded. "You are fucking crazy!"

"And you have no choice!" Nate shot back. Then he calmed himself, smiled, and started again. "I'm not talking about an outright gift. I was thinking about some sort of long-term, low-interest sales deal. I'll bet your accountant there can come up with a way to make it work out, for both of us."

"Certainly," Quiet said. "A low-interest small-business loan for you, a tax write-off for the Senator. Not to mention good publicity here in the heart of his district, helping a sick man get back on his feet."

"Right," Nate said. "Do we have a deal?"

Langer grimaced, then nodded. "But that's all!" he said. "I'm only gonna give in so much."

"I think that's about all, Senator Langer," Quiet said. "Unless someone else has a question?"

"I do," Harry said. "What about the *Miss Behavin'?*" He gestured lovingly toward the boat behind him.

"Well," Quiet said. "Legally the boat is registered to the Cinco de Mayo Sailing Club, which exists only as a front to the Honduran Hall of Heroes Association, which doesn't exist at all. That means the boat is pretty wide open to any prior claim. The prior owner was Langer

Seafood"—he gestured toward the sullen Senator—"but I suspect the Senator has long since reported it stolen or sunken, and collected his insurance money, so I doubt that he'll be filing a claim." Langer nodded. "That would leave the boat open to any substantial salvage claim."

"I don't know the salvage laws," Harry said. "But I've been in sole possession of that boat for almost two months now. Does that count for anything?"

"That, Mr. Harper, counts for quite a bit. If you like, I could file the necessary paperwork for you in Tallahassee." He looked at Jane Ellen and smiled. "It's the least I could do."

Jane Ellen slipped over to Harry and put her arms around him. Harry, too happy to speak, simply nodded.

"How very nice," Carlos said. "Now if we are all finished here, could we get out of this hot sun? And Oscar, would you please remove that irritating pistol from my temple?" The gang lord's words were polite enough, refined even, but Jane Ellen sensed a tightly controlled tension in his voice. She found herself quietly relieved that Carlos's snake-black eyes were focused on Quiet, and not on herself.

Quiet, who seemed too pleased with it all to notice Carlos's ice-cold stillness, glanced over at Boulder. Boulder nodded, and Quiet slowly, reluctantly, lowered the gun.

"There is one more thing," Jane Ellen said. Everyone turned to look at her expectantly. "Harry was hired to bring that boat up from the Dominican Republic—and he did it. Someone owes him five thousand dollars."

"No!" Langer said. "You already got my house and my boat, I won't give any more. Besides, I don't have that kind of money with me."

"No," Boulder said. "But your partner does. You wouldn't go this far from home without a nice fat stash, would you, Carlos?"

"I am not afraid of having my picture in the paper," Carlos said. "Why should I give this man anything?"

"Consider it a matter of honor, Carlos," Boulder said. "A business debt. I know how you feel about unpaid debts."

Carlos and Boulder looked at one another, unblinking as statues. Finally Carlos looked away. He reached into his jacket pocket, produced a black eel-skin wallet, and pulled out a handful of bills. "You know," he said, without looking at Boulder, "that you will never work in Florida again."

"I know," Boulder said. "And that's fine. I'm sure you won't be surprised to hear that I have just retired."

Carlos glanced sidelong at Boulder, then walked over to Harry and handed him the money. He turned without speaking, walked past Boulder and started down the dock toward the shore.

"Madre de Dios! Would one of you crazy *yanquis* please get me out of here?" It was the thug in the water, Rey, still clinging to the side of the dock, waterlogged and unhappy as a drowned cat. Billy Byars grinned and extended an arm to the complaining Cuban; the rest of the crew smiled and turned to watch the fun.

Everyone, that is, except for Jane Ellen, who couldn't

shake the uneasy feeling that Carlos had one last mean trick in him. While everyone else laughed at Rey's clumsy attempts to climb onto the dock, Jane Ellen kept her eyes glued on the retreating gang lord. She watched as he walked past Harry, past Quiet. She watched Carlos come to a sudden halt and reach inside his coat. And she saw him spin around and stride quickly toward Quiet, raising toward the heavens one wiry arm holding something that glittered in the sun like silver death.

Jane Ellen screamed.

All eyes turned toward her, and then toward Quiet and Carlos. Boulder dropped into a shooter's crouch and whipped up his gun hand—but Rey, who was out of the water and not nearly as clumsy as he had seemed, slammed into the big man and jerked the arm down. Tiny grabbed Rey by the scruff of the neck and tossed him aside, but everyone knew he had delayed Boulder long enough. Long enough for Carlos to kill.

"Traitor!" Carlos screamed, his face contorted with raw fury. He raised his second hand and wrapped it around his weapon, rising on tiptoes, clearly intending to drive death downwards into Quiet with all his manic strength. "Traitor!" he screamed again, and then—

—and then a fist smashed hard into Carlos's right cheek. His head snapped sideways, a silver ice pick fell from his fingers, and Carlos dropped to the dock at Quiet's feet.

Cool, Jane Ellen thought. Of all the people on this dock, the giant Tiny and the professional assassin Boulder and her own Special Forces brother Nate, it was her dear sweet Harry Harper who was standing over the stunned killer, staring in surprise at his own clenched fist.

Jane Ellen pulled her arms dramatically to her chest and tried not to laugh. "My hero," she said.

And then she laughed anyway.

Harry looked up and grinned at her. Tiny let out a great happy belly laugh and casually tossed Rey back into the water. Even Quiet let out a deep breath and managed a nervous smile.

But Boulder Baker was not amused. He stomped over to stand astride the fallen Carlos. The gun came out again, this time pointing straight down toward Carlos's head.

"Enough," Boulder said.

It was Tiny who stopped him. Tiny who said, "Now, Boulder . . ." and when Baker didn't move, said it again, "Now, Boulder," and Boulder Baker slowly looked up. Tiny was a good eight or ten feet off, too far, Jane Ellen knew, to stop Baker from firing. But Tiny didn't even move. He just stood there, shaking his great ugly head gently from side to side, looking for all the world like a disappointed hound dog. And to Jane Ellen's great surprise, Boulder lowered the gun.

Boulder slipped the pistol back inside his coat, never taking his eyes off Carlos. Then he slowly undid the thin black tie hanging around his neck and let it drop on top of the prone Cuban.

"You remember this," Boulder said. "These are my friends. If anything should happen to them—to any of them—I will come out of retirement.

"Now go back to Miami, Carlos. Where you belong."

Carlos stared up at the impassive giant staring back down at him. He raised one hand to wipe away the line of crimson blood running from the side of his mouth. Then he turned away from Boulder, away from those merciless frozen shark eyes, and slowly nodded his head.

They all walked up to the house then, and, supplied with the best lemonade Jane Ellen had ever tasted, sat down to work out the details. It took them a while to get the paperwork sorted out, but Quiet clearly knew what he was doing, and the ominous presence of Boulder Baker kept the Senator and Carlos from protesting much. Nate and Gush went roaring off in Nate's new boat as soon as the Senator signed the bill of transfer; the Senator himself left with two of the three rolls of film Al had shot, unhappy but stuck with Quiet's promise that the final roll would never be printed as long as the Senator did all he could to keep the Apalachicola Bay safe and clean. Baker had a long private conversation with Tiny, then went upstairs to pack his few belongings. Carlos, speaking carefully around a badly chipped tooth, gave Tiny one hundred dollars each to carry his unconscious assistants up from the dock and load them into his waiting car while the dripping wet Rey looked on from a safe distance.

Jane Ellen and Harry made their own farewells, listening to Quiet profoundly apologize one last time, before leaving the house for the dock and their waiting boat. To Jane Ellen's surprise, Billy Byars was still sitting there, his feet dangling over the dock, staring at the bay and looking morose.

"Why, Billy Byars, what's the matter?" Jane Ellen said. "You look like you just lost your best friend. Aren't you happy with how everything turned out?"

Billy looked up at Jane Ellen, stood and dusted the sand off his overalls. "Sure I'm happy, for you, and for Nate, and for this man of yours here," he said. "But I ain't happy for me. I mean, Nate's got his boat, and he's gonna go off into his own business, and you got your boat, and you're gonna go off God knows where. I'm right back where I started from! I lost my best waitress, and I lost my morning fry cook, and now I'm about to lose them both again! Who's gonna bring my customers in? Who's gonna open for me at 5 A.M. in the morning?" Billy threw back his head and wailed at the sky like a coyote in mourning. "Who's gonna cook my goddamned omelets?"

Jane Ellen felt the dock shake beneath her, and a dark shadow passed over Billy's distraught face. It was Tiny, with the last of Carlos's henchmen thrown carelessly over one shoulder. Billy opened his eyes and looked up uncertainly at Tiny, like a Chihuahua staring awestruck at a Great Dane. Jane Ellen could see the concern on Billy's face as he watched the mountain of a man looming above him.

And then the mountain smiled.

"'Omelets'?" he said.

Harry ran the *Miss Behavin'*'s engines until he got out into the bay, well away from the shore. He was sure he could tell the difference in the way she ran without the weight of the coffin and its contents. The crabs and eggs were in three metal trash cans at the house, soaking in gasoline and destined for immolation. Despite Harry's misgivings, he and Jane Ellen had manhandled the coffin overboard just a few hundred yards offshore. Harry had been reluctant to do so until Jane Ellen explained that the junk was just the sort of hardware that young oyster spat loved to latch onto. They were forming an artificial reef, she said, that would someday supply the very oystermen Carlos and Senator Langer had hoped to drive off.

"Sooner or later," Jane Ellen had said as they watched the heavy coffin sink below the waves, "the bay makes good use out of everything."

The mainsail was up and just beginning to catch the wind when Jane Ellen emerged from the cabin. She was wearing a thigh-length T-shirt Boulder had left behind and, Harry suspected, not much more.

Jane Ellen joined Harry at the helm, and he slipped an arm under the T-shirt and up around her waist to confirm his suspicions. He couldn't believe how good he felt. He had his own boat beneath his feet, cash money and a bill of ownership in his pocket, his beloved Jane Ellen at his side. He kissed her, long and lovingly, and then turned back to the wheel.

"Well, Janie my love," he said. "We've got our own boat now, forever and always ours, and enough money to keep us going for a nice long while. Where to?"

"East, until we clear St. George Island," Jane Ellen said without hesitation. "And then south."

"South," Harry said. "Back to Tampa, down to Miami, or through the Straits of Florida and on across the Atlantic to Europe?"

"Actually," Jane Ellen leaned in and gave Harry a mischievous nip on the neck, "actually, I was thinking about this quiet little cove I know on the other side of St. George. We could drop anchor, and no one would even know we were there for a long, long time."

Happy Harry Harper looked at Jane Ellen Ashley and thought his heart would burst with joy. He grinned at her and she grinned right back. The sails tightened with the clean evening wind, spreading wide and welcoming like the pages of an unwritten book, and the *Miss Behavin'* went darting over the bright Apalachicola Bay.

POCKET BOOKS
PROUDLY PRESENTS

TATTOO BLUES

Michael McClelland

COMING IN HARDCOVER IN MARCH
FROM IBOOKS

Turn the page for a preview of
Tattoo Blues. . . .

The ornate Chinese symbol tattooed on her practically perfect left breast—Desiree Dean liked to tell anyone who was curious or crude enough to ask—translated to "Quit staring at my tits, asshole!" What it really meant—she knew in her secret heart—was "golden dragon," which she thought was sublimely sexy. Desiree had no idea that a more precise translation would be "with hot sauce." She had labored under her pleasant illusion for several weeks now, and was likely to continue doing so for quite some time. After all, how many Florida Gulf Coast beach town topless Chinese-food waitresses—or topless Chinese-food waitresses' customers, or topless Chinese-food waitresses' tattoo artists—could actually read Chinese?

Certainly not Pimlico Phil, Desiree's artist, who couldn't tell calligraphy from tire treads, or Cantonese from cat calls. But Phil did know a hot trend when he saw one, and Phil, as he so often said, was nothing if not a businessman. This was why he kept a stack of purloined Chinese restaurant menus in the back of his tattoo parlor and a handful of dramatic translations in the forefront of his opportunistic mind. This was also why the summer of 2002 saw a great many bright-eyed and bronzed beauties returning north from their summer side trips to quaint little Cedar Key, sporting tattoos that proudly proclaimed "extra spicy," "with noodles," or "gratuity not included."

Pimlico Phil saw no harm in any of this; in fact, he wouldn't have done the tattoos if he had. Phil was at heart a gentle old soul, a barrel-chested, sleepy-eyed gentleman who in another life could pass as a slightly swarthy Santa Claus. But Phil had been in the business a long time, long enough to know the cyclical nature of the beast, long enough to know that he'd best strike while the fad was fresh. And he had spent quite enough time eking out a living gouging anchors, snakes, and "I Love Mothers" into the biceps of drunken sailors and greasy bikers, always one city ordinance or a prissy new base commander away from exile and bankruptcy. That was, in fact, how he'd ended up in Cedar Key—run out of Okaloosa County and the lucrative Eglin Air Force Base market by an uptight new commander with vengeance on his mind. One little hepatitis scare—probably not even Phil's doing—and suddenly there was talk of civil fines and background checks. Phil probably could have paid the fine and maybe even passed the background check, but he knew that being on the commander's shit list meant his days in Okaloosa were limited. Best to get while the getting was good.

And that had turned out just fine. There wasn't much of a market for tattoos in Cedar Key, but costs were low, and Phil had gotten a break on the rent by agreeing to let his landlords store supplies for their busy restaurant in his back room. He liked the slower pace here, the little arts and crafts stores and the island-time feel to the place. And he liked students much more than soldiers. That was the bulk of his Cedar Key clientele—bored University of Florida students who'd driven the sixty miles from Gainesville for a weekend blowout, or snowbirds from up north seeking a low-cost alternative to the neon-lit Panama City Beach strip—and, for the most part, Phil genuinely liked his youthful customers. He didn't understand them, not one bit. It still embarrassed the hell out of him when a voluptuous young woman would pop open her shirt to discuss the aesthetics of a breast tattoo as if they were considering how to best dress a turkey. He wouldn't do piercings, though God knew he got plenty of requests. In tattoos he could see beauty and self-expression, even if that self was expressed as a snarling Tasmanian Devil or a blood-spattered, flame-covered human skull. But piercings struck him as desecration rather than decoration. Phil had discussed that with some of his clients until a sweet little thing young enough to be his granddaughter explained to him she wanted her tongue pierced so she could give better blow jobs. Phil had blushed furiously and never discussed that with his clients again.

Still, Phil was a businessman. Everything he knew he'd learned from his father—and Pop had always stressed the importance of keeping up with the times. "Three things," his pop would say. "Spot the trends before they get there, stay liquid, carry plenty of insurance." To that mantra, Phil had added, "Go with your strengths." In his case, that meant admitting to himself that he was a solid craftsman, that on a good day his work could rise to the level of art, but that he really did not have much imagination. So he studied the work of other artists, and he kept a close eye on what he saw on the barely dressed human canvases that paraded by his door every sweltering summer day. And he had placed a large placard in his window, promising that "You bring it in, we'll put it on." That worked well; half his customers came in carrying pictures they'd ripped out of magazines or copied off a CD case. For the most part, they left satisfied.

For the other half—the impulse buyers—Phil had a dozen thick black binders packed with images and ideas to choose from. The walls of his outer shop—the back shop was where he actually did the work—he kept postered with blowups of his most popular designs. Leaping dolphins, leering demons, cartoon characters, and big-breasted, sword-swinging women warriors—there was something there for everyone.

But even so, one night in early spring—a late night at the end of a long day, when Phil really wanted to close the shop and head upstairs for a hot-plate meal of tomato soup and beanie-weenies—an obnoxiously drunken frat boy from Memphis State had wandered in, taken up residence in front of the display case and gone through four or five of Phil's books, scornfully trashing each and every page. Phil had been right at the point of tossing him out—Pop's admonitions be damned—when the kid pushed aside a just-finished binder, stopped, and then emphatically said, "That one!"

Phil looked at the exotic design the boy was pointing at and frowned in exasperation. "You can't have that one, son," he said.

"Why not? What's it mean?"

"It means that you are fucked up beyond all recognition."

"Perfect! Fucked up beyond all recognition! Do it."

"No, I mean—"

"Do it, old man, do it! Right here, around my biceps, big, in black ink. I got the money right here."

And he had, he'd produced a fine leather wallet and spread it open for Phil to see, to see all the cash his poor deluded parents had no doubt intended for textbooks and tuition. The money alone might not have convinced Phil to do it, but that "old man" crack . . . Phil shrugged, swabbed the boy's arm down good, and set to work producing a perfect copy of the Oriental characters embossed on the back of the Chinese take-out menu that had been left sitting on the counter. He'd done a nice job, and did it in good time, too. The boy sweated a bit and winced once or twice, but he'd strutted like a banty rooster when he left the shop, his biceps proudly proclaiming, Phil would later learn, that he was a "Great Buffet."

Phil had felt a little bad about that. The next day, when he looked up to see that same boy striding into his shop with two muscular friends in tow, he'd felt sure he was about to receive his well-deserved punishment. He was wrong.

"My homies want 'em, too," the boy said, while his two friends nodded their emphatic agreement. "Fucked up beyond all recognition, just like me."

Phil stood staring out his shop window for a long time after the freshly tattooed trio left, gazing out at the sun-drenched streets and thinking about things like artistic integrity and business ethics and his pop's thoughts on trends and times. It was a slow morning, as usual, and

Phil closed up for an hour at noon, as usual. But when he left, he didn't walk down to the Dancing Dolphin Drinks and Diner for chicken salad and sweet tea. Instead, he got into his battered Dodge Dart and drove over the bridges and bayous of Levy County, east to Otter Creek and then south through Gulf Hammock, Lebannon and Inglis, on into Citrus County, one-and-a-half hours of slash pine shadows and winding roadkill highway to cover the 56.2 as-the-crow-flies miles to the not-big-but-getting-there tourist town of Crystal River.

There was a new Chinese restaurant there that Phil wanted to check out.

Pimlico's Pinprick Palace had been transformed from a sleepy backstreet shop into a thriving business with a near-cult reputation by the time Desiree Dean tentatively stepped into the crowded store several weeks after the boys from Memphis strutted out. Like most of the other college-age customers packing the small shop that afternoon, Desiree had learned of Pimlico Phil by word-of-mouth. Easily half of Phil's clients told him they had specifically sought him out, that they had been told by proud former clients the only place to get one of the uniquely self-expressive, personalized character tattoos was at a hole-in-the-wall joint in an end-of-the-line town way the hell off the spring break circuit. The Memphis boys, it seemed, had stopped at every frat chapter house from Tallahassee to Tennessee to bum gas money and show off their tattoos. In Atlanta, a Georgia Tech brother with an Internet scanner and a love for dramatics had sent the Tiger Trio's tattoos, along with some cock-and-bull story about a genius artist hiding from the world in a Florida fishing village, skittering all across the Internet. Now college kids from Denison to Dartmouth were showing up at Phil's doorstep, demanding a tattoo just like the one his/her girlfriend/boyfriend/sorority mate/fraternity mate/teammate/classmate or professor was now sporting. Or better yet, a carefully calligraphied character picked out just for them, so they could be unique just like everybody else.

At first, Phil had said no. Even if he couldn't bring himself to admit the truth, that the trio of Tigers were wearing nothing more than an advertisement, he just didn't like the idea of scamming his trusting young clients. He tried to steer people toward his more traditional offer-ings, toward the leaping dolphins and dancing girls. He'd actually turned several people away, despite his borderline finances and the nagging voice of his father's "Give 'em what they want" echoing through his head. But that had backfired. Somehow, word got out that it took more than money to get one of Phil's calligraphies, that you had to deserve one. Next thing he knew, potential customers were quoting Eastern mysticism to him, or boasting of their good works, or offering him outrageous sums of money. And suddenly, he was doing calligraphy.

Because he had an innate understanding of what his customers were really after, Phil would, in his sagely grandfatherly way, carefully study each such client, find some clue as to what that person thought of himself, and then tell that person pretty much what he or she wanted to hear. This was a talent that had served Phil quite well over the years, a talent born of long nights watching his pop play poker and longer days listening to clients tell their life stories while he drilled away stoically at an arm, leg, or other appendage—and now it was paying off big-time. It all reminded Phil of a short-lived but lucrative business Pop had once started, a cosmetics and toiletries business he dubbed New Generation Ventures. Phil had spent many after-school hours emptying economy-size bottles of cheap perfume into tiny bottles bearing big price tags and the NGV label. "Remember, Phillip," Pop had said. "What you actually sell 'em doesn't matter. It's what they *think* they're getting that counts." And then Pop would tap sagely on the NGV label and wink. Phil knew what he meant, and he knew what NGV really stood for. The only three reasons anybody in America ever spent money on anything, Pop said, were need, greed, and vanity.

Years later, Phil was employing exactly that philosophy, along with some flattering talk and a few stolen symbols, to give people just what they wanted. Phil felt a little guilty about it sometimes, but he was making a killing.

And Pimlico Phil was a businessman, after all.

Desiree Dean didn't know any of that, of course. All she knew was that she was in desperate need of a change, in her life, in her lifestyle, in her very soul. She had been in Panama City Beach for the last week, despondently watching her decidedly dull Spring Break dribble away in a mocking miniature of her deadly dreary life. Her sorority sisters had spent that week getting loaded and laid, and Desiree—well, Desiree had not. Mostly she'd sat at a beachfront ice cream stand, nursing cherry slushies and dreading the day she'd have to return to Ohio and school. Not that college was that much worse than where she was. Truth is, Desiree carried her misery with her wherever she went. Desiree knew that about herself. And, like most everything else about herself, she hated it.

What she needed, Desiree told herself time and again, was a dramatic change. She needed a new life, a new future, a new body, a new past, a new self. She needed everything she was to become, everything she was not. And she would start, she decided, with a tattoo.

Not just any tattoo. Not a fairy princess on her shoulder or a rainbow on her rump, not some generic graphic that would fit just as equally well on anyone's random stretch of skin. Desiree wanted—no, *needed*—something uniquely hers, uniquely special. She needed a constant reminder to herself of what she wanted to be, and what she did not want to be. She needed something that would shout to all the world, "Look out, people, there's a new Desiree in town!" Well, maybe not shout. Nothing obnoxious. Something subtle but strong, like a good perfume. She wanted something people would admire, but mostly it was to be a message to herself. She didn't need a billboard, she didn't need a spotlight.

"What I need," Desiree said to the genial white-haired gentleman smiling at her over the countertop at Pimlico's Pinprick Palace, "is a symbol."

"Ah," Phil said, "a symbol. A symbol of . . . ?"

"Independence. Strength. Daring. Courage."

"Hmmmm . . ." Phil studied Desiree closely, one finger propped up thoughtfully on a hairy cheek. "A lion, perhaps? Or a lioness, in your case? A brave beast, strong, free . . ."

"An animal, yes, that's good. But I was thinking maybe about one of those Chinese characters you do. Something that would mean something to me, but not necessarily to everyone else. Mysterious and meaningful at the same time." Pimlico Phil nodded and, Desiree thought, hesitated just a bit before reaching behind the counter to produce a hefty, unmarked black folder. The famous black book, source of Phil's legendary designs.

Desiree caught her breath, flashing back to the hushed words of Keith Wade, a way-cool upperclassman from Michigan State who had spent much of the prior week in the arms and bed of Desiree's sorority sister, Irene. "It's a Pimlico Phil original," Keith had said to the group of people staring reverently at the fist-sized Chinese character freshly embossed on his left shoulder. "It means, 'Thunder Lover.'" Irene had blushed furiously at that, but Keith either didn't notice or didn't care. "I drove all the way to Cedar Key," he said, "which is like practically out in the swamps, and I tracked down his shop and walked in and told him I was ready for the world to see the real me. He just looked at me and knew just who I am.

It's like he's psychic or something, just like everybody says. Like he can see right into your soul."

Psychic, Desiree had thought then, that sounds like what I need. So she spent thirty bucks and six sweaty hours on a bus ride to Cedar Key, which was not in a swamp at all, but on a lush green island separated from mainland Florida by a delightfully scenic system of inlets and bayous. But now, flipping through the black book Keith had praised so lavishly, she was a little disappointed. According to Keith Wade, Phil and his famous book ranked up there with Moses and the Ten Commandments. Desiree had expected something more than a stout old man wielding a black plastic business binder.

"Something wrong?" Phil said. He started to pull the book back away from Desiree. "This is your first tattoo, correct? Perhaps you'd prefer to start with something small, something simple. I do a very nice daisy, very dainty, almost painless . . ."

"A daisy?" That caught Desiree by surprise, instantly making her reconsider her evaluation of Phil. Daisies were her favorite flower, always had been. Her room back in Dayton was covered with them, dazzling white-and-yellow flowers painted on the walls and the ceiling, plastic daisies in plastic flowerpots, daisies on her sheets and pillowcases. Even at college, in sleepy little Springfield, Desiree's notebooks and book covers all featured the golden flowers. The thought brought with it a sudden surge of nostalgia, a sense of longing and loss and—

Desiree shook herself mentally and pulled the Black Book back toward her. "No," she said firmly. "No flowers.

No kittens, no bunnies, no rainbows or puppies or smiley faces. Something strong, something bold. Something with teeth, metaphorically speaking."

Phil studied her again, shrugged, and flipped the book open about one-third of the way through. He turned the pages, slowly, watching her take in each of the half-dozen or so twisting black characters on each page. The calligraphy was wonderful, some drawn in a strong, masculine hand, others delicate, almost feminine. There were no translations; each character held a message, a meaning known only to a few. Desiree studied each one intently, waiting for one to call out to her. Some were too massive, others twisted this way or that in spirals and curves that intrigued but did not captivate. Phil turned the pages in a slow rhythm, almost hypnotically. And then—Desiree took a sharp breath and leaned forward even closer over the book. Phil hesitated, then took his fingers away from the page he had been about to turn.

"Yes, of course," he mused. "I had thought about that one, about what you said about strength and independence. Certainly it fits. But—no, perhaps not. This is a symbol of great power, of frightful strength and raging passion. On a delicate, sweet young lady such as yourself . . ."

Desiree tore her eyes away from the calligraphy and glared at Pimlico Phil. Was he mocking her? Could he really look at her big-boned gawkiness, her klutzy walk and coke-bottle glasses, and see delicacy? Or was it simply that this Guru of the Gulf looked at her and saw nothing but daisies?

"What's it mean?" she said. She stared Phil right in

the eyes as she said it, trying to keep her voice steady and strong.

Phil returned her gaze for a long moment before he answered. "Golden dragon," he said ominously, in a voice so low it was almost a whisper. He let the words dangle in the air for a moment, evaluating the determination Desiree was forcing into her heart and her gaze. She boldly nodded her assent, lips pursed tight, fearful that Phil might not think her worthy of such a powerful symbol. She reached into her purse and dropped a fat wad of bills on the counter, not knowing or caring how much a golden dragon cost. Phil glanced down at the money and then back up at her. Desiree thought she saw a flicker of distaste dart through his eyes, and was instantly horrified that she might have just insulted him. The hazy future she was imagining for herself teetered on the brink. So much depended on finding this perfect symbol of what she could and would become. It was her declaration of independence, her starting place for a new life. If she lost it now . . .

But then Pimlico Phil shrugged, scooped up Desiree's dollars, and gestured for her to follow him. Desiree stood shakily and hesitated no more than a second before hurrying after Phil. Into his parlor and into my new life, Desiree thought, all on the wings of a golden dragon.

Visit
❖ **Pocket Books** ❖
online at

....

www.SimonSays.com

....

Keep up on the latest new
releases from your favorite
authors, as well as author
appearances, news, chats,
special offers and more.